Award-winning author **R**[...] stopping suspense and poignant romance, coupled with her adoration of high-tech weaponry and covert ops, encouraged her secret inner commando to take on the challenge of writing romantic suspense novels. Robin loves to interact with readers. You can catch her on her website, www.robinperini.com, and on several major social-networking sites, or write to her at PO Box 50472, Albuquerque, NM 87181-0472.

Julie Anne Lindsey is a multi-genre author who writes the stories that keep her up at night. She's a self-proclaimed nerd with a penchant for words and proclivity for fun. Julie lives in rural Ohio with her husband and three small children. Today, she hopes to make someone smile. One day she plans to change the world. Julie is a member of the International Thriller Writers and Sisters in Crime. Learn more about Julie Anne Lindsey at julieannelindsey.com.

Also by Robin Perini

Finding Her Son
Cowboy in the Crossfire
Christmas Conspiracy
Undercover Texas
The Cradle Conspiracy
Secret Obsession
Christmas Justice
San Antonio Secret
Cowboy's Secret Son

Also by Julie Anne Lindsey

Federal Agent Under Fire
The Sheriff's Secret

Discover more at millsandboon.co.uk

LAST STAND IN TEXAS

ROBIN PERINI

SHADOW POINT DEPUTY

JULIE ANNE LINDSEY

MILLS & BOON

First Published in Great Britain 2019
by Mills & Boon, an imprint of HarperCollins*Publishers*
1 London Bridge Street, London, SE1 9GF

Last Stand in Texas © 2018 Robin L. Perini
Shadow Point Deputy © 2018 Tyler Anne Snell

ISBN: 978-0-263-27397-7

0119

MIX
Paper from
responsible sources
FSC® C007454

This book is produced from independently certified FSC™ paper to ensure responsible forest management.

For more information visit: www.harpercollins.co.uk/green

Printed and bound in Spain
by CPI, Barcelona

LAST STAND
IN TEXAS

ROBIN PERINI

This one's for all my Carder, Texas, Connections readers. Your letters and encouragement urged me to tell more CTC stories. This book wouldn't exist without you. Thank you for loving the Carder, Texas, world as much as I do.

Prologue

The humidity weighing down the late spring breeze buffeted against Burke Thomas like an unwanted lover. At least the burning Texas sun would be at his back on his return to the civilized side of Dallas-Fort Worth.

The curtains from his ex-wife's dilapidated house shifted and she peeked out. At the sight of her, an exploding ache burst at the base of his skull. If killing Faith were a viable option, his life would markedly improve. He wanted nothing more than to break through the front door and give in to his desire.

Instead, he bit the inside of his cheek to rein in the unfeasible need.

Burke forced himself to take a slow, deep breath before turning on his heel and striding calmly to his Mercedes. He could maintain control. He *was* in control.

He opened the car door, but the new-car smell didn't possess the crisp, clean scent he savored. He peered down at the seat. A small streak of mud marred the leather.

Zoe.

His nails bit into his palm, piercing the skin.

Dirt from his daughter's jeans had soiled his car.

Unacceptable. His child needed etiquette lessons. Now. If it wasn't too late already.

He removed a plastic bag from the glove compartment and pulled out a clean rag and leather conditioner. Carefully, he swiped the mud away. His movements grew frantic, back and forth, back and forth, back and forth. The shine would reappear. It had to.

Zoe. Zoe. Zoe. Zoe.

With each swipe his daughter's name circled in his mind. He had to get control of her. If he could instill appropriate behavior in her as a seven-year-old, perhaps she wouldn't take after her mother. He'd come to the obvious conclusion that delayed training had been the problem with his ex-wife. Before he'd fully molded her, she'd ruined everything and forced him to divorce her.

After one last, vicious swipe, he studied the glistening surface. It would do.

He slid into the Mercedes and with a quick turn of his key, the engine roared to life. He glared at the now-closed curtains and screeched away from the house.

No more delays. He tapped his phone.

"Mr. Thomas?" his lawyer answered.

"Deliver the document. Now."

"It's Friday night after five. Our couriers have left for the evening. We can accommodate you first thing Monday."

"Tonight. Within the hour. Or do you want me to take my family's business elsewhere?"

Burke smiled. He could almost hear the man choke through the phone.

"Of course not, sir. The revised custody agreement will be in your ex-wife's hands within the hour."

"See that it is."

With a curse, he threw his phone across the seat, the frustration hammering his skull. His skin itched as if a rash bristled just beneath the surface. It was happening again. It always happened when Faith defied him.

Burke needed relief.

Sweat popped against his brow. He gripped the steering wheel. The familiar urge rose through his spine and into his head. The need settled and expanded, impatient and undeniable.

Why not celebrate Faith's latest punishment with his own personal gift to himself? Hadn't he denied himself enough tonight?

Burke jerked the steering wheel and guided his vehicle straight to the ideal hunting ground. He needed a woman.

With each passing stoplight, his skin prickled in ever-escalating anticipation. More often than not, he relished foreplay more than the act itself.

Tonight would be memorable. For both of them.

The search wasn't quick or easy, but Burke possessed remarkable patience. After two hours, his entire body brimmed with eagerness. He opened the car's passenger door for his choice, rounded the vehicle and joined her in the front seat.

Burke flipped on the air conditioner and sent his guest a sidelong glance. She was perfect for his plans tonight. Her eyes, in particular, had caught his attention. Big, emerald-green and noteworthy. Plus, she possessed the lithe figure Faith had lost the moment she'd gotten pregnant.

The woman's blond hair was just the right color, as well. It probably wasn't real, but he could live with one flaw. Besides, the dye job wasn't half-bad.

Either way, she would do nicely; she'd give him exactly what he needed.

She settled against the upholstery seat cover with a sigh and shot him a come-hither look. What was her name again? Randi, Brandi, Candi? It didn't matter. He'd just call her *sweetheart*.

He ran his hand through her long blond locks. She

hadn't caked them up with hair spray like some women did. He let the silky strands slip through his fingers and bent his head to her ear. "It's too public to do what I want to do to you. How about a ride?"

"You got the money, I'm all yours," she said, her voice husky with need, her words slurred with intoxication.

His gaze scanned the road and surroundings. No police cars or cabs. He didn't worry about cameras. He knew exactly where they were located, and he'd paid well to disable those on his preferred route. He'd seen to the necessary detail the first time he'd used the Shiny Penny Bar as one of his selection zones. Tonight, all the vehicles were dark. No witnesses. He was safe.

She placed her hand on his leg. "Where are we going?"

"A midnight drive."

"How about a little preview?" She ran her fingers high on his thigh and sent him a flirtatious glance.

He gripped her arm to stop her from exploring too soon. "Not yet, sweetheart. I have big plans for you."

By the time they reached an elaborate garden park, Burke's heart pounded with anticipation. He pulled onto a side street and grabbed the prepacked supply kit from behind his seat. He held out his hand to her. "Come with me. I have something to show you."

He pulled her close, his arm pressing her rail-thin body against his. He led her to a locked gate and shimmied through the rails.

She grinned and slipped through after him. "You're so bad."

"I haven't even begun."

He wound his way through the English-style hedges to a small wall of trees. He pushed a branch aside. "After you, my dear."

She ducked through the lush oaks. He followed. They

were enclosed in a small clearing, hidden from prying eyes.

"We're alone." She smiled and leaned against him, crushing her breasts into his chest.

"All alone," he whispered quietly, staring down at her, studying his choice.

The moon shone down from the break in the treetops. The gleaming light made her skin appear smooth and ageless, blurring her face so he could ignore the discrepancies with the woman who haunted his dreams.

Perhaps this one would quash the hunger inside of him.

He stroked her cheek with his thumb, across to the cleft in her chin. His heart kicked up a notch. The flaw proved she wasn't his dream lover. She wasn't even Faith.

His pulse raced, his breathing quickened. He should've been disappointed, but he wasn't. His body hardened with excitement of what was to come.

"What are you waiting for?" she whispered, nestling closer, grinding her hips against his.

"Almost," he whispered. He removed a plastic-lined sheet from his bag and spread it out, before guiding her a few steps to its center. His body tingled. "It's time."

She reached down to his zipper. He slapped her hands away, grabbed her hair and yanked, forcing her to look into his eyes.

She clutched at his hands. "Ow! What are you doing?"

With a smile, he tugged harder. Her eyes blurred with tears before the true nature of her predicament dawned on her less-than-Mensa intellect.

Burke smiled when fear, then panic widened her eyes.

He pulled a knife from the sheath at the small of his back and whipped the blade around. With joyful precision, he sliced long and deep across her throat. She clutched at her neck, but he knew his business. He'd studied. Diligently. For years.

She was dead in seconds.

Her body dropped to the ground. Her eyes stared sightless at the moon. He looked down at her and sighed. The cut had been deadly accurate, but life always left too soon. The efficient kill was a necessary sacrifice. He couldn't afford for her to resist too much. Scratching and fighting might result in evidence, something he refused to tolerate.

Burke knelt and tugged over his supply kit. He'd been looking forward to this one. The Eyeball Killer had fascinated him since the man's first mention during Burke's research.

He laid out his tools and studied her face. Green eyes were the rarest in the world. They would be a nice addition to his collection. He would have liked to collect brown, gray and blue, and maybe even hazel, as well. Too bad his discipline only allowed him the one opportunity to copy a unique modus operandi.

Discipline and preparation. That was what made him successful. And uncatchable. Regardless of his father's concerns.

Burke pushed her hair aside. Clutching the knife oh so slowly, he pressed the blade at the corner of one of her beautiful, blank and lifeless eyes.

Everything up to this moment had been foreplay.

Now for the main event.

THE MORNING LIGHT broke through the space between the kitchen curtains.

"Can I take the tablet Daddy gave me to school?" Zoe ran into the room at full speed and skidded to a stop in front of her mother, a huge smile on her face.

Faith folded the legal-sized paper and returned the custody agreement to the envelope for the umpteenth time. She rubbed the bridge of her nose to ease the building headache. She couldn't believe Burke had filed for full custody.

Undeniable proof she'd been a first-class fool. How many years had she believed she'd married Prince Charming, that he'd swept her out of the Shiny Penny, where she'd barely made enough to pay rent, and into a fairy tale? The only good to come of her marriage with Burke was her daughter. And the lesson Faith's mother had tried to teach her—never rely on anyone but yourself.

With a sigh, she gulped another swallow of coffee. She'd left Zoe with her neighbor half of Friday night hoping to find Burke, praying to talk some sense into him.

She'd finally located him near the bar where they'd first met, but not before he'd hooked up with another woman. Must've been some night, because he'd been incommunicado ever since.

Not that she cared. She'd stopped loving him long ago, but Zoe's well-being was at stake. Zoe irritated him more than anything. She couldn't imagine him taking care of her every day, seven days a week. He wanted a perfect china doll for a daughter. A child he could show off and then shoo away. Zoe would never be that. Faith's daughter was a tomboy through and through. She was messy, eager and independent. And definitely not a wallflower. Faith loved every inch of her.

She slid the rubber band off the morning paper. She'd have to fight the Thomas family machine to keep her daughter. To do that, Faith needed a job with more regular hours than her diner gig.

Intent on searching the classifieds, she spread the paper out. Below the fold on the front page, a photo screamed out. A familiar-looking blond-haired woman smiled at her. The caption chilled Faith's soul.

"Local Woman Murdered. No Suspects."

Quickly, Faith scanned the story and stopped at a single paragraph. Mandy Jones's time of death was estimated between seven and ten.

Faith dropped the paper on the kitchen table, her body frozen in shock and disbelief. Faith had seen Mandy that night. She couldn't make herself believe this was possible, and yet, she knew what she'd witnessed.

Mandy Jones in the passenger seat of her ex-husband's car.

Chapter One

Three months later

The gray clouds threatening the West Texas sky earlier in the day had turned black. The air sizzled with electricity, and a rare drizzle of rain seeped into Stefan's skin. He peered at the sky. Strange, but the weather matched his mood today, so he'd go with it.

He ducked his head and darted up the Carder Texas Public Library's steps. Rain rolled off the brim of his Stetson, the incessant damp reminding him of the mountains of the tiny European country he'd once called home. A home on the other side of the globe. A home he hadn't visited in years. A homeland that believed he'd been assassinated along with his older brother during a failed coup d'état.

Instead, he was alive and well and impersonating a native Texan so convincingly he sometimes forgot he wasn't one.

"Hey, Léon, how's it going?"

"Can't complain." Stefan didn't blink at the use of his long-term alias. He tilted his hat in acknowledgment as the deputy limped past the library. Smithson had almost died a few years ago. Now he and his wife had a couple of kids and the guy never stopped smiling.

Something Stefan could never see happening for himself.

He couldn't afford connections or family. Which was why last night he'd made one of the toughest decisions of his life.

Stefan tapped his Stetson to remove the water and pushed through the double doors of the library.

A small girl sat at the front desk. A too-big baseball cap cocked to one side on her head. Her light brown hair fell halfway down her back. She looked up at him and smiled. "May I help you?"

He really should ignore her, or scare her with a terrifying frown, but instead he walked over to the desk. "Just browsing. Worked here long?"

"Do you have a library card?" she asked in a very professional tone. "You can't check out a book without a library card. My mom told me that."

Stefan fought back a smile at the girl's confident antics. "Nope. I like to read here."

"I don't have one, either." She leaned forward. "It's a secret."

He bent down so he could make out her whispered words. "I'll keep your secret."

"You're funny. I like you." She grinned up at him.

"Zoe." An urgent whisper sounded from his left.

"Uh-oh." The little girl bit her lip. "That's my mom. I'm not s'posed to be up here."

A woman hurried over, an adult version of the imp in front of him. However, instead of Zoe's charm, she wore an expression that froze him.

He recognized the look. Not apologetic, not angry, not worried. Panic laced her eyes and had tightened her mouth.

Stefan took a step back from Zoe, putting space between them.

Zoe's mother scooted between her daughter and Stefan in mama-bear mode. "I'm sorry if she bothered you."

"Zoe was very helpful," he said with a wink at the little girl. "I definitely need to get a library card."

"See, Mom." She straightened her shoulders. "I told you I could help."

Her mother closed her eyes for a moment and pinched the bridge of her nose. "Do you need any assistance?" she asked him, entire body taut, practically begging him to refuse.

If he had any sense, he'd walk away right now. Most women would have smiled at him with warm eyes, but she did the opposite.

Retreat would be the best option. These two weren't any of his business, but something made him hesitate. Should he break his own rules, just this once? They looked like they could use someone in their corner.

The grip on his hat tightened. He couldn't believe he was even considering the idea.

"I'm browsing for now. I expect I'll see you around." With a quick nod at Zoe, he headed to the fiction aisles, keeping the pair in his peripheral vision.

As soon as he'd turned away, Zoe's mother ushered the little girl toward the back of the library.

Interesting. The sleeves of the woman's shirt showed a bit of fraying. Her shoes were scuffed. He recognized the Magic Marker polishing up the toe, but she colored her hair. The brown was almost too perfect. She'd fastened her locks away from her face with a clip, the strands hanging long and silky and infinitely touchable down her back, but with a slightly uneven edge, as if she'd cut it herself. Her gold-colored small hoop earrings might have appeared real at one time, but the tinge of green peeking through revealed the truth.

Her gaze had darted back and forth, hyperaware of her surroundings. He'd like to have seen her smile. He'd bet her eyes would light up just like her daughter's.

Stefan caught himself in his poetic musings. Okay, so she was attractive. Very attractive. Her body filled out her jeans very nicely with just enough curve to make a man notice twice. And he had. He'd also bet she was on the run and low on cash.

His curiosity—and interest—aroused, he worked his way down the book stacks. He could use a bit of intel, and he knew just who to ask. After he completed his primary task.

He scanned the sea of authors' names and even flipped through a couple of books. Surely one of the monikers would appeal.

A new identity came with a new name.

He'd be relieved to get rid of Léon Royce. He'd never liked it, but he'd been almost dead when it had been decided so he'd made the best of it. In some ways he already regretted this decision, but he didn't have a choice.

If he were honest, at first, he'd loved the CTC job: danger, excitement, helping people no one else could help. But ever since the Jennings fiasco, he'd volunteered for every dangerous, out-of-the-way job that CTC could throw at him, praying the next challenge would reignite a spark. Something inside of him had broken when that family had died.

Truth was, he should've left sooner. Would have, if not for the connections he'd made at Covert Technology Confidential. Except those relationships that kept him here also made him vulnerable.

He needed a new start, a new life, which made his curiosity about Zoe and her mother all the more odd.

Stefan wandered the stacks and each time he rounded

the south end, his gaze veered to the woman. Definitely an upgrade from the middle-aged, sour-faced library assistant who'd stalked him when he'd visited several months ago.

The sound of creaking footsteps stiffened his spine before he recognized the rhythm of the familiar gait of the head librarian.

"Léon. You're back. I haven't seen you all summer," a familiar voice said.

He faced her and feigned surprise. "Mrs. Hargraves, how do you sneak up on me in those boots?"

Not that she really had, but they both played the game. Still, she'd realized he'd been gone for months, which meant she'd been watching for him. His behavior had become too predictable. Another sign he should move on.

Mrs. Hargraves smiled, a beam of pleasure in her eyes at his compliment. "Practice. If I'm going to avoid wearing quiet, ugly librarian shoes, I'd better be able to walk this place without making a sound."

She could probably sneak up on 99 percent of the clientele, too. According to Carder legend, Mrs. Hargraves had been the librarian since the 1960s. Dressed in jeans, Ropers and a flannel shirt, she sure didn't dress or act like any librarian he'd known, but the woman knew her books.

Over the last couple years, he'd let her pick out one book for him whenever he visited. She rarely went wrong. His favorite to date was *Inherit the Stars* by James P. Hogan.

"I've been saving this for you," she said, handing him *The Prince* by Machiavelli.

He nearly choked. He jerked his chin to meet her gaze. Did she know? Or did she think he needed lessons in being authoritative? Either one made the back of his neck itch.

"Thanks." He took the book, forcing a smile.

"I can see there's something wrong." She frowned at him. "Are you okay after your…trip? Not like that last one, I hope."

Okay, so she was observant, too.

"Or…" She paused for a moment and glanced behind her. "Is it my new assistant you're interested in?"

A small sense of relief loosened his neck muscles. So his favorite octogenarian had matchmaking on her mind.

He returned the book to the shelf. "You caught me. I *may* have noticed both of your new helpers."

Mrs. Hargraves rocked back on the heels of her boots. "The last one quit and Faith needed a job. I liked the look of her. Been here a couple of months. She's always on time, she's no trouble, and that girl of hers is a pistol. Reminds me of myself when I was a youngster."

Faith. Her name suited her.

"You're collecting strays."

"Maybe." She crooked her finger at him, and he bent closer. "Faith's in big trouble. Skittish as a newborn colt. I don't know what kind of problem, but I get the feeling whatever she's running from is about to come to a head. You could help her." She narrowed her gaze. "I have a strong suspicion of what you folks do out at that ranch."

He didn't respond. "Thanks for everything." He kissed her cheek and started to walk away.

She grabbed his shirt. "She needs you. Don't ignore your gut."

Muffled whispers sounded from the tables at the back of the library. Stefan sent Mrs. Hargraves a subtle nod and followed the noise. He paused just out of their sight.

"What have I told you, Zoe? We can't draw attention to ourselves, and you promised you'd work on your reading."

"I *hate* reading. I'm bored. I want to go home and play

baseball with Danny. I can't miss the next season of Little League. He'll kill me."

"Look, Slugger, we need to stay here just a little longer. Then…"

"You keep saying that. I want to go home with Daddy. I know he doesn't like you, but he likes me. *He* wouldn't make me sit hours and hours and hours reading stupid books all the time. He'd buy me stuff to play with. Cool stuff." Zoe jerked away from her mother and plopped down at a table scattered with crayons, construction paper and children's books.

Ouch. Faith's daughter could strike a bull's-eye.

Faith stared at Zoe with tortured eyes. Stefan had seen it before. The heartache. The dejection. He didn't know exactly what was going on, but they clearly needed help.

Seeing a woman that afraid of being found didn't sit well with him. They needed help. Help he could give. If he could convince them to trust him.

THE RAIN PELTED Carder with no signs of letting up anytime soon. A rainbow crossed the gray sky of the horizon, leading to nowhere. Faith stood in the doorway of the library and studied the expanse of dark clouds. They portended the future much more than the pink and blue and green. Rainbows were supposed to hold magic and hope. She'd lost count of the days since she'd believed in either.

Zoe still did, of course.

Faith attempted to cloak herself in optimism. Maybe their luck could change, but somehow she doubted it. From the morning she'd realized what her ex-husband had done to her car breaking down in this middle-of-nowhere town, she and Zoe hadn't caught a break. She'd fought against the panic of being discovered every day. Sometimes she succeeded, but she'd been unsettled since the stranger had shown up at the library today. Something to do with how his gaze had pierced right through her, how he'd seemed to see too much and how Zoe couldn't stop talking about him.

She didn't know how long she waited before the rain finally tapered off. The library had closed an hour ago, but Faith couldn't afford for their clothes to get wet or dirty. She didn't have the money to go to the Laundromat twice in a week.

"Looks like it's letting up," Mrs. Hargraves said.

"Thanks for letting me stay." Faith shifted on her feet. She didn't like making small talk. It led to relationships, and relationships meant being noticed.

"I don't mind driving you home, honey."

"That's okay. I have to hit the store first. I'm out of your way."

"Nothing's out of the way in Carder."

Faith didn't respond. Mrs. Hargraves had hired her off the books. It was best no one knew where she lived, not even someone as seemingly honest as her boss. Faith had to be careful. If no one knew where she lived, she could relax enough to close her eyes at night. At least for a few hours. "Pack up, Zoe. We're going home."

Her daughter ran up to her with a frown. "It's not home, you know."

Before Faith could respond, her daughter rushed to the back of the library. Heat flushed her cheeks and she glanced at Mrs. Hargraves. "Sorry."

The librarian patted her arm. "Don't you worry about it. She's a good girl, just a little frustrated today. Rain'll do that. I couldn't ever live in Seattle or somewhere like that. I'd be in a bad mood all the time."

"Thank you." Faith met the older woman's gaze. She'd saved their lives. "For everything you've done."

"You've helped *me*, honey. I'm not getting any younger. Speaking of which, I'm telling you, if I had fifty years back, I'd be all over that man who took a shine to you today." She winked. "You know who I'm talking about."

Faith didn't pretend not to know. "He barely said a word to me."

"He was watching you all right."

"Watching me?" A chill froze Faith. "Why?"

"The fact that you're a very attractive woman might be the reason." Mrs. Hargraves arched a brow in disbelief. "Come on, Faith. I saw that look you gave him. Besides, Zoe certainly liked our Léon."

Léon. So her boss knew him. Faith relaxed a bit. Burke had no connection with Carder, so he wouldn't know Léon, either. She was being paranoid. Again. "I couldn't place his accent."

"If you find out, let me know. Every woman in town from seven to seventy would like the answer." Her boss chuckled. "That boy is easy on the eyes…and the ears."

Faith couldn't deny he was attractive. Tall, with a rugged square jaw, that sexy, unshaven look and piercing blue eyes. He could be the hero in a fairy tale, his dark hair highlighted with sun-kissed blond streaks. Except this stranger had a sad, lonely darkness in him, and that kind of need pegged him as a troublesome cloud, not a rainbow.

What struck her as odd, though, was how he'd taken Zoe's playacting as a librarian seriously. The girl had fallen in love with him after two minutes. Faith didn't blame her daughter. Faith wasn't dead either, but since she preferred staying alive, she had to stay as invisible as possible.

Besides, he seemed too good to be true, and she knew better than to believe all those trimmings. She hadn't seen the danger in Burke, and look what had happened. "If you say so."

"Of course I do, and so do you." Mrs. Hargraves took Faith's hand. "Look, I'll let you in on a secret. If you need help sometime, Léon is a man who knows what to do."

Faith bit her lip.

"Don't ask me for details. I don't have all the answers. I just know if I were in trouble, Carder is where I'd want to be. We take care of our own."

Chewing on that interesting tidbit, Faith grabbed the large tote that doubled as her purse and waited. Zoe took her time but eventually dragged her feet through the front door.

Faith took her daughter's hand.

"Be safe, honey," her boss called out.

Faith waved to the librarian and the woman locked the door behind them. Zoe skipped along, jumping in a large puddle. Water splashed up her jeans.

"Stop it. You're getting your clothes dirty."

Zoe stilled and turned to her mother. "That's what Dad always says."

Faith's heart ripped in two. She knelt down in front of Zoe. "I'm sorry, Slugger. It's just… I'm trying to find us a new home, a place where we can be happy. I need money to do that and it's expensive to wash our clothes. When we get our own place, you can dirty up those jeans all you want. In fact, I'll roll in the mud with you."

Zoe didn't meet her gaze for a few moments and then peeked up. "You promise to roll in the mud with me?"

"Pinky swear." Faith held out her hand. Zoe grinned and linked little fingers.

"I won't jump anymore, then."

"Thanks, Slugger."

Luckily, the family grocery store, which also served

as the feed store and gas station, was only a half mile down the road. She and Zoe ducked in and grabbed one of the five carts sitting just inside the door.

Faith pulled out her small calculator. She picked up a loaf of bread, on sale, thankfully, and looked over at the peanut butter. Full price. They could probably make do another week with what they had if she kept the coating thin. Maybe it would be on sale next week.

"Can we get some chips?" Zoe asked.

Faith bit her lip. She shouldn't. "Maybe a small one. We'll have to wait and see."

Zoe gave her a huge grin, and the sight caused Faith's heart to sink. Her little girl shouldn't be so excited to buy a small package of chips. She loved Zoe's enthusiasm, but her reaction made Faith feel like a failure as a mother.

Every day she asked herself if she'd made the right decision, and every night she recognized she'd had no choice but to leave. Not once she'd realized what Burke was. She couldn't risk losing custody to a serial killer.

She tapped the cost of the small bag of chips into the calculator and scanned her list. Was there anything she could take off?

A scuff sounded behind her. Faith straightened and turned around. No one there. She clutched her purse tighter, hoping to push down the foreboding that laced her every thought. She picked up a bag of beans on sale and placed them in the cart, then paused.

Another rustle fluttered at her back.

A prickle skittered down her spine. Zoe examined a box of cereal, making an enthusiastic attempt to whistle the jingle. Faith glanced behind to her left, then her right. The store was small, a quarter size of the grocery store she'd frequented at home. She should have a visual on everybody.

Gripping the cart's handle with white-knuckled fists, she prodded Zoe along and hurriedly maneuvered through the last two aisles, placing the final four items into the cart. Maybe the weather had impacted her more than she thought. Maybe the fact that she hadn't heard any updates from her fake ID supplier in weeks had rattled her. Or maybe it was the man Mrs. Hargraves had told her she could trust. Léon. He'd come out of nowhere. He'd shown too much interest in her and Zoe. What if he *did* work for Burke?

She had to trust her gut. "Come on, Zoe. We need to leave." Faith couldn't hide the urgency from her voice.

Zoe frowned at her mother. "What's wrong, Mom?"

"Nothing. It's getting late." She headed toward the checkout.

"It's still light outside," her daughter protested, hurrying beside her.

"It won't be for long and we have to walk home."

Zoe shifted her knapsack, heavy with all her treasures stored inside.

The checker smiled at them. "How's it going, Faith?"

"Fine. And you, Maureen?"

The woman grinned, her face open and joyful, something Faith envied. "Can't complain. My boy just graduated. He's headed for boot camp."

"Congratulations. I'm sure you'll miss him."

"Yep. They grow up fast. Enjoy this one while you can." Maureen nodded at Zoe.

"I will." Faith scooped up the two bags and glanced over her shoulder yet again. She couldn't shake the being-watched feeling.

She had truly become paranoid. She wasn't made for being on the run. She wanted a normal life back. She just prayed that would happen once she could afford to leave Carder.

The sun hung low in the sky when she and Zoe walked out of the store. They had a two-mile trek to the shack she'd rented.

She started out slow. Not many walked in this town. She didn't even see a bicycle. Carder, Texas, was ranch country. Pickups ruled the streets.

The sheriff's office loomed in front of her. She crossed away from it, telling herself that she was simply making her way to *her* side of the street. It had nothing to do with the fact that Burke and his family's political allies could very well have convinced someone to put out a warrant for her arrest. She just prayed dyeing her hair brown would fool everyone long enough for her to disappear.

Whatever Burke was thinking or doing, it hadn't made headlines in the *San Antonio Express-News*. Much less the Carder weekly paper.

That strange unease settled between her shoulder blades. Faith didn't believe in ESP, but if she did, her spidey sense was going crazy. She picked up the pace.

"Mom, you're going too fast. I'm tired."

Faith slowed and turned around. Her daughter had taken to dragging the pack behind her. "Hand me the knapsack, Slugger."

Zoe held it out with both hands.

Faith took it and nearly dropped the bag. She hadn't expected it to be so heavy. "What have you got in here?"

"The books you made me bring. Plus my baseball, my favorite games, chalk and my shiny stones for hop-scotch." Zoe shrugged. "So I wouldn't have to read the whole time."

An incessant pounding pulsed behind Faith's eyes, but she shoved aside the pain. "I don't want to get caught in

the rain, Zoe. Let's hurry. I bet you can't beat me home."
She fought to form the smallest smile.

Her daughter took off, and Faith jogged behind her.

"Stop before crossing the street," Faith shouted.

Zoe glanced back and grinned. "You won't catch me!"

Even so, her daughter slowed down a bit. When they
settled in a new place, she'd make sure she enrolled Zoe
in softball or baseball or maybe even soccer. Her daughter needed a way to work off all that energy.

By the time they reached the two-room shack she
called home, Faith panted and bent over to catch her
breath.

Zoe waited outside the door, shifting from one foot
to another.

Faith slipped her hand into her pocket and dug out
the key. She pushed it into the lock and opened the door.

Zoe rushed in, whirled around and raced back at her
mother, plowing into her. The shopping bags flew out
of Faith's hands. Zoe's knapsack dropped like a stone.

"What—"

Zoe's face made Faith's heart drop. "Mom, someone's
been here."

Faith pushed her daughter behind her and peered inside the open door.

The sofa had been overturned; bookcases toppled. The
few items they had left were spread on the floor.

Their place had been ransacked.

"Zoe, we need to leave. Now!"

THOMAS, INCORPORATED OCCUPIED the top three floors of
the downtown Dallas office building. Oil made the fortune, but Burke's father had diversified. They were now
in distribution, energy storage and financial institutions.
If you lived or worked in Texas, you dealt with one of

Thomas, Inc.'s companies or subsidiaries. The business would be his someday, and Burke had big plans for the future.

For now, the company's reach equated influence, and influence translated into power. It also meant when his father called, Burke had no choice but to appear. He inserted his executive key into the elevator panel and pressed the button to the penthouse. The elevator zoomed upward.

A finely tuned bell chimed and the doors opened. Burke exited and crossed the thick carpet, ignoring the latest administrative assistant. Bracing himself, he knocked on his father's office door.

"Enter."

Burke took a cleansing breath and stepped inside.

His father raised his head and frowned. "Shut the door."

The older Thomas didn't smile. This wasn't going to be fun, and Burke had a feeling he knew the subject of the latest lecture. He closed the door quietly, as was expected, and strode across the room. "You wanted to see me?"

"Are you over the latest *incident*? Have you regained control of your *urges*?"

"Yes, sir." He met his father's gaze. "You know, it wouldn't hurt if you'd help me out a little with this Faith situation."

Gerard Thomas shot to his feet. "How dare you speak to me that way. Help you? I've saved you from going to prison more times than you'll ever know. It's only been two weeks since the previous *problem* occurred. Two weeks. Have you *no* discipline?"

Burke ground his nails into one palm. "I keep getting calls from investigators and lawyers. It's…frustrating. I need to relieve my…stress."

"Then go for a run. Lift some weights, but don't..." His father scowled and slugged a shot of whiskey. "Your mother wants to see Zoe. I'm running out of excuses."

"I'll visit Mom, make up something." Burke shrugged with indifference.

"You think this is a game?" His father slammed the glass onto his desk. "You're too impatient. You have no self-discipline. You should have waited until we nailed down the case against Faith before serving the proposed custody agreement."

"You're the one who told Mother we were ready." Burke lifted his chin. "How could I predict she'd run?"

"How many times have I told you to run any decision that affects this family by me first?" His father rubbed his eyes. "Faith might not be fit to raise my granddaughter, but neither are you. I needed an airtight case of neglect to ensure you get custody."

"Well, she's taken Zoe without my permission. That's a plus."

"*If* we find her."

"I can fix this," Burke said under his breath. "If you give me the leeway, when I find her—"

His father slammed his hand on the desk. "Do not even *think* about harming Faith."

Burke's lips pursed.

"The cost of cleaning up your messes just doubled. If my team hadn't gone in behind you, you would've been caught. Your DNA was there, Burke. You're getting sloppy.

"If you do something to your ex-wife, I won't be able to protect you, or our family name. My sway only goes so far." His father took a seat, steepled his fingers and stared over the tips at Burke. "Get control of yourself and get back to work."

The stinging words pierced Burke's skin with the force of icy knives, but he said nothing. He simply nodded and crossed the hall to his own office.

Once inside, he slammed his fist into the wall. How had his father found out about his latest indiscretion so fast?

His head pounded in a rhythmic crashing against his skull. He placed the heel of his hand against his temple. This was all Faith's fault. She was the one who'd taken Zoe, and because of it, his mother was a basket case. His father...

He didn't give a damn about Gerard Thomas or how he felt.

Burke rubbed his face. Faith had been gone three months. She wasn't smart enough to disappear completely. She would make a mistake. And then he'd have her. No matter what his father said.

He sagged into the leather chair behind his desk and tossed his phone onto the perfectly polished mahogany. He unlocked the top drawer and pulled out a folder containing his plans for the future. When *he* ran Thomas, Incorporated.

He flipped through the pages. Burke would expand the company's power nationally, and then internationally. There would be no limits.

His cell vibrated to life.

He glanced at the caller. Orren better have some good news. "Report."

"Mr. Thomas. We found her."

Chapter Two

Stefan's SUV bounced over the West Texas badlands, putting his back-road driving skills to the test. He glanced at his GPS. He should be there soon. A strip of vivid purple and orange winked at him from the western horizon, the only color except for a few blooming cacti. The harsh landscape didn't mince words; dramatic, beautiful in its own way, but nothing like his home country of Bellevaux, strewn with lakes and rivers, lush rolling green hills and vineyards.

His vehicle kicked up dust from the parched earth. He'd been traveling a cattle trail for a half hour, and he just hoped he'd picked the right path. He'd never rendezvoused with Annie in the same place twice. The woman put his own paranoia to shame.

On the other hand, she survived when by all rights she should be dead.

They both lived in the world of gray shadows, where light and dark, truth and lies, right and wrong fused into a strange, inseparable muddle.

The vehicle rose in elevation just enough to see another mile or so into the distance when he made out the top of a nondescript tow camper.

Right where she said she'd be.

He pulled his SUV about fifty feet from her makeshift

home and exited, hands raised, leaving his SIG Sauer in the vehicle. Annie had her rules about guns, after all.

She didn't show herself, but he knew she could see him. Probably had her sight trained on him right now.

"Annie?" he called out.

She didn't answer, so he waited.

And waited.

A figure finally rose from the protection of a group of saltbushes. Annie cradled an Uzi, her favorite weapon, and strode toward him. She'd piled her loose curly hair on top of her head, not the dark brown he recalled from their first meeting or the auburn from their last appointment. No, this visit, golden brown kissed with blond framed her face, highlighting an unexpected softness to her appearance. Maybe her natural color. He couldn't be certain, but it suited her.

She wore her usual black jeans and a too-large black T-shirt. By the time the sun set she'd be practically invisible.

Her smile widened when she reached him, a smile that revealed the hidden beauty she made an effort to conceal. He'd never understood why.

"Léon, you look good for a dead man."

"And you look too beautiful to be dead."

He bent down and kissed her cheek gently. They'd been friends for about five years now. She knew him as well as anybody, but even she didn't know his true identity. When CTC had smuggled him into the United States to save his life, they had provided her the information for his Léon Royce persona, but the company had never revealed his real name.

"How've you been, Annie?"

A shadowed expression he recognized all too well crossed her face. "Not bad. And you?"

Just the sort of conversation friends with benefits had when they kept each other at arm's length. Two people with major trust issues and on the run didn't make for a good long-term relationship. They'd recognized the reality early on, so they performed the identical dance each time they met.

"You planning on coming out of hiding anytime soon?" He always asked.

"Probably not. I just got my hair done for the apocalypse," she said with a sad smile. "You and I made our choices years ago. This is my life now—helping troublemakers like you and innocent people who have nowhere else to turn."

Faith and her daughter flashed into his mind. He shoved them aside. He really shouldn't care.

Except he did.

"So, business has been good?"

"Better than ever." She sighed. "Power corrupts everything. Law enforcement and government included. Sometimes disappearing is the only answer."

"Truer words."

"So why the smoke signal?" she asked. "Ransom usually contacts me for a job."

"This is personal." Stefan shifted his weight and met her gaze, direct and unwavering. "I need to disappear."

She let out a low whistle. "You're leaving CTC?"

He nodded.

"I see." She strode across her campsite and unlocked a series of padlocks she'd attached to the reinforced door of the camper. "Come inside."

He removed his hat and ducked inside. The last time she'd invited him in, they'd headed straight to the bedroom. This time he took the opposite turn to a sophisticated set of equipment, a high-tech wizard's dream.

Annie could forge any identification card needed. She could backstop an elaborate past, or tap into satellite imagery and even street cameras—for a price. He didn't want to think about what other intel she could lay her hands on.

She slid behind her desk.

"Léon needs to die a public death," he said, sitting across from her. "I want a new identity. A fresh start. A clean slate."

She quirked an eyebrow. "Does Ransom know?"

"You're the first."

She smiled in that knowing way of hers. "Yeah, right. He knows something is up."

"Probably."

Her fingers flew across a keyboard. "I can kill Léon without too much trouble. Creating someone brand-new could take a bit longer. Are you at risk?"

Her forehead furrowed. He recognized the worry. "I'm not in imminent danger, but it's only a matter of time. I've gotten sloppy, made too many connections. It could be dangerous if—"

"The people wanting to kill you ever found you," she finished. "Why do you think I live out of a trailer? I can't afford long-term anything." Annie leaned back in her chair. "Starting over isn't all it's cracked up to be, either."

Like Faith was obviously trying to do. Her terrified expression suddenly came to mind. Helping people like her was what CTC did—and what Annie did. What *he* tried to do.

"I can't go back to who I was." He drummed his fingers on his leg. How could he put his desire into words that didn't sound ridiculous? "I want—"

"A normal life." Annie chuckled and he met her gaze. Despite her laughter, commiseration laced Annie's eyes.

"The minute you chose to play spy guy, you hung up the normal hat."

"You have no idea how true that statement is." He'd become Léon Royce because of his undercover work. He'd become a ghost to his family and his country because of his own choices. Now, he had to live with the consequences.

She rounded her desk and hitched her hip on its edge. "I may not know your true identity, but I doubt you were ever ordinary. That's what you'll have to become for this to work."

Stefan flicked the brim of his Stetson. "Ordinary. I like the sound of that."

THE LITTLE SHACK they'd called home wasn't safe. Faith nails bit into her palm, trying not to let Zoe see her true panic. Her gaze raced through the room. Nothing had been left untouched. Even the bookcase shelves had been strewn across the floor. The coffee table lay on its side. Faith's heart raced as she surveyed the damage. She couldn't move. She couldn't breathe.

She could only protect her daughter.

In her old life, she would've immediately rushed to a neighbor's house and called the police. She didn't have that luxury now. They were alone, and everything they owned was inside that house. She couldn't walk away.

Faith stepped just inside the door and reached to her left. Zoe's baseball bat was still propped in the corner. She snagged it and curled her fingers around the wooden neck.

"If you're still here, get out. I'm armed," she shouted.

No one answered. The shack was eerily quiet. She circled and her gaze scanned every inch of their small, furnished rental. Nothing had been left untouched.

There went her security deposit.

"Stay here," Faith whispered to Zoe. "If anyone comes, run and hide in the trees behind the houses. I'll find you."

Her daughter gripped her knapsack and nodded, her small face terrified.

Clutching the bat with all her strength, Faith tiptoed into the small kitchenette. Everything had been chucked out of the cupboards. What had they been looking for? If it was money… Oh, God.

She rushed into the small bedroom. The mattresses she and Zoe slept on had been tossed; their clothes were scattered across the floor.

Her gaze stopped at the closed closet door. The blood pounded against her temples. Slowly, carefully, she approached. Her fingers folded into the recessed handle and she yanked open the door.

The wood slid on the rails and rammed into the wall at the other end with a clatter.

Empty. No one was here.

She couldn't breathe yet.

After checking the bathroom and shower, Faith sank onto the bed. Now, she could breathe. "Come here, Zoe," she called. "It's safe."

The little girl ran in and leaped at her mother. Faith held her close and rocked her for a few moments. "We're okay. That's all that matters."

"Did they steal anything?" Zoe asked from her lap. "Did they take Rainbow?"

"Your unicorn? I don't think so."

"Where is she?"

Faith's gaze scanned the room. No stuffed toy. "Maybe under the bed?"

Zoe slipped out of Faith's arms and got down on her hands and knees. She peered under the rickety bed frame and squirmed underneath before popping out, holding the colorful animal.

"I got her. Rainbow was hiding from the bald man. She's smart that way."

At her daughter's words, Faith stilled. "Zoe, did you see someone?"

Her daughter shrugged.

"Zoe?"

"I saw a big man with a bald head follow us in the grocery store. Whenever you turned around, he hid. I thought he was playing a game."

Faith rubbed her eyes as the realization hit her. "Was he tall like Daddy?"

"Yes. With a mermaid drawing on his arm."

The tattoo. She'd seen the man before, but not in Carder. The more Faith racked her brain, the more her memories coalesced. In Weatherford. He'd been hired as the bouncer at the Shiny Penny about the time she began dating Burke. What were the odds that a man working at the bar would end up at a grocery store in Carder?

Only one person could be responsible for this happening.

Burke had found them.

They had to leave Carder. Now.

Knees trembling, Faith knelt beside the bed and shoved aside the nightstand. She pried up the carpet. An envelope was tucked beneath the poorly installed rug. Hands shaking, she pulled it out and fingered through the bills.

Her entire body sagged in relief. She plopped down in the middle of the bedroom, grasping the envelope, their lifeline, the money she'd raised to pay for the car repairs so they could leave Carder.

At one time, there had been two envelopes hidden here. In the first one, she'd placed all the money she'd scraped together from selling her wedding ring and all the jewelry her husband had given her. Most of which had been fake.

It hadn't been enough to pay for new identities for her and Zoe. Her contact had required $10,000 up front. To make up the difference, she'd been forced to sell the small diamond ring her mother had given her before her death.

The money represented their escape, their chance to get away from the past, and from Burke.

If he ever discovered that she knew what he'd done, he wouldn't just take Zoe from her. He'd kill her to keep his secret.

"Mom? Are you okay?"

Faith swiped at her eyes. "I'm fine. We're fine."

"Why are you crying?" Zoe hugged her unicorn, the vulnerable expression breaking Faith's heart.

She pulled her daughter close and hugged her tight. Everything they were going through would be worth it. It had to be. "Sometimes I just need a good cry, Slugger. Do you know what I mean?"

Her daughter's forehead wrinkled with worry. "I've never seen you cry before. Not even when Daddy hurt your feelings."

"Everybody cries, honey. Even moms."

Zoe laid her head against Faith's chest and wrapped her arms around her mother's body. "Do we have to move again?"

Faith looked around the room. "I'm sorry, sweetie. We're packing up and getting out. Tonight."

THE DARK PANELING closed in on Burke. He hated this office, a mirror image of his father's. The mahogany desk, the leather chairs. All his life his father had wanted a carbon copy of himself. Burke had lived up to those expectations. He'd been happy to. In Burke's childhood eyes, his father had been the greatest man he'd ever known. He'd believed that until the age of sixteen.

Burke threw down the latest balance sheet. That was the year he'd fallen in love for the first time. With the *perfect* woman.

That was the year he'd uncovered his father's feet of clay.

That was the year Burke had been forced to kill the woman he loved.

He walked across the plush carpet and poured a drink.

The door opened without a knock. He whirled around, ready to tear into whoever dared interrupt his planning until he saw the woman who walked in with a smile on her face.

"Burke, darling, you shouldn't be working this late. I've told your father not to foist his bad habits onto you."

"Mother." Burke walked across the room and gently pulled her close. "I wasn't expecting you."

Her sweet smile tilted the corners of her mouth. "I'm dragging your father to the club for a late dinner. Do you want to join us?"

"I have work to do."

His mother pouted her lips. "You're too much like Gerard."

No, I'm not! he wanted to scream. "You always say that." He smiled.

She kissed his cheek and he released her. His mother deserved the world for putting up with his father all these years, for helping Burke survive his childhood. He'd do anything to protect her and to give her whatever would keep her life content and happy.

That had been true all his life. His vow had been put

to the test when he'd discovered his father's weakness for other women, but Burke had passed the test.

She picked up the photo of Zoe on his desk. "I can't wait for your little girl to visit. Did she like the dress I sent her? I've been looking at a catalog. I think I'm too old-fashioned. I want Zoe to have a hip grandmother."

Inside, Burke winced. Until Orren brought Zoe back to him, he'd have to lie, and he hated lying to his mother. "You don't need to change a thing, Mom. Zoe loved the dress. She's planning to wear it next time she visits."

Of course, sometimes lies were necessary.

His mother frowned. "How long will Faith's trip last? I miss my granddaughter. I'm sure it's good for Zoe to attend a camp to help with her reading, but she's been gone all summer. School starts soon."

Burke hugged his mother to his side. "Zoe will be back before long. I promise."

She let out a slow sigh and replaced the photo. "I'm sorry your marriage to Faith didn't work out. She seemed like such a nice girl." She patted his cheek. "You look tired, Burke. You should find someone who can make you happy. Your father worries."

Hardly.

He kissed the perfectly coiffed hair. "I have work, and you have a date."

She flushed and patted his arm. "Don't work too hard, my sweet boy."

Burke escorted her to his office door and gave her one final kiss.

"I'll do what I have to do."

SEVEN IN THE morning didn't come early enough, especially when you'd bedded down the night before in a small grove of trees. Thank God Faith had made an emergency plan in case something like this happened. Zoe was safely hidden. Faith had stayed up all night clutching the bat, staring at the back of the shack where they'd lived for the past few months.

She stretched, and her body protested with every movement. Each time she blinked, she could have sworn sandpaper scraped off a layer of her eyelid.

Burke hadn't shown up, though she'd caught a glimpse of a couple of figures lurking around. Unfortunately, she hadn't been able to get a good look except that one appeared to be bald. Just like Zoe'd said.

If she'd harbored any last hope, it was gone. Burke had definitely found them.

Her daughter squirmed out of their hiding place and crawled over to Faith. "Is it time to get up?"

"Afraid so." She wrapped the blanket she'd been forced to steal from the shack's bedding around Zoe.

Her daughter rubbed her eyes and let out a yawn as big as Texas. "My stuff is still in the bag, isn't it? We got everything? My unicorn? The baseball Daddy gave me?"

"It's all here."

"What if we left something?" Zoe asked.

"We didn't." Faith had no plans on ever going back to that shack. "Let's get ready."

Using water from a bottle, they cleaned up as best they could before the long walk into town. Faith took the backstreets and traveled across a vacant lot or two. No need to make their presence visible.

Zoe didn't skip along like normal, and Faith found it tough to smile or fake any optimism. They were in deep trouble. She tucked her money into her pocket except for one hundred dollars for gas. She just prayed the mechanic would cut her a break on the car repairs. Especially since he already had the ten grand she'd prepaid for the IDs.

Finally, Faith made out the siding of the auto shop. She gripped Zoe's hand and rounded the back of the building. A shiny new vehicle sat outside the small repair shop. At least Ray was early. She scanned the empty streets and tried the doorknob, but it was locked.

She pounded on the front door. It yanked open.

The guy looked like he'd done an all-nighter. Oil and grease streaked his jeans and work shirt.

"Oh, it's you," Ray said with a frown. "Come back next week. Car's not ready."

He moved to shut the door on her, but she stuck her foot through the crack.

"Not an option. I need to leave town." She shoved her way inside. "Zoe, stay out here, but where I can see you." She turned on Ray. "I need the car. And the other items. Today."

Faith crossed over to the counter and laid the envelope down.

Ray followed her. He fingered the bills and clicked his tongue. "You're $500 short."

"I know. But we have to go."

He shook his head. "No can do. Besides, I found another problem. It's gonna be another $750 before it's drivable. Parts, you know."

His twisted smile challenged her. Faith tried with everything in her not to react, not to cry out in defeat. She straightened her back. "This is all I have. You gave me a quote, and I've paid you a lot of money. You know I'll come through with the rest."

"Sorry," he said, though he didn't look sorry at all. "I can't give you the car without the full amount." He moved closer, his face just inches from her. "Besides, it don't matter. No IDs yet."

Her knees buckled. She gripped the counter to keep

from sinking to the floor. "I need those IDs," Faith said, her voice rising.

His gaze scraped up and down her body. A horrible feeling slithered through Faith. She stepped away from him and crossed her arms over her chest. Lifting her chin, she met his gaze. "Then the deal's off. I want my money back. All of it."

She grabbed at the cash but he yanked it away.

"Hold on now." With a slimy smile painting his face, he leaned toward her. "I'll get the IDs in a couple of days. As to the car, well, maybe we can work something out." His smiled broadened. "A trade wouldn't be a bad idea."

"Mom?" Zoe called through the cracked open door.

Days? Faith stilled. Impossible. They couldn't return to the shack. Her mind whirled with possibilities. Mrs. Hargraves *might* help. Or maybe they could sneak in after closing and sleep in the library.

His smile broadened as if he knew he'd won. He leaned forward and lowered his voice. "Ditch the kid. Come back at noon. We'll have a little fun for the next few days until the documents arrive, and I'll give you the car when it's ready."

Faith swallowed deeply. She couldn't believe she was even entertaining the proposition.

Ray fingered a stray piece of her hair. "Just so we're clear, I've been very lonely lately. Your enthusiastic company would square the account. A fair trade."

He scooped up the cash from the counter and pocketed it. She now had $100 to her name. Ray had everything else.

"Mom?"

Could she let him touch her? For Zoe?

"I'll see you at noon, sweet cheeks." He leaned close and licked the edge of her jaw to her ear. "If you're not here, the sheriff will get an anonymous tip, and I don't think you want him to wonder about you. Sheriff Redmond's the curious type."

She couldn't hide her shudder. She hated that he assumed she'd comply. As much as she loathed to admit it, she wasn't sure he was wrong.

Faith would do anything for Zoe.

THE SUN HAD fully risen when Stefan paused outside the Carder Diner, his empty thermos at his side. He'd grown tired of burning his morning brew over a campfire. Besides, Carla had a way with coffee beans.

The post-dawn glow gave the huge expanse of sky a soft tint. The angry clouds of yesterday were a distant memory. He'd been forced to get used to the constant sun and blue sky here. He missed the rain of Bellevaux, but the truth was, he'd grown to like the drama of the West Texas landscape. He hadn't decided where he'd go after this, but he might want to stay where the sun wasn't constantly hidden by clouds.

He pushed through the restaurant door at eight in the morning. The sizzling of hot bacon and scent of fresh coffee evoked a groan of temptation. Out of habit, he scanned the seating, lingering on the rear exit and timing his escape from the building. He didn't anticipate trouble, but he doubted he'd ever break the habit. It had saved his life more than once.

When his gaze landed on the booth closest to the back door, he paused. Faith and Zoe sat at the table. Seemed he and the pair had one more thing in common.

Zoe dug into a plate of bacon and eggs while Faith watched her daughter, sipping on coffee, no plate in front of her. He walked over to his standard seat at the counter and took a sip from the cup Carla had placed at his usual stool before setting his thermos on the counter. Carla scooped it up to fill, but he didn't attempt a conversation with her. He had every intention of eavesdropping.

"Mom? Aren't you going to eat?" Zoe asked.

"Not today, honey." Faith's voice whispered with a quick look under her lashes at him. She flushed and dipped her gaze, stirring her coffee longer than anyone would need to.

So she'd seen him come in. No need for pretense. He grabbed his cup and slid into the booth adjacent to theirs. Her eyes widened. He lifted his cup and smiled at her.

"I don't like camping out in the bushes," Zoe complained. "I got prickles down my back. Will we get the car back today so we can sleep on the cushions?"

"Hush, Zoe. You know the car is broken. How about you use your inside voice and finish your breakfast. Please, Slugger."

The little girl shoveled more food in her mouth while Faith avoided his gaze. She clearly would have preferred he sit anywhere but within listening distance. Too bad. If she was homeless, he could at least do something about that.

He didn't bother to ask himself why he cared. Maybe she and Zoe reminded him of Jenny Jennings and her daughter. He'd been too late to save them. Was he simply trying to redeem himself?

Could be.

Faith lowered her head and stared into her coffee cup. Dark circles shadowed her eyes. Her mouth was tight with stress. Something was wrong, something more than yesterday.

"Will that man fix the car? That would be good. I'm tired of walking everywhere."

"Me, too." Faith cleared her throat. "You let me worry about the car."

"What did the man want to trade?"

Faith's gaze jerked up to her daughter's.

"You're going to go see him at noon. He said he was lonely and you could help him, but I don't get it. He wants to talk? He must be really sad. Maybe I should go with you. I'm a great talker. Everybody says so. I always get in trouble at school."

A lot of words in one breath. Stefan would be impressed with Zoe's soliloquy if Faith didn't appear quite so mortified.

"I know very well." Faith's skin tinged a strange green and her gaze darted around the room.

Stefan could have told her no one else but him heard Zoe's revelation. The moment he'd walked in, he'd mapped the location of every person in the diner. He studied his coffee so she wouldn't have to see the fury he doubted he could hide.

Zoe swallowed another bite. "We could play baseball with him. Baseball helps me when I feel lonely," she said between chews.

"I don't think baseball's what he has in mind."

No doubt there. Stefan had never liked Ray, and had never let him touch his SUV. Rumor was the man had a reputation of gouging customers who couldn't afford to take their car to San Angelo or San Antonio for repairs.

"You leave him to me, Slugger," Faith said. "And don't talk with your mouth full."

For Stefan, the bigger question was why hadn't Faith sought help from the law? He knew the answer. He and Faith had a lot in common. He'd never go to the law if he had a choice. There were too many questions he couldn't answer. The idea of Faith feeling like she had no other options made Stefan want to knock most of Ray's teeth out. That she was considering giving in—and he could tell she was, just from the sick expression on her face—made him want to do even more damage. Preferably something that would cause Ray not to walk straight for a month or two.

Carla walked over to his table. "Changing things up on me, Léon?"

He pasted his standard charming smile on his face. "What can I say? I'm a man of mystery."

"I won't argue there. What'll you have?"

He ordered his usual, a couple of eggs, some bacon and a biscuit—he'd really miss her biscuits.

He motioned Carla closer and whispered his instructions in her ear. She grinned and hurried to the kitchen.

"I'm done," Zoe said, shoving her plate away. "I need to go to the bathroom."

Faith started to stand.

"M...o...o...om! I can go by myself."

Stefan bit back a smile. Faith's daughter made him smile. The girl had backbone.

For the next few minutes, Faith avoided looking his way by watching the door of the restroom.

Stefan emptied his coffee cup. He wasn't quite sure how to approach Faith. If their positions were reversed he certainly wouldn't want some stranger to stick her nose where it didn't belong.

Before he could solve the dilemma, Carla set the filled thermos in front of him, followed by his breakfast. The aroma of bacon caused his belly to rumble.

He tucked into his eggs, keeping an eye out for Carla. The waitress better hurry before Faith and Zoe left.

The little girl rushed back from the bathroom. Instead of sliding into the next booth, she stopped right beside Stefan. "Hi. I saw you in the library yesterday."

"That you did." Stefan smiled at the little girl. "You were a big help."

"Zoe," Faith hissed.

The little pistol shrugged at him and slunk back to their booth.

"How was your breakfast, sweetie?" Carla asked Zoe.

"Yummy."

The waitress placed a full plate in front of Faith.

"What's this?" she asked.

"Breakfast," Carla said.

"I… I can't afford it," Faith whispered.

"It's already been paid for, honey. Accept the gift." Carla winked at Stefan and walked away.

Faith stared over Zoe's head at him. "You did this?" she asked.

"Sounds like you're having a rough morning." Stefan hesitated, but truth was, he didn't have the time or patience to be polite, and if she had a noon deadline, neither did Faith. "Ray's got a reputation. I can talk to—"

"Zoe," Faith interrupted. "Wash your hands."

"I already did—"

Faith quirked her brow. "Really?"

Zoe bowed and shook her head. "No."

"That's what I thought. Now go."

Once Zoe was out of earshot, Faith pinched her nose. "Look, I appreciate the gesture, but…"

"I get it. You don't know me from Adam…or Ray, but I can help you. If you'll let me."

Chapter Three

Dishes crashed behind the counter. The entire diner went silent except for the pop of splattered oil from the grill in the kitchen.

The sound of shattering plates had nothing to do with Faith going speechless, though. Léon deserved that honor. She forced herself to close her mouth, fallen open from utter shock.

"Sorry, folks," Carla said with a sheepish grin. "Go back to your breakfast."

The volume of low conversation and clattering silverware rose at a steady pace in the busy eatery.

Faith couldn't stop staring at the man facing her.

Léon—like she'd ever forget that name—didn't avert his gaze; he just sat looking at her, unflinching, his expression deadly serious. Faith couldn't believe a man she'd barely met—who had obviously been eavesdropping—would show any interest in them, much less offer to help. Things like that didn't happen. Especially not to her.

The one time she'd bought into a too-good-to-be-true offer, she'd found herself married to Burke.

Léon left his half-eaten plate and scooted into Zoe's seat. "Who are you running from?"

"This is crazy. You're crazy." She placed her hands flat on the table. "You don't even know me."

Léon leaned against the seat, too relaxed from her perspective. "I have a job that puts me in contact with people who are in trouble, and Faith, you're wearing trouble all over your face. I'd like to help because I think you need it."

He reached across the table and took her hands in his. "Talk to me."

Stunned by his action, she didn't immediately pull away from him. His hands held hers with gentle warmth, not the harsh force Burke had used. For a moment, she allowed herself to feel that unfamiliar human touch even as she knew she couldn't ask for anything. Despite Mrs. Hargraves's endorsement yesterday, Faith couldn't risk trusting anyone else. Burke was too dangerous. More dangerous than she'd ever thought a human being could be.

She tugged her hands away and he let her go. "You're just guessing. You can't know."

He didn't say a word, just quirked a brow.

"I appreciate the offer, but I can't. I won't. You won't want any part of my troubles."

A glint of humor lit his eyes. "I can handle myself. I've faced more bad guys than pickups in Carder."

She couldn't stop the small smile. "You've been busy, then, since every other car I've seen in this town is a pickup."

"You get my point then." He leaned toward her. "I have significant resources at my disposal. You don't have to go into this battle alone."

At one time Faith would have given anything to find someone to share her problems with, someone to rely on, but she didn't believe in fairy tales anymore, and she'd accepted the truth. She was on her own. She and her daughter.

Zoe opened the bathroom door. Faith stood up. "I appreciate the offer, Léon, but it's not fair to drag you into our problems. Zoe and I are leaving Carder today. It was nice to meet you. And thank you for breakfast."

She grabbed two backpacks and held out her hand to Zoe, trying not to let her panic show. She recognized the questioning furrow of her daughter's forehead, but after a well-understood look, Zoe bit her lip and took Faith's hand.

They'd been out in public far too long. Hopefully if anyone came asking for her, Carder would live up to its reputation and be silent. Faith had until noon to figure out what to do about her car. Either way, as far as Léon and Carder, Texas, were concerned, Faith and Zoe would be gone. "We're leaving."

She made her way to the back door and walked into the heat of the late summer morning.

Zoe gave Léon an apologetic smile. "Bye."

He followed them out the back of the diner. "Whoever's after you knows you're here, doesn't he? That's why you're leaving today."

She ignored him and shifted one backpack on her shoulder before handing the smaller one to Zoe. "Goodbye, Léon."

Faith led her daughter down an alley leading to the library. She forced herself not to look behind her until she'd walked a full block. Work started at nine, and she had until noon to make an untenable decision.

With a quick pause, she allowed herself to glance back.

"He's gone," Zoe said from beside her. "I liked him. He was nice."

"Maybe." Faith knelt in front of Zoe. "But for now it's you and me, Slugger. Okay?"

"Okay, Mom. You and me."

WELL, THAT HAD gone well. The morning air carried the scent of rain, but for the second straight day Stefan didn't take the time to notice. He rounded the diner and stalked to his SUV. Faith had schooled him a new lesson on women in trouble: offering to help was the quickest way to scare them away. Particularly if she was on the run.

What got him was she really believed she was somehow protecting him. He rubbed his brow to alleviate the headache starting to build behind his eyes. She'd made herself perfectly clear. She didn't want his help. He should listen to her.

Besides, in three days, Léon would be dead.

In three days, his life in Carder would be over and his new life would begin.

In three days, he'd leave Faith and Zoe behind.

His vehicle's engine revved, and he pulled into the street. He should stay on the road out of town and drive straight to CTC's headquarters, let Ransom know his plans and prepare for a new future.

He didn't have anyone to tell. Only two members of CTC along with his sister and her husband even knew he was alive.

Maybe he could leave a gift for his nieces and nephew since CTC was located on the Triple C, his brother-in-law's ranch. Eventually his sister and her family would make their way to the spread. Maybe he could even risk calling his sister Kat before he vanished again.

That's exactly what he should do. Instead, when he drove past the library, he slowed down. Faith and Zoe hurried toward the front door. Faith glanced over her shoulder every few seconds. Her gaze paused at his vehicle. She turned her back on him, knelt down and whispered at Zoe before knocking on the library door. Mrs. Hargraves opened up with a smile.

Faith ducked inside and Zoe gave him a cheery wave before placing her finger over her lips and disappearing after her mother. That smile and mischievous attitude reminded him of his niece.

Of course, the last time he'd seen Lanie in person had been years ago. She didn't know him except from photographs. He didn't know if his sister had told her kids he was dead, or just never mentioned him.

Lanie was fearless from what he remembered. Zoe put on a good front, but he could see Faith's fear clouded her daughter's outlook.

With a curse, he jerked the vehicle into gear and made a U-turn toward the auto repair shop.

The siding had seen better days, but Stefan caught sight of a brand-new Land Rover out back, so money was flowing from somewhere.

Stefan peered through the glass on the front door. Ray counted bills at his counter, a satisfied smile on his face. Eager to wipe away the grin, Stefan slammed open the door.

The bell thwacked against the glass. Ray shoved the money into his cash drawer. He looked up. "Can I help you?"

"I hear you've got a car back there you've been holding hostage for a trade? Did I get that right, Ray?"

The man flushed. "What's it to you?"

Stefan leaned across the desk. "Oh, it means a lot to me, actually. What does she owe?"

"A thousand bucks."

"Show me the invoice," Stefan ordered.

Ray dug through a large pile of papers and thrust a document at Stefan. "It's not complete. We found a leak—"

"Save it. I know exactly what you're doing." Stefan scanned the list of repairs. "She's paid you enough. Give me the keys." He held out his hand.

"But it's not fixed. I don't got the parts."

"You want to play this hard, I'm happy to oblige." Stefan turned and flipped the Open sign to Closed. He locked the front door and pulled down all the shades.

Ray's face paled. Stefan crossed his arms in front of him. "Let me explain the situation so even you can understand it, Ray. Faith is a friend of mine. I don't like it when my friend is gouged by a small-time criminal." He rounded the counter. "Do you know who I am?"

The guy shook his head.

Stefan smiled. "Let's just say that I know how to make a man beg for his life and still not do any visible damage. Would you like me to demonstrate?"

Ray's eyes widened with terror.

"I didn't think so. Now get out there and finish those repairs. In fact, I'll watch you."

Stefan followed a shaking Ray out to the car. Within thirty minutes the mechanic had the car purring as well as a thirty-year-old car could. He shoved the keys into Stefan's hand. "So, why are you going to all this trouble for her? She putting out for you?"

Stefan didn't hesitate. He grabbed the idiot's collar and shoved him against the wall. "You disrespect her like that again, and I'll teach you some manners. Oh, and Ray. You might want to straighten up your act. I'm paying a visit to Sheriff Redmond the moment I leave this place."

Ray lifted his chin in misplaced defiance. "I wouldn't

do that if I were you. Not unless you want your lady friend to get into trouble."

Stefan stilled before tightening his grip. "And why would that be?"

"W-we have a side deal. She hasn't received delivery."

"What deal?" Stefan's words came out clipped. He should have known there was more to this than a car. "I'm waiting."

Stefan didn't remove his hand, but pressed his forearm against the man's windpipe.

"N-none of your—" Ray clutched at Stefan's arms and sucked in a breath. "Business."

"I'm putting about eleven pounds of pressure against your trachea. At thirty-three pounds, I'll crush it, and don't think I can't. I'm not even breaking a sweat."

"Wh-who are you?"

"I'm a ghost," Stefan said with a small grin. "I don't exist."

Ray clawed at Stefan's arm. He didn't budge.

"You're turning blue, Ray. I suggest you talk. I wouldn't risk testing my patience."

"I'll...call...the...sheriff," he gasped.

"Go right ahead. We'll see what Sheriff Redmond thinks about you gouging your customers and running an illegal business out of your shop."

"You don't have proof."

"You told me your customers don't mention your deals with them. You admitted you have the leverage to gouge them and they don't have anywhere to go. Simple math, Ray."

The mechanic sagged, clutching at Stefan's hands to keep upright. "I can't breathe. Let me go. I'll tell you everything."

"That's better." Stefan eased the pressure some, but not completely. "I'm listening."

"You don't understand. I do business with people who... Well, they expect a certain amount of volume. This is a small town. Sometimes, I run short, so I—"

"Blackmail people who can't afford to say no. I understand. I want names."

Ray shook his head. "I can't. They'll kill me."

"And I won't?" Stefan asked.

"No offense, but they scare me more than you do. I get the feeling you play by a set of rules at least. These guys? They got no rules."

Stefan released Ray. The man bent over, sucking air as if his life depended on it. Stefan had to end-run his fear. "What did Faith buy from you?"

Easy question to answer, and the floodgates opened. Ray told him everything. In fact, he wouldn't stop talking.

After listening to the idiot for a solid fifteen minutes, Stefan kneaded the back of his neck. "Shut up, Ray."

Stefan picked up the phone and dialed a familiar number.

"Léon." Ransom Grainger, his boss and head of CTC, answered. "What's up? You got something to share?"

CTC's boss man was damn spooky. "You figured out I'm leaving." Stefan couldn't keep the resignation from his voice.

"I had a feeling. Annie helping you?"

"It's the only way," Stefan said. "I've been living on borrowed time, and we both know it."

The crick of a chairback filtered through the phone.

"You sure you want to start over completely? Last time, you were able to keep a little of your past alive.

Similar job, we kept you in the know about your sister and her family…"

"If I stay my life will always be in the shadows. Eventually I'll bring my trouble to Carder. We both know that."

"Maybe. But if it comes we can handle it."

"I won't take the risk, Ransom. You and CTC have too much to lose. Now, do you want my tip or not?"

Ransom bit out a curse. "This conversation isn't over, Stefan."

"Yes, it is." Stefan cleared his throat. "Got a lead on some smugglers who deal in guns and stolen identities and have a contact in Carder. You interested?"

"Definitely. And Léon, we'll talk soon, I assume?"

"Of course." He'd miss working with Ransom. With everyone.

"Good. Now back to business. Firepower?"

"Unknown, but a lot," Stefan reported. "They've got a pipeline through the auto shop in town."

"Ray." Ransom let out a harsh curse. "I should've known. Consider it taken care of."

Stefan ended the call and pinned Ray with his gaze. "You'll be receiving a visit from a couple of my friends. You tell them everything. You do exactly what they say, and you may get out of this alive. Do you understand?"

Ray nodded his head.

"If you cooperate, you may, and I stress *may*, be able to escape this mess without jail time. Do you understand?"

He nodded again.

"If you so much as step a toe out of line from now on, I'll be back, and this time you'll wish you were facing your business partners. Do you understand?"

Ray shook his head up and down. "Yes, sir."

"Good." Stefan punched him in the gut and kneed him so he'd sing soprano for a week.

Ray dropped to the floor and held his groin. He looked up at Stefan.

"That's for insulting Faith." Stefan stared at the man. "And by the way. She'd never let a toad like you touch her."

THE MORNING WAS half over already, too quickly as far as Faith was concerned. She sat at the side of the library, strategically perched behind a tree, ever watchful of her surroundings. She hadn't noticed any unfamiliar vehicles and no strangers had come into the library so far, but she could barely breathe for the tension knotting her back.

What was she going to do? They couldn't stay in Carder, and she had one hour to make her decision.

Even if she agreed to do what Ray wanted, could she trust him to keep up his end of the bargain?

Stupid question, with an obvious answer. Of course not.

Faith's entire body shook with strain. She couldn't let Burke get to Zoe. She needed a solution and making Ray angry meant not getting their new identity. She'd paid $10,000 for a new life—the only way she could protect Zoe.

She was trapped.

Léon's offer reverberated in her mind, but she'd be taking a huge risk. Could she trust him?

Why was she even considering his offer?

Her head hurt as the flurry of questions pounded against her skull. She gripped her hair. She knew why: because one hour and one hundred dollars wouldn't get her out of town and away from Burke.

Zoe raced past her. "I found the bunny, Mom. I'll catch

it this time." She held up a small box and dove behind a hedge. Faith wasn't too worried about the bunny since Zoe and the rabbit played the identical game every day.

The city hall clock chimed eleven like an alarm sounding a warning. Faith rubbed her face with her hands. The key to the front door of the library burned in her pocket. She'd taken it from Mrs. Hargraves's desk. The betrayal ate at her, but she couldn't ask Zoe to sleep outside again. They'd been lucky last night, but more thunderstorms were coming in from the east.

They could leave and sneak in after her boss closed up then be gone around daylight. The food she'd packed might last a few days.

Only one problem left. Giving in to Ray, or tucking her tail between her legs and asking Léon to help.

Zoe hopped from behind a tree and ran across the sidewalk at full speed, skidding on her sneakers to a halt. She knelt down on the sidewalk in front of Faith, drew a hopscotch board with chalk, then grabbed one of her polished rocks from her knapsack.

"Wanna play, Mom?" she asked.

"In a minute, Slugger."

Zoe sidled up to her mother. "What's wrong?"

Faith clung to her daughter, the warmth of her small body filling her with comfort and hope. "It'll be fine. You play one round, and I'll join you."

Zoe bounced over to the game and slid the rock along the concrete.

The library's front door opened. Mrs. Hargraves stepped out and peered around before catching sight of Faith tucked behind the tree. She made her way down the library steps and over to them. "You're looking worried."

Faith chewed on her lip. "We have to leave."

"He found you?" the librarian asked, her eyes dark with concern.

Faith nodded.

"Then why aren't you already gone?" Her boss's eyes widened with realization. "Your car?"

"It's complicated." She watched Zoe jump through her hopscotch board. Faith sent the older woman a sidelong glance. "Léon offered to help me. I turned him down."

"Why would you do a fool thing like that, girl?"

The incredulity in Mrs. Hargraves's voice would've made Faith smile if she'd had it in her. "I don't know him. No one offers a handout without wanting something in return. And you know what I mean."

Her boss plopped down on the planter next to Faith and crossed one boot over the other. "Ninety percent of the time, you're probably right. If you're talking about Ray the auto-moron, you're definitely right. That boy was a problem from the time he was three. I kicked him out of the library permanently when he turned thirteen. Selling joints between the stacks." Mrs. Hargraves huffed in disgust, snagged a stone from the ground and flicked it into the adjacent rock garden. "Léon is different. He wouldn't have told you this, but he works with those boys out on the old Triple C Ranch. They've accomplished more than one miracle. If I was in bad trouble and needed someone...special, I'd call them up."

"I don't like relying on other people," Faith admitted. "I've been burned every time."

"At least you divorced him, honey. I had to wait for mine to die on me." Mrs. Hargraves winked.

Faith couldn't help but chuckle. "That's a story you haven't told me."

"Oh, it's not worth telling. He was an SOB and I married him because I was a ninny of nineteen." The librarian stood up, her spine stiff. "Call Léon."

She rounded the front of the library before freezing, her gaze pinned toward Main Street. "Faith, you said you turned Léon down?"

She nodded.

"I don't think he listened."

Faith peeked out from behind the tree. Mrs. Hargraves pointed down the street.

Her hunk-of-junk car headed their way with Léon at the wheel. He pulled in front of the library and stepped out of the vehicle. Ray followed in a large SUV. He parked behind Faith's car and without a word, hightailed in the direction of his garage at full speed, noticeably panicked.

Zoe ran over to Léon. "Our car! Look, Mom. He brought it back."

Faith's mouth opened wide. She didn't know what to say.

He ruffled Zoe's hair and strode up to Faith. "We need to talk." He handed her the keys and glanced down at Zoe. "In private."

Mind spinning, Faith gave a quick nod.

"I'll watch her, dear," the older woman said. "In fact, I may join her. You go inside to my office. And be nice. He's a good boy."

He arched his brow at Mrs. Hargraves, but she simply laughed. "You be nice, too, Léon. She's had a rough morning."

Side by side, they walked into the library and headed to her boss's office.

"I don't understand," she said once she'd closed them inside the small room. "How did you get my car? It was undrivable."

"Ray fixed it in thirty minutes. He's no longer an issue."

Faith sank into the chair in front of Mrs. Hargraves's desk. They *could* leave, if only for one thing.

"Did Ray give you anything else?" she asked in a hesitant voice.

"You mean your $10,000 deal?" Léon hitched his hip on the desk. "That's a bit of a problem. His business partner wanted double or you wouldn't get the IDs, and I've got to be honest, I doubt they'd pass for authentic."

Faith twisted her hands in her lap, denial running through her. "This can't be happening." She wrapped her arms around her body and rocked back and forth, her mind awhirl.

"Am I safe in assuming you don't have the money?"

With a sarcastic laugh she pulled a few crumpled bills from her back pocket. "This is it. One hundred bucks. That's all I have. Ray might as well want a million."

Léon plucked Mrs. Hargraves's chair from behind her desk and sat across from Faith. "Why do you and Zoe need new identities?

The keys dug into Faith's palm. She shook her head.

He took her hands in his and squeezed her chilled fingers. "Who are you running from, Faith?"

"You don't understand. His family is too powerful. We have no choice but to disappear."

"I may have a solution—"

She shook her head side to side. She couldn't listen. "We *can't* stay. He knows where we are. He trashed our place last night. I'll have to find another place to hide until I can raise the money. Maybe if I were closer to Mexico, I could find someone—"

"Take this." Léon released her hands and pulled out a thick folded envelope from his pocket. "You're making a mistake, but here's your $10,000." He pressed it into her hand.

She opened the envelope and peeked inside. "I don't understand."

He shrugged. "Ray realized he wasn't doing the right thing."

She slapped her hand to her mouth. Her eyes glistened. "I don't think you could possibly know what this means. You've saved our lives."

Impulsively, she leaned over and hugged him. "Thank you. Again."

For a moment he stiffened against her, before folding his arms around her. She'd meant the embrace to be a quick thank-you. Faith didn't expect the warmth that seeped through her body as he held her.

He bent his head to her ear. "Let me help you."

The breath behind his soft words tickled her ear. Her heart thudded against her chest in an anticipation she hadn't experienced in a very long time.

"You've done enough." She eased away from him. "You've given us hope."

"Stop! Leave her alone!" Mrs. Hargraves shouted.

Faith's eyes widened. She sprinted to the library door, and Léon raced past her in a full-on run. He slammed the heavy oak open. Faith stared in horror at the street.

An old Cadillac idled half on, half off the sidewalk. Mrs. Hargraves lay sprawled on the concrete, struggling to get up. A bald man held Zoe in his arms next to the vehicle. Her daughter fought like hell against him, kicking and screaming.

"Stop!" she shouted. "Zoe!"

Léon sprinted down the steps, but before he could reach Zoe, the man shoved her into the back seat of the car and dove into the vehicle. Zoe fought to open the door, but he must've locked it. She pounded her fists against the glass, but no sound penetrated.

With a shout, Léon vaulted onto the hood and reached around to the driver's side. The guy twisted the steering wheel hard. Léon grabbed on. The car swerved again. He flew off and skidded across the asphalt.

Faith raced at the vehicle, but it was no use. The Cadillac sped away.

Her knees shook. Panting, she bent over and stared down the road. This couldn't be happening.

Zoe's panicked face peered through the back window. And just like that, her daughter was gone.

Chapter Four

Tar and rock pressed into Stefan's palms. A wild screech sounded and the Cadillac disappeared around the first corner. He heaved to his feet, and without hesitation, sprinted to his SUV.

"Are you okay?" Faith rushed over, meeting him at the vehicle.

He'd love to slam his fist into the jaw of that bald-headed kidnapper. He couldn't believe he'd been too late. Again.

This time, though—unlike the Jennings family—he had a chance to save Zoe. He yanked open the car's door and cranked the key. Faith jumped into the passenger seat and buckled her seat belt.

He didn't try to argue. If Zoe were his, he'd have done the same thing.

"They'll be heading out of town." Stefan gunned the accelerator and swerved around the corner. "Where's he taking her?"

"Dallas," Faith said, her voice thick with unshed emotion. "That man was following us yesterday. His name is Jerry. I think he works for my ex-husband."

"Zoe's father?" A flood of curses coursed through Stefan's head.

"It's not what you think," she rushed out.

A man who'd pay a thug to terrify his child didn't win any Father of the Year awards. Stefan would figure it out later. First things first. He had to get Zoe back.

He headed east, but the car wasn't visible. He had a fifty-fifty chance and needed to up the odds. Stefan grabbed his phone and dialed.

In one ring he received an answer through his earpiece.

"Sheriff Blake Redmond."

"It's Léon." He quickly gave Blake a sitrep. "Best guess is the kidnapper's headed to Dallas. Can your deputies cut off his exit routes?"

"Cops?" she whispered, clutching his arm.

"We don't have a choice," Stefan mouthed. He hit the outskirts of Carder and floored the accelerator. The SUV zipped down the narrow road, the flat brush whizzing past. "I'm headed that way now."

"I don't have enough cars to cover all the roads," Blake said. "I bet he'll take Highway 113 to 67, unless he knows the area."

The squawk of a radio shrieked through the phone. "Deputy Smithson's patrolling west of town. I'll head your way." Blake shouted instructions to inform the other deputies of the situation. Drawers and cabinets slammed. "What's he driving?"

Stefan provided the make and model of the car and a description of the perp. "Plates were splattered with mud," he said. "Contact CTC for a chopper and some men. They'll give us more eyes surrounding Carder. And can you patch me through to Smithson? I've got an idea if he's not too far from Old Mine Road."

"I like the way you think," Blake said.

A few clicks signaled the call forward. Stefan glanced at Faith through the corner of his eye. She'd leaned forward in her seat and gripped the dashboard, straining as if ready to catapult through the window.

"Where is she?" Faith bit her lip, her eyes lined with worry.

"Not far." If the guy hadn't doubled back. Stefan couldn't push the car any faster. "Is Jerry from Dallas?"

"He was a bouncer at a bar in Weatherford."

"Which means he won't know the shortcuts." They had a chance.

"Léon, what do you need?" The deputy's voice came through Stefan's earpiece.

"A roadblock across 113. I want to force the guy onto Old Mine Road."

"The arroyo will box him in." Sirens sounded through the phone. "How far ahead is he?"

"I'm doing ninety. He had about four minutes on us."

"I'll set up at the fork on 113. You know it?"

"Perfect." Stefan yanked the steering wheel onto a dirt road. Six-foot-tall rows of sorghum nearly ready for harvest lined the route.

Faith bounced in the seat. "What are you doing? He wouldn't have gone this way."

"Trust me. It's a shortcut."

"What if you're wrong?" Faith gripped the armrest. "What if he didn't come this way?"

"There aren't that many ways leading out of Carder." Stefan winced at his reassurance. He'd made mistakes before, but this could be their only shot.

Within a few minutes a sheriff's office SUV, lights flashing, appeared on the horizon behind them.

"It's taking too long." Faith searched the horizon around them. Dirt flew from the rear wheels.

"If Jerry's taken the fastest way to Dallas, he'll go

through San Angelo. Deputy Smithson's car will block the road just a few miles as the crow flies. We'll get him."

Stefan's phone rang.

"Cadillac in sight," the deputy said. "He's slowing down."

"Almost there," Stefan whispered.

"He turned, Léon."

Stefan made a quick right. Deep arroyos lined one side of Old Mine Road. He had to be smart about this. Zoe was in that car. He planted his truck in the center of the narrow road. Like clockwork, over a small rise, the Cadillac sped toward him.

Faith gasped. "You were right."

The car heading straight at them didn't swerve. Stefan braced himself, his foot hovered over the gas pedal.

The kidnapper veered at the last minute away from the deep ditch. His vehicle skidded across the dirt and into the brush before shuddering to a halt.

Stefan didn't hesitate. He grabbed a rifle from the back seat and rushed to the driver's side. He aimed at the guy's head. "Hands on the steering wheel," he shouted. "Use your elbow to roll down the window and unlock the doors. Don't try anything." He tapped the windshield with the barrel. "I won't miss."

Jerry's hands quaked as he complied. Still holding his weapon on the man, Stefan opened the back door. "Go to your mom, Zoe."

The little girl sprinted, arms pumping as hard as they could, to Faith. She hugged her daughter and ran her hands up and down the girl. "Are you okay?"

Zoe wrapped her arms around her mother and nodded.

Certain they were safe, Stefan studied his prisoner. Hired hand at best. He yanked the door and it bounced open. "Who ordered you to take the girl? Was it her father?"

"I can't." The man shook his head. "He'll kill me."

Flashing lights screamed toward them. Stefan cursed. He wanted the guy's name, and he didn't have confidence Faith would tell him. Come to think of it, he didn't even know Faith and Zoe's last name.

The realization conjured a twinge of admiration. She'd been more than careful. Faith had shown herself to be smart and savvy. More so than he'd given her credit for.

Deputy Smithson limped over and cuffed Jerry. The guy glared at Faith. "It won't matter," he shouted at her. "We're both dead anyway."

"Not yet, I'm not," Faith countered, positioning herself in front of Zoe. "And I don't plan on giving you or him the satisfaction."

Stefan strode over to her. "Take Zoe to the truck," he said with a tilt of his head. "I'll deal with this guy."

Faith led her daughter away, and Stefan followed her with his gaze. He liked Faith. He liked how protective she was of Zoe. He liked her fighting spirit. He'd also learned a very important detail about the gravity of her situation: Faith's ex-husband evoked real fear in a man who wasn't exactly a lightweight. Stefan needed to get the truth out of Jerry—hopefully enough to arrest Faith's ex.

Before he could begin questioning his prisoner, Blake Redmond's SUV rounded the curve and pulled to a stop near Stefan. He exited the vehicle. "Everyone okay?"

"Zoe is fine. So is her mom. Unfortunately, our friend Jerry, no last name—" Stefan indicated the kidnapper "—doesn't have a scratch on him."

Blake grabbed his phone and ordered the searchers and the CTC chopper to stand down. He pulled out his notebook. "I received a call from dispatch. Mrs. Hargraves is at the clinic. She's doing well. Of course, she's arguing with the doctor. She wants to go back to the library, but they're keeping her for observation for a bump on the head."

"Sounds just like her. Faith will be relieved."

The sheriff tipped his Stetson back from his brow. "She know who did this?" He stared at Stefan's vehicle where Faith and Zoe huddled in the back seat.

Stefan didn't blink. Blake was a straight-arrow kind of law officer, but he also understood about family, and justice.

"Her ex."

"I hate custody disputes." Blake's forehead furrowed in concentration. "What's your take?"

"She's got reason to be scared." Stefan stroked his jaw. "Can you hold this guy without their statement? At least until I get the full picture."

Blake hooked his thumb in his belt loop near his badge. "I *should* take her in now. You know that."

From the tone in Blake's voice, Stefan could tell he understood. CTC had worked with the sheriff before. He valued the law's intent—and justice—more than the letter.

"Give me a day or two, Blake. This is more than a straightforward custody battle. If I'm wrong, I'll bring her to you myself."

Blake slapped his hat against his thigh. "Our prisoner abducted a child in front of witnesses in broad daylight. He won't be leaving my jail anytime soon." The sheriff paused before meeting Stefan's gaze. "You've got two days. After that, I won't be able to stop the legal wheels."

Stefan glanced over his shoulder at Faith's skittish expression. "I hope it's enough."

MIDMORNING LIGHT BOUNCED off Burke's immaculately polished mahogany desk. His feet sank into the thick carpet. He'd been here all night, waiting for word. He hadn't stopped pacing. Any minute now he should get the phone call that his daughter would be coming home.

Once he got hold of her, he could control her.

Of course, Faith would never see Zoe again. Burke would make certain of it.

His cell phone rang.

"Thomas."

"Jerry got caught. He's in jail in Carder, Texas, on kidnapping charges."

Burke let out a stream of curses. "How could you let this happen?"

"Don't blame me. You're the one who recommended the guy. *You* said I could trust him. Well, he's not as advertised. The idiot ransacked her house. To intimidate her, he told me. Instead, she ran. Made things twice as difficult to grab your daughter."

"Where's Zoe? Did you get her?"

"Jerry had her for all of fifteen minutes before the local sheriff returned her to her mother. We're on the sheriff's radar, and I haven't identified any Thomas, Inc. strings you can pull."

"What's this Podunk sheriff's name?" Burke picked up a letter opener and slid the edge across his palm. In his mind, he imagined blood oozing from the wound. The image transformed into his ex-wife's throat, exsanguinating her until her lifeless body fell to the floor. "My father doesn't need to know about this. You understand?"

"Double my fee, you'll buy my silence, and I'll take care of Sheriff Redmond. And my loyalty."

Burke's neck muscles bunched in protest, but for now he needed Orren's expertise.

"Have you located Faith and Zoe?"

"They left the scene with some cowboy playing hero. No intel on him. He's a wild card."

Burke fell into his leather chair and drummed his fingers across his desk. The guy was a loose end he couldn't afford. In fact, there were too many loose ends all the way around. They'd *all* have to be taken care of eventually. "Clean up this mess. Jerry knows me."

"You pay me to make problems disappear. But from now on, I do the hiring. I do the terminating."

Burke spun in his chair and peered across the Dallas downtown skyline. "Fine."

"I'll take care of Jerry and bring your daughter to you." Orren paused. "If your ex gets in the way?"

"I want *my* wife gone. Disappeared. With no trace."

"You certain about that? Your father—"

"Faith is *my* business. Not his," Burke said, his shoulders tight with anger. He pitched back two fingers of whiskey. "Just make certain I'm not implicated."

"Triple my fee and I'll take care of her myself. Within twenty-four hours your daughter will be with you and your ex-wife will be dead."

THE WEST TEXAS landscape surrounding Stefan's vehicle stretched out for an eternity. The midday sun beat down on them. When he'd first arrived in West Texas, he hadn't realized the horizon rested sixty and in some places even one hundred miles away. Most didn't.

Stefan glanced in the rearview mirror. Faith held Zoe snuggled in her arms. The little girl had fallen asleep clutching her mother. Faith stroked her daughter's hair, tension lining her mouth. He didn't blame her for being scared. He might not be a father, but he couldn't imagine anything worse than having a child taken from you, even if it had only been for a half hour.

Zoe stretched and blinked open her eyes. "Where are we going?"

"Camping," Stefan responded, meeting Faith's gaze in the mirror. "Do you like camping?"

"Will we sleep in your truck?" Zoe asked. "Mom and I went camping in the car after we left home."

Faith winced at her daughter's words.

"We'll stay in a tent."

"Cool. I spent the night in a tent in my best friend Danny's backyard." She yawned again.

"Try to sleep, Zoe. We didn't get much rest last night," Faith whispered.

The little girl sagged against her mother and soon her breathing evened out. Faith, on the other hand, fought back a yawn and kept her gaze focused out the back window.

Stefan turned onto another dirt road, searching the landscape for any signs of dust that wasn't caused by his SUV.

"So far so good," he said in a low voice so as not to wake Zoe. "We're not being followed."

He'd taken all the precautions he could. He'd stowed everything they owned in the back of his truck only after he'd swept the items for tracking devices. Since her ex possessed enough resources to hire a man to locate them in Carder and to kidnap Zoe, he could only think of two places where they would be safe. His camp or the CTC compound. The moment he'd mentioned CTC and the ex-military covert operatives who frequented the place, Faith had shut down, so he'd piled them into his SUV.

She met Stefan's gaze in the mirror, apprehensive at best. "Does the sheriff know where we'll be?"

Her concern for law enforcement hadn't been lost on Stefan. He needed to understand why. They'd be having a long conversation soon. "No one knows. I like my privacy."

"Good." Finally, Faith relaxed against the seat. Within minutes, her eyes had closed, her lashes fanning the shadows beneath her eyes. For the first time since Stefan had met her, the tightness around her mouth eased a bit, and her face took on a softness he found far too appealing.

Stefan drove for another half hour and took several more intentional wrong turns before doubling back. If anyone had wanted to track him, they wouldn't be able to.

Just after noon he felt comfortable enough to exit a dirt road. He headed toward the small rock outcropping that protected his campsite from the weather. A small stream trickled through a creek bed to the north. It hadn't been easy to find a water source out here, but Stefan had managed.

He pulled up near the midsized tent and opened the door. A blast of hot air hit him full throttle. "We're here," he said, exiting the SUV.

Faith yawned and helped Zoe out of the truck.

The little girl's eyes widened in surprise and she spun around. A huge grin split her face. "This is awesome. Can we fish?"

"The creek's not deep enough," Stefan said.

Her smile fell.

"We might find some frogs," he offered. "And I've seen a horned toad or two wandering around."

"Neat."

The midday Texas sun burned bright in the sky, beating down. His campfire lay dormant, his cooler in the tent to keep it from being pelted by the summer day. Stefan pulled out a couple of camp chairs from the back of his SUV and placed them in a small shaded area. He retrieved cold water from the cooler and handed one each to Faith and Zoe.

After sitting down, Faith took a swig. "How did you ever find this place?"

"I spent a lot of hours searching the backcountry. One night after a long day's ride, an afternoon storm blew in. The sun was setting and I headed toward these rocks. I stay here when I come to town."

"You don't have a house?" Zoe bent down and picked up a piece of quartz and shoved it into her pocket.

He doubted she'd consider the palace where he grew up quite the same thing. He sat across from them. "I travel a lot for my job. It's easier to camp out than worry about keeping up a place. Besides, there's never a no vacancy sign out here."

The corners of Faith's lips lifted, and her eyes crinkled. She lit up when she smiled. He shouldn't notice, but he couldn't help himself. Something about her...

"I like it here. Maybe we should camp out, too, Mom." Zoe sipped her water and handed the bottle to her mother. "Can I explore?"

"Make sure you can always see the tent." Faith took the beverage and set it on the ground.

Zoe huffed an exasperated sigh. "I'm not a baby." She raced around the camp, bending to pick some flowers, then checking out a cactus.

"She doesn't stop, does she?" Stefan said, watching the little girl dart when anything new caught her attention. "How do you keep up?"

"I don't."

He glanced over at Zoe practicing opening and closing the tent's zipper. At least she played far enough away for him to ask a few questions.

If only he could find the right words not to send an

extremely skittish Faith back behind that protective wall she'd erected so carefully.

"I temporarily delayed the sheriff questioning you, but I can't protect you from his questions forever. Not unless I understand what's going on." Stefan leaned forward in his chair. "Give me the unvarnished truth, Faith. Did you take Zoe without her father's permission? Is that why you need to avoid the sheriff?"

Faith's head snapped to check on Zoe, obviously confirming that her daughter couldn't eavesdrop on their conversation. She crossed her arms in defiance. "Look, I'll never be able to thank you enough for saving Zoe, but I can't allow her anywhere near law enforcement. If that's not possible, take me to my car right now. We'll disappear and you can forget we ever met."

Her tone didn't leave room for negotiation and neither did the stubborn expression on her face.

"Forgetting about you isn't an option." He didn't want to ask his next question, but he had to know. "Did your ex-husband hurt you? Did he hurt Zoe? Is that why you ran?"

"It's complicated." Faith twisted her fingers in her hands and touched the ring finger of her left hand. "He didn't hit me. Or Zoe. But he *is* dangerous."

Stefan studied her every microexpression, attempting to piece together her secret. He couldn't read her. What wasn't she telling him? "How dangerous? Would he kill Jerry or you?"

She didn't speak for a moment. "If I tell you, will you promise not to take us to the sheriff's office?"

Every instinct within Stefan urged him to agree. He hadn't survived the last decade without trusting his gut. "Agreed."

Her gaze bored into his, as if trying to gauge his honesty. He could tell her not to bother—he excelled at lying, yet another reason he was still alive. She didn't move for several moments. He dug into his pocket for the keys to his SUV and waited for the request to take them to the library to retrieve her car.

"I don't know how Burke found us," she said, chewing on her lip.

Her eyes darted back and forth. Stefan could almost see her mind playing out worst-case scenarios.

"We're in trouble," she finally admitted. Her leg bounced with nerves. "You saved Zoe's life, and I'm out of ideas."

"You can trust me."

"I hope so," she said with a long sigh. She sucked in a deep breath. "Zoe's name is flagged in the system. The sheriff would have to send her to her father, and I can't allow that to happen."

At her admission, a silent curse slammed through Stefan's mind. "So this *is* about custody?"

"Not exactly." Faith rubbed her face. "I should start with Burke."

Finally. The moment she removed her hands from her eyes, Stefan nearly gasped aloud. He didn't think he'd ever forget her haunted expression so he simply waited, still and silent.

"I was so stupid to marry him," she bit out. "I wasn't good enough for him. Not thin enough, not blonde enough…just not enough. He divorced me and used Zoe to keep his parents happy. They want to make her into a little debutante. They can't see her for what she is."

He hadn't liked this guy from the moment he'd seen the fear on Faith's face, but her tone of defeat urged him to fold her into his arms and simply hold her. How could anyone believe Faith wasn't enough, that Zoe shouldn't be treasured?

"The last few months, Burke started laying ground-work to get full custody." Faith looked up at him with despair in her eyes. "I'm pretty sure someone called in false reports to Child Protective Services. They were at my door asking if I'd paid my bills for the month. When I reported Burke late on his child support they mumbled a few words, but nothing ever happened. Burke and his family have the money and the power. They want full custody. Someone like me can't fight them and win. I knew I could lose her. I was terrified."

"So you ran."

"I hadn't planned to." Faith rose and stared off into the desert. "I never wanted this."

"CTC has a lot of connections in the state and across the country. My team could help you fight your ex-hus-band's family. The right way."

She shook her head. "It's too late for that. A few months ago I would have jumped at the offer, but now—"

He joined her at the edge of camp. Gently, he turned her toward him. The fear in her eyes wasn't an act. Her ex-husband terrified her. Stefan placed his hands on her shoulders and squeezed lightly.

"What aren't you telling me, Faith?"

She averted her gaze from his.

"I'll wait for an answer as long as I have to." Stefan tilted her chin up with his finger. "I can help. If you'll just trust me."

She took a shuttering breath. "I haven't ever said it out loud. I still can't believe it."

"Tell me."

Conflict whirled behind her eyes. Finally, she swallowed. Stefan didn't know what else he could do. What terrified her so much? Why couldn't he convince her to tell him?

Faith stared at him, still obviously struggling. She glanced at the tent and her brow furrowed. "Where's Zoe?" Frantically, she scanned the camp.

He followed her line of sight. "She can't have gone far."

"Zoe!" Faith called.

Stefan ducked his head into the tent. Not there. He perused the landscape, but the little girl had wandered out of sight. She couldn't have gone far. It had only been a few minutes.

His mind flashed to a horrifying possibility. "The creek," he shouted, racing toward the water.

"Is it deep?" Faith chased after him.

Before he could answer a horrified scream sounded through the desert air.

"Oww! Mommy! Mommy! Help me!"

They headed toward her voice and slid down the embankment. Zoe danced around, slapping her legs.

"What's wrong?" Faith shouted.

Stefan looked down. A swarm of red ants surrounded Zoe's feet.

"Fire ants." He grabbed Zoe and set her away from the nest she'd stumbled onto. Quickly, he flicked away the ones still crawling on her.

She cried out. "They hurt."

"I know," he said, scooping the lightweight into his arms. "I've got something that will help."

The little girl clung to his neck. Hard. For a tiny thing, she certainly had a grip.

"It hurts, Mommy. Hot prickly burns."

"I know, Slugger."

Stefan tightened his arms around her and ran back to the camp, Faith at his heels.

He passed a sobbing Zoe to her mother and knelt down in front of his cooler. Every cry twisted his heart a bit. "Where did they sting you?"

"My l-legs," she sobbed.

"Get her pants off," he ordered and dug into the chest for some ice.

Faith removed Zoe's pants, shoes and socks. Stefan crouched beside her and cleaned her legs with cool water and a bit of soap.

The moment the liquid touched Zoe, she sighed. "That feels better. I like the cool."

Red welts erupted on her legs. They had to hurt like hell. "They're fire ants. You can tell because they're reddish brown. They don't have an opening on the top of their nest so they fooled you. That's why you stepped on it."

Big tears slid down Zoe's cheeks. "I didn't mean to step on their house."

Stefan dug into his tent for a T-shirt and wrapped an ice-filled baggie inside. "Hold this on the welts. It should help. I'll get some cortisone cream."

Faith pressed the cold pack against Zoe's leg. She sucked in several shuddering breaths and leaned against her mother. Stefan returned with a small tube.

"Do you have the kitchen sink in that tent?" she asked.

"Necessities when you're living outside." He spread the cream on Zoe's feet, ankles and calves. "Did they get anywhere else?"

Her daughter wiped her eyes and shook her head.

"Okay, then. How about you go into my tent and we'll elevate your feet. Do you think you can do that?"

"What's elevate?"

"It means we'll put a pillow under them so they're above your heart. It'll help the swelling go down."

"The ants won't come inside the tent, will they?" Zoe asked, frowning at the ground in suspicion.

"We'll close the screen. You'll be safe."

Faith carried her daughter into the tent and settled her. She lay next to Zoe. The sound of Faith humming to her daughter filtered through the camp.

Fifteen minutes later, she sneaked out.

Crossing the camp, she grabbed her water bottle and plopped down across from him. "She's out, poor thing. Neither one of us slept well last night. Not after the house was ransacked."

She lifted her gaze to his, her eyes red and tired, her expression defeated. Stefan fought his instincts to push her. Sometimes stillness could extract the truth far more effectively than the most compelling persuasion. He longed to ask why, if her ex had the political upper hand, had Jerry torn through their things. Why had he tried to kidnap Zoe? It didn't make sense.

Instead, he waited.

Would he finally hear the truth she'd obviously kept to herself for quite a while?

Faith took a deep breath. "Burke has secrets."

Stefan nodded with encouragement.

"He killed someone," she rushed out. "In fact, he didn't murder just one person.

"My ex-husband is a serial killer."

Chapter Five

Burke paced the floor, his feet sinking deep into the carpet. A pile of unreviewed reports littered his desk. He'd been unable to focus since Orren had called. Damn Faith. She'd caused him more trouble than he'd thought possible.

Soon it would be over. If Orren could be trusted, within twenty-four hours she'd be dead. The thought didn't thrill him like it should have. He paused at his office's panoramic window and peered across the Dallas skyscape.

The room went hazy. An image of Faith appeared in the glass. His smiling, low-class, treacherous wife. Before his eyes, a stream of blood washed her away.

Burke shook his head and the vision dissipated. *He'd* wanted to be the one to make her disappear. He'd been dreaming about taking his favorite Bowie to her since she'd let herself go after Zoe had been born. Her hair no longer the perfect blond, she'd fattened up at least twenty pounds. She was no longer the trophy he'd molded from that waitress at the Shiny Penny. She wasn't *his* Faith any longer. She'd forced him to divorce her.

Faith needed to be gone on *his* terms, not hers. And to discover she had some fool cowboy helping her. The very thought made Burke's head pound with each beat of his heart. He couldn't take it. He'd bet she'd given the guy her body. That she'd squealed underneath him like the low-class Jezebel she was. He just knew it. He might not want Faith anymore, but he damn sure didn't want anyone else to have what had belonged to him. He didn't share.

Burke grabbed his coat and walked out of his office, forcing his voice and demeanor to remain calm and controlled when inside he longed to scream. "I'm leaving for the day. Cancel my afternoon appointments."

Before his administrative assistant could ask him any questions, he walked into the elevator. The doors slid closed, leaving him in peaceful silence.

Finally alone.

Burke let out a loud curse. His ex had found herself another man. The guy must not have any class to want someone as broken down as Faith.

His body trembled, prickles of irritation flicked under his skin. He rubbed his arm until it turned red. It didn't help. Nothing would. He'd have to find a way to calm himself. His father wouldn't like it, but Burke was past caring.

He needed release. His bag was packed. His plan in place. The Acid Bath Murderer had always fascinated him. The original had been caught. Burke didn't plan to be.

Now all he needed was the right woman.

The elevator door slid open and he quickly blanked his expression even as he wanted to claw each inch of his body.

A woman stepped onto the elevator and acknowledged him with a nod. Her blond hair turned under just above her shoulders, sleek and smooth.

Polished.

Nothing like Faith.

He shoved his hands in his pockets, digging his thumbnails into his palms. Sometimes pain would drive the urge away for a while. He had rules he followed. One was not to hunt near where he worked or lived.

He glanced down at her hands. She wore a ring on the left one. She had someone else.

Blood pounded at the backs of his eyes. He closed them.

"Are you all right?" she asked in a husky voice that made his body harden in anticipation.

"Low blood sugar," he said, thinking quickly.

He loosened his hands. The pain dissipated. He'd made his choice.

Burke frowned and plastered a worried expression on his face. "I don't know if I should drive. Could you take me home?"

She looked at him, surprised. "I can call you a cab."

"Never mind. I'll find a way."

They exited the elevator at the parking garage level, and he stumbled through the doors.

She reached out to help him catch his balance.

He smiled up at her and plunged a syringe into her neck.

The shock on her face caused his body to pulse with pleasure, and he groaned at the release. He scooped her into his arms.

Sometimes rules were made to be broken.

Serial killer.

The desert horizon tilted. The campsite surrounding Faith faded away. The persistent trill of the cicadas drowned out the frantic beating of her heart. She pressed her fingers to her mouth. She'd said the words aloud for the first time since she'd called in an anonymous tip the night she and Zoe had left Weatherford.

As far as she could tell, nothing had come of her call. She couldn't be sure why, but it reinforced her decision as the right one. No one could stop Burke. He was untouchable.

Faith stared down at her hands before chancing a glance at Léon. She hadn't known him long. He'd been tough to read from the first time they'd met, but she recognized the surprise on his face.

Who wouldn't be shocked? Burke Thomas came from a wealthy family. He had money, good looks, and power. She'd run away for two reasons: no one would believe her, and she was terrified for Zoe.

Despite his promise, she half expected him to smile and cart her off to the sheriff—or maybe a psychiatrist's office.

His silence made her shoulders tense.

"How did you learn the truth about him?" he asked, brows drawn together.

Léon hadn't laughed in her face. He hadn't immediately dismissed her claims. In fact, he actually seemed to take her seriously.

"By chance." She twisted her hands in her lap, her nerves still jumping with dread. "He'd brought Zoe home after a weekend with him and her grandparents. Less than a half hour after he left, a lawyer delivered a new custody agreement." Faith couldn't stop the ironic chuckle from escaping her. "I'd hoped I could change his mind, so I tried to find him. My last stop was the bar where we'd met. I saw a prostitute getting into his car. Two days later, her photo appeared in the paper. She'd been murdered."

"It could have been a coincidence."

"That's what I tried to tell myself," she said with a frown. "For a while. A few weeks later, we argued about child support. He was behind again. I threatened to call his father. Two days afterward, the police found a body a couple counties over. The victim had blond hair and resembled the first woman, but she'd been killed in a completely different way."

Léon picked up a stick from the ground and poked at the cold ashes from the previous night's campfire. He didn't say anything for a moment. He thought she was insane. He had to.

"I know what you're thinking." She forced herself to stop fidgeting and met his thoughtful gaze. "I'm not crazy."

"Actually, I was waiting to hear what else you'd found. I have a feeling there's more."

For a moment she froze. Every time she'd pictured going to the cops—or anyone for that matter—she'd imagined being on the receiving end of condescending questions with an oh-so-reasonable tone that grated on her like a karaoke singer a half step off key. Léon's encouragement shattered the dam of silence.

The words, the thoughts held in confidence for so long, poured out. "I reviewed the newspapers, searching for murdered women. I found over a dozen tall, blonde, very thin women in the counties surrounding the Dallas-Fort Worth area. Almost all of the victims lived or were killed in different cities or towns. I recorded the dates. They all happened on days that Burke and I had a huge argument."

"You remember every argument?"

She bristled a bit. He didn't understand. Would he ever? Someone like him, who was clearly in control of his world. "I know which days Zoe stayed with Burke. When he brought her home, he pushed me. I pushed back."

Faith didn't mention how every encounter had ended with her dry heaving in the bathroom. Their arguments had upset Zoe, too. The love between her and Burke may have died, but she'd kept hoping they could both put their daughter's well-being first.

A scratching filtered through the air from the edge of the campsite. Léon shot to his feet and palmed his handgun. She'd never seen anyone move with such precision and economy of movement.

A prairie dog scurried at the edge of the campsite. He returned to his seat across from her and leaned forward. "You're convinced after each fight he walked out your door and committed murder?"

"I know it sounds crazy, but yes. That's exactly what I believe."

He rubbed his neck and the camp went silent for a few seconds. "Did you ever call the police?"

"I left an anonymous tip from a pay phone." She tucked one leg underneath her. "I couldn't think of anything else to do. The police knew about the custody battle. They'd come out several times on bogus calls—a tree branch crossing the property line, someone falsely reporting screaming. I'm pretty sure Burke called in as part of his plan to get full custody.

"I didn't think they'd believe me."

"Could you be wrong?" Léon propped the heel of his boot on the edge of a rock.

"I wanted to be wrong, but I'm not." Faith glanced over to make certain Zoe still slept and lowered her voice even further. "When we married, Burke tried to transform me to look like the women he killed."

Léon stilled, his eyes laced with incredulity. "Some might say a custody battle would be an excellent reason to suggest your ex is a murderer."

She didn't bother responding. Why should she? Instead, she retrieved a bag hidden beneath her things and dug out a thick expandable folder. "Maybe you'll believe this," she challenged.

Faith removed the rubber band holding her evidence in place. She passed over a newspaper clipping of the face of a blonde smiling into the camera. "The woman I saw Burke with outside a bar a few hours before she died." Faith pulled out an article she'd printed from the woman's social media site. The image still made Faith shiver. In color, the victim's hair was styled the way it had been that night, her dress designed to show off her prominent collarbones and very thin frame.

"Obviously the same woman."

His deep voice tugged Faith back to the present. "She was murdered on a Saturday night, the same night Burke and I argued. A few weeks later, Burke came over out of the blue. We had an arbitration scheduled about the custody agreement, but he wanted Zoe to stay with him all week. His father had some kind of event planned. I think Burke wanted to show Zoe off to his clients. I told him no. She had two baseball games she had to pitch. We had another fight. A couple of days later, I saw this article in the paper."

She passed the newspaper clipping, taking in every expression, every nuance as he read the article.

"There's a definite resemblance," he said, pointing at the grainy photo.

He met her gaze, and she followed the first two with another social media printout. Faith couldn't help but hold her breath. She'd never shown these documents to anyone.

Léon fingered through the items. "No doubt. They could be sisters." He returned the papers to her.

Faith clasped the evidence to her chest. "The photos

made me nauseous. I think I must've known in that moment what was going on, but I didn't want to believe it."

His brow furrowed. "There's something you're not telling me."

He wouldn't understand until she showed him everything. Faith dug into the folder. "I went to the library and searched old papers." She slapped another woman's photo in his hand. "Two days after our divorce was final." Another photo. "Three days after he didn't receive sole managing conservatorship of Zoe, which is basically sole custody." She placed a stack of photos in his hands. "I found nine more. Every time I saw another photo I thought I was going to be sick."

Léon flipped through the pages. A low whistle escaped his lips. "Have the cops connected Burke? Surely they see the pattern?"

"I don't know." Faith shrugged. "There's been nothing in the paper. Maybe they're investigating after I called in my tip, but not one of these bodies was found in the same town. None of them were killed the same way. From what I've read, most serial killers have a pattern. Burke's pattern is that he *doesn't* have one."

She hesitated over the remaining two photos. Her skin tingled every time she stared at these images, but she handed them over anyway. "This is me."

Léon gripped the photos tight and fell back into his chair. She got that. When she'd first seen all the photos together, she'd sunk to the floor, unable to stand.

Faith knew exactly what he saw. Her, smiling, with a bone-thin figure hugged by the formfitting gown her husband had chosen, hair golden blond, piled on her head in an elegant chignon. She'd been Burke's image of perfection. He'd told her so. She'd been so happy; she'd had no doubt she'd finally found her very own Prince Charming.

She'd found a monster disguised as a prince.

Léon studied the second picture of her poured into a skin-tight designer dress, her hair straight, with wisps of bangs. Faith winced at her emaciated body. She looked sick and starving.

"He chose my clothes. He dictated the cut and color of my hair." She let out a self-deprecating laugh. "He said it was because he wanted me to be the best I could be. That he wasn't trying to change me, just make me better. I believed him. I thought I was lucky he cared. For a while."

Léon tugged a cooler over to them and used it as a small table. He laid the photos down with Faith's picture in the middle. To Faith, the images shocked her as much now as the first time she'd seen them.

He let out a soft, low whistle. "You could *all* be sisters."

"And they're all dead." Faith met Léon's gaze. "Except me."

A SMALL BREEZE furled the photos spread out in front of Stefan. When he'd first met Faith, he'd assumed she'd been running from an abusive relationship, or someone showing a twisted interest in Zoe…anything but a man who was obviously murdering Faith over and over and over again in his twisted mind.

Crazy made it a tough capture. An organized psycho was easier to track due to their predictable nature. Burke seemed to be a very dangerous combination: an organized killer mimicking a disorganized one. The worst of the worst.

Faith sat across from him and chewed on her lips; a guarded expression settled in her eyes. She was waiting for his judgment, as if she feared he'd laugh at her.

"I'm impressed. I understand why no one identified

the pattern. Until you." He couldn't give her enough credit. "If my company had compiled this package, we'd be on the cops' or district attorney's doorstep with high confidence the perpetrator wouldn't see the outside of a prison for the rest of his life. With all this—" he swept his hand across the pile of evidence "—why run?"

"Haven't you been listening?" Her voice grew urgent. "Burke and his family have too much influence. The Thomas family doesn't lose." Faith shook her head, the movements strong and emphatic. "I can't take the risk. I could *never* put Zoe in that kind of danger."

Her entire body shook. Stefan knelt in front of her, gripping her hands. He rubbed her ice-cold fingers between his. "You and Zoe are safe here."

"Because of you, but we can't live here forever." She didn't pull her hands away. "My plan to escape Burke is in the toilet. He found us in Carder, a town I'd never even heard of before my car broke down. How am I supposed to disappear without new identities for me and Zoe? He'll track us down. I just know it."

The despair in her voice struck his chest like a bayonet. More than that, he could see the loneliness in her, echoing his own.

CTC could help Faith. Ransom's contacts had to be as influential as the Thomas family's. His challenge was, after fighting against power for so long, would Faith ever trust him enough to let them help?

He pulled her to her feet, determined to try. She stood stiffly. Ever so slowly, giving her ample opportunity to escape him, he trailed his hands up her arms to her shoulders and cupped her cheeks. His gaze held hers captive. "Listen to me, Faith. Whatever I have to do, however I have to do it, I'll make certain you and Zoe are safe. I promise you that. I think you should let me help get Burke the legal way, but if that fails, I have a friend. Her name is Annie. She can create new identities that Burke can never track. I promise."

"Really?"

He nodded.

She leaped at him and threw her arms around his neck in a grateful hug. He wrapped his arms around her, but within seconds, the warmth of her body tugged at him. He fought the instinct until she stilled. Faith cleared her throat and stepped out of his arms.

He couldn't speak. His gaze fell to her lips and he dragged his attention back to her eyes. Her pupils had dilated. Awareness sizzled between them.

She swallowed deeply and wet her lips.

Stefan nearly groaned in response. He shouldn't feel this way. He couldn't. He only had three days, though he'd already admitted to himself that however long it took, he'd see Faith and Zoe safe and secure before he carried out his own plans.

Faith gripped his shirt. She blinked once, then twice and shook her head. "This can't happen," she whispered under her breath.

She stepped out of his embrace. Stefan let her go. She was so very right, but the moment she backed away, his heart chilled a few degrees.

He couldn't remember ever having such an intense reaction to a woman.

"I...umm... I think I'll rest," she said softly. "It's only three, but it's already been a very long day." She nodded at the tent where Zoe still slept.

He didn't say anything, and after one long look back at him, she ducked into the tent and zipped it closed.

Stefan let out a long sigh. Man, he was in more trouble than he'd thought.

He forced himself back to the makeshift table, familiarizing himself with every photo, every case file, everything Faith had compiled on her ex-husband. She might believe there was only one choice, but he would convince her to let CTC help. He'd run through every scenario.

He wouldn't risk Faith and Zoe to a madman.

By the time he raised his head, the afternoon sun beat down on the campsite. He stood and let out a long groan. He couldn't find a hole in her theory, and he was no lawyer, but her case wasn't a slam dunk. She'd fit together a plethora of damaging coincidences and the closest fact she had to a smoking gun was her own eyewitness testimony. A defense attorney would not only tear her apart, her discovery also placed a crosshair directly on her back.

Maybe she *should* run. Maybe he should call Annie right now, except imagining Faith and Zoe looking over their shoulders for the rest of their lives didn't sit well. He understood the pitfalls all too well. No, he needed more time. There had to be a way to eliminate Burke as a threat.

After a last glance at the tent where his guests still slept, Stefan wandered over a couple of small dunes, through the shrub bush, until he was out of earshot. He dialed a familiar number on his sat phone.

"Sheriff's office," the dispatcher's voice answered.

"Blake Redmond, please."

"I'd recognize that smooth, mysterious accent anywhere. How are you, Mr. Royce?"

"Waiting for you to accept my proposal, Miss Iris."

She chuckled. "My husband of fifty-five years might not like that. The sheriff's pacing in his office cursing at the walls, I'd venture to say. That jerk he brought in for kidnapping that sweet girl ain't talking and Blake's spittin' mad. Hold while I connect you."

A click sounded through the earpiece.

"Redmond." The terse greeting didn't leave any doubt as to the sheriff's frustration.

"He won't talk, huh?" Stefan asked.

"You charm Iris out of that information?"

"Of course." He didn't have to tell Blake his dispatcher was also the town megaphone when it came to gossip.

"I should fire her, but she wormed her way in here after we lost Donna several years back. She's kind of like mold. Once she's there, she's tough to get rid of." A wooden creak indicating Blake sat in his chair filtered through the phone. "The guy's clammed up. I'm getting nowhere. I need to interview the girl and her mother."

"Look, Blake—" Stefan rubbed the base of his neck.

"Damn. I recognize the tone in your voice," the sheriff said in exasperation. "Let me guess. Things are worse than we thought, and she needs to hide and can't come into the station."

"You're good at this."

"No, I'm not, but every time I get involved with CTC I end up sitting back and doing nothing and the problem just vanishes. Am I going to uncover a bunch of dead bodies on that ranch someday?"

"I doubt it. Ransom doesn't leave evidence."

A long sigh escaped from Blake. "I know you guys help people I can't, but it gets old."

"You could always join up. There might be an opening soon." Stefan deliberately allowed his words to reveal more than he usually did.

Blake didn't respond for a few seconds. "You thinking about leaving?"

"Let's just say it's time for a change."

"I'm happy with my family and my life here, thank

you very much. Why don't you quit trying to veer me off my target? What's going on?"

"You'd be a good operative," Stefan acknowledged. He kneaded the back of his neck. "Between you and me, her ex is searching for her, and he doesn't wear a white hat."

"Sheriff!" Iris's voice squealed through the phone. "Come quick."

"What the hell?" A wooden crash erupted through the phone. "I'll call you back."

The phone went silent.

Stefan waited for a few moments, but when Blake didn't immediately get in touch with him, he made his way back to the campsite. He'd try again later. Hopefully the emergency had nothing to do with Stefan's witness, but he had a bad feeling.

His footsteps soundless, Stefan crossed to the pile of evidence and took out the wedding photo of Burke Thomas and Faith. The man oozed charm and an easy smile. Of course, so had Ted Bundy.

"That's my daddy when he was nice to my mom," Zoe said from his side.

Stefan jerked in surprise. He quickly shoved the other photos into Faith's folder. The kid was light on her feet. Or he had already become too comfortable with his guests. Both possibilities disconcerted him.

He forced his shoulders to relax. "You'd make a good spy, Zoe."

"Thanks." She grinned. "Is that what you are, a spy?"

Stefan looked down at her, her face so open and eager. Strangely, he found himself not wanting to lie to her. "I guess you could say that."

"Really?" Her eyes gleamed with excitement. "Like in the movies?"

"Well, investigating isn't as exciting as in the movies." Okay, that was a half-truth. He'd been tortured in a dungeon, almost blown up on more than one occasion, nearly outed during several undercover ops and forced to play long-range sniper to save the lives of his CTC teammates. "Mostly I read a lot and figure stuff out. Kind of like homework."

Zoe wrinkled her nose. "That doesn't sound like fun."

"Catching a bad guy and sending him to jail is fun."

Her eyes cleared. "That's good. Bad people should be in jail so they can't hurt good people."

"Exactly right." Stefan knelt to face her eye to eye. "Are you feeling better?"

"I've got little white bumps where the ants bit me." She lifted her pants leg and showed him. "They're itchy."

"How about we use some more medicine?"

"Okay." Zoe nodded and plopped in the chair across from Stefan.

She lifted her legs, and he rubbed the cortisone cream onto her ankles and calves.

"Thanks. You know how to put on medicine real good. Do you have kids?"

That all-too-familiar pang of regret twisted inside his chest. "I have two nieces and a nephew. In fact, my niece and nephew are twins. They're about your age."

"Could I play with them?" Zoe practically bounced in her seat. "Are they nearby?"

"I wish they were, kiddo. They live across the ocean." He rubbed the last inflamed spot and pulled her pants legs down.

"Do you fly on a plane to visit them?"

"Not as much as I'd like." Now there was an understatement. "Sometimes families are complicated."

"What's com...pli...cated?"

That had Stefan stumped. "Confusing," he settled on.

"Sometimes we don't get to do what we want to do because it's hard to figure out the right thing to do."

Okay, that didn't make a whole lot of sense to him, but Zoe nodded her head.

"Yeah, I understand. My life is complicated, too. My daddy likes me to wear dresses with lace. I like jeans and T-shirts. But since my grandma gets me the dresses as a present, I gotta wear them. It's hard."

Stefan chuckled at the horrified expression on the little girl's face. "You don't like frilly dresses?"

"They get in the way. You can't play baseball in a dress. It'll get dirty and then you get yelled at." She swung her feet back and forth. "If I didn't have to wear a dress, I'd like to go on a plane with my dad. He promised to take me, but he's really busy. Did your daddy take you on a plane?"

So that was another very complicated question Stefan wasn't quite sure how to answer. The good memories of his childhood had been overtaken by a devastating truth. He couldn't imagine his father would have been part of the plot that had cost Stefan's brother his life, and Stefan his freedom. He wished Zoe would never have to deal with the same disillusionment, but she would learn her father's identity someday. He hadn't actually asked, but Faith's behavior and Zoe's actions had made it clear the little girl knew nothing about her father.

The phone interrupted them. He glanced at the screen. Not a number he recognized. "Zoe, stay here. I'll be right back."

He walked out of the girl's earshot. "Léon Royce."

"It's hit the fan here," Blake said. "My prisoner keeled over dead, and I don't know how."

"Heart attack?"

"He's young for that. Maybe he took a pill or poisoned himself, but I can't tell. One visitor who used a fake name, but that was hours ago. I called the medical examiner in from Odessa. We'll know soon enough."

"Damn it," Stefan said. "I was hoping he could confirm Faith's story."

"Well, he's not talking now. On the other hand, I have some surprising news for you. I just received a call pretty high up in the state attorney general's office. They want me to verify the identity of my kidnap victim as a seven-year-old girl named Zoe Thomas. But get this, I'm supposed to keep it on the down low if I find her, and just get back to *him*, and no one else. Of course, the guy included a not-so-subtle threat to audit my budget and the past five years of cases if I don't cooperate."

Stefan let out a low whistle. If he'd needed proof to support Faith's story, Blake had just given him solid testimony of the power of Faith's ex-husband.

"Her ex is tipping his hand. Why?"

"I don't know, but I don't like being pushed around. I sure as hell don't like a prisoner dying on me."

"This entire situation's uglier than I expected," Stefan admitted.

"It's a cover-up of a different kind, that's for sure." Blake's voice lowered. "I called on a burner phone, and I didn't say this to you, but don't call me back. I don't know where you are and I don't want to know. Whoever's after that little girl has some powerful friends. I'd stay as far away from the law as you can."

Chapter Six

Something hard and pointed pressed into Faith's lower back. She lay still and rubbed her eyes. For a moment, she didn't know where she was.

A breeze blew across her face and she opened her eyes to the view of the top of Léon's tent.

Léon.

Zoe.

She snapped her gaze to the empty space next to her and shot to a sitting position. A rock ground into her hip, but she ignored the pinch. She vaulted out of the tent and lifted her hand against the late-afternoon sky.

The bright sun beat down, heating her face. She winced at the glare and crinkled her eyes to search the campsite.

Léon and Zoe were both gone.

Faith's heart seized in panic until joyful laughter wafted from somewhere behind the tent. When had she last witnessed true happiness in her daughter's voice? A pang of guilt weighted down Faith's shoulders. Zoe deserved so much more than what Faith could give her right now.

Homeless, on the run, without a plan. What kind of mother was she?

Zoe erupted in another trill of laughter. Faith trudged

toward the noise, tracking the sound to the creek. The sight made her pause.

Léon hovered near Zoe, pointing at the ground. She crouched and looked up at their rescuer, unadulterated adoration painted on her face.

Faith's heart melted. Who wouldn't be enamored with the man who had saved her life, and in this moment treated her as if she were the most important person in the world?

He'd made Faith feel that way when she'd very nearly fallen into his arms. He'd believed her when she'd thought no one would. He'd offered to help, and he'd promised to find a way for Zoe and her to be safe.

Faith's head might doubt, but her gut actually trusted him.

Léon smiled at Zoe and softly patted her cheek. The gentle movement caused Faith's heart to flip in her chest. If she let herself, she could fall for him, too.

Scooching behind a rock, she peeked out to watch them. She needn't have bothered to attempt to be inconspicuous. From a side view, Léon gave Faith a quick wink before focusing on her daughter.

"You know a lot about camping." Zoe perched on a rock by the stream. "Can I tell you something?" Her daughter's voice had turned serious.

Faith strained to hear.

"Sure." Léon knelt in front of Zoe. "Is something wrong?"

"I got lost today." Zoe bowed her head. "I stepped on the ants because I didn't know which way to go. I was scared."

Faith eased out from her hiding place, ready to comfort her daughter, but the tender expression on Léon's face made her pause.

He pushed his hat back and met Zoe's gaze, unblinking and serious. "It's okay to be scared. Everyone is afraid sometimes."

"Well, I didn't like it." Zoe crossed her arms and took a stubborn stance Faith recognized all too well. "I didn't know what to do. What if I hadn't yelled? I might have gone the wrong way and lost you and Mom. I can barely see the camp from here."

"Hmm." Léon stroked his chin. "Well, I camp out a lot, and I know the rules for getting lost. Want to hear them?"

Zoe's eyes widened a bit and she nodded, giving Léon her devoted attention.

"Okay." He held out his hand and Zoe grabbed it. He led her a few feet from the edge of the creek. "First, you stay on a trail, like this one." He pointed to a path in the dirt. "Animals made this to drink water. If I'm looking for you, I'll go down all the trails first to find you."

"What if there's not a trail?"

"You find a place out of the cold and wind, like over by those rocks, and wait for me and your mom to find you. And whatever you do, don't wander around at night. There are no streetlights when you're camping."

"What if you don't see me?" Zoe asked, her forehead furrowed with worry.

"That's where your orange backpack comes in." Léon grinned. "Put it outside wherever you're hiding. It's so bright, I'll be able to see it. And while you're waiting, make a lot of noise as often as you can."

Zoe took all the information in, then frowned. "But what if I'm hiding from bad people? Mom always says to stay quiet. What do I do then?"

Faith's heart broke at the question. Zoe shouldn't have those thoughts.

"Good point." Léon paused for a moment, as if trying to form his answer. "You leave me a sign that I can follow."

"What kind of sign?"

"Well, I'd recognize one of your shoelaces, or even a pen or pencil from your bag. I'd know it's you, and since we've had this talk, I'd know where to look." He clasped her daughter's shoulders. "I'd find you, Zoe. I promise."

She bit her lip, scanning the trail over to the rock before finally nodding her head. "I think I can do that. Thanks, Léon."

"We're not done yet," he said. "Which direction are we facing right now? North, south, east or west?"

She pursed her lips and twisted her mouth. Faith recognized the face. Zoe shared it often enough while doing her homework when she wasn't quite certain of the answer.

"Take your time," he said, scratching the dirt with a stick. "You don't have to panic. Just be logical. Where's the sun right now?"

Zoe's eyes brightened. She pointed in the sky. "You told me the sun rises in the east and sets in the west. That way's west, so..." She knelt and dragged her finger through the dirt. "We're facing north."

"Excellent." Léon smiled and lifted his hand. Zoe slapped him a high five. "When you know which way you're headed, you won't go in circles if you're lost."

Her daughter sighed, loud and long. "There's a lot to remember about getting lost." She peeked up at Léon.

"Then how about we practice? I'll go over to that rock." He pointed to Faith's hiding place. "You pretend you're lost and figure out what to do."

"Like a game." She scampered off.

Léon walked over to Faith and met her behind the rock. "Survival 101?" she asked.

He shrugged. "It was something to do."

"It was more than that," Faith said. "Thank you for helping her not be afraid." She leaned back against the boulder, one eye on Zoe's adventure. "Do you like living this way? In the middle of nowhere?"

"I miss a hot shower on occasion. I have a system jury-rigged, but it's nothing compared to high-pressure water pounding on your back. Other than that, yeah, I like the silence. How it gets totally dark and I can see all the stars in the sky." Stefan propped himself beside her. "What are you thinking?"

"I'm wondering if I could live like this with Zoe for a while. Just until I can figure out what to do next."

"You can stay as long as you need to," he offered.

Faith's entire body relaxed. At least she didn't have to worry about shelter or food. Today anyway. "Thank you. You're saving our lives."

His gaze shifted away, almost as if he were embarrassed. "Zoe," he called out. "I'm coming to find you."

They rounded the large rock. Faith scanned the area. Zoe was gone. "Where is she?"

"Don't worry. I haven't let her out of my sight. She's testing me. She wants to make certain I really will find her." Léon glanced at the ground. "We follow the trail." He held out his hand. "Come on."

Faith linked her fingers with his. They wandered down by the creek to a narrow dirt path.

"It's a sheep trail. Livestock graze on both public and private land out here."

They picked their way among the shrub bushes to the rocky outcropping. Right next to a large boulder, in plain sight, Zoe's backpack gleamed in the afternoon sun.

"Help!" a voice cried out. "I'm here."

They raced over to the rock. Zoe sat grinning in a small indentation.

Léon gave her a second high five. "Great job. You'd be out of the wind and rain if you hid in this little hole."

Zoe looked at Léon. "Well?" she asked, her hands on her hips, an eager expression of expectation on her face.

He made a show of hemming and hawing and finally sighed. "Okay, I guess you've earned it."

"What's going on with you two?" Faith asked, biting her cheek to keep from smiling at their antics.

Léon placed something in Zoe's hand. She ran over to her mother. "Look. A little flashlight to keep with me. And an arrowhead. Léon found it near the creek. I earned them for doing a good job."

Faith hugged her daughter. *Thank you*, she mouthed over her daughter's head.

A slight flush tinged his cheeks and he glanced at his watch. "Are you hungry?"

"I am," Zoe shouted out. "We missed lunch and we're out of peanut butter."

"I think we may do a little better than peanut butter." He led them back to the fire pit and dug into a sealed cooler. "Salmon okay?" he asked.

"You've got to be kidding." Faith's mouth fell open.

"I may live out in the middle of nowhere, but I like a good meal at the end of the day." He adjusted the rocks surrounding the ash-laden hole in the ground.

"Can I help?" Zoe asked.

"Sure. First I have to build a fire."

Zoe's eager expression made Faith want to wince. One look at her face and Léon sent her a stern look. "No fire-starting without an adult. Do you understand, Zoe?"

Much to Faith's relief, her daughter nodded and hunkered down beside him. Faith pulled one of the chairs closer to the pit. She studied Zoe's awestruck expression as she hung on Léon's every word. He pointed out the magnesium fire starter; he showed her what grass made good tinder and how to pick out small, dry sticks for kindling, and even how a half-gutted log would help the fire grow at first. Within a few minutes, the flames gleamed brightly.

He pulled out foil, some corn ears and asparagus, a grill and two iron skillets, and a bag of what looked like cooked apples, and quickly threw a meal together.

"You come prepared."

"Necessity breeds skill."

As their dinner cooked, Léon poked at the blaze. "So, Zoe. Another quiz. If I walked toward the sun for a whole hour, how would I get back here?"

"Is this a trick question?" she asked.

"Nope. What do you think?"

Zoe stood up and started walking a few paces. She turned around to look at them. "You go backward," she said with a triumphant smile. "You walk the same time with the sun behind you."

"You're a definite pro," he said with a grin.

"What if there's no sun?"

"Then you can find a special star and do the same thing."

"Will you show me?"

"When it gets dark."

"I like it here with you, Léon. Can we stay?"

"As long as you want," he said quietly, sending Faith a sidelong glance. She shivered under his stare. She couldn't deny the attraction between them. She hadn't expected it, and could only see trouble if she gave into the feelings, but it was there just the same.

He clearly felt it, too. He strode over to her. "You okay?"

What was she supposed to say? She cleared her throat. "I appreciate everything you're doing for Zoe. You've made her feel safe for the first time in months."

"She's a great kid."

Faith cleared her throat. "You've let us horn in on your privacy when you didn't have to. I don't know what to say, how to…" Her voice trailed off and with a tentative touch, she reached for his hand. She wasn't sure why. He didn't pull away. Her heart skipped a beat. Faith raised her gaze to his. She recognized the awareness, the heat in his eyes. Another time, another place, she would lean into him and let him hold her all night long.

Zoe raced up between them, destroying the moment. "Is dinner ready yet?" she asked. "I'm hungry."

Faith cleared her throat and turned to her daughter, shoving back her own desires.

Léon stood statue still and studied her with that inscrutable expression she'd come to recognize. What was he thinking? Did he want to hold her as much as she wanted him to? Even though she shouldn't.

"Dinner's not quite done, but soon. I need to gather some more firewood and make a call," Léon said. "I'll be back."

Before Zoe could offer to go with him he disappeared behind a small hill.

Faith dropped her head in her hands.

"Mom? Are you okay? Your face looks hot."

She forced herself to look at her daughter. "I'm fine, sweetie. Just figuring out where we're going to go next."

"Since that bad guy's in jail, can we go home? Then can I call Danny? There's a new coach for baseball, and I have to try out again."

"I'm sorry, sweetie…" The impact of Zoe's words hit Faith. "How do you know about the new coach?"

She grasped Zoe's arms, but her daughter glanced away. "Zoe? Have you been in contact with Danny?"

She swallowed. "I know I wasn't s'posed to, but I… I sent him a video message from the library computer."

Faith froze. "D-did you contact your father?"

Zoe dug her shoe into the dirt. "I… I thought about it."

"Did you?" Faith held her breath. "I'm not going to be mad, Zoe, but I need to know."

"I didn't, Mom. I promise."

Somehow Burke had traced the message Zoe had sent to her best friend. That was how he'd found her in Carder. Faith hadn't even known Burke knew about Danny.

Her knees buckled and she fell into the chair behind her. "Zoe, I know it's hard for you to understand, but it's important your father doesn't know where we are. Not yet."

"Because Daddy wants me to live with him?"

The words skewed Faith's gut. "How do you know that?"

Her daughter refused to meet her gaze. "I'm not s'posed to talk about what I hear by accident. You said so."

She clasped Zoe's shoulders. "This is important. Tell me, Slugger."

Her daughter scuffed her toe in the dirt. "One time I heard him tell Grandpa that if you were in an accident, I could go be with them forever."

THE THOMAS FAMILY'S palatial estate stood well off the main road in the exclusive neighborhood of Preston Hollow. Burke strode up to his parents' home, livid. He'd never been more embarrassed in his entire life than when the waitress at the most exclusive restaurant in all of Dallas had refused to return his credit card. He couldn't believe his father's audacity.

The butler answered the door. "Good evening, Mr. Burke."

"Where is he?" Burke asked.

"His study." The butler cleared his throat. "He's not in a good mood."

"Neither am I."

Burke stalked into his father's domain. When he was a child, he'd never been allowed inside. Sometimes entering the dark, mahogany-lined room made him feel like a ten-year-old kid.

Of course, his father treated him like one.

"You cut off the money," he said, slamming the door closed.

His father leaned back in his chair. "You didn't control your urges, did you? And this time you picked someone from *my* company. The whole place is freaked out. I had to bring in a damned psychologist for grief counseling. Do you know how much productivity you've cost me? And all because you couldn't keep your hands off that woman."

The vein on the side of his father's temple bulged; his mouth tightened. Burke hadn't seen him so upset in a long time. He narrowed his gaze. "Did you know her?"

His father's cheeks flushed.

Burke recognized the guilty expression. "Unbelievable. You were sleeping with her." He crossed the room and poured two fingers of Scotch. "I should've known. She's your type." He downed the shot in one large gulp. "Does Mom know?"

His father bristled. "She doesn't need to. I give your mother what she requires of me. Always have."

At the words, Burke rushed across the room and grabbed his father by the throat. "You betray her every day."

His father shoved him away. "And what do you think she'd do if she learned that her precious son is a murderer?"

Burke found his footing and glared at his father. "You wouldn't."

"Don't push me, son. I could stop protecting you and send a very informative envelope of evidence, complete with photographs and video, to the district attorney."

Burke dug his fingernails into his palms.

"That's right. I caught you on videotape. And I'll use it."

This couldn't be happening. Burke stared down at the floor. His father had to be bluffing.

"Don't worry. It's safe. The camera equipment was damaged…somehow."

Burke's head jerked up. What was his old man playing at? His father had threatened more than once to hold Burke's *hobby* over his head. He'd gone so far as drafting commitment papers, though he doubted the old man would ever use them. If he did, the world would learn too many secrets about the Thomas family, and his father couldn't have that.

Burke glared at his father; the veneer of civility had vanished. "What do you want?"

"Control yourself and get my granddaughter back permanently so she's no longer poisoned by her low-class mother. Can you do those two simple things, or do I have to take care of you like always?"

"I'm dealing with Faith. You'll have Zoe back soon."

"And the other?"

"Fine. I'll find another outlet for my…urges. You happy?"

His father sighed, that disappointed sigh that made Burke's belly burn with resentment.

"I'll have to be. Your mother only gave me an heir, not a spare."

Burke spun on his heel and stumbled on the carpet. The barb shouldn't have fazed him, but instead had made him appear vulnerable. He dug his fingernails into his palms again so hard a bead of sweat popped on his forehead. He straightened his back and strode across the room, careful with each step.

"Burke, don't screw up again. You'll find me to be a difficult enemy."

So am I, old man. So am I.

THE GENTLE COOS of quail pulled Faith out of a death-like night's sleep. Zoe slept curled next to her mother, cocooned in Léon's tent. Even though they had no walls, no solid door and no alarm, Faith felt safe.

She liked the feeling.

Easing away from Zoe, Faith stretched her arms and shoulders. Keeping her movements as silent as possible, she quietly drew down the tent's zipper and peered outside.

Dawn peeked over the horizon, with brilliant purple and orange and pink meshing in a kaleidoscope of color.

One thing about sunrises in the desert, they really couldn't be topped. The scent of coffee wafted over to her. She rubbed her eyes and a figure in black, loose-fitting pants that rode low on his hips and no shirt made her freeze.

Léon shifted his foot forward, his movements deliberate and practiced. He threw a series of vertical punches, his arms straining, muscles quivering. He drew in a deep controlled breath and executed two complex sliding kicks before finally bringing his hands slowly together.

She'd never witnessed anything quite so beautiful. He controlled every movement with precision. His chest was dusted with hair and gleamed with sweat. Her belly quivered in response.

Since falling for Burke she'd been turned off by a pretty face, but Léon made her rethink that position.

His body relaxed and he blew out a long, slow breath. He adjusted his stance and turned away from her. She gasped. His back was covered in scars. They crisscrossed all over. Several long, thick discolorations appeared near his kidneys and they disappeared below his waistline.

He whirled around, cursed and grabbed his T-shirt, yanking it on.

They couldn't pretend she hadn't seen them.

"Coffee?" he asked, walking over to the fire as if nothing had happened.

"Sure." What was she supposed to say?

He handed her the cup. She looked down. "Do you have sugar?"

In silence, he opened a tub and pulled out several packets. She dumped one in and stirred.

She stared at the swirling dark brown liquid.

"I was captured. It happened a long time ago," he finally said. "My own choices led to my predicament." Léon shrugged. "Part of my old job. My previous life."

She lifted her gaze. She blinked slightly to clear the emotion from her eyes. "I'm sorry."

"I survived. I have a new life now. It's over."

His words closed that conversation, but Faith let his statement reverberate in her mind. The warmth of the cup filtered through to her hand, but it didn't touch the chill that had settled around her gut. "I've been thinking a lot about my future." She held the warm cup in her hands. "Tell me more about Annie."

That she'd brushed aside the idea that he and CTC could help her stung. "Are you sure?"

"I don't want to run. I want Burke to pay for what he's done, but I can't trust the system. It's stacked against us." She raised her gaze to his. "I don't have a choice."

He sat beside her. "Your past will follow you. If not physically, emotionally. The question is, can you live in the present? Your new present? Without wishing for what might have been?" He took her hand in his. "It won't be easy with Zoe. She's old enough to remember, but not old enough for you to be sure she can keep this secret. She'll have to get used to a new name, a new place. She won't be able to tell anyone about her past."

His words vibrated with truth…and with firsthand knowledge. She searched his gaze. "You've found a new life, haven't you? You have friends, people who care about you? People you count on?"

Léon didn't speak for a moment.

"Haven't you?" she asked again.

He cleared his throat. "Do you have family besides Zoe?"

She didn't like that he refused to answer the question. Maybe she'd assumed too much. "My folks died when I was twenty," she said. "Right before I met Burke. I have some cousins, but we never saw them. They live back east. Vermont, or maybe New Hampshire."

"That will make the transition easier. A new identity won't weigh on you as much." Léon sighed. "Annie's a pro. I ought to know. She can help you and Zoe disappear. As long as you follow her rules, you'll be okay. And safe."

"Will the $10,000 I have be enough?" Faith had a feel-

ing Annie's services were much more valuable than anything Ray had offered.

"She owes me a favor. It'll be enough. And you don't
have a choice, Faith."

"And you know she's the best." Faith shifted in her
chair. "Is Léon your real name?"

He tilted his head. "What do you think?"

She studied his closed-off expression. "You know too
much about what Annie can do for us. Besides, I've never
thought Léon fit you somehow."

"You're smart, and beautiful and very intuitive." He
cupped her face in his hand, holding her captive with his
gaze. "I don't let people see through me often. I don't
know what it is about you."

She leaned in closer to him. "This isn't a good idea.
I'm leaving."

"I know. Which is why I'm not fighting the temptation."

He lowered his mouth to hers, exploring her with a
kiss that was gentle and powerful at the same time.

Faith shivered under the touch of his lips. He didn't
press her body close. He held her face between his hands
and his lips and tongue seduced her.

She couldn't have stood if she'd wanted to. She finally knew what the phrase *legs feeling like jelly* meant.

He raised his head and looked deep into her eyes.
"That was…surprising."

The moment his lips left hers, a strange coldness in-
vaded her. She hoped her mouth wasn't hanging open
in shock. Her heart raced, thudding against her chest.
Her entire body trembled. She gripped his collar. "Don't
stop."

Faith pulled him back to her. With a groan, he wrapped
his arms around her, pressing her tight against him. His

kiss wasn't gentle this time. But neither was hers. He demanded. She wanted.

The flames licked at her very soul. She couldn't stop touching him. Her hands worked their way beneath his shirt, and she pushed it up. He lifted his mouth just long enough to let her toss his T-shirt away. She explored every inch of skin. His body was hard and firm. His back marred with scars. He sucked in a breath.

He'd been through so much, and he hadn't hesitated to help her, to protect her. To save Zoe.

The worry and fear disappeared with the touch of his hand on the bare skin of her back. She couldn't catch her breath. She'd never wanted anyone the way she wanted him.

She didn't know his real name, but she knew enough to know she trusted him.

Suddenly, he lifted his head. His heart thudded against her palm. She took a shuddering breath.

Before she could ask why he'd stopped, a soft buzzing sound filtered through her fuzzy brain.

The noise got louder, closer. He stared up into the sky and let out a curse. "A drone."

He grabbed her hand. "Head for cover. Now." He dragged her to the tent and they ducked inside.

Zoe shot up, immediately awake. "What's wrong?"

Faith pulled Zoe toward her, pressing the little girl close.

Léon crouched inside the tent and peered out. The buzzing swooped down closer. The drone flew over them, then circled in for another pass.

Faith's heart slammed against her ribs. She could barely process what was going on.

Had Burke found them again? She had no other explanation. This was why they had to run, why they needed new names. If only she could make Zoe understand they truly had to disappear. Forever.

Otherwise, they'd never be free. He'd always find them.

She looked over at Léon, not caring if he saw her fear. His jaw tightened. "Someone's found us."

Chapter Seven

The morning sky offered no clouds, no cover. The drone had pinned them down. Stefan shoved his hand through his hair and peered through the tent's mesh screen.

"It's Burke, isn't it?" Faith's face had paled to the color of milk.

He wished he could reassure her, but he didn't know. Besides, whether it was her ex or Ray's contacts or even Stefan's enemies, it didn't matter. They'd been compromised.

All he could do now was minimize their vulnerabilities. Most drones recorded their information on an SD card and didn't necessarily go wireless. Either way, the machine had captured too many images, including Faith and Zoe, Stefan's face, the scars on his back and their license plate. If there was a chance he could keep the images and location from being disseminated, he had to take it. Hell of a shot, though, given the speed.

"You two stay here," he ordered.

Keeping his head low, he raced to his truck, dug into the cab and pulled out his rifle case. Within seconds he'd yanked open the zipper and lifted the Keppeler KS-V. His obligatory stint in his country's military had highlighted his unusual skill at long-distance shooting. It'd been the reason CTC had approached him for covert operations in the first place.

The drone made yet another pass over the camp, its camera visible at the bottom of the machine. He pressed the butt of the weapon to his bare shoulder and swept the barrel toward the drone. Whoever flew the machine may have recorded the location of the camp, but if they hadn't written it down or if they were counting on the drone's memory to keep the info, Stefan might be able to buy them some time.

He'd just have to hope the footage wasn't being recorded remotely.

Stefan sighted the drone and estimated the speed. He couldn't hesitate, not while his target kept on a steady path. He lined up the target, and anticipating its speed and trajectory, took in a slow breath. His instincts took over. He exhaled, and in between heartbeats, squeezed the trigger.

The loud crack echoed across the landscape. The drone broke apart in midair, its remains plummeting onto the desert floor several hundred feet to the south.

He swept his weapon along the landscape in a circle, searching for any vehicles. Nothing for at least twenty miles in any direction. He had a few minutes, but they couldn't hang around long.

"You can come out now," he called. He grabbed his T-shirt from the ground and tugged it on.

Zoe barreled out of the tent and raced to him. "You shot it? Right out of the sky?" Her eyes shone with awe.

"It's one of my jobs." Stefan returned his rifle to the case and met Faith's gaze over the girl's head. "We're leaving in ten minutes. Pack your things as fast as you can."

"Zoe," Faith said, nodding her head toward the tent. "Go ahead. I'll be right there."

Surprisingly, Zoe didn't argue or resist. Maybe it was the flat order from Faith, or the urgent tone in her mother's voice. Whatever the reason, the little girl raced to the tent while Faith followed Stefan out of the camp.

"Where are you going?" she asked, hurrying to his side.

"To check the camera and retrieve any memory chips that could identify us or the vehicle."

She paled and clutched his arm. "Are you telling me Burke may have *seen* us?"

"If it was Burke at all. The drone may not be your husband's. It could be Ray or the men he hasn't paid for your ID. Or, as you may have inferred, I have my own set of enemies." Stefan glanced over his shoulder. Zoe had set her knapsack outside the tent.

"You don't really believe that, do you?" She matched him step for step. "After everything, I don't need to be placated, Léon."

He scowled at her use of his alias. Before they parted he'd really like for her to call him by his given name. Just once. Strange how badly he wanted what he'd never wished for in the past.

Stepping up his pace, he picked through a thick group of shrub bushes. "I think chances are better than even that your husband is using some rather extraordinary means to find you and Zoe."

He knelt beside a twisted mess of plastic and metal. The drone hadn't been military quality. He popped out the hard drive and SD card and filtered through more wreckage. He let out a curse. The transmitter was expensive. He took a series of quick photos with his phone. "I can't tell if the video could live-stream ten miles out. I'll find out. Either way, they know our coordinates, so we're out of time."

They rushed back to the campsite. Zoe had taken it upon herself to pack up her mother's duffel and she'd even placed Stefan's makeshift kitchen items in a box.

"Are you sure you're not twenty instead of seven?" Stefan kept his tone joking and light, but even as he said the words he grabbed the duffel and box she'd packed and shoved them into the back of his SUV.

She poked her chest out and placed her hands on her hips. "I'm a big help. Just ask Mom."

Faith knelt and hugged Zoe. "I don't know what I'd do without you, Slugger." She rose and looked around the campsite. "Let's load everything into Léon's truck. I'll race you."

Zoe chuckled and they darted around the area, folding up camp chairs and putting away his kitchen staples. Faith laughed with her daughter, but Stefan recognized the tension lining her mouth, the stiffness in her back and shoulders.

Nothing could be done about that. Except to get them to safety.

They disappeared into the tent once more. The moment they began talking, Stefan grabbed his sat phone and called a number he rarely dialed.

The phone rang once, twice, three times. What if Daniel wasn't home?

A click sounded.

"Stefan?" Daniel Adams asked, his tone surprised. Maybe even shocked. "Is that you?"

For a moment Stefan simply closed his eyes. Daniel was the only person to use his given name these days. The man who had saved his life daily for weeks.

"How's your family?" Stefan tucked in his earpiece and pocketed the phone so he could finish loading the SUV. He shoved several tubs filled with tracking equipment and weapons and moved on to the boxes Zoe and Faith and closed.

"Unbelievable. The girls are into everything, and Hope's still in remission. We're going on almost four years now. I think we've beat it. Knock on wood."

"That's terrific." Stefan grabbed a bag of tools and the camp chairs, stowing them away. "How are the flash-backs?"

The last time he'd communicated with Daniel, his friend had still been struggling, though he'd improved a thousandfold since he'd vanished from a VA hospital and walked across the country to clear his head. Of course, he'd met his wife, fallen in love and found a family in the process. Not to mention all the headwork.

Daniel didn't answer for a moment. "Under control. I doubt they'll ever go away but I'm managing." He paused. "Are you having them?" his friend asked quietly. "Is that why you called?"

Only Daniel knew what had really happened to Stefan in the dungeon. Stefan had spent months in the hidden catacombs below his family's castle in the small coun-try of Bellevaux. He'd expected to die, but the handoff to the terrorist leader who'd paid for the privilege had been delayed. Stefan's brother-in-law-to-be and a few others from CTC had rescued them before the exchange could be made.

"Sleeping outside helps," Stefan said. "Seems to me you gave me that advice."

"A bed isn't a bad way to spend the night. You should try it, my friend."

The sound of soft footsteps coming up behind him caused Stefan to pause. Faith cleared her throat.

"Hold on, Daniel," Stefan said. He faced Faith. "If I take down the tent, can you fold it up while I get the rest?"

"Sure." She set down two more bags. "That's the last of it."

Stefan glanced at his watch. "I'm back, Daniel."

"Distracted by a lovely female voice. Sounds like your life is improving," Daniel said with a smile in his voice. "So why this phone call out of the blue?"

"I need a favor." He loaded the last two bags and quickly toured the area.

"Anything for you, Stefan. You know that."

"You may change your mind. I need a place to hide for a few days. Somewhere no one can find us."

"Us?"

"I'll be bringing a woman and her daughter with me. They're on the run. They're in trouble, Daniel. I'm involving Annie."

His friend let out a slow sigh. "Bring them here. No one but CTC knows of our connection. Besides, Raven would love to see you."

Stefan strode across the camp where Faith and Zoe still struggled with the tent. "I'll owe you one."

"That's what friends are for, Stefan."

"Thanks, Daniel."

His friend hung up, and Stefan slipped his earpiece back into his pocket. They folded the tent and he loaded it, slamming the back end shut. "That took fifteen minutes. Come on, we're out of here."

Faith and Zoe jumped into his SUV and he joined them. "We have a place to lie low," he said, yanking the car into gear.

"We'll be safe?" Faith asked. "You're sure?"

Stefan sped across the desert, the sand kicking up behind him. "He won't find you. I promise."

THE TEXAS MORNING sun hadn't peeked over the tall buildings of downtown Dallas. Burke's Mercedes whizzed west, leaving the city behind, past too many exits to count. He headed through Fort Worth and finally came upon the Weatherford exit, but he couldn't return to the Shiny Penny. It was too soon.

He gripped the steering wheel until his knuckles whitened. Every nerve ending under his skin fired until he could hardly bear the stinging.

His father didn't understand. Burke wasn't some self-indulgent child. He had to feed his needs or he would explode.

He gripped the armrest just as his cell phone rang.

Burke tapped his Bluetooth receiver on the steering wheel. "Thomas."

"It's Orren. I found them."

At the news, Burke's heart raced. "You have Faith and Zoe?"

"I said I found them. And their cowboy friend. He shot down the drone and knew enough to take the hard drive and memory card before they bugged out. Their camp has been scrubbed clean. We caught a few fuzzy images during streaming, but there was a delay. We were too far away for clear reception."

Burke's knuckles whitened. "Who *is* this guy?"

"I got no leads. No one in this town talks to strangers." Orren cursed. "It's damned spooky. I couldn't even get the waitress at the diner to gossip."

Burke's neck and shoulders clenched. He gripped the steering wheel with a death-like force. "How will you find them?"

"Leave it to me. Your ex-wife doesn't have any family or friends, so my best bet is tracking this guy. I'm sending you several photos. We need your father's contacts to run them through enhancement and facial recognition software. Someplace that has military records. This guy is no cowboy."

"Done." Burke couldn't ask his father for a name, of course, but he had access to his father's files. He'd find someone.

"By the way, boss. Your ex and the cowboy are *very* close, if you know what I mean. I have a photo of them in a lip-lock that practically melted the camera."

Burke's hands jerked. The car veered. He cursed before straightening out and pulling off the road.

He banged on the steering wheel, the fury rising up his neck. "I'll take care of the photos. You find Faith. I don't care how, just do it. Because if you don't, I'll find someone else who can. And you know what a canceled contract means."

Orren gulped through the phone. Burke relished the fear he could evoke with the simplest of words.

A woman in a convertible passed his Mercedes and pulled over. Her blond hair whipped in the wind as she backed up on the side road.

She turned to him and smiled. "Need some help?"

Burke grinned back. Just his type.

He glanced in the back seat. His kit was packed. The Smiley Face Killer had been his latest research project. He'd even included yellow chalk to mark her.

His father could go to hell.

"My phone died," he said. "May I use yours?"

She glanced at him and then his car, the smile in her eyes deepening. "I think I can trust a Mercedes man."

"You can." He pasted on the expression that had gained him trust from all of his victims. "My name is Burke."

"I'm Shanna."

"Well, Shanna. You have a beautiful smile."

Noon in West Texas brought the sun beating down, especially in late summer. Faith leaned forward and turned up the air conditioner. They'd been traveling over dirt roads alternating with paved for hours, and she had no idea where they were headed. The West Texas landscape didn't hold a lot of distractions, much less unique landmarks. No matter which road he turned onto, nothing changed.

Faith sent Léon a sidelong glance. "You haven't told me exactly where we're headed." She didn't like getting the silent treatment.

"We're meeting my boss to switch vehicles in case the drone picked up the license plate." Stefan glanced at his watch. "After that, I'm taking you to a friend's house."

Faith couldn't stop the gulp that seemed to echo through the car. "My situation has already caused you to leave *your* home." She scooted across the seat closer to him and lowered her voice. "Zoe and I should disappear. Like we planned."

"He's got the scent now, Faith." His low voice rumbled in his chest. "I'll hide you until I can connect with Annie. In the meantime, I'd like to see if there's a way we can stop *him*—" he glanced over his shoulder at Zoe "—without you two being forced on the run for the rest of your lives."

"It can't be done," she whispered with a tone of resignation lacing her voice. "Just give me Annie's contact information. It's the only choice. We both know it."

"Give me the chance to fix this for you. I have the resources. In the meantime, I can keep you two safe. I promised, didn't I?"

His voice rose a bit, and his challenging scowl caused Faith to sigh inside. Just what she needed. Another person even more stubborn than Zoe in her life.

"Léon always keeps his promises, Mom. He told me." Zoe munched on a bag of chips behind them.

Faith's head whipped around to stare at her daughter. How much had Zoe heard? Faith couldn't read her face. Zoe simply looked at Léon with complete adoration. She was his biggest fan.

"Good to know," Faith muttered. "I can't be in the dark like this. I need—"

"To control your life. I get that." Léon had the grace to wince. "Sorry. I'm used to working alone. We're closing in on the first rendezvous point to meet the head of CTC, Ransom Grainger. I'll give you Annie's number then."

They turned down another dirt road. Dust kicked up behind them, leaving a visible cloud ten feet in the air.

Two vehicles waited just ahead. Léon pulled up beside them, before reaching across her to snag a notebook out of the glove box. He scribbled a phone number. "Don't use this until I have a chance to call Annie," he warned. "She takes her privacy very seriously."

Faith pocketed the number and nodded.

"Wait here," he said, and exited the vehicle.

He crossed over to the two men. Faith rolled down the window. She wasn't about to be in the dark about her own situation.

"Ransom," Léon said, and shook a tall man's hand.

From what Faith could see, Ransom Grainger would intimidate most people. His black hair added to his intense demeanor, and his dark brown eyes were cold and calculating. His appearance alone made Faith shiver. She wouldn't want to be on the wrong side of that man.

She strained to hear what they were saying.

"What's their story?" Ransom asked Léon with a skeptical frown.

Léon's brow arched. "Why are you asking?"

"Because about an hour ago an image of you popped up in a federal-agency-wide facial recognition sweep."

Léon paled. Faith couldn't have imagined him ever appearing scared, but he did.

"What's wrong with Léon, Mom?" Zoe asked. "He looks like he's going to be sick."

"Shh, Zoe. Let me listen."

"Damn it. The drone." He rubbed his face. "Faith was right. Her ex-husband's family's got a lot of contacts." He looked at Ransom. "So, how bad is it?"

"Let's just say it's a good thing you've got Annie working on a new identity, even though there was no reason for you to leave Carder," Ransom said in a curt voice. "Now there's every reason. You've been made."

The statement hit Faith in her chest, forcing the air from her lungs. He was in trouble just like her. He had to disappear, too.

"Are you just assuming? Maybe—"

"The chatter's up, and I'd say in the next twenty-four to forty-eight hours, your enemies will be landing in Texas to vie for a $20 million price on your head. There's even a $1 million reward for proof you're alive."

Faith pressed her hand against her mouth. What had she done? She should never have agreed to let Léon help them. The Thomas family had put Léon's life in danger, but it was her fault.

"He's that desperate?" Léon asked. "Twenty million will buy just about anyone." He paced back and forth and looked over his shoulder right at her.

She made her expression go blank. He narrowed his gaze slightly, but she simply stared out the window, struggling not to show the anguish shredding her heart. She didn't want him to know she'd heard every word.

"Do Logan and Katherine know?" Léon asked with a frown.

Ransom nodded. "Your sister and brother-in-law are

upset. They'd hoped to rendezvous with you on their next visit to the ranch. They know if you leave, they may never see you again."

"They're in danger now that my enemies know I'm alive. They'll go after anyone who cares about me for leverage. You know that."

"Luckily, your sister has the best security in place. Logan won't let anyone near her or the kids."

Léon crossed his arms, his expression more intense than Faith had ever seen.

"There's only one way to protect my family, Ransom. Someone needs to earn that million dollars and I have to die again. Publicly."

"I know."

Faith turned her head and looked at Zoe. Her little brow had furrowed. "Is Léon in trouble, Mom? Can we help him?"

"I'm going to try, Slugger." Faith's mind whirled with possibilities. She had her money back. She stuffed her hand into her pocket and fingered the piece of paper he'd given her.

"You have a day to help me get Faith and Zoe into a safe house," Léon said. "Then I'll worry about me."

"Eighteen hours," Ransom countered. "I'll scrub your vehicle. The license plate number appeared in the chatter. You can take one of mine. It's clean."

Léon rubbed his chin. "Deal."

Ransom dropped a set of keys into Léon's hand and glanced over at the car, meeting Faith's gaze. She swallowed hard. His expression had turned thoughtful, contemplative. Faith shifted on the seat. What was it with these men in Carder that made her shiver? It's as if they could see right into her mind and soul.

"Running isn't the answer for her and the little girl,"

Ransom said, as if he were speaking to her, not Léon. "We can help. That's what CTC does."

Léon shook his head. "I offered several times. She doesn't trust that *anyone* can guarantee their safety. I have to honor her wishes, Ransom."

"At the expense of your life?"

Léon didn't answer. Faith leaned back in the front seat and closed her eyes. She'd been right to run in the first place. She'd been wrong to get him so involved, and she could only think of one way to fix the problem. It wouldn't be easy. But it might work.

If she was smart and quick.

"Let's transfer your belongings into my truck," Ransom said.

Faith twisted in her seat and lowered her voice. "Slugger, I need you to pretend you're asleep for a few minutes, okay?"

Her daughter's eyes grew confused. "Why?"

"We're playing a little trick on Léon, okay? Don't let him know you're awake."

She grinned. "Okay, Mom."

Faith hated lying to Zoe, but it was for Léon's own good.

He walked back to the vehicle. "We're taking the white truck. No one will be able to track us."

With everything inside of her, she struggled to remain calm. He was too intuitive not to guess her intentions. She couldn't let anything slip. "Good."

At her staccato response, he narrowed his gaze at her. "Are you okay?"

She let out a small yawn and blinked at him. "Just tired. Like Zoe." Faith nodded at the back seat.

"Asleep?"

"She couldn't stay awake any longer. It's been a tough couple of days."

"I'll carry her."

"No, I'll take her. Keys?"

Léon handed them to her. Faith opened up the back door and pulled Zoe into her arms.

Ransom tipped his hat to her. "Ma'am."

She didn't know what to say to him. She slipped Zoe into the vehicle and hurried back to the SUV. Her timing had to be just right. She grabbed her duffel and Zoe's orange knapsack.

Luck was with her. Léon, Ransom and another cowboy headed to the back of the SUV to unload the camping equipment.

With hands shaking, Faith scooted into the front seat and shut the door as quietly as she could. It closed with a soft snick.

She turned the engine on and without hesitation slammed it into gear and took off across the desert.

Léon stared after her, stunned, along with the two other men.

Within a few hundred yards she hit pavement. She never looked back.

Someday, she'd send money to pay for the truck, but for now, she had to protect Léon.

She'd head to Mexico and disappear. She refused to let anyone else get hurt because of her.

Chapter Eight

The sun hung low in the sky and shadows painted the desert. Stefan slammed his hand against the steering wheel. Faith and Zoe had vanished. He'd been a fool to try to help. He was still a fool to search for them.

Faith had left no trail to follow.

A very small part of him admired the hell out of her gumption. He kneaded the back of his neck. As a last resort he'd asked Zane, CTC's computer expert, to run a background check on Faith's ex-husband. Except for a few late child support payments, he'd come up squeaky clean. Too perfect, actually.

He squinted through the failing light. He was out of options and no closer to finding them.

His phone rang. After a quick glance at the screen, he tapped his earpiece. "Ransom?"

"Did you give her Annie's number?"

The curt question caused Léon to groan. "I instructed Faith not to call the number until I spoke with Annie personally."

"She's not too happy with you. Her number is a sacred trust. What were you thinking?"

"That Faith is hiding from a serial killer who found her in the middle of nowhere." Stefan winced despite his excuse. "I'm in deep trouble with Annie, aren't I?"

"I'd get used to permanent groveling. *If* she forgives you." Stefan recognized the frustration in Ransom's voice. "On the other hand, Annie normally would've left us in the dark. Instead, she called to let me know Faith and her daughter were at the trailer."

The world had just tilted on its access. "Annie never reveals her clients. Even if we're the go-between. Why?"

"She discovered a $250,000 reward on the dark web. Too many people are looking for them."

"Annie would've already moved her camper by now. Where are they?"

Ransom gave Stefan the GPS coordinates. He cut a sharp U-turn. Next stop: Annie's.

Two hours later, the sun had set and Stefan's headlights pierced the night. He drove over a small rise and when he hit the top, a lantern beamed at him from the distance.

Almost there.

What was he supposed to say to Faith when he saw her? She was an adult. She could make her own mistakes. Why in the hell was he driving in the middle of nowhere trying to find her when she clearly didn't want his help?

Because he was an idiot, and for some reason Faith and Zoe had inserted themselves into a soft, squishy place he'd believed he'd eradicated a long time ago.

He parked his truck next to the one Faith had stolen and exited the vehicle.

Annie stepped out of the trailer, hands on her hips. He winced at the expression on her face. He raised his hands. "I'm sorry, Annie. I just—"

"I know exactly what happened. One look at Faith and that kid of hers and you melted into a puddle of primordial ooze. Just so you know, I've changed my number, and you don't get it." She opened the door and shook her head in disgust. "Swallow your apology and come in. Zoe's going to be happy to see you. Faith, not so much."

"She stole Ransom's truck," he said with a bemused shake of his head.

Annie chuckled. "I'd have loved to have seen his face when she took off. And yours."

"We weren't expecting her to do something so damned crazy." Stefan scowled at her, but Annie simply smiled and led him inside.

At least she wasn't angry enough to shoot him.

He followed her into the camper.

Faith sat at the makeshift table with Zoe. When he strode in, she shot to her feet. "What's he doing here?" She whirled on Annie. "You called him! I thought I could trust you."

"Zoe," Stefan said with a wink. He held the latest and greatest handheld device up. "I brought you a game and some earphones."

Zoe's eyes got big. "Really? Danny had one at home, and I used to play—"

Stefan placed it in her hands and she shot a pleading glance to her mother. "Please?"

"Just for a while." Faith shot Stefan a withering glare while Zoe bundled down in the recliner with her new game. "Are you trying to buy her off? That's one of Burke's tricks."

"Maybe I didn't want her to hear that every criminal on both sides of the border is looking for you both to earn a nice finder's fee."

"How much?"

When he told her, she lost all color and sank into a dining chair. "What can we do?"

"What you should've done in the first place. Let me

help you." He faced Annie. "How long to create a new identity for them?"

"I can turn the birth certificates and driver's license around in a day. It'll take longer to backstop her identity, though."

"I can work with that. We'll disappear for a few days." Stefan stared down Faith. "You're coming with me. No more running."

"Can't we stay with Annie?" She sent a pleading glance to the woman.

The plea shouldn't have hurt, but it cut Stefan to the core. Why couldn't she trust him?

"I'm sorry, honey," Annie said. "I've got clients whose lives depend on secrecy. It just wouldn't work." She glared at Stefan.

"What about a motel?" Faith chewed on her bottom lip and met Stefan's gaze. "I know people are coming for you. I heard your boss. Your life is in danger because of me. If you're not with us you can disappear."

"Faith—"

Annie let out a sharp curse.

"It was only a matter of time before my previous life caught up with me." Stefan forced an uncaring shrug. "Speaking of which, is my new passport ready?"

Annie shook her head. "You said you weren't in a hurry, but I can have it the same time as theirs."

Stefan crossed his arms and glared at Faith. "You blew my cover, darlin'. You owe me and I'm collecting. For now, we stay together, we get out of town and we hunker down. Agreed?"

"I think you're making a mistake." Faith sank into the bench behind the table. "I was only doing what I thought was the right thing. I was trying to protect you."

"That's my job. Not yours." He studied her, baffled.

When had anyone ever cared enough to sacrifice for him? He knelt next to the table and took one of her hands. "Let me finish this, Faith. Let me keep you and Zoe out of Burke's hands."

She lifted her head and he met the tired gaze in her red-rimmed eyes "I should be able to handle my own problems. Burke was mine."

"We all need help sometimes," Annie said quietly. "Léon knows what he's doing."

Stefan squeezed her fingers. "You may have believed you were fighting this battle alone, but you're not anymore. Burke's my problem now, too."

THE WOMAN'S DEATH hadn't satisfied. Burke struggled to slip the key into the lock of his condominium. His hand trembled. Drawing that stupid smiley face near her body, mimicking the Smiley Face Killer, had been anticlimactic at best. He needed a more hands-on approach to the body. More up-close-and-personal time.

Burke pushed open the door of his home. The place was elegant, pristine and perfect. White, black, glass and metal. Without a stick of mahogany anywhere. Exactly how he wanted his life.

He set down his kit on the entryway table. The thrumming in his veins had dissipated, but it hadn't left him. The urge remained.

He now understood. He needed a more personal kill. He relished witnessing the life fade from their eyes, hearing them beg for mercy, but he needed more time with them. To touch them, to cut them, to make them his own.

The urge, the desire, grew stronger by the minute. He'd have to find someone else. Tonight.

"You broke your promise to me." His father's voice pierced the darkness. "Again."

Burke spun around.

His father flipped on the lamp in the living room. A tall glass of whiskey sat in front of him. He took a sip. "Why?" he asked. "Why can't you stop?"

The fatigue on his father's face surprised Burke. Weakness? His father never showed anything less than strength.

Gerard Thomas swirled the drink around. "Maybe I should have told the authorities about Heather when you were sixteen. That was a mistake, I think. I thought you'd grow out of it. I thought you'd learn self-control."

Heather. When was the last time Burke had heard her name aloud? His one true love. His first. In everything. She'd just turned eighteen when she'd gone to work for his father. Burke had been doing time in the mailroom when he'd first seen her. Beautiful, pure blond hair, a waiflike figure who wore clothes like a New York model. Passionate lips and hands that had brought him more pleasure than he'd ever known. His ideal. His passion. His only love.

His father set the glass down with a clink. "I can't cover for you anymore, Burke. You need help I can't give you."

Burke straightened his back, shoving the past away. "I'm *fine*. I don't need your interference. I can see to my own affairs."

"You're not fine. You killed again. You've hired a man who can't be trusted to deal with your ex-wife. You've become reckless." He paused. "I've decided you need professional help."

"What have you done?" Burke stilled and knotted his fist.

"I found a place overseas. They'll be…discreet. They

will teach you discipline, how to control your urges. When you're better, you can return."

"You're sending me away? To what? Some hospital?"

"It's a facility that deals with…difficult cases."

"You SOB." Needles of fury pricked the back of Burke's neck. "You're committing me, aren't you? You want me to disappear."

"Just until you're better."

The placating tone grated on Burke's already-raw nerves. He paced back and forth, shaking his head with force. The man would ruin all his plans. He needed to think. He had to clear his brain from the roar echoing in his skull. He faced his father. "I'll have Faith soon. I'll stop her. I'll get Zoe back for Mom. That's what you wanted, isn't it?"

"You're taking too many girls. They're being noticed." His father rose and grabbed Burke by the shoulders. "Look me in the eye and tell me you can stop."

"Of course I can."

"That's what you said after Heather."

"You don't get to talk to me about her. She threatened to tell Mom about your affair with her," Burke spat out. "What was I supposed to do?"

His father's head snapped around. "What?"

"She was mine!" Burke shouted. "You had to put your filthy hands on her, and she threatened to tell. I couldn't let her hurt Mom. I killed her *because of you*." Burke crossed the room until he loomed above his father. When had the man gotten so old? "You didn't call the cops because you *knew* Mom would find out. She'd divorce you and her family's money would drive you out of business."

His father's face slackened with shock.

"I didn't know then, but I'm in the company now. I'm

good at what I do, Father. I studied the history, believing you were something you're not."

Burke walked over to the bar and pulled a small leather pouch from a drawer. He'd been prepared for this day from the moment he'd divorced Faith. He poured himself a double and downed the whiskey in one gulp before unzipping the kit. A syringe and small vial lay protected inside.

Filling the syringe didn't take long. He returned to his father.

"You're taking drugs now?"

"This isn't for me," Burke said with a smile.

He grabbed his father's left hand. The whiskey fell to the floor. In one motion Burke jabbed the needle at the base of his ring finger and plunged all the way.

His father stared at his hand. "What have you done?"

"What I should have done years ago."

His father shot to his feet. Burke shoved him back to the sofa. He recognized the fear lacing his father's eyes. His chest swelled with satisfaction.

"I protected you." His father clutched his chest. "I've saved you countless times. You'll get caught without me."

"You taught me well." Burke pinned the man he'd hated for fifteen years to the sofa. "I'll never get caught."

FAITH COULDN'T STOP staring at the white center lane on the West Texas road. The blurring line mesmerized her. Or maybe it was the lack of sleep. She'd tossed and turned in the fold-out bed Annie had provided her and Zoe until about four this morning.

The dreams had come feverishly. Léon reaching out to her and someone jerking him away. The visions had all ended the same way, with them lying on the ground in a pool of blood, Burke standing over them laughing, Zoe at his side.

She'd called out at least once because in the early morning hours, Léon had lain down beside her, pulled her into his arms and held her close the rest of the night. He'd been nothing but a gentleman. She'd finally settled in and given in to sleep.

Three hours hadn't been enough to wash away the dreams, though. Her entire body felt as if she'd been chewed up and spit out by a harvester. Faith rubbed her tired eyes just as Stefan turned the truck down a long, winding driveway. He paused briefly in front of an iron gate. It swung open and the truck shuddered when they crossed a cattle guard.

They'd been on the road for at least four hours, but following his indirect route had been impossible. She had no idea where they were. She didn't want to ask.

A ranch-style house sat at the end of the paved road. There had to be at least five acres around it. Faith could even make out a barn behind the main house. The lawn surrounding the house appeared a bit odd, actually, in the midst of the desert plants.

Two girls, a year or two younger than Zoe, ran through a sprinkler system in the front yard. Every few seconds a huge reddish dog forced his face into the water before shaking all over and sending the girls into fits of laughter.

Léon pulled into the driveway. "We're here."

Faith glanced at him, worry weighing down her shoulders. "What if Burke—?"

"Do you think I'd do anything to place this family in danger?" he asked, his tone sharp.

She bit her lip. Faith should trust him. She did, actually, but Burke... She'd never known him to give up. He always won.

Could this time be different? With a sigh, she sent him a sidelong glance before finally nodding.

Zoe looked through the car's window with longing. "Can I play?" she asked, though from her tone she expected another *no*.

Léon turned in his seat. "You can play all you want here," he said. "We're staying for a day or two."

"Good. I'm tired of driving." Zoe grinned at him.

A tall man with a slight limp walked toward the truck. Léon rolled down the window and smiled. The first truly relaxed smile Faith could remember seeing on his face.

"Daniel. Good to see you, my friend."

The faint accent thickened with his greeting. Maybe because Léon had let his guard down?

"And who might you have with you?" Daniel asked, peering into the SUV, the scar down the side of his cheek taking nothing away from his compelling features.

"This is Faith, and the girl eager to jump into the fun is Zoe. Faith and Zoe, this is my friend Daniel Adams." Léon flicked the unlock button on the console and opened his door. "You're free, Zoe."

Her daughter nearly bounced out of the back seat onto the ground and raced around the truck to stare at the front yard with longing.

Faith couldn't remember her daughter being so excited since the first day of baseball practice earlier this spring. A familiar wave of guilt settled in her gut. She'd wanted so much more for Zoe than being on the run the rest of their lives.

Faith exited the vehicle and rounded the truck. She placed her left hand on Zoe's shoulder and reached out her right to Daniel. "Thank you for taking us in."

He smiled at her. "Any friend of Léon's." Daniel

turned to the yard and cupped his hands around his mouth. "Christina. Hope. Come here, girls."

They veered from their play and the dog followed. He bounded toward Faith and Zoe.

"Trouble. Sit," Daniel ordered.

Before the dog could jump on them, he dropped his rump. His tail wagged and the huge animal had what appeared to be a smile on his face. His entire body vibrated with excitement.

"He won't bite. He's just excitable. And yes, he was named after the town." Daniel smiled down at the two girls. "These are my daughters, Christina and Hope."

"It's so nice to meet you," Faith said. "This is Zoe."

Her daughter took a few steps until she was toe-to-toe with the little girls. "You look alike."

Hope grinned. "We're twins. We're five. Do you want to play?"

Zoe glanced over her shoulder at Faith.

"Sure. Just stay close."

Zoe grinned wide.

"Come on, Trouble," Hope called.

A woman joined Daniel and she gave Léon a hug. "It's good to see you."

"This is my wife, Raven," Daniel said.

Raven gave Faith a welcoming albeit sympathetic smile. "From what I gathered you've had a tough few days. How about some sun tea?"

She hesitated, glancing at Zoe.

Léon gave her a small nod. "Daniel has a surveillance system. If anyone opens the gates without permission, he'll know it. Zoe is safe here."

Raven squeezed Faith's arm. "Daniel and Léon will watch over them. Come on inside."

Zoe ran through the sprinkler, laughing and shaking her head. Water sprayed from her. How long had it been since she'd heard that kind of carefree laugh from her daughter?

Until Léon came into their lives?

Faith followed Raven into the house, through the welcoming living room and into the kitchen. She poured tea over ice. Faith sat at the large rectangular oak table and took a long sip.

She could breathe in this house. No one could tie her to Daniel and Raven Adams. And who would come looking for them in a house outside of a town she'd never heard of? She hadn't known Trouble, Texas, existed.

"Delicious," she said with a sigh.

"You can't beat sun tea," Raven said, wiping down the counter. "Barbecue okay for a late lunch? That way Daniel does most of the cooking." Raven grinned. She placed a stockpot of water on the stove and dumped a bag of potatoes into the sink.

"Can I help?" Faith asked.

Raven scooted over and handed her a potato peeler. "I never refuse an extra pair of hands."

The women worked silently for a while. Raven placed a clean potato off to the side. "If you're wondering, Léon didn't tell us what you're going through, just that you're in trouble." She picked up another vegetable and slid the peeler along the skin. "Daniel and I met because he saved my life. He and Trouble found me buried alive. You can trust my husband and Léon to protect you and your daughter. I have the experience to prove it."

Faith gaped at Raven.

"Long story, but we found my daughters and have a good life. We're even adopting a little boy next month." Raven placed her hand on Faith's. "My point is life can get better. You've found a good man willing to do whatever it takes to help you, and that man has some friends who've gotten people out of more trouble than you can imagine."

Faith had rarely seen the kind of confidence Raven displayed in anyone, much less experienced it. She'd come with Léon because she couldn't figure out another way to protect Zoe. Inside, that wall she'd built around her heart had weakened a bit. Her response to him terrified her.

Burke's betrayal had practically destroyed her. She'd vowed not to rely on anyone else. She couldn't afford to give away her power like that.

Faith's head hurt from all the scenarios she worked through in her mind. She and Raven continued in silence until the three girls rushed into the kitchen.

"Mom, when are we eating?" Zoe asked.

"Not for a while yet."

The twins groaned. "We're hungry," they said in unison.

Raven nodded toward a bowl of sliced fruit and cheese. "I know my daughters well. Sit at the table to eat."

Three chairs scraped the floor. The girls giggled and scarfed down their snack. Soon they were whispering quietly.

"What do you think that's about?" Faith asked Raven in a low voice.

Raven frowned. "Trouble, if I know my girls."

ZOE SAT AT the table, eyeing her mom before examining the last nectarine slice. Today had been the best day in a long time. She'd gotten so tired of being cooped up in the library all the time. Especially when her mom made her practice her reading all day long.

"You take it," Hope said with a smile, pushing the plate to her.

Zoe didn't usually play with girls, especially not little girls who were only five, but Hope and Christina weren't like other girls. Plus, it was so cool that they looked exactly alike.

With a smile, Zoe popped the nectarine slice into her mouth.

Hope shoved back her chair. "Come on," she said. "Let's go to our room. We can play there."

Zoe stood up, but paused for a moment. "Do you ever talk?" she asked Christina.

The girl nodded.

"Not really," Hope interrupted. "She doesn't like to."

Zoe followed the girls to a large room. Twin bunk beds lined up against one wall opposite huge shelves with tons of toys. Zoe wrinkled her nose. Mostly dolls and girl stuff on the left side, but on the right side, a bunch of board games were stacked up, along with a soccer ball.

A soft scratch sounded at the door.

"Trouble!" Christina shouted.

The dog trotted in and plopped in the center of the floor.

Christina climbed onto his back and hugged him. "My daddy said you don't have a place to live."

Zoe's eyes widened. "I thought you didn't talk."

Hope grinned. "She talks, just not much. And mostly when Trouble's nearby."

Christina stroked his fur. "Do you miss your house?" She stared at Zoe from astride the huge dog.

A small pang in the center of her chest made Zoe sad for a moment. "I miss playing baseball with my friend, Danny. And I miss my daddy. He promised to take me to a baseball game this summer, and summer's almost over. Plus, he buys me neat toys. He got me a tablet a while back and it wasn't even my birthday."

The twins' mouths dropped open. "Wow. Where is it?"

"My mom made me leave it when we ran away. She and my dad don't like each other." Zoe sat in front of Trouble and patted his head. "You're lucky you have a dog. I wish I had one. My mom said I could get a puppy, but then we left home. I don't know if I'll *ever* have one now." She let out a long, drawn-out sigh.

Hope grinned and stared at her sister.

Christina nodded at her twin. "Wanna see something?"

From the expressions on the twins' faces, Zoe knew whatever they were going to look at had to be good. She followed her new friends out the back door, across the lawn and into a big barn. Christina put her finger over her lips. "Shh. We have to be quiet. We might wake them up."

They shut the door behind them and opened up a gate just inside the building. A bunch of squeaks erupted and a half-dozen balls of fur zoomed at them.

A dog that looked kind of like Trouble lay in the corner and sort of smiled at them.

"Puppies," Zoe said, her eyes wide. "You have puppies."

"Come on. Sit down."

Hope and Christina plopped down on the hay in the center of the pen, and Zoe joined them. The puppies scrambled all over them.

Zoe giggled. The smallest puppy pushed its nose into her side. She picked up the reddish brown furball with big eyes and white splashes around her eyes and mouth. In less than a minute, Zoe fell in love.

She held the puppy in her arms and the little animal buried itself in her shoulder.

"Mom said we have to give them all away to good homes," Christina said with a frown. "So other little girls and boys can play with them."

"Do you want one?" Hope asked.

Zoe jumped to her feet and hugged the little furball tight. "I want this one. She likes me."

"Zoe!" her mother's voice sounded panicked.

She ran out of the barn and skidded up to her mother. Her mom was scared, and Zoe felt bad. Her mom didn't smile anymore, either. Except when Léon was around.

The puppy would cheer her mom up.

"Look." She cradled the little dog in her arms and walked over to her mother. "Hope and Christina said I could have her. I'm going to name her Catcher, 'cause she kinda looks like she has a face mask on."

Her mother knelt down and Zoe got that twist back in the pit of her stomach. She recognized the look on her mom's face.

"Zoe. We're moving around a lot. A puppy needs a backyard to play in."

It wasn't fair. They used to have a backyard. Her grandma and grandpa had a huge yard. Her daddy had a yard, even though Zoe had never seen him go outside at his house.

"You're just saying that. We could go home and have a place for Catcher. You took away my house and my friends and my daddy. I hate you."

Zoe shoved Catcher at Christina and ran into the house. She'd had enough of this so-called vacation her mom had taken her on. She wanted to go home.

Chapter Nine

The barn went awkwardly silent. The screen door slammed against the jamb, and Zoe's footsteps pounded away. Faith took in a shuddering sigh and pinched the bridge of her nose.

Raven placed her arm on Faith's shoulder and gave her a sympathetic smile. "She's probably gone upstairs to the girls' room. If I'm right, here comes the door."

Sure enough, a second door slammed closed.

Faith closed her eyes. "I'm so sorry."

"I may not know much about what you're going through," Raven said, "but it's obvious Zoe's been through a lot."

"Thank you for being so kind." Faith wanted to sink into the floor despite Raven's understanding. "I need to talk to her."

Faith left Raven and her daughters and headed inside the house. She trudged up the stairs. She hated this. Why couldn't she have said *yes*? She wanted to give in. Zoe had lost so much, and was about to lose more even though she didn't realize it yet. Faith's head throbbed from the base of her skull all the way to her temples. Maybe she'd ask Raven and Daniel if they could take one of the puppies once she and Zoe settled.

Except, that wouldn't work. With new identities they

wouldn't be able to contact anyone from their past life. Annie had been very clear about the rules...and the consequences. She and Zoe were stuck, painted into a corner by Burke—and her own choices.

Faith hadn't felt so insecure as a mother since the first day she'd brought Zoe home from the hospital. Or maybe the day she'd left Burke's mansion and taken Zoe to the rental house Faith couldn't really afford.

She reached the top of the stairs. Of the five doors she could see, only two were closed. Faith knocked on the first one and cracked it open. She peered into the guest room, searched the closet, the bathroom and even under the bed. Zoe wasn't anywhere to be found.

One room down, one to go. She rapped on the door. No answer. She knocked again. "Zoe, I know you're in there. Come on, let's talk about it."

Her daughter didn't respond.

She inched open the bedroom door and stepped into the twins' room. Faith wanted her daughter to have a room like this one, except maybe she'd have sports equipment and Erector Sets instead of dolls and board games.

Faith crouched down and glanced under the bed. Zoe wasn't here, either. She rose, scanned the room and her gaze honed in on the closet. Perfect hiding place. Zoe had been known to disappear in small spaces from the time she was a toddler.

Faith pressed it open. Zoe sat on the floor, her back facing her mother. With a long inward sigh, Faith sat cross-legged next to Zoe.

"I'm sorry, but we can't go home, Slugger. And we can't bring the puppy with us. Not until we have a place to live. I promise, when I find us a house—"

"I didn't want a dog anyway," Zoe said, her voice catching with emotion. "They're too much trouble."

She tugged some blocks from the corner of the closet. "I'm busy right now. I want to be alone."

Zoe swiped at her face.

Faith placed her hands on Zoe's shoulders. "Honey—"

"Can I be alone, Mom? I don't want to talk right now."

The words were so quiet, so disheartened, but Faith knew her daughter well. Sometimes she needed space. Kind of like her mother. Faith rose to her feet. "I *am* sorry, Zoe. Soon, everything will be better."

"Sure."

Her daughter ducked her head. The flat tone hurt Faith's heart, but it couldn't be helped. She had no other choice. With one last backward glance, she exited the room and headed downstairs. She met the twins racing up. They stopped and looked at her.

"Is Zoe okay?" Hope asked.

Faith forced a smile. "She'll be fine. Maybe you'd like to play with her? I think she could use a couple of friends."

The girls ran to their room and burst inside before closing the door behind them. Faith hovered outside for a moment, but she couldn't make out what the girls were saying.

"Tough love?" Léon asked from the top of the staircase.

"The toughest." Faith met his sympathetic gaze. She rubbed the bridge of her nose. "I hate this. I want to let her have that puppy more than anything. She's been a trouper since all this started."

A dose of giggling sounded through the door, and Faith recognized Zoe's voice if not what she said. "At least she's talking to the twins."

Léon held out his hand. "Come with me. Hope and

Christina are just what she needs right now. Maybe her mom needs a break, too?"

Faith gnawed at her lip, but after one last glance at the door, she followed him. He led her to the guest room and closed the door behind them.

Léon opened his arms, and she walked into them. Her body sagged, leaning against him. She shouldn't do it. She couldn't depend on him to comfort her, but she'd been alone for too long. Really since Zoe was born. She needed so badly to be held.

He stroked her hair.

"Going on the run isn't fair to Zoe," Faith whispered. "Nothing that's happened is her fault and she's paying the biggest price. How do I explain it?"

"She's a tough kid. She'll survive not having a puppy. She'll even survive this move. Kids are resilient. My nephew was kidnapped when he was little. He came through. So will Zoe."

Faith shook her head against his T-shirt. "I don't know. She's lost everything in the last few months. What if she's not okay? What if I'm ruining her life?"

"You're doing what you have to do to protect her." He cupped her face; his blue eyes captured her gaze. "She loves you. She trusts you. You won't let her down."

"You really believe that?" Faith swiped at her eyes.

"She's got an amazing mother and role model. That's what I know."

"Thanks." She wanted to look away, but standing there, so close to him, she didn't want to move. She placed her hands on his arms. Her body leaned toward him.

"Léon—"

The blue of his eyes transformed to dark cobalt as he

stared at her. He cupped her cheek and stroked down her skin. She leaned into his touch and took in a deep breath.

Ever so slowly, he lowered his mouth. She parted her lips and pressed against him. She wanted him to kiss her. Once more.

"Dinner," Raven called from down the stairs.

Léon stilled, his lips hovering just above hers. "Saved by the gong."

The deep, husky tone of his voice made her shiver. He didn't pull away. His hands drifted down her shoulders, past her elbows, until he threaded his fingers through hers.

She couldn't let this moment pass. She rose up and kissed him. The moment their lips touched, Léon groaned and folded her into his arms, pressing him hard against her, breast to chest, hip to hip.

He overwhelmed her with his mouth, claiming hers.

Her knees shook, and she clung to him, pulling him even closer.

"Hope, Christina. Now," Raven called out in that I'm-serious mom tone Faith used all too often.

With a reluctant moan, Léon lifted his lips. Faith couldn't mistake the hunger in his eyes, the want, the need. Her heart raced; her body tingled from her lips down deep into her belly.

He pushed her hair back from her temple. "I guess that means us, too."

Faith simply nodded.

A long sigh escaped him. "I shouldn't have. You know that."

"Maybe." She closed her eyes briefly. "But I'm not sorry, Léon."

He pressed his lips firmly against hers one last time. "Neither am I."

BURKE PACED BACK and forth. His father sat on the sofa, head lolled to the side. The man's breathing was shallow. His lips had turned blue and he'd grabbed his chest.

He was still breathing.

The bastard shouldn't have survived this long. And there he sat, in Burke's living room, still alive.

Damn it.

Burke itched to slice his throat. His hand reached behind him to the knife sheath. He could imagine each action. He relished the feel of the blade slicing through skin, the warm blood bathing his hands.

The light of life leaving the eyes.

It soothed him, drove away the needles of anxiety that prickled his skin.

Unfortunately, he couldn't use his father to provide the release he longed for. The world must believe Gerard Thomas had died of a heart attack.

That meant hands off.

Burke rubbed his temple. From everything he'd read at the medical school library, the potassium chloride should've worked. Really, it was the perfect poison. When they tested the old man's blood, the drug's metabolites would appear elevated, but the medical examiner would simply blame the levels on the muscle damaged caused by the heart attack.

What had gone wrong?

Had Burke made a mistake on the dosage? He picked up his phone, then paused. No, he couldn't search the internet. He'd watched enough cop shows to know they might review his browsing history.

He smiled. Maybe he could use his father's phone.

At that moment, his father convulsed on the sofa, his body twitching and jerking. He groaned once before going limp. His bowels emptied all over Burke's sofa.

The odor erupted through the house. Burke gagged. His father was still, but was he dead?

Burke stared at the grotesque image of his father lying in his own filth. The stain would never come out. He'd have to get a new sofa.

After rounding the couch, he reached out to feel for a pulse.

Nothing.

A flurry of triumph shot through his veins. Job done. He should have done this a long time ago.

The phone in his pocket vibrated. Hopefully Orren with good news.

He glanced down at the screen. Blocked call. He scowled. Perhaps the man had switched phones.

"Thomas."

"D-daddy?" Zoe's voice filtered through the earpiece.

Burke shook his head to clear his mind. "Zoe! Thank goodness you called. I've missed you so much, honey. Are you having fun on your vacation?"

"No. I miss you, Dad. Did you go to the baseball game like we planned?"

Burke cursed. He'd forgotten all about that stupid promise. "I couldn't go without you, Zoe. It wouldn't have been any fun. We all miss you and want you to come home. Your grandpa and grandma miss you, too. Where are you?"

She let out a sob. "I don't know. Outside a little town somewhere. We don't have a house anymore, Dad. We're staying with other people. They have puppies, and I want one, but Mom said no because we don't have a backyard."

"I have plenty of room for a puppy, Zoe." Burke gripped the phone tightly. "If you come home."

"I could bring Catcher with me? He's so cute and soft and—"

"You can have the puppy, Zoe, but I need to come get you if you're going to bring him home."

Zoe paused for a moment. "Mom wants me to live with her."

His daughter's voice had gone quiet and hesitant. Burke had to play this carefully.

"Your mom and I disagree, Zoe. But that's okay." He let out a long, slow breath and considered his next lie. "I love you enough to let you have a puppy. Maybe your mother doesn't."

A small sob and snotty sniffle escaped from Zoe. Kids really were disgusting.

"I don't know, Daddy. Mom would be all alone."

Some high-pitched whispers filtered through the phone. "We know our address," a little girl whispered.

Burke could've cheered. "Zoe? Please come home. Your mom can visit if she wants to." Of course, that would never happen.

His daughter had given him a gift. Once he knew Zoe's location, he'd know Faith's.

"I can bring Catcher?"

"Absolutely." Burke paused. "Where are you, Zoe?" He glanced over at his father's body. Everything was going to be fine.

THE KITCHEN BASKED in the scents of Southern barbecue and banana pudding. Stefan set down his spoon. "I don't know what you put in that ambrosia, Raven, but I could die happy now."

"Hey, what about me?" Daniel groused. "I grilled the chicken."

"She's domesticated you, that's for sure." Stefan leaned

back in his chair and patted his belly. "If I hung out with you for a month, I'd weigh three hundred pounds."

The twins leaned toward each other and whispered. Stefan may not have children, but he recognized a plan being hatched. He leaned toward Christina. "What are you up to, little lady?"

Her eyes grew wide and frightened. "How did you know?"

Hope shushed her sister and Stefan forced himself not to grin. If only the bad guys he chased were as transparent as Daniel's twins. And Zoe.

Christina squirmed in her chair before turning toward her mother. "Can we be excused? Pleeease."

The plea went first to Raven, then Daniel.

"One more bite of green beans each," their father ordered.

They didn't even argue. Christina and Hope shoved a forkful of the vegetable in their mouths and stood up. They stared at Zoe.

Faith looked over at her daughter's nearly untouched plate. "Not hungry, Slugger?"

She shook her head, avoiding Faith's gaze.

"Okay," Faith said with a sigh. "I'm not going to force you."

Zoe shot to her feet. All three girls raced to the back door.

So that was their plan? Return to the barn? He wasn't sure it was a good idea for Zoe to get even more attached to the puppy. A little girl's heart was fragile, and Stefan didn't want it broken.

A bit shell-shocked at how the idea of her being hurt pained him, he stilled. He'd never allowed himself to connect as quickly as he had with Zoe and Faith. No doubt his own heart would be battered and bruised by the time they parted ways.

The girls opened the back door, ready to escape the house.

"No more visits to the barn," Raven said, as if reading his mind. "Go upstairs and play."

Christina's face fell. "M…o…m."

"The puppies need their sleep and so does their mama." She glanced at her watch. "You have thirty minutes to play before bath time. I'd take advantage of it before I change my mind. Or you can always sit and listen to the grown-ups talk about the state of the economy and politics."

The three girls didn't hesitate. They closed the door and raced up the stairs.

"So, our conversation would bore them that much." Daniel chuckled.

Faith's gaze followed the girls' path. "I'm sorry Zoe's so moody. I just can't give her what she wants."

Daniel and Raven chuckled in sympathy. "Multiply it by two, and welcome to our world. She'll be okay."

Faith bit her lip. "I hope so."

"How about we take this into the library?" Daniel stood up. "Anyone want a drink?"

"Are you breaking out the good bourbon?" Stefan asked, escorting Faith and Raven through a set of French doors.

"While you're here, I can't go with the cheap stuff," his friend parried, sidling up to the bar.

"Then I'll sample a glass." Stefan touched the small of Faith's back. When she didn't pull away, he left his hand there, awareness rising within him.

"None for me," she said to Daniel's offer. "Sleep deprivation and alcohol don't mix."

Raven sat on one corner of a loveseat and tucked her feet underneath her, frowning in sympathy. "Do you know where you're headed?"

"Even if I did, I couldn't tell you. For everyone's safety." Faith glanced over at Stefan. "We'll disappear, and somehow, after we're gone, I have to explain to Zoe what her father is. I have no idea how to do that."

Stefan squeezed Faith's knee in comfort. "You're a psychologist, Daniel. Maybe you can help."

Faith gave Stefan a small nod and Stefan shared the basics of her dilemma. "Any suggestions?" he asked Daniel.

His friend let out a long whistle. "It's tough. I'm dealing with mostly veteran PTSD patients while I finish up my dissertation, so my expertise isn't child psychology, but I'd suggest being as honest as you can about what's happened. She must know your ex-husband had issues."

"If I didn't see it the entire time I was married to him—" Faith stared down at her nails "—how can I ask a seven-year-old to accept that the man she loves and trusts most in the world is a man who has murdered so many people?"

Daniel leaned forward in his chair. "The problem is, running away doesn't make sense to her. If you're going to make a success of your new life, your decisions need to be understandable to her, especially since protecting each other is the way your life will be. At least until he's caught."

Stefan slipped his hand into hers and squeezed. "There *are* other options."

He met Daniel's gaze, and his friend nodded.

"CTC can help," Daniel said. "Ransom Grainger, the head of CTC, has powerful connections. He'll use them if it means justice wins out."

Faith squirmed on the sofa. She tugged her hand from

Stefan's grasp and crossed her arms. "So Stefan said, but I can't wait. Not with Burke so close to finding us. Not with the law on his side. If it goes wrong, he could take Zoe from me. I'm sorry. I can't risk it."

She glanced toward the stairs leading to the twins' bedroom and rose. "I've got to check on Zoe, then I'm going to bed." She turned to Raven and Daniel. "Thank you for putting us up. We appreciate it."

Raven stood and gave her a quick hug. "Trust them," she whispered. "They can help you."

Faith met Stefan's gaze and left the room.

He watched her leave and sipped on his bourbon. "I don't think she appreciated my PDA."

Daniel slapped him on the back of the head. "What were you thinking? As far as she's concerned, she'll never see you again once she leaves. Unless you two have agreed to be friends with benefits."

"Not Faith's style."

"Exactly," Daniel said.

"And that's my cue to exit and give the girls their bath." Raven stood and kissed Stefan on the cheek. "You've changed since the last time you visited. Faith and Zoe are good for you. Don't let the baggage stand in your way. You two could have something."

She kissed Daniel a little too long for comfort. Stefan cleared his throat as she sashayed out of the room.

"I'd say the passion's still there."

"You could say that." Daniel cleared his throat. "Raven doesn't understand the risks staying together would bring to Faith. There've been too many CTC weddings in the last half-dozen years. My wife wants everyone to be happy."

"That's because you married an amazing woman. And one who's far too insightful."

"Truer words, but our path wasn't easy. You know that as well as anyone." Daniel closed the doors behind Raven. "What's going on with you, Stefan? You're involved. More than I've ever seen you."

Stefan paced the floor. "I don't know what I'm doing. Zoe… That little girl is fearless. She doesn't hold back. Faith…" He set his empty glass on the end table. "She's smart, she's beautiful and she's real, even while she attempts to keep everyone at arm's length. I look at her and I see her heart. How many people can you say that about?"

"Very few."

"I want what I can't have." Stefan paused at the end of the room and faced his friend. "Her ex destroyed her trust in others and herself. She knows she can't trust me—"

"You're wrong about that. She's put her life in your hands by coming here. She trusts us by extension. She's let her guard down for you, Stefan."

He shoved his hand through his hair. "What am I supposed to do with that?"

Stefan stared at Daniel, more uncertain than he'd been since they were in that dungeon in Bellevaux, facing certain death.

"I make a round of the grounds every night, just to be safe."

"Paranoid much?" Stefan said.

"When it comes to my family," Daniel said, "absolutely."

They walked in silence for a while. The summer night's heat weighed upon Stefan, clinging like the past. The stark darkness made the world seem infinite.

Once they'd walked the perimeter they re-entered the house. "I can't tell you what to do, but I will remind you she took a leap of faith for you. You may want to do the same." Daniel strode over to Stefan and squeezed his shoulder. "Loving someone is the most terrifying risk I've ever taken."

More exasperated than ever, Stefan headed up the stairs. Raven and Faith met him outside the girls' bedroom.

"They asleep?" Stefan's body pulsed with frustration at how much remained out of his control.

A small fit of giggles filtered through the door.

"Pretending." Raven smiled.

"Though Zoe is still sulking," Faith said with a frown. "I'll give her until the morning, but she's got to accept my decision."

Stefan turned to Faith. "Can we talk?" Of course, he had no idea exactly what he was going to say to her.

Daniel joined them at the top of the stairs. "The house is locked up."

"Then we'll see you tomorrow morning." Raven held out her hand to Daniel, and he followed her into their bedroom.

Faith faced Stefan. He could see the indecision in her eyes.

"You don't have to be nervous," he said.

"How do you know what I'm feeling? It's kind of annoying."

"Because I'm feeling the same hesitation." He touched her cheek. "The truth is I'm tired of thinking."

"Me, too."

She pressed into his touch and her action made his heart swell. He led her into the guest room. "Let's sit."

Stefan pulled her to the edge of the bed and sat beside her, his knee touching hers. He twisted to face her. "I want to be with you, Faith. More than anything I've wanted in my life."

Her cheeks flushed. "I… I want you, too, but it's complicated."

"Another time, another place. It would still have been complicated." He cupped her cheek. His thumb grazed her silken cheek. He lost himself in her eyes. Those trusting eyes. "God, you look at me, and I forget everything. My past, my future. Your future."

"Maybe that's okay. We could forget everything. Just for tonight." She leaned into him. "Touch me before I change my mind, Léon."

The moment she uttered his alias, Stefan's entire body stilled. He met her passion-filled gaze and took in a deep breath.

"Not Léon. My real name is Stefan, Prince of Bellevaux."

Chapter Ten

A prince?

A loud gulp echoed in the guest bedroom over the cacophony of crickets outside. For a brief, horrifying moment, Faith realized it came from her.

"This is a joke, right?"

Stefan shifted, more uncomfortable than she'd ever seen him.

"Unfortunately, no. My real name is Stefan, Prince of Bellevaux."

Her mind whirled in confusion. "But… I remember the news story. There was a revolution. The two heirs to the throne were murdered. A woman from Texas became queen."

"My half sister, Kat." He cleared his throat. "I didn't know about her until after I was captured. She's Queen Katherine now."

Faith rubbed her temple. "You're a prince. Hiding out as some kind of spy?"

This couldn't be real.

"Why did you become Léon in the first place?" Her mind tried to understand, but she kept running into the obvious. "I know why I'm doing it. Because Burke is too powerful to fight. But why would a prince want to disappear? You have money and power."

"Not as much as you'd think." He removed his hand from hers and scratched his brow. "I never thought I'd be king. I was the stereotypical playboy second son until I completed graduate school in the States."

"I remember seeing your picture in the checkout line at the grocery store." She refused to tell him she'd always taken a second look at him. A real-life Prince Charming.

"I sold a lot of newspapers in those days." A chuckle escaped from him. "Everything was simple before I went home and served my two years in the military, like every other young man in my country. During my training they discovered I had a gift for long-distance shooting. I got pegged for a mission to verify rumors of a terrorist attack and stop it if we could."

"You succeeded." She didn't have to guess.

He shrugged. "I discovered I was good at black ops. My father was furious, but I'd found my calling. Until I killed the son of one of the terrorist leaders."

She gasped.

"A price went out on my head. Soon after the coup in Bellevaux took place, and the revolutionaries dumped me into the prison, sending out press releases I had been killed. They were planning to sell me to help fund their takeover of my country. Daniel and his team rescued me, but I was almost dead, and the hit was still in place. Even more so when the coup failed. They couldn't keep me safe."

He stood and paced the floor. "I had no choice. The people trying to kill me were in the shadows, they had operatives everywhere. Anyone near me would be at risk." He frowned at her. "Something for you to remember. If someone wants you dead badly enough, eventually they'll succeed. No matter what the security. You always have to be on your guard."

Faith shuddered at his flat statement because she knew he was right. But sometimes running was the only option.

Stefan stared out the bedroom window. "The palace didn't contradict the information that I'd been killed along with my brother. Kat became queen. I went into hiding."

She walked over to him, forcing him to face her. She studied his face. "You don't resemble the prince I remember from those papers or television."

He touched a small scar on his cheek that she'd barely noticed before now. "During my captivity, they broke a few bones. The shape of my face changed a little and I wear my hair longer and darker. I don't look completely different, but enough. Even if I tried to go back, I'm not sure the public would accept me. I not only look different, I am different. I can't be what they'd accept."

Faith took his hands in hers. "I'm so sorry. Because of the Thomas family, you have to start over again. After you've made friends and connections in Carder with CTC."

He lifted her fingers to his lips. "This is not your fault. Léon Royce has become someone I don't even like anymore. A black ops, sharpshooting expert who makes too many mistakes." He drew his knuckle down her face. "I would give anything to be normal again."

"Léon…" She shook her head. That wasn't his name. "Stefan." She chewed on the moniker. "It's not going to be easy calling you that. Léon saved Zoe's life. He's who I thought maybe…" Her voice trailed off.

What was she supposed to say? That somewhere in her mind, before she'd realized she'd put him in danger, before she'd realized who he was, she'd wondered if Léon would go with them? That she'd have a partner on this crazy journey she was about to embark on? She'd been more a fool than she'd thought. She'd done the worst thing she could possibly do. She'd come to rely on him.

"Do you prefer Léon?" he asked in a too-calm voice.

At his odd tone, she raised her gaze to his. Tension lined his eyes. His normal self-confidence had vanished. Discomfort and hesitation remained. For someone who'd lived under a false identity for years, he seemed oddly concerned by her response. "Léon's the man I grew to trust."

"Does my name matter that much to you?"

She chewed on the question for a moment. What was he really asking? "No matter what my name, I'm still me, right?"

He sat silent for a moment, not answering until she squirmed.

Her throat thickened. "Is Léon different from Stefan?"

Stefan considered her for a moment. "Do you want the truth?"

She nodded, now afraid of the answer.

"Changing your name changes you. Your new identity will change you. No matter how much you fight it, or how much you wish it didn't."

"Is it your life that changed you," she asked, "or your name?"

"Touché. It's hard to know after years of being Léon. Stefan is dead in so many ways. He died in that dungeon."

In a flash of insight she understood. They both felt trapped. "If you could do anything, go anywhere, what would you want your life to be like?"

She'd been afraid to ask herself that question.

"I'd want to have a chance to be with you," he said in a husky voice. "I'd want you and Zoe to come away with me, to be free from fear, free from looking over your shoulder."

He slipped his arms around her, and she rested her head against his shoulder as if she'd always meant to be there. With gentle hands, he stroked her hair and she didn't move. He felt strong and warm and solid. She never wanted to leave his embrace.

The cadence of night sounds filtered through the window. A soft breeze, the hoot of an owl, the buzz of cicadas.

"Why can't this last forever?" she whispered.

"Being in hiding doesn't give us the freedom to follow our hearts," he said softly. "Being smart will keep us safe."

"Am I a coward?" she asked. "For running."

"Power can be destructive. It can twist justice into something perverted, but power used for good can level the playing field. I've always believed that."

From the tenor of his voice, she got the message. "You're talking about your friends," she said. "CTC couldn't help you?"

"It's different. Burke is one man."

Before she could respond Stefan's phone rang. "Speaking of which…" He tapped the screen. "What's up, Ransom?" Stefan frowned. "She's right here. I'll put you on speakerphone."

Faith leaned closer to the phone.

"Faith, I've been looking into your ex-husband to see if we can help you in your situation."

"I… I know. Stefan told me."

"Stefan. I see." Ransom paused for a moment. "I have some bad news."

Faith's heart stuttered. "What's wrong?"

"Gerard Thomas is dead. It appears to be a heart attack."

Her body went numb. "I… I don't understand. He was so healthy."

"You were close?" Ransom asked.

Faith shook in Stefan's arms. "Not really. He never wanted me to marry Burke. I think his wife, Janice… oh my gosh, she must be devastated. He and Burke are her entire world."

Ransom cleared his throat. "I need to ask you an awkward question. Would you say Gerard protected Burke? Maybe intervened over the years on his behalf?"

Grabbing the phone, Faith stepped away from Stefan. "What do you mean?"

"Your ex-husband's life is too…perfect."

"I… I don't understand."

"No one gets to be thirty without having some transgression on their record. A parking ticket, a few unpaid bills, a few photos that are less than flattering, but Burke's records are too clean. Which, frankly, has us wondering about some bought and sold influence."

"Mr. Thomas had friends across the state. People owed him favors. Burke threw the family name around a lot to get what he wanted. There was even talk of a run for governor."

Stefan joined her, and she hadn't realized how much she'd come to rely on his presence. His warm body pressed close to hers and he clasped the phone. "Ransom, if Gerard Thomas was willing to help Burke get custody, what if he helped his son in other ways, too?"

Faith turned in his arms. "Are you saying Mr. Thomas knew about Burke?"

How could anyone know about what Burke had done? Faith couldn't fathom it.

"All I know," Stefan said, "is my father smoothed over a few things he probably shouldn't have when I was a teenager. Fathers don't always make the best choices for their kids."

"Burke is a serial killer."

"And with his father gone, Burke doesn't have anyone to protect him anymore."

Ransom's words sent a chill through Faith.

Stefan squeezed her shoulders. "This could be an opportunity. Ransom may have the bigger hammer."

Not liking where this was going, Faith let out a long, slow breath. "I don't think—"

"This can work, Faith. Send your proof to CTC. All of it. Give them every piece of ammunition you have, and let them run with it. Without your father-in-law's influence, we have a chance to get Burke behind bars."

The energy and certainty in Stefan's voice reached into Faith's heart. Her mind whirled with unforeseen possibilities. For the first time in a long time, a small pinprick of hope filtered through the darkness.

Could she take the risk?

She met Stefan's gaze. She trusted Léon. And no matter what Stefan argued, his name changed nothing.

Faith placed her hand on his chest. "Okay," she whispered into the phone. "Let's end this."

Two hours later Stefan pressed the scanner button in Daniel's office, sending the last page of Faith's evidence to CTC. She sat on the sofa, her feet tucked under her, chewing on her nail as she watched each piece of paper feed through the scanner. He returned the last page to her, and she slipped it into the folder and secured it.

"That's everything," he said. Stefan's phone sounded and he pressed the speakerphone. "You're on with both of us, Ransom. What do you think?"

"I'm impressed," he said. "After the first batch I had Zane do some preliminary digging. Since Faith went into hiding, there's been one murder—of a woman who worked in Burke's office. Not to mention six women disappeared from the Dallas-Fort Worth and surrounding areas. All of them match the description."

"That's crazy."

"It gets worse. Three of the disappearances occurred in the last two weeks."

"He's escalating." Stefan couldn't stop the worry from his voice.

"It doesn't make sense." Faith rose from the sofa. "He killed after we fought, when he got angry with me. Why is he getting worse? I never meant for it to get worse."

"He was a murderer before he met you." Stefan forced her to meet his gaze. "This isn't your fault. You can't allow yourself to believe it is."

"Stefan's right, Faith." He paused for a moment. "I just learned another fact. Burke was with his father when he died."

Faith's eyes widened with shock.

"What was Burke's relationship with his father?" Ransom asked through the phone, his voice quiet.

Stefan recognized the moment Faith understood the implication of the question.

"You can't believe Burke killed his own father?"

"We need to consider whether or not this is a spree. If he's lost control, he'll take risks he wouldn't normally take, he'll do things he normally wouldn't do."

"Like make mistakes." A flood of curses circled Stefan's head.

"With too much collateral damage," Ransom added. "Faith, did Gerard control Burke?"

"Yes." Her voice croaked the words. She turned pale. "Burke complained about the tight thumb he kept on the business, the money."

"Have Daniel do a psychological profile on Burke,"

Ransom ordered. "It wouldn't surprise me if there are murders back to his college days." The tapping of a keyboard sounded through the phone. "I have a few good friends in high places who I trust. Just hold tight. And stay safe. Don't give him an opportunity to find you. If he's on a spree, he's deadly. To anyone. And Stefan," he added. "Pick up."

The tone in his boss's voice froze Stefan. He tapped the screen and placed the phone to his ear. "What's wrong?"

Faith threaded her hand through his. He squeezed her fingers. With CTC's help, Faith and Zoe might end up with that happily ever after they wanted.

"Nothing's wrong exactly," Ransom said. "I debated whether or not to tell you, but you have a right to know before you leave Léon behind for good."

Stefan gripped the phone, bracing himself for bad news. His boss didn't prevaricate over good news. "Just say it."

"There's movement on the terrorist cell that put the hit out on you." Ransom lowered his voice. "They showed their hand too quickly when the Thomas photo went public. Your brother-in-law has a strong lead."

Stefan had been expecting a blip. He was surprised it had taken this long. Normally he would bail immediately and disappear until he could hook up with Annie, but one look at Faith made him pause. He had to think this through. "How solid a lead? Did they make it to the airport? Are they in Texas already?" His enemies bringing the fight here changed everything. No way would he risk Faith and Zoe. Or Daniel and his family.

"Logan's fairly certain they stopped them from boarding. They have three men in custody."

"Timeline?" Stefan asked.

"According to the itinerary, they would've made it to

DFW in about twelve hours. Eighteen to reach Carder. If they had the location."

Stefan's neck muscles twitched. Terrorist groups were like roaches. Even if they appeared to be exterminated, they popped back up in greater numbers. "What if there were four? One could be on the way. You know better than most I can't count on hope."

"Logan's got them talking. The organization's been decimated by Katherine and Logan's anti-terrorism efforts. This is the best—if not the only—opportunity you'll get to come back from the dead."

Stefan couldn't think. If it were him alone, he might grab the opportunity with both hands, but he had others to consider. "I put a target on everyone around me."

"Give us twelve hours," Ransom countered. "It might be different this time."

"Don't bother." Stefan held Faith close. "Direct all your energies to helping Faith. I need to know she's safe."

"Twelve hours. Please." Ransom ended the call.

Knowing his luck, it probably wouldn't go well. Maybe plastic surgery. A more radical transformation?

He glanced down at Faith's worried expression. The modicum of hope he'd nurtured deep inside him, that maybe they could be together, that maybe they could find a future in some anonymous place with some anonymous name, had disintegrated.

"What did you just do?" She frowned at him. "Is everything okay?"

Stefan forced a confident smile to camouflage his worry. "Let's focus on you and Zoe staying safe. I'll worry about me later."

He texted Daniel and relayed Ransom's request, leaving the file on the desk.

"Talk to me," she said. "What's going on?"

"Catching Burke is Ransom's first priority. I made sure of that. It's going to be fine."

Faith sighed in resignation. "I guess that's it then."

Stefan didn't like the disappointment on her face, but he couldn't share the truth. She'd run right into danger, and he couldn't live with himself if something happened to her.

He wasn't ready to say good night—or goodbye. Still, he hesitated. When he said nothing, with heavy footsteps, she walked to the office door.

Before opening it, she turned to him. "Thank you, Stefan. For everything you've done. You didn't have to get involved, and you did." Her gaze warmed. "You reminded me that there are good people in the world."

Her footsteps faded up the stairs, leaving Stefan standing alone in Daniel and Raven's home. In that moment, he'd never felt more alone.

Nothing could be done about the situation until another lead popped. He trusted CTC to find one.

Tonight might be the last sleep he'd get for a while.

Heart heavy, he trudged up the stairs. Twelve hours from now he'd be forced to say goodbye, whatever happened.

Everything inside his body screamed not to leave her.

He had no choice. Neither of them did.

At the landing, he froze. Faith stood there, just outside the twins' room, looking beautiful and vulnerable and tempting.

She delicately closed the door and the lock snicked closed. "Zoe's asleep. Finally." Her lips turned down. "I'm worried about her. Something's not right. She usually bounces back from a pout before now."

He couldn't say a word so he touched her cheek. "Why aren't you closed safely behind that bedroom door, Faith?"

Her eyes flared with recognition. "I... I didn't do it on purpose." She tugged on his hand and pulled him down the hall to the guest room, closing and locking the door behind her.

Stefan swallowed deeply and covered her hand with his. "If things were different—"

"I know," she said softly. She cupped his face and pulled his lips down to hers. "Stefan."

When his real name whispered from her soft lips, he didn't resist. He couldn't.

He lowered his mouth to hers and wrapped her in his arms. All the wishes and hopes and dreams he'd been searching for the last several years came washing over him. They came alive in Faith's arms.

When Faith's hands tugged his shirt from his jeans, his heart thudded. He pulled back from her. "Are you sure?"

"I need you, Stefan. I need you now."

"Even if it's only for tonight? I don't know what tomorrow will bring."

"Tonight's all I'm asking for."

Stefan tugged his T-shirt off and slipped his hands under her blouse. She raised her arms and he pulled the shirt over her head. He touched the smooth skin at her waist before removing her bra and pressing her chest against his.

Skin to skin.

Her hands danced around his back. She lingered on the scars. He tensed under her touch, but she didn't shy away.

"How did you survive?" she whispered.

"Had no choice," he said, cupping her breast in his hand. Her nipple pebbled beneath his touch and she let out a low groan. "You don't have to touch them. I'd understand."

She hugged him tight. "They're part of you."

Stefan backed her toward the bed. He threw off the covers, scooped her into his arms and laid her on the cool sheets. His hands hovered over the button of her jeans, and with a flick of his fingers unfastened them.

He slipped his hand low on her belly and caressed the skin there. She shivered and he slipped the zipper down and removed the rest of her clothes.

Heart racing, he shucked his own jeans and followed her onto the bed, pressing her into the mattress.

His body throbbed with heat and he stared into her brown eyes. She wrapped her legs around his hips and pulled him closer.

"Don't stop," she said into his ear. "Don't ever stop."

"Protection," Stefan said, his voice gravelly while he dug into the pocket of his jeans. He slipped on the condom and turned back to her.

With a groan, he joined them together.

Faith was like coming home. She wrapped her arms and legs tighter. With each movement she clung tighter. He reveled in her response, his body seeking out every untouched inch of her. Her nails scraped his shoulders, and he shuddered. Higher and higher they flew together.

Beneath him, Faith cried out in completion and he followed, relishing the pulsing caress of her body surrounding his. He had no wish to leave her or this bed ever again.

He'd found what he'd been looking for in Faith's arms. A strange peace settled over his heart and he shifted to his side. She followed him, plastered to his body.

She said no words, but they weren't needed.

Stefan stroked her hair and rested his chin on the top of her head.

He was complete with her in his arms. She was everything he wanted, everything he'd dreamed of, everything he'd hoped for.

And now he knew exactly what he'd be missing for the rest of his life.

STEFAN'S WARMTH SEEPED straight into Faith's soul. She cuddled against his strong, hard body and he squeezed her. His heart thudded against her ear. He'd been so tender, so loving, so giving.

That's what she'd been missing all these years.

Stefan had shown her the world when he'd loved her, as if he'd read her mind. He'd touched her places no one else had touched, made her feel things no one else had, made her want more. Made her want forever.

Except it was only one night. She'd promised.

She wanted to take the vow back.

Should she even ask? How could she? She'd been ready to run.

"What if..." Her voice trailed off.

His fingers toyed with her hair. "Don't," he said.

"Stay the night." She kissed his chest, letting her lips linger there for a few moments. "We have tonight."

"Even though in a few hours it'll be morning." He rose above her. "Tonight lasts until daylight."

Stefan lowered his lips to hers, taking her mouth. Faith couldn't stop the groan coming from deep within her belly.

"Tonight."

What she wouldn't give for tomorrow, over and over and over again.

THE SUN HAD been up for a while, but it was only seven in the morning. Burke had driven most of the night. He looked at his map and turned down a dirt road. A figure stood on the roadside. He pulled over and rolled down his window.

"Want a lift?"

Zoe smiled at her father, holding Catcher in her arms. "Hi, Daddy."

Chapter Eleven

A strange buzzing filtered through Faith's sleep-logged mind. She threw her arm to the side. It landed on a hard chest.

She blinked. Stefan. Her cheeks burned at the memory of last night right before a wave of sadness washed over her. One night was all he could promise.

Stefan passed her phone to her.

"No one calls me except Zoe," she said, her voice still husky with sleep. She pressed the phone's screen. "Hello."

"Good morning, Faith."

Her body went numb before she jerked to a sitting position. "Burke? How did you get this number?"

Stefan tilted the phone toward him and tapped the speaker icon.

"You didn't think you could hide from me forever, did you?"

Burke's voice sounded smug. The way it did when he knew he'd won. Her heart froze and she swallowed down the horrifying foreboding.

She clutched Stefan's hand. "What do you want?"

"Nothing." Burke's voice held a self-satisfied smile. "I have everything I want." A rustle filtered through the speaker. "Zoe, don't let the puppy run too far."

Faith's entire body froze in terror. "It can't be."

"Okay, Daddy," Zoe's voice called out.

Stefan jumped out of bed and raced from the room. Within a minute he returned. "She's gone," he mouthed. "And a puppy's missing."

"How?" Faith asked. How had he found them?

"You don't know your daughter as well as you thought," Burke taunted. "Zoe called me. She needed to be rescued. Remember when I rescued you, Faith? You let me down. I'm going to make certain Zoe can't betray me."

His words strangled her breath. Faith's mind whirled, remembering everything Ransom had said. "Please, Burke—"

"Shut up, Faith. Here's the way it's going to work. I have Zoe. We're done with custody. If you want to see *my* daughter again, I'll let you say goodbye to her. Then you can go wherever you want, but Zoe is mine. No negotiations."

Faith choked back a sob. "Please—"

"Don't bother begging. Drive toward the Guadalupe Mountains. I'll text you instructions along the way. Oh, and Faith, come alone. Whoever you're sleeping with, he'll just make me angry. Maybe you won't get to see Zoe after all."

The phone went dead.

Faith wrapped a robe around her nude body and stood. "She called him? How? How did this happen?"

Stefan shook his head. "Daniel and Raven are working on the twins in the kitchen. Your instincts were right yesterday."

"I ignored my gut because I wanted to spend time with you." Faith hugged her arms. "I knew something was off with Zoe."

He placed his hands on her shoulders. "This isn't your fault. It's Burke's. You couldn't have known. You're not psychic."

"I'm a mom. I'm supposed to know when my child is thinking of doing something like this." She rubbed her eyes. "Why would Zoe call him?"

"One way to find out."

They dressed quickly and walked down the hall to the kitchen. Daniel and Raven faced two solemn little girls.

Raven had her hands on her hips. "Where did this plan come from?"

Christina swung her feet back and forth. Hope refused to meet her parents' gaze.

Faith walked over to the table and knelt in front of the twins. "I'm worried about Zoe, girls. I need to know why she left."

The twins met each other's gazes. Hope gave Christina a quick nod.

"Zoe was really mad. She wanted to go home so she could play baseball with Danny and have a backyard for Catcher. You told her if Catcher had a backyard, she could keep him. So she called her dad."

"Not on my phone," Faith said.

"On mine." Raven passed over the cell. "They called late last night. She snuck out at daylight and took Catcher with her. The girls turned off the security system."

Daniel placed his hands on his hips. "You two are in big trouble. Zoe's mom is scared for her."

"But she's with her daddy. Daddies take care of you," Hope said.

"Not all daddies," Daniel said quietly. "Go on. You're grounded. No puppies today. No games. Your mother will come up with a list of chores. Until then, I want you sitting quietly in your room."

"Yes, Daddy," they said together and walked out of the kitchen, heads held low.

Daniel faced Faith. "I'm so sorry."

"It's not their fault. It's mine. I didn't know how to tell Zoe about her father, and why we were hiding. She still trusts him because of me." Faith rubbed her eyes. She had no idea what Burke would do. "I need a car to rendezvous with my ex. Maybe I can convince him—"

"You're not going alone. I'm coming with you," Stefan interjected.

She shook her head. "He said I should come alone."

"He's a killer."

Faith whirled on him. "You think I don't know that? I have to do whatever it takes to keep Zoe safe."

Stefan held her hands in his and squeezed until she met his gaze. "We'll get Zoe back, but you can't do this alone, Faith. You don't have to. You have me." He pulled her in his arms and held her close. "We can do this smart. I'll follow you. We'll set up a tracker on your phone. You'll never be alone. I promise."

"It's not right to put you in danger," she whispered. "It's not right."

He smiled at her. "It's what Léon Royce does."

"And Stefan?"

"Stefan protects the ones he cares about most. No matter the cost."

THE CRAGGY ROCKS of the Guadalupe Mountains could hide a multitude of sins. The crevices might come in handy today. Burke hiked past the trail and scanned the rugged terrain. Too many hiding places here. This wasn't the right place for his rendezvous with Faith. He checked the first possibility off his list.

"Daddy, I'm tired," Zoe whined behind him.

He gritted his teeth to keep himself from yelling at her. "Not much farther."

"Catcher is tired, too."

He glanced at Orren. "If this is going to work, I need her away from the meeting."

Orren nodded. "We could hole up in a cave."

Burke pulled out a series of photos from his bag. The satellite image showed an old miner's shack just over that ridge. "Take her there. It's far enough away she won't hear anything, and she can't call out."

The man nodded. Burke pulled out his canteen and knelt in front of Zoe.

"I need you to be a big girl. I have to meet someone and it's far away. Orren is going to take you to a place where you and your puppy can rest, okay?"

"But I don't know him," she said with a frown at Orren. "I want to be with you, Daddy. You promised."

Burke gritted his teeth to hold back his instincts. He fought against the inclination to shut her up. His skin prickled with irritation.

"Zoe, we're going to be together all the time soon. Just do this for me, honey? Then we'll go back to my house and your puppy can have a big yard."

She crossed her arms in front of her and glared.

"I thought you were brave. Was I wrong?" Burke winced at the whining in his voice.

"I'm not scared. I'm tired and hungry. Mom wouldn't make me wait to have my breakfast."

Burke's nails dug into the heel of his hand. He couldn't lose control. "Can you be brave for me and climb some more? Then you can have a snack."

"I guess." Zoe sighed, cuddling the puppy in her arms.

"Let me have the puppy," he said.

She backed away.

"I'm going to put him in your backpack, honey. That's all."

Reluctantly, Zoe let him.

He slipped the backpack on her shoulders. "Follow Orren, sweetie." Zoe trudged after the man. As they reached the top of the hill, she looked back at Burke.

He waved at her until she no longer turned around. Finally.

With his daughter out of the way, he could get down to business. He'd know soon enough if paying for the high-def photos via drone surveillance had been worth the money.

He veered toward a group of pines. He pushed through the grove and came to a clearing. His heartbeat picked up a bit. The prickles snaked down his spine. He scanned the perimeter and his gaze stopped at a spot where a strange gap appeared between the rock formations. He walked toward the fissure and peered over the side.

His heart leaped. He couldn't even make out the bottom of the ravine.

Perfect. Nowhere for Faith to run. All he had to do would be to maneuver Faith toward the edge. No one would ever find her.

THE DRIVE TO the base of the Guadalupe Mountains took far too long. Each mile, Stefan's mind lingered on Zoe in the hands of a madman. He'd orchestrated his share of drop-offs, but nothing compared to this. Usually, his partner had been trained, and was as deadly with any weapon as he was. Faith didn't have those skills, but she had more heart than he'd ever seen.

She sat next to him, stiff and unyielding, because she blamed herself.

He understood, because he felt the same way for not protecting Zoe. He'd promised. What could either of them say?

So, they said nothing.

They sped past the latest mile marker. The road was deserted. Not many frequented this side of the Guadalupe Mountains National Park, making it a great meet site. The mountains could be brutal, and Burke had chosen this location for a reason. People disappeared. Permanently.

Stefan knew Faith's ex had set a trap. She just hadn't realized it yet.

She would.

"We're going to find her," Stefan repeated.

"I can't believe anything else, but…" Faith stared out the window. "My heart's breaking. Zoe possesses this light inside her. That trust you have when you're a kid. I don't want her to lose it, and I don't know how to stop it from happening."

He tucked her hand in his and squeezed. She didn't pull away, to his surprise. "You can't protect her from the truth, Faith."

"I can want to."

He caressed her palm with his thumb, and she leaned her head back against the car seat. His sidelong glance revealed the tension around her mouth, the stark paleness of her face.

"What's Burke's plan?" she asked, eyes still closed.

Stefan didn't want to tell her, but she had to be ready. "He knows you'll never let Zoe go willingly and with his father dead, he can't risk you causing him any trouble."

"He wants me gone," she said, "so he forces me to come out here alone, in the middle of nowhere." She paused for a few seconds before her jaw tightened. "He doesn't plan on letting me leave these mountains, does he?"

"That would be my guess." Stefan tightened his grip on her. "He believes you don't have help. That you're alone. He doesn't know what you know or how strong you are, Faith. He won't get what he wants. We'll make certain of that."

"I'm afraid for Zoe." Faith swallowed. "Would he hurt her?"

Stefan didn't want to answer. "Do you think Burke's capable of love?"

He wouldn't mention Daniel's initial opinion, that Burke possessed antisocial personality disorder. Stefan preferred the term *sociopath*. Fewer syllables.

Faith shifted in her seat. "If he loves anyone, it might be his mother. He's devoted to her. And Burke's mother loves Zoe."

"Interesting." Stefan mulled the new information. "If he's focused on his mother being happy and occupied—and ignorant to his true nature—he might use Zoe. Without you in the way, his mother takes care of Zoe and he has a clear field to kill whenever he wants. As long as he doesn't get caught."

"Even if something happens to me, he'll go to prison." She gripped his shirt. "You promised."

"Ransom called in a few favors in the state attorney general's office. From what I hear, more than one official was trying to cover their tracks. They're running. Burke doesn't know it yet, but he's trapped with no way out."

"And what happens when he realizes I've turned my evidence over to the authorities?"

"We get Zoe out of there before he knows."

Burke would become a trapped animal. A cornered

serial killer wasn't someone Stefan wanted to try to reason with.

His phone rang and he tapped the screen.

"You're nearing the turnoff," Ransom announced over the speakerphone. "Zane's cast a little computer voodoo. We've got Faith's phone on a satellite tracker. We'll be able to ping her location anywhere, as long as it doesn't get too cloudy."

The Guadalupe Mountains loomed ahead, and he veered the vehicle toward the hiking trail.

"What about backup?" Stefan asked.

"Sheriff Galloway will be your closest resource. I'll have a helicopter on standby in Trouble, Texas, in an hour. They'll be able to reach you in less than thirty minutes. The rest of the team is on their way, but they're two-plus hours out. Unless you can delay."

"No can do." Stefan cleared his throat. "They didn't have to drop everything."

"You've saved their lives more than once. You're part of CTC. You always will be. No matter what happens. We're family. Besides, I couldn't stop them trying."

With that, Ransom ended the call.

"You have good friends," Faith said.

"They have my back." Stefan eyed his odometer. They should be getting close.

Sure enough, two vehicles sat off to the side of the road. He pulled next to the sheriff's car, behind a second SUV.

Sheriff Garrett Galloway exited his car and walked around to the side. Stefan rolled down his window, and Garrett dropped the keys into his hand. "Gassed and ready," he said.

"Thanks, Sheriff."

"I'm taking a side route. I'll be nearby. Just send up a smoke signal. I'll get there as quickly as I can."

Stefan exited the SUV, leaving it running. He met Faith's gaze. She looked scared, but determined.

"You won't be alone," he said.

She slid into the driver's side. "I know."

Stefan leaned into the open window, grabbed her face and kissed her. "I promise. Come nightfall, Zoe will be back with you."

She smiled weakly. "I know."

THE WEST TEXAS road snaked across the desert with shrub bushes peppering the landscape. Faith's fingers ached from her grip on the steering wheel. She was close to the base of the large mountains.

Burke could very well kill her the moment she arrived. She knew that. Stefan knew that. The only thing that gave Faith comfort was the fact that Stefan would see to it that Zoe was safe.

She pulled over to the mile marker that Burke had mentioned in his last text. The hot sun pounded her through the windshield. She waited. And waited.

Moments ticked by. Fifteen minutes. A half hour.

Where was he?

She wished she knew where Stefan was located. She believed he was watching. She had to believe it.

Finally, a truck pulled over. An old man looked at her from the driver's side.

"You Faith?" he asked.

She nodded.

"Your husband said he's waiting for you at the mile two marker of the Guadalupe Peak Trail."

"Where is that?"

"Up fifteen miles. Veer to the right. You'll see a small

visitor's center. There's a trail that leads up toward Guadalupe Peak. It'll take a while to walk, but you'll find him."

The man cleared his throat. "He told me your cell phone doesn't work. He wants you to give it to me."

"What?"

"He said you have to give your cell phone to me or you won't be able to meet him." The guy stroked his beard. "Seemed a bit weird to me, but he wants us to trade phones."

She forced a smile. Was he watching? She glanced behind her. She didn't have a choice. At least if Stefan followed her phone, he'd get the information of where she'd gone.

She handed the phone over and the old man dropped an old flip-style cell in her hand.

"Good luck." He shuffled toward his vehicle.

Faith bit her lip. "Ummm…what did the man who gave you the directions look like?"

"Don't you know your own husband?"

What was she supposed to say to that?

"Can't be too careful these days."

"Brown hair. Scar on his face."

In other words, not Burke. He'd left nothing to tie him to her. No witnesses. And she had no way to contact Stefan, unless she used Burke's phone. Could she risk it?

Before she could respond, the phone rang.

"You received the instructions?" Burke asked.

"Yes. Is Zoe okay?"

"Of course. Why wouldn't she be? Now drive."

The old man had heaved himself into his truck and his engine gunned to life.

She pulled off the highway. "What now?"

"Follow his instructions." Burke paused. "And Faith.

Don't detour, don't contact anyone. I'll know. This is between you and me, no one else. I need your promise."

A promise used to mean something in their marriage. Faith had never broken her word to Burke. This would be the first time. "I promise."

"Excellent."

A loud explosion pierced the sky. Faith's hands jerked the steering wheel. Behind her a pillow of black smoke erupted into the sky.

"Throw the phone out of the car. Now."

Oh, God. Had Burke killed the old man?

"I'll only say this once more. Get rid of the phone. If you're not at the mile marker in thirty minutes, you'll be too late," Burke said. "You'll never see Zoe again."

He was watching. Where was he? Not that it mattered.

She couldn't believe he'd blown up the car. The poor man. And her phone was destroyed.

Which meant Stefan had no way to track her.

She tossed Burke's phone along with an earring out of the car. She drove on the side of the road, hoping Stefan or Garrett or someone might see which direction she was going.

The odometer ticked away the miles. Every couple miles she tossed something else out of the car. Another earring; a lipstick, anything she could find that he'd be able to recognize as possibly hers. After thirteen miles, her entire body reminded her of a tightly wound rubber band ready to break. She tossed out a hair tie of Zoe's just as she turned off to the visitor's center.

Around her, shrub bushes and pine trees lined the building. She didn't go inside. Why bother? There were no cars, no people, no nothing.

Deserted. No one to see her enter the national park. She glanced at her watch. She was running out of time.

Uncertain if Stefan had seen any of her signs, she had to trust him and his ability.

A wooden sign delineated the trail's beginning. She could make an arrow with rocks, but it would be obvious. If Burke brought her back this way, he'd know what she was doing. Instead, she used her foot to scratch an arrow in the dirt.

She started up the trail, walking slowly, digging into a baggie of Zoe's clips and elastics she kept in her purse, dropping them like a trail of breadcrumbs. If Stefan were looking for her, he'd know which direction to head.

About a quarter mile into the walk she made a show of slipping on the trail to offer another sign, then struggled to get back up. She brushed off her pants and hiked another mile. Fifteen minutes later, she rounded a curve in the trail.

A figure stood at the top of the hill. She hadn't seen him in months. Just the sight of him made her gut twist in revulsion.

Burke waited for her, arms crossed, his dark hair perfectly slicked back, his khaki pants ironed with a stiff crease, and his button-down starched just as he preferred. Perfect. Cool, composed and calm.

Who went hiking dressed like that? A crazy serial killer, that's who.

Faith stared at him, trying to see behind him.

"Where's Zoe?"

Burke grinned, a smile that at one time had blinded her to the deadness behind his eyes.

"She's not here." He raised his hand. "Before you start, she's safe. I decided you and I should have a reunion first. Just the two of us. We have a few things to discuss."

Chapter Twelve

This place was worse than the ugly house her mom had made her stay in. Zoe took Catcher out of her backpack. The puppy wriggled in her arms. She hugged his soft fur and buried her face deep. She wanted her mom.

The man—Orren was his name—had practically dragged her up the mountain. Her father shouldn't have made her go away. Not with this man.

Zoe frowned at the tall figure glaring at her. He didn't like being stuck in this wooden hut, either.

Catcher whined in her arms and nibbled at her finger.

"Ouch," she muttered. "Your teeth are sharp."

"Keep the dog quiet," the man rumbled in a low voice.

"He's just a baby."

Orren muttered something under his breath. "Burke has lost it." He paced back and forth like Zoe's mom did when she was worried.

"What do we do now?" Zoe asked.

"None of your business. Just sit on the floor and stay quiet. Your dad will be here soon."

"You were supposed to give us something to eat," Zoe said.

He whipped around and growled at her, like a wolf. "Shut up and sit down or you'll be sorry."

Catcher wiggled in her arms and jumped out of them.

The puppy charged at Orren with a loud yip. The high-pitched bark hurt Zoe's ears.

Orren pulled a big gun out of his pants—just like on television. He pointed it at Catcher. "Shut up, dog!"

"No, you can't hurt him." Zoe ran over and grabbed the man's arm.

"That dog will ruin everything," the man said, shaking Zoe off. "I'm not losing my payday. Not for a mutt."

He kicked out at Catcher. Zoe gasped and dove for the puppy. The man's boot hit her shoulder, but Catcher didn't get hurt.

Zoe's back throbbed. Orren's face had turned red. He looked real mad. She wasn't staying here.

With a shout, she scooped up the puppy. The man lunged for her. No way would she let him hurt Catcher.

Zoe scooted backward across the old wood floor. Orren loomed over her, his arms reaching for her like a monster. She kept scooching until she caught sight of a missing board that left a gap in the side of the shack. She wasn't staying here. She had to find her daddy. Orren wasn't nice. He was bad.

He bent over close. She held her breath, hugged Catcher and squeezed through the opening.

Orren yelled a very bad word. "Kid! Come back here."

Zoe didn't look back. She held on tight to Catcher and ran as fast as she could.

The man slammed open the front door. "Stop, kid. Your dad will be mad. You can't run away."

No way was Zoe answering him. She remembered what Léon had taught her. She darted between some big trees and bushes and searched for a placc to hide. A wall of rocks shot up into the sky. She squinted through all the grass and saw a small cave just at the bottom.

The man's huge footsteps were chasing her. They

pounded somewhere behind her. She couldn't outrun him, even if she was faster than Danny. Orren was a grown-up.

She darted into the hole and took a few steps inside. It curved around. Her eyes widened. The room got really big and very dark. She held Catcher tight.

"Go inside my backpack, Catcher. I need both hands."

She couldn't lose him or she'd never find him in this scary place. He whimpered, but settled in okay. She slipped the backpack on and took a step forward.

The ground below her crumbled and disappeared.

"Mommy!"

SMOKE BILLOWED INTO the sky from the explosion. The blast had stopped Stefan's heart. His SUV skidded up to a blazing truck in the middle of the road. He slammed on the brakes. The fire charred the metal and his entire body went numb.

"You're sure this is the last location of her phone?" He could barely enunciate the words.

"Yeah." Ransom's voice was solemn. "Then we lost all signal."

"What's Faith's phone doing in a truck?"

He didn't want to think, didn't want to move. His mind kept flashing to another burned-out home. The Jennings house. He'd lost all of them, including the bastard who'd blown them up. Jenny and her kids. They hadn't deserved to die, and he'd been too late to stop it.

Shoving the past out of his mind, he stepped closer. A wall of heat slammed at him. This wasn't her vehicle. It couldn't be her.

He squinted at the charred body inside and his eyes centered on the metal socket in the man's shoulder.

"Not Faith."

His knees shook and he stumbled back to his car. He

sucked in a couple of deep breaths. Their plan had gone to hell.

"It's not her," he said, his voice choked. He slammed his fist into the side of the vehicle.

"Thank God." Ransom barked some orders on his side of the phone. "We'll trace the signal backward as far as we can."

"I promised her, Ransom. I promised her I'd keep them safe."

"We'll find them."

Ransom's words were a jumbled mess. Stefan's head swirled with fury. Burke had done this. Covering his tracks. He had to track her down.

"…stopped at mile marker twelve," Ransom said through the phone. "The phone reversed direction. We assumed he was testing for a tail."

"I'm headed for the mile marker where she stopped. Call everyone in. We've got to find her."

Stefan drove down the deserted West Texas road like he'd entered Le Mans. When the marker was ten feet ahead of him, he stopped. Faith's car wasn't in sight.

He strode down the road, searching for anything out of place. A glint of silver caught his eye.

An old flip phone. And something else next to it.

His breath caught. He knelt down and picked up a gold hoop earring and squeezed it tight. Oh, yeah, baby.

She'd been wearing these the day they'd met at the library. She'd never taken them off, probably because they were her only pair. She'd been here. He scanned the gravel at the edge of the road.

One thing about Faith, she could think on her feet. He walked on the side of the road for a half mile.

The other earring gleamed from the black tar.

He scooped it up, activated his phone and ran back to

the SUV. "She's headed toward the mountains. She left me a damn trail of breadcrumbs.

"Call Daniel. Have him bring Trouble. We might need the dog if I can't find her fast."

Stefan jumped in and started toward the mountains. Every mile he caught sight of a small clue. When he saw the lipstick he practically cheered.

"I'll find you, Faith. I promise."

He drove along the side of the road and paused at an obvious turnoff, but he didn't see any signs of recent activity or of a car turning off. The weeds growing in the middle of the road hadn't been disturbed.

He was taking a chance, but Faith was smart. If she could, she'd guide him. That was a big *if.* Maybe Burke had stopped her. Maybe he'd forced her into the back seat.

Shoving the worst case into the recesses of his mind, Stefan tried to treat this like any other mission, except it wasn't. He'd fallen for Faith. More and harder than he'd ever imagined. Not to mention Zoe. That little girl held his heart in her baseball glove.

After a couple miles of nothing, he almost stopped. Should he retrace his steps? Maybe try that turn? His foot tapped the brakes just as a glint shined in the road ahead.

A hundred feet later he hit pay dirt. A compact. He'd seen her use it when they'd been driving to his campsite.

He could breathe again.

Man, she was tough.

Another couple miles and a white SUV appeared abandoned near a small building. Stefan palmed his weapon and slowly pulled up to the vehicle. He peered into the back and called Ransom. "She left her car at the base of Guadalupe Peak Trail. She's not here, but she started hiking."

"How far behind her do you think you are?"

Stefan knelt down beside the arrow she'd scratched into the hiking trail and the pattern of grass and oxidation beneath her steps. "Too long. No sign of a second set of prints, though. She was alone."

"The team is still an hour away. Unless you want Garrett to fly in on the chopper."

"I don't want him spooked until I'm in position. Give me a half hour. If you don't hear from me, send in the cavalry."

"You got it." Ransom paused. "And Stefan. Don't get dead."

"Will do."

Stefan ended the call and trudged up the trail, searching for any more signs from Faith. Every so often he'd pick up a tie for Zoe's hair, a button. At the top of a hill two miles in he stopped. A man's shoe print. Size eleven.

Burke.

Stefan clutched his weapon and followed the trail until the footprints ended. He swept the area of pinyon pine and Southwestern white pine on each side.

Above him, thunder cracked across the afternoon sky. Black clouds hovered over the mountain, streaks of gray dropped to earth. A hell of a summer storm high up, which meant flash floods heading down.

"Where's Zoe, Burke?"

Faith's shout pierced the air from Stefan's left. He raced toward the sound and burst into a clearing.

Burke hovered over Faith. Blood zigzagged across her forehead.

Stefan raised his gun.

"You move, and you're a dead man." He glanced at the bruise darkening Faith's cheek. "Hell, I may just kill you anyway."

Faith scrambled to her feet and stood between Stefan and Burke, holding her hands up.

Stefan froze. "What are you doing?"

She swiped her face and the blood smeared across her forehead. "Zoe's not here and Burke's the only one who knows where she is."

STORM CLOUDS COVERED the sun. The sky had turned angry and violent.

Faith stared at Stefan's weapon. Behind her, Burke let out a curse and grabbed Faith around the waist. He plastered her to his body. Cold metal pressed across her throat. She glanced down. He held a knife against her skin.

"Throw your weapon down or she dies."

"Burke. You can't do this."

"Of course I can," he said. "Who's going to stop me? You? My father?" Burke chuckled. "Father's dead and can't protect you any longer. Mother doesn't know a thing. And you, you're going to end up at the bottom of that gorge along with your lover. If they ever do find you, they'll assume you both died in a lover's quarrel. All the better for me."

"Burke, Zoe needs me."

He scoffed. "Zoe needs a woman to raise her who knows what it means to be a woman. You, you're nothing. I was a fool for thinking you could ever learn to be my consort."

She struggled against his tight grip, but his grip only tightened. "Have to tie up all the loose ends. Then life will be perfect again."

He really was insane.

Burke dragged her to the right. Stefan followed step for step.

"Please, Burke. Where is Zoe?" she begged.

"There's no need for you to know. You don't get to see her again. She's mine. Didn't I tell you that?"

"She's alone, afraid. Please. She's your daughter."

Faith wanted to duck down, let Stefan do what he was obviously willing to do, but she couldn't. What if they were unable to find Zoe?

Burke chuckled. "Oh, she's not alone. If I don't come back, he'll take Zoe away. You'll never see her again."

He jerked her toward rocks at the edge of the clearing, using her as a shield against Stefan.

"You don't have to do this," Stefan said quietly. "We just want Zoe to be safe. We can all walk away."

Burke shook his head. "Father was right about one thing. No loose ends is the only way."

Stefan chuckled. "You don't believe that, do you? We know all about you, Burke. Faith figured out your little hobby. Why else do you think she ran away?"

Burke gripped her even tighter. "It's not possible."

"Faith is smart and resourceful. She figured out your twisted game, and she gave me the file."

Burke gripped Faith's throat and squeezed. She gasped for air. "You're lying."

"Cassandra. Allison. Mary Ann, Brittany, Alexandra. Do those names sound familiar?"

With each name, Burke's grip tightened. His hands shook. Faith could feel the fury. Spots circled in front of her eyes.

"We know." Stefan glanced at his watch. "In fact, as we speak, a very influential member of the state attorney general's staff is perusing the documents right now. It's over, Burke. Your best move is to let Faith go and tell us where to find Zoe. If you do that, I'll put in a good word for you."

"No. Not possible."

Faith held her breath. Burke had stopped moving. He'd turned slightly. She met Stefan's gaze. He gave a slight nod of his head toward the ground. Did he want her to try to get away?

Burke bore down on her throat again. "I don't believe you. Father covered my tracks. I killed him and the men who helped him. No one's left. No one can prove anything." Burke pulled out a knife from behind his back. "Except you."

"Now!" Stefan shouted.

Faith wrenched her body forward, but she couldn't break Burke's hold. The knife sliced her skin. Warm fluid trickled down her neck.

She tumbled to the ground. A loud gunshot echoed through the woods. Faith's gaze flew at the noise. Stefan held the gun in his hand.

Burke screamed. He dropped the knife. One arm hung limp at his side. Blood dripped down his arm. He stared at Stefan in shock.

"You shot me?"

"Be thankful I wasn't aiming at your head. Now where is Zoe?"

Burke shook his head. "This isn't the plan."

His hand jerked. He twisted, looked at Faith and then behind her. "This is all your fault. Everything is your fault," he screamed. "You were supposed to be perfect for me. You were supposed to replace my true love. My Heather."

He gripped her arm with his good hand and dragged her backward. She tried to wrench away, but she couldn't escape his grip.

"Give it up, Burke. It's over," Stefan said.

"It's not over," he said. "Not until I have control."

He shouted out a curse and rammed her with his body. She stumbled toward the rocks.

Stefan let out a loud curse and rushed toward them.

His eyes wild and desperate, he lunged at Faith. She rolled to her side to avoid him. He pitched forward and let out a loud yell.

"Move!" Stefan yelled.

Faith lurched to her left. Burke tripped and couldn't regain his step. He hurtled over the cliff.

"No!" Faith shouted. "Zoe!"

DIRT RAINED DOWN on Zoe. She blinked up at the hole she'd fallen through. No way she was climbing out that way.

"Damn it, kid. Your dad's gonna kill me. Wait right there."

The puppy squirmed in her backpack. She peeked inside, but she could barely see in the dark. "You okay, Catcher?"

She nuzzled the dog. A flash brightened the hole she'd fallen into. Thunder clapped and echoed.

"We're not getting out that way," she whispered. "And I'm not waiting around for that bad man to hurt you." She dug into the pocket of her backpack. "Stefan gave me this." She pulled the mini flashlight out in triumph.

A rope dropped down through the hole in the ceiling.

Zoe swung on her knapsack and flipped on the flashlight. There were railroad tracks on the floor of the cave. It was a very small train. Her mom had taken her onto a big train once. She swept the flashlight around. No way would that train fit in this cave.

A glint blinked at her through the light. She tiptoed through the cave. A big pile of dirt had come down. "Look, Catcher. Another tunnel."

She peered around the mound that was twice as tall as she was. A bunch of shiny gold rocks were piled high in a corner. She picked one up that was the size of a baseball. It was way heavier than her ball.

"Cool." She stuffed it into her backpack with Catcher.

A loud curse echoed through the cave. She whirled around. The man's feet came through the hole. "We gotta go."

She hesitated. There were two tunnels. "Which one, Catcher?"

Zoe squinted down the one with the yellow rocks. Dirt sprinkled down from the ceiling. The other one was bigger. Catcher whined.

"I think you're right," she said. "Let's go that way, boy."

"Kid. You better stay right there," the man shouted.

She'd waited too long. Zoe took off running beside the railroad track. A trickle of water followed her.

Her heart beat fast. Her pants for breath echoed against the rocks around her.

"Kid! Stop. There's a flash flood coming."

She didn't know what he was talking about, but she knew she couldn't trust him.

A loud rumble sounded behind her. Rocks came down. The man shouted. Zoe didn't care. She kept running, the light from her flashlight bobbing in the dark.

"Kid. Stop!"

She glanced over her shoulder. He was gaining on her. A huge wall of rocks rumbled down behind him. Water rushed through a small hole at the side. She looked down at her feet. The whole cave was wet. Zoe stared into the blackness ahead of her. She was trapped. There was nowhere to go.

Chapter Thirteen

Through the sprinkling rain Stefan stared over the side of the cliff. He couldn't see Burke's body, but no one could have survived a fall hundreds of feet down. He turned to Faith. She sat on the ground, her eyes wide with shock.

"Is he—?"

Stefan nodded and crouched beside her. He pulled her into his arms. Her nails bit into his skin. "Zoe."

"We'll find her."

He helped her to her feet. "Let me look at your neck."

She slapped his hand away. "I'm fine."

The cut wasn't deep, but still oozing. He tore a strip from his T-shirt and pressed it against the wound. "This should stop the bleeding."

"Zoe!" Faith shouted, while he tied the makeshift bandage around her neck.

"Don't call out to her," he said. "You heard Burke. Someone's with her."

"Then how will we find her?"

He glanced around the clearing. The trees just to the northwest were disturbed. "This way," he said.

"Are you sure?"

"As much as I can be." He took her hand and led her out of the clearing.

She glanced back to the cliff.

"We'll find his body. After we find Zoe," he said.

Thunder growled ahead of them. Angry clouds hovered over the mountain. "The water'll start coming through the canyons soon," he said. "Looks like a huge rainstorm up there."

"Zoe doesn't know anything about flash floods. We've got to find her."

Stefan stared at the ground. The wind and rain would compromise any trail he might have followed if they didn't find her soon.

The sky darkened even more. Stefan stopped. The mountains were too quiet. He could only make out the sound of the wind through the branches and the pattering rain. No Zoe. No sounds of human activity at all.

He looked around him.

"She's with some kidnapper. What if he—"

He recognized the panic in her voice. He understood, but they had to stay focused. "Burke's a powerful employer. The guy doesn't know Burke's dead. He has to keep Zoe safe."

Faith nodded. "Right. Janice loves Zoe. He'll want her safe."

Stefan didn't mention Burke's erratic behavior. Faith knew. They both did.

Before long, the signs Stefan had been following had disappeared.

Stefan walked a few steps forward. He bent down, then craned his neck to look back the way they'd come.

"You don't know which way, do you?" Faith said. "What are we going to do?" She rubbed her arms quickly.

Stefan pulled her close. She was chilled to the bone. "Burke wouldn't have wanted her too far."

"But maybe far enough not to be heard? Or to hear him."

"Exactly." Stefan grabbed his sat phone and verified his location. Thank God for CTC.

"Are you okay?" Ransom asked.

"Burke's dead. He's hidden Zoe. Who knows these mountains?"

"Sheriff Galloway." Ransom didn't hesitate. "He's on his way. About thirty minutes from your location."

"Can you patch me through to him?"

"Want me to send the chopper?"

"We need everyone you can spare, but it's raining in the mountains. Warn them about flash floods."

Ransom let out a curse. "I'll patch you through to Garrett."

Faith plastered herself against Stefan. He wrapped his arm around her. "We've got help."

She gave him a stiff nod.

"Galloway."

"This is Léon. We've got a missing child—"

"Ransom filled me in. I'm heading your way."

"The guy hid his daughter out here somewhere. I need likely locations. The weather obscured any signs."

Stefan fed Garrett his GPS coordinates. Paper rustling filtered through the phone. "Okay, I'm looking at the map."

"There are a lot of old mine shafts," Garrett said. "They're not safe, though."

The phone went silent. "This looks interesting. There's an old hunting cabin a mile or so northwest from your current location."

Stefan could have cheered. "Thanks, Garrett. I'll be in touch."

"We'll send searchers up your way. Good luck."

Stefan ended the call. "This way," he said, and led her up another hill.

A quarter mile in, the rain let up, but thunder and lightning still hid the top of the mountains.

He fingered a broken branch. "Someone came this way, and not that long ago." He turned to Faith. "We're headed in the right direction."

"I want to call for her," Faith muttered. She dug her hand into his arm. "I want her to know we're coming for her."

"You can't."

Stefan could tell Faith was near her breaking point when they reached the cabin. It was nestled back in the woods. Stefan pulled out his weapon. He slowly turned the doorknob and shoved into the one-room shack.

Empty.

Faith turned to Stefan, her eyes devastated. "Where is she?"

ZOE TOOK A step back, her foot sloshing through cold water. The puppy whimpered from her backpack. The yellow rock weighed it down.

She shined the light through the rocks. The side of the man's face was bleeding. He looked really mad.

"You've killed us, kid," he growled.

Water streamed behind him. It started getting deeper and deeper.

He pushed aside the rocks and came closer and closer. Zoe didn't wait for him to catch her. She whirled around and ran.

"Nowhere to go, kid. I'm gonna to do what Burke was too scared to do. Before I die, you're dead."

Zoe heaved forward. She tried to run, but the water was at her knees now. She lifted her legs, but she couldn't get any traction. The water pushed her forward. Soon it was up to her waist. The flashlight slipped through her wet hands and blinked off.

Dark surrounded her. Rushing water carried her forward in the small cave. She blinked. The backpack weighed her down. Catcher barked at her. Her teeth chattered.

This wasn't good.

The man behind her sloshed closer. She rounded a curve and blinked. A little twinkle of light shone from one end, like a star in the rock.

She headed toward it.

"Got you," the man growled.

His hands gripped her shirt. She squirmed, but he had her. The water climbed higher.

The man held her down, below the water. She couldn't breathe. The water shoved her forward and suddenly she was free. She lifted her head and sucked in a deep breath.

"Damn it," he groaned. He floated close to the ceiling. Blood dripped from his head.

Zoe only had one chance. She let the water carry her toward the hole with the light. It wasn't very big.

She pulled herself up. "Don't worry, Catcher. We're almost safe," she panted.

Something grabbed at her foot.

"Oh, no you don't."

THE EMPTY CABIN sucked all the life out of Faith. Her gaze swept the floor.

"Someone's been here recently," Stefan said.

A glint of string caught Faith's attention. "Zoe," she said, picking up the red tie. "This was on her backpack."

Stefan tilted his head. "There's a trail across the floor." He grinned. "That feisty little sweetheart." He glanced over at Faith.

"She escaped. Zoe ran away. Come on," he called.

They ran through the back door. Stefan headed for the edge of the clearing. "Broken branches," he said.

Faith raced after him. The wind had slowed down. She could even hear the songs of a few birds.

A high-pitched yip pierced the air.

"Stop," Stefan said.

The yip sounded again.

"The dog," Faith shouted. The dog she'd denied Zoe. They ran toward the noise.

"Let me go!" Zoe shouted.

"Zoe!" Faith yelled. Her legs pumped harder as she scrambled over the rocks. They rounded a bend and she gasped.

Zoe's torso came out of a hole in the rocks and water poured out on either side. Her orange backpack lay on the ground. Catcher raced around in circles, yipping at Zoe.

"Mommy. Help. I'm stuck."

Stefan positioned himself in front of her. "I'm going first. We don't know where our friend is."

Faith scrambled over the rocks behind him.

"Zoe!" she shouted.

"Mommy. Hurry. The man's going to get me."

"Where is he, Zoe?" Stefan asked.

"He's grabbing at my feet."

Stefan shoved his gun away. "Start digging," he shouted.

Two rocks in and they were able to pull Zoe out. Water rushed from the hole.

Faith picked her up and rocked her. "Are you okay?"

Zoe nodded. "Catcher and me escaped the bad man. We got wet."

"I see that."

A man's arm stuck out of the hole. "Help," he gurgled against the churning water.

Stefan grabbed a large tree limb and dug away at the edges of the small hole. Water rushed out, and the man squirted through. He lay on the ground, gasping for air.

He looked over at Zoe and glared at her. "Kid, you ruined my life."

Zoe glared at him. "Then you shouldn't have been bad."

STEFAN STOOD OUTSIDE the room at the medical clinic in Trouble, Texas. Waiting. Daniel walked up to him and placed a hand on his shoulder. "Ransom called. They found Burke Thomas's body at the base of the cliff. He died on impact."

"It's for the best. Faith and Zoe have their lives back now." Stefan didn't think too hard about the emptiness lingering in his heart. He couldn't change reality. "What about the guy we brought in?"

"He's in custody. Singing like a canary. He worked for both Thomases. Cleaned up a lot of messes. He's added several names to Burke Thomas's kill list. Not to mention more than one politician who will be resigning. Starting with a couple of police commissioners who looked the other way."

"Good riddance." Stefan shot a glance at the closed door.

"How are they doing?" Daniel asked.

"Zoe's a tough kid. Faith's a tough woman. They'll get through this."

"So what are you doing out here?"

Stefan shook his head. "Nothing's changed. Faith has her life back. I never will. I need to rendezvous with Annie soon."

The thought depressed him. He didn't think he'd ever get over Faith and Zoe.

"I wouldn't be so sure about that." Ransom Grainger walked into the hallway.

Stefan quirked a brow. "I didn't expect to see you here."

"I'm here for a couple of reasons. First, I wanted to meet the woman who put together the research that would've nailed Burke Thomas if he hadn't taken a nose dive."

Stefan narrowed his gaze at his boss. "What are you thinking?"

"I can always use a good researcher in CTC. I'm planning to offer her a job."

"Like hell you are."

"What's it to you?" Ransom said. "You're taking off anyway. Besides, the pay's great. I don't think she'll turn me down."

Stefan glared at his boss. "I don't want her in danger. She needs a normal life. I don't know one member of CTC who has a normal life."

"I do," Daniel said.

"You quit," Stefan reminded him. "And I don't have a choice. You know that. The Thomases outed me. My cover's blown."

Ransom cleared his throat. "If you weren't in danger, would you stay?"

Stefan's jaw throbbed so hard it ached. "It's not a choice I have."

Ransom started to speak, but Stefan just shook his head. Before his boss could say anything, the hospital room opened.

"How's Zoe?" Stefan asked, placing his hands on Faith's arms.

Faith shook her head in bewilderment. "A few scrapes and bruises, but she's not even fazed. She thought the whole thing was a big adventure. And of course, she and Catcher have bonded."

Faith smiled at Daniel. "Thanks for coming."

He kissed her cheek. "I guess we know where that puppy's going. I'm glad you're both okay."

Faith frowned. "I haven't told her about her father yet. I don't know what to say."

"Tell her as much of the truth as you can. Over time, you can fill in the blanks," Daniel offered. "You'll know what she can handle."

She glanced at Stefan. "She wants to see you."

"Sure." Stefan followed Faith into Zoe's room.

"Stefan." Zoe smiled at him. "I like your new name best of all."

He winced at the bruises on her head and the scrapes on her arms. "How you doing, Slugger?"

"That's what my mom calls me."

"I know. But after you escaped from that bad guy, I've decided it's the perfect name for you."

She beamed at him. "Mommy, where's my backpack?"

"Here, sweetie. It's heavy."

"I know. That's what I wanted to show Stefan." She unzipped the front pouch and pulled out a large rock.

Stefan let out a low whistle. "Where'd you find that, Zoe?"

"In the cave. A bunch of rocks fell and there was this tunnel. A big stack of yellow rocks were just sitting there, piled up. I almost went down that tunnel, but the ceiling was coming down."

"You did the right thing. Can I hold it?" he asked.

"Sure." She shrugged. "I'm going to keep it in my collection."

Stefan weighed it in his hand. "Zoe, I think this is a very large chunk of gold. Real gold."

Faith gasped. "You're kidding."

Zoe took the stone from him. "It's worth a lot of money? Enough for me to buy Catcher? Please, Mom. Can I have him?"

Faith looked over at Stefan. "His bark led us to you. Of course you can keep him."

"Yay! I can't wait to show Daddy. He said I could keep Catcher at Grandma and Grandpa's house. Where is he?"

Faith cleared her throat. Stefan hurt at her struggle, but this was one thing he couldn't protect Zoe from. She sat on her daughter's bed. "Slugger, I have something to tell you."

Looking at her innocent face and open expression, Stefan tensed. He placed his hand on Faith's shoulder and squeezed. He felt a shudder run through her, and then she stilled.

"Zoe, your daddy was in an accident in the mountains. He got hurt. Really bad."

Zoe bowed her head. "Is he in the hospital?"

"No, honey." Faith pulled Zoe into her lap. "Zoe, your daddy is gone. He didn't make it off the mountain."

Zoe looked at her, eyes tearing up. "I won't ever see him again?"

Faith hugged her close. "I'm sorry, baby."

Zoe cried for several minutes. She bit her lip and looked over at Stefan. "Was my daddy a bad man?"

"What do you think, Zoe?" Stefan asked, his voice quiet. He didn't want to lie to Zoe, but he didn't want her to hear the truth. Not yet.

"He gave me to that bad man. That wasn't nice."

"No, it wasn't." Stefan knelt down next to her. "My dad did some bad things, Zoe. But I still loved him. It's okay to still love him."

Tears fell down her cheeks and she leaned into Stefan. He wrapped his arms around her and rested his cheek on her hair. God, he was going to miss her.

He met Faith's gaze over Zoe's head. He was going to miss them both so much, his heart might never be the same.

FAITH'S HEART BROKE for Zoe. She rested her hand on Zoe's head as her daughter hugged Stefan. He cradled her daughter close. Tears welled behind Faith's eyes.

Stefan had kept his promise. He'd saved them both. She nestled next to them on the bed. They sat there for a few minutes, just being quiet. No words were necessary.

It was over.

Faith didn't know how long they sat there when a nurse entered the room with a wheelchair. "Miss Zoe. The doctor wants to do an X-ray of that arm."

Zoe lifted her head from Stefan's chest and bit her lip. "Will it hurt?"

"Not at all. You just have to lie there and he'll take a picture."

"I'll come with you," Faith offered.

"I have to be a big girl." Zoe lifted her chin. "I can do it by myself, Mom."

Faith didn't know what to say to that. She and her daughter were so alike. Faith wanted Zoe to grow into a self-sufficient young woman, but not so she wouldn't let herself accept help when she needed it.

She looked over at Stefan. He'd taught her that sometimes you could actually count on someone else to have your back.

Stefan ruffled Zoe's hair. "You don't have to do everything on your own, Zoe. We all need help sometimes."

"Not you."

"Even me. How about your mom and I come with you?"

"I can do it myself. I'm not scared."

Stefan raised his brow. "What if we want to be with you because we missed you?"

Zoe let out a long sigh. "I guess that's okay."

The nurse chuckled, but Faith caught a bit of relief in her daughter's eyes.

Zoe winced as she got out of bed. The large bruise showing from the sleeve of her hospital gown had grown even darker purple.

"That arm looks like it hurts, Slugger."

"It's okay, Mommy. The water shoved me into the rocks. Or it coulda been when I fell in the hole. Lots of stuff happened in that cave."

"You've got a tough daughter," the nurse said.

"I know." Faith smiled down at Zoe. "She's the best."

The nurse wheeled Zoe out of the room. Faith and Stefan followed.

"Well, it's clear both of you love her very much," the nurse said. "I may be old-fashioned, but that's always the best medicine."

Faith's gaze flew to Stefan's. Did they really look like a family?

When they reached the X-ray room door, the nurse stopped them. She wheeled Zoe inside. When the door closed, Faith sighed. "Is she handling all this too well?"

"I don't know. She's something else, that's for sure."

Faith sat down, and Stefan moved a chair around to face her. He took her hands in his. "Look, I don't know how much longer I can stay. The men who want to kill me will start coming. You and Zoe need to be safe. I couldn't live with myself if anything happened to you."

"You're leaving? Now?"

"I have to. I don't have a choice, Faith."

She bit down on her lip. "You know, I've just realized my daughter is braver than I am." She met his gaze. "So

I'm just going to ask. If things were different, would you want to stay with us?"

Stefan touched her cheek gently. "Oh, yeah. You and Zoe brought me back to life, Faith. I was dead inside before you came into my world."

She took in a shallow breath. "Then take us with you. Nothing is stopping you."

He shook his head. "I can't let you give up everything. It's not fair to you. Or to Zoe. She needs a future, not a life on the run."

Faith couldn't stop the tears from rolling down her cheeks. "I love you, Stefan."

She held her breath. He closed his eyes, then opened them. "I love you, too. More than you'll ever know. That's why I can't let you come with me, Faith. You and Zoe deserve a normal life. A happy life."

"Zoe and I deserve to be loved. And that's you." She grabbed his hand and held it to her heart. "I've never met a man who was willing to drop everything just to help two strangers. You saw we were in trouble and didn't take no for an answer. Why won't you accept the same from me?"

Stefan groaned, rose from the chair and pulled her close. His body trembled against hers. She couldn't believe she made him shake with longing.

He kissed her eyelids, her cheeks and finally her lips before holding her against him. "I shouldn't. It won't be fair to you."

"Leaving us isn't fair, either."

The nurse wheeled the chair back out. Zoe looked from her mom back to Stefan. She smiled. "I like you like that."

"We'll take her back to her room," he said as he cleared his throat, his voice rough with emotion.

"The doctor will be up soon to give you the results," the nurse said.

Stefan wheeled Zoe down the hall while Faith walked beside her.

"Slugger," Faith asked. "What would you think if we went with Stefan when he leaves here?"

She frowned. "Could we take Catcher?"

"Of course."

"And you'd be there, too?"

"Yes."

"Forever?"

"Absolutely."

Zoe grinned. "I like that idea. He makes your eyes smile, Mom. And you always look happy."

Stefan knelt down in front of her. "Zoe, there's a catch. If you come with me, we can't see our friends again. We'll start a new life."

"But you'll be there? You promise? You'll take care of Mom so she's not alone and sad anymore?"

Stefan met Faith's gaze. "I'll take care of both of you. I promise."

Zoe grinned. "Okay. We can do that. As long as we have a backyard."

Epilogue

The crisp air on the Triple C Ranch was soaked with a hint of pine and cinnamon. Christmas had its own special aroma. Stefan hadn't thought about such things in, well, ever, but Zoe had brought the fact out to him, so…

He paced back and forth in the small room where he waited.

A soft knock sounded at the door and his best man walked in. Daniel Adams grinned. "I've seen you waiting to infiltrate a terrorist organization and be less nervous than this."

Stefan frowned. "After five months hiding out, testifying against Orren, and learning how many women Burke brutalized over the years, Ransom's got our second set of new identities ready, but this time it'll be permanent. No going back. I just don't know if Faith and Zoe really understand what this change will mean. Zoe will miss her grandmother. The poor woman lost her family and had no idea what was going on. The truth is, I don't know if I'm doing the right thing taking them away from everything they know."

Daniel shook his head. "How about you trust your soon-to-be wife to make that decision?"

"She loves me," Stefan said, still unnerved by that fact. "She wants to be with me wherever I am."

"Definitely a crazy woman who doesn't know what she's talking about," Daniel said with a smile. "And what about you? Can you imagine your life without her?"

Just the words made Stefan's heart twist. "She brought me back to life."

"Then quit worrying. I'll tell you from experience, whatever your name is, wherever your life, it won't be perfect, but it'll be an adventure."

Daniel left the room, but Stefan couldn't let the doubts recede. He had to give her one more chance. One more opportunity to come to her senses, even if she shattered his heart in the process. He loved her too much not to give her the chance to live a normal life.

He peeked out into the foyer of CTC's headquarters. He heard a lot of voices. The house was filled with his friends and coworkers. Surprising how many he'd made over the years.

Faith was just down the hall getting help from Mrs. Hargraves, Raven and a couple other CTC wives.

He walked quietly down the hallway and tapped lightly on the door.

"Come in," Faith said.

He walked inside and his breath stopped.

She stood before him, shoulders bare, lace hugging her body and flowing to the floor in a pool of iridescence. She was his dream. He swallowed and the sound seemed to echo through the room.

Her eyes grew wide, frantic. "What are you doing here?"

"I have no idea," he said. "You are…more than beautiful."

She flushed, pink lacing her cheeks. "Thank you. Burke…uh, Burke picked out a poofy, pastry-shaped monstrosity. Marrying you. This is *my* fairy tale."

Stefan knew he should walk away, but he couldn't. He took her hands in his. "Last chance for a normal life."

She tilted her head. "I have no doubts." She frowned at his transparent expression. "Do you?"

"Every moment of every day. I want you and Zoe to be happy. What if we have to move during the middle of baseball season?"

"Then we'll survive. As long as we're together. Whatever else happens, we'll take as it comes."

He leaned down and kissed her lips, feeling the warmth under his mouth. "I have something for you," he whispered.

"We can't." She grinned. "Not before the wedding."

He reached into his pocket and pulled out a small velvet pouch. "I found this for you. I wanted you to have it back." He tilted the fabric and a small silver ring dropped into his hand. The traditional wedding ring had two small diamonds on either side of a modest square-cut.

Faith gasped. "It can't be. I pawned Mama's ring." Her gaze flew to his. "How could you have possibly found it?"

"It took a little searching, and a little bit of digging where you'd been from Zoe."

Her hands trembled as she slipped the ring on her right hand. "Thank you, Stefan. I can't—"

"You don't have to say anything. I'd do anything for you and Zoe."

"I never had a doubt." She straightened. "So, are you going to marry me and then disappear into the ether? I'm ready if you are."

"Well, I'm not."

Stefan whirled around. He couldn't believe who was standing there in the doorway, looking every inch a royal. "Kat?"

Queen Katherine of Bellevaux grinned and raced

across the room to hug him tight. "Did you think I was going to let my big brother get married without the family?"

Two six-year-olds ran across the room. "Hi, Uncle Stefan. 'Member me? I'm Hayden."

"I'm Lanie," a precious little blond-haired girl said, hugging his leg. "Mama told us all about you. You're a hero." She looked up at Faith. "You're dressed like a fairy princess." She straightened. "Did you know I'm a princess, too?"

Stefan froze. "What are you doing here? It's not safe."

"Don't worry… Stefan," Logan Carmichael said as he stepped into the room, holding a year-old cutie pie in his arms. The man who'd married his sister, who'd become Prince Consort of Bellevaux.

"I don't understand."

Ransom Grainger walked in.

"Well, everyone, just come on in," Stefan said.

Logan handed his daughter to his wife. "The last few years we've been working to break up the group who put the hit out on you. We captured Chanteaux last week. There's nobody left who wants you dead, Stefan. You can come home."

He staggered back. "Home?" He looked at Faith. She appeared to be in a state of shock. He definitely was.

"But—"

"I'll step aside, Stefan. Logan and I have discussed it. The throne is yours if you want it."

Stefan's mind whirled with shock. *Throne.*

"No, Katherine. Our people have embraced you and Logan. You've already done so much good. Besides, I never wanted to be king. If I have to legally abdicate, I will, but I want a normal life." He kissed Faith's hand. "With the woman I love."

"You're still a prince," Kat reminded him.

"What's going on?" a voice demanded. Zoe stood there, dressed in a tuxedo, not a hint of lace anywhere. A large reddish dog hovered by her side.

Stefan knelt down. "Zoe, how would you like to be a princess?"

She looked at him like he was crazy. "No, thanks. I like baseball better."

"Me, too." Stefan laughed. "Thanks for the offer, Kat, but you can keep the throne. I've already found my dream come true."

He pulled Faith into his arms. "My fairy tale began the moment I met you."

"A normal life," she said softly. "Are you ready for that?"

Stefan smiled down at her. "With you and Zoe in my life, it will always be an adventure."

* * * * *

SHADOW POINT DEPUTY

JULIE ANNE LINDSEY

Dedicated to cat ladies.
You are my people.

Chapter One

Rita Horn parked her new pickup truck in the muddy gravel lot across from the docks. She dragged a bag of dry kibble from the bed and squinted at a dozen feline silhouettes framed by the sunset. It was a shame so many cats were homeless in Shadow Point. She'd take them all in if she could, but the three she already had were sure to protest.

"Here, kitty, kitty," she called, shivering against the brisk autumn breeze. Feeding the strays seemed a decent compromise to adopting them all, but it didn't minimize the guilt she experienced every time she stopped to check on them. If they had to be on their own, she supposed the abandoned factories along the waterfront made a decent haven. There was camaraderie, no natural predators and plenty of mice to sustain them when Rita worked late and missed her usual stop.

The cats swarmed her ankles as she rounded the building's edge, mewling and climbing over one another to get to the food. She stopped at a line of cement bowls she'd purchased from a local landscaper when the pet store versions had insisted on blowing away.

"Who's hungry?" She tipped the bag over the bowls, filling each to its rim. "Ah-ah-ah." She nudged a growling pair apart. "No fighting. There's plenty for everyone."

The bag was nearly empty when a latecomer trotted into

view. The little orange-and-white tabby had something smeared over its face and down one side.

"What is that?" Rita crouched for a closer look. Deep crimson streaks flattened the kitty's fur into matted stripes. Rita clutched her chest. "My poor baby. What happened to you?" She reached for the tabby, but he jumped free with a hiss. It was easy to forget many of the cats were feral, not abandoned. It had taken weeks to get some to come out and see her at dinnertime. She clucked her tongue and extended a hand with the last of the kibble on her palm. The little guy wouldn't survive long with an injury that had bled so much. He needed the wound cleaned, antibiotics and probably stitches.

"Kitty," she cooed. The injured cat darted away, and Rita dashed after him, leaving the empty bag behind.

"Kitty, kitty, kitty." Her sensible three-inch heels clicked and snapped against the cold ground as she gave chase. She stopped short at a fence marked NO TRESPASSING. The cat paused a moment beyond the chain- link barrier before screeching out of sight.

"Darn it." She dropped the kibble from her palm and scanned the scene, debating the importance of her flawless, law-abiding record when that kitty needed a doctor.

A line of bloody paw prints knotted her tummy and propelled her to action. If she was caught, at least she could give a good explanation. Surely no one would fault a woman for trying to help an injured animal.

Rita shored up her nerve and tugged the gate where a thick chain and padlock held it loosely to the fence. There was enough space to slip inside if she held the gate and ducked beneath the chain, so she took a deep breath and went in. She followed the trail around the factory's edge, admiring the soft cotton candy glow of a setting sun as it gave way to twilight. The cat stared down at her from a windowsill eight feet in the air. "Are you even hurt?"

She scanned the scene for another injured animal. Where had the blood come from, if not from the cat who was wearing it? A dark puddle drew her forward, toward a narrow object several yards away. The air seemed to sizzle with danger as she scooped an expensive-looking pen off the ground. An odd thing to find at an abandoned factory, unless developers had been here. Maybe the state was finally going to make good on the promise to renovate the area. She froze as the tip of her shoe slid against the slick cement and swallowed a scream when the puddle came clearly into view, red as the sun burning its last rays of daylight off the water.

Rita raked her cell phone from a coat pocket with trembling fingers. There was far too much blood to have come from a cat.

A sudden splash sent ice fingers down her spine, and the low murmur of voices pushed her back to the building's edge. She closed her eyes to summon a thread of bravery, then peeked toward the sounds with caution.

The angle of the sunset reduced both figures to faceless silhouettes. They were clearly male with broad shoulders and strong gaits, but they were of strikingly different heights. Together, they strode beneath a cone of security light, revealing one man's dress shirt and the other's official-looking jacket, complete with patches she couldn't read from that distance. Rita's heart took off at a sprint as a dark stain down the front of the dress shirt began to look a lot like the puddle she'd just seen. The man with the stained shirt wiped his hands on a rag. A gun holster nestled safely against his side.

A black sedan seemed to manifest from the shadows, parked silently beside a line of blue barrels. The trunk popped open as the men approached, revealing what appeared to be more blood and a number of firearms. The man tossed the rag into the trunk, then dragged a suit jacket out. He threaded his arms through the sleeves and fastened two buttons over the broad crimson stain.

Rita swiped her phone screen to life. The little device rocked unsteadily in her sweat-slicked palm. Her breaths shortened and her heart rate spiked uncomfortably. There wasn't enough air, and she couldn't swallow. Rita gripped her phone tighter and fought the wave of panic quickly taking control. Not since she lost her mother had anxiety come on so quickly.

She pressed her back to the wall and returned the phone to her pocket. She needed to sit down before she fell over. Her eyelids slid shut for an internal pep talk, and she reopened them with purpose. She'd make the call from someplace safe. Someplace she could breathe. She forced the last ounce of bravery from her bones and tiptoed back through the shadows, along the building's edge, careful not to let her heels smack against the ground.

The snick of a closing trunk and soft purr of an engine were behind her. A set of low growls rose before her near the food bowls. Rita's muscles tensed. *No fighting*, she prayed. *Not now.*

The sound grew steadily into the familiar squawks of a feline brawl. A beam of light flashed over the ground before her, sweeping and narrowing as it drew nearer.

"Who's there?" The man in the official-looking jacket moved in her direction. The familiar Cade County Sheriff's Department logo was on his chest.

That could not be good.

Rita burst into motion, running as quickly as her trembling legs would carry her toward her truck, through the chained gate and across the gravel lot.

"Stop!" the man's voice boomed behind her, punctuated by the echoes of heavy footfalls.

Not today, officer, she thought as she dived behind the wheel. Something bad had definitely happened at the docks tonight. She didn't know what, and she wasn't about to become another puddle on the concrete.

Chapter Two

Rain poured over Deputy Cole Garrett's hat and slicker. Heavy storm clouds had masked the sunrise, but Shadow Point was still in motion. The blue-collar town had risen with the sun for a hundred years. Farmers. Bus drivers. Factory workers. Somehow the body pulled from the river wore a watch worth more than Cole's first truck.

He peered through the downpour at his older brother and current Cade County sheriff, West Garrett. "Recognize him?"

West's frown deepened. "Nope."

Dressed like he was, no one probably would. Folks with that kind of money drove right on through Shadow Point. "Maybe he was visiting family," Cole suggested, "or was here on business."

West shot Cole a look. "By the looks of the bullet hole in his forehead, business wasn't good."

Members of the local coroner's office loaded the waterlogged body onto a gurney and covered it with a white sheet. The medical examiner presented West with a clipboard. "We'll do our preliminaries and get back with you."

West followed the coroner back to the van.

Cole flashed his light over the scene, seeking anything that might explain how a stranger wound up murdered and floating in the water before dawn. The river had surely stripped the body of any clues, but maybe the killer had left footprints or the shell casing on land.

He moved methodically upriver, toward a set of abandoned factories by the docks. The shielded space seemed a more likely location for an execution than the sodden, unobstructed field where the body had been pushed ashore.

He returned the flashlight to his belt as the storm peeled back its efforts. A swarm of cats came into view near the largest building, gathered beneath a broad metal awning. They cried at the sight of him, and Cole changed trajectories, drawn to the mass of complaining felines.

The coroner's van motored away in the distance, rounding a bend and drifting out of sight. West's cruiser rolled quietly into a muddy gravel lot near the factory.

The world grew brighter by the second, finally relieved of the relentless storm.

"A bit off the path, aren't you?" West called, slamming the door behind him.

Cole stared at a line of cement bowls and a shredded cat food bag. "I don't think so." He nudged the soggy paper with his toe. "Someone fed the cats. Wasn't the first time, either. They didn't scatter when they saw me."

West cast a glance at the crowd of furry spectators, then turned his attention to the cruiser. "There were some tire tracks where I parked. They're washed out. Tread marks are gone."

"Let's measure them," Cole suggested. "Could be something. Might be how they brought the body here." Cole moved toward the cats, shooing them and scrutinizing the only patch of dry ground for miles.

"West." A set of bloody paw prints and the pointy outline of one shoe appeared beneath a broad awning. A white slip of paper clung to the sheet-metal door. A receipt dated the night before. The rest of the print was blurred away but he was certain it said cat food. "We've got a witness out there somewhere."

RITA STARED AT the clock above her fireplace and debated leaving for work an hour early. She'd been dressed since dawn, having given up on sleep hours before. The raging storm had rattled her windows and her mind. Each time her lids had grown heavy, she imagined the man from the docks trying to break down the door, only to wake again with the realization it was just the wind.

The same carousel of questions ran endlessly around her mind. What had she really seen? What sort of thing would involve so much blood, the docks and the local sheriff's department? Did the man giving chase recognize her? If so, what would happen next?

She'd watched the news on the edge of her seat, waiting for reports of whatever had happened at the docks, but there were none. Nothing in the morning paper, either.

A sharp pounding on the front door nearly sent her out the back. She inched across the living room and peeked through the curtains. Her little brother, Ryan, stood on the porch rubbing his palms together and puffing into his hands. The temperature must've dropped after she'd left the docks.

She opened the door with a forced smile, then jerked him inside. "Hey, what are you doing here?" She secured the door behind him and flipped the lock, hoping to look more normal than she felt.

He dragged his gaze from the locked door to her. "You said I could borrow your truck. My new roommate is moving in." He tented his dark brows, green eyes flashing in suspicion. "Are you okay?"

Ryan was nineteen and a sophomore at the university one town over. He was a full seven years her junior, with a misplaced big brother attitude. She'd helped raise him, and not the other way around.

"Yep." She tugged her ear and hefted a passing cat into her arms. The sight of her feline family usually brought her great comfort, but today they only delivered flashbacks of the docks.

"I thought you didn't have to be at work for an hour," Ryan said.

"I don't."

He scanned her freshly straightened living room, the result of too much time and anxiety with zero sleep. "Since when are you up and dressed by now, and why is your place so clean? What's going on?"

Rita's cheeks ached from the forced congeniality. What she wanted to do was cry. "Nothing." She dropped the act and pinched the bridge of her nose with one hand while cradling her kitty with the other. "I had trouble sleeping. Can I get you some coffee? Are you hungry?" Her gaze jumped again to the hands of the clock that never seemed to move. Going to work early wasn't a bad thing. It was normal, really. Not for her, but lots of other people did it. Maybe she could finally make some headway with the files on her desk, and the distraction would keep her mind off the slew of questions that she had no way of answering.

Ryan's hand danced before her. A US Army key ring swung from one finger. "Did you hear anything I just said?"

"What?"

He cocked a hip and dropped his arm. "Did someone hurt you?"

"No. Of course not." That was funny. Self-defense was a mandatory course of education in the Horn family, had been even before they'd lost their mother. Though no amount of self-defense training could've saved her from the drunk driver who'd taken her from them.

Rita dropped the cat on the couch. "Let me grab my purse." Her breath caught as she pulled back the zipper, revealing the pen she'd found at the docks inside. She'd considered throwing it away when she found it in her coat pocket, but decided to keep it until she knew what had happened. Maybe it was evidence.

"Give me one more minute," she called into the living room.

Rita grabbed a sandwich bag from the lazy Susan and wrapped the pen in tissues before stuffing it inside. If being trampled by thirty cats at an abandoned dock wasn't contamination enough, one night in her disaster of a handbag had surely ruined the pen's chances of being useful. But with technology these days, maybe someone could do something with it. If only she knew who to give it to or if she should. She rubbed her forehead and swallowed a lump of emotion. Was it evidence? Was she crazy? Maybe both. She sealed the bag and stuffed it back into her purse.

"Found it." She dropped the bag on the couch beside her white Himalayan rescue. The other two cats leaped onto the sofa and stuck their noses into her bag.

She presented the key to her new truck on one palm. "Take care of my baby."

He made the trade with enthusiasm, dropping the key to his twenty-year-old yellow hatchback into her newly empty hand. "And you take care of Suzie Sunshine."

Rita snorted and dragged one finger in a small X shape over her heart. "Do you need money for gas or lunch? How are your grades?"

Ryan backed toward the door. "I'm good. Grades are fine. I am meeting the guys for a cram session, though. So I should get going. I've got two morning exams. All those professors want me to learn things." He pretended to choke himself.

Rita clapped slowly, and a genuine smile formed on her lips. "The future of America, ladies and gentlemen." Education had always been high on Rita's priority list, but never on Ryan's. It had been all she could do to convince him to get a degree before enlisting in the army alongside their father. With a degree he could at least enter the service as an officer and be prepared for a career afterward.

He turned for the door.

"Wait." Rita pried the pile of cats from her handbag and set them aside. "I'll walk you out." She stroked the kitties' heads and scratched their chins. "Try to behave."

A thick fog had settled in after the night's heavy rains, making it impossible to see the stop sign at the end of the block and adding a Hitchcockian feel to her already pear-shaped world.

Ryan angled her silver Ford smoothly out of the driveway.

She coaxed his rusty hatchback to life. The stench of exhaust bit her nose and the air.

Ten minutes later, she set her purse on the municipal building's security scanner and nodded at the guards. She collected her things on the other side and walked quickly away, feeling irrationally conspicuous, knowing the pen lay inside.

Her heels snapped and cracked against polished marble as she crossed the cavernous foyer and climbed the wide, sweeping staircase. Cade County wasn't small, but it was rural, and the population was low, making one grand building a sufficient hub for the courthouse and local government offices, including hers at the County Treasurer. Oil paintings of the governor, senator and US presidents lined the second-floor hallways.

Rita ducked into her office and dropped onto her rolling chair with determination. Once she cleared the clutter from her head and desk, she'd give the sheriff's department a call. Anonymously. She'd been trespassing, after all, and she wouldn't be in this predicament if she'd obeyed the law and heeded the sign. She dropped her head into waiting palms. What would she say? She suspected that something bad happened? The storm had surely erased any evidence, and hadn't a deputy been there last night?

Why, yes. He had. And she'd *run* from him. A groan escaped her lips.

"Good morning, Rita!" A perky voice split the silence.

Rita jerked upright. "Hello."

The receptionist stared expectantly. "You're here bright and early." She fluffed giant blond hair and straightened a spray of stiff bangs.

"Hoping to catch up." Rita motioned to the pile of folders on her desk.

"Any luck?"

"Not really." She shouldn't have come in today. The office didn't feel like a distraction. It felt like a prison. "I think I'm going to make a coffee run before I get started." Maybe a little fresh air would help. "Can I get you something?"

The woman raised her steaming mug higher. "Kinda got that covered."

"Right. Sorry." Rita grabbed her coat and purse. "I won't be long." She straightened her white silk blouse and black pencil skirt, then hustled downstairs, taking the side exit into a public garden to catch her breath.

A slight drizzle forced her to stay near the door, where a small overhang served as shelter. The benches were wet. The ground waterlogged. Narrow puddles filled the spaces between walkway paving stones. She inhaled the cool, misty air and shook her hands out at the wrists. She didn't need fresh air or caffeine. She needed answers, and the only way she'd get them was to call the police like she should have done last night. It was better to report something that turned out to be nothing than to not speak up and find out later that her call could have helped someone.

She marched back inside with resolve and climbed the stairs to her office. Her steps slowed at the sight of a deputy speaking with the receptionist inside her glass office doors. If she truly planned to report what she'd seen, this was the time, but her muscles seemed to atrophy at the thought. There was something unsettling about his stance. She hadn't seen the faces of the men at the docks, but this deputy seemed familiar in a way that raised the hair on her arms.

She slipped into an alcove and waited. When the deputy reappeared on the steps to the building's front doors, she dialed the main line to the receptionist.

"Cade County Treasurer. This is Cyndi."

"Hi, Cyndi, this is Rita."

"Rita? Talk about timing! A deputy sheriff was just in here looking for you. Did he find you? I told him you went for coffee. Probably at that diner around the corner. Is that where you went?"

A cold sweat broke over Rita's brow. "Yes. Did he say what he wanted?"

"No. Only that he'd hoped to catch you."

"Did you get his name?"

Cyndi paused. "No. Honey, are you in some kind of trouble?"

Rita moved double time down the rear staircase. "No. Not at all. I'm feeling sick, though. I think that's why I was so distracted earlier. It's really hitting me now."

"Oh, well, then you should go home. I can't afford to get sick. Remember when I got that stomach flu last spring?"

How could she forget? Anytime anyone complained about so much as a headache in Cyndi's presence, they were reminded of her personal near-death experience in March. "Mmm-hmm. You know what? I think I have that."

"Oh, dear."

"Yep. I'm going to head home. Rest." Rita jogged through the door and across the employee lot toward Ryan's decrepit compact. "Cyndi? I've got to go. I think I'm going to be sick."

"You need lots of fluids."

"Okay." She dropped behind the steering wheel and gunned the little engine to life. What she really needed was to go home and pull herself together. "Thank you. Goodbye."

The phone rang in her hand, and she tossed it aside. The only person she'd answer for today was Ryan, and that wasn't his number. Everyone else could get in line.

She made a bunch of paranoid and probably unnecessary turns before arriving on her street almost twenty minutes later. Several neighbors stood on her lawn beside a cruiser in the driveway. Fear and panic bubbled in her core.

She cranked Ryan's window down and hooked an elbow over the frame. "Mrs. Wilcox," she stage-whispered. An elderly woman turned to face her. The woman hustled in her direction.

"What's going on?" Rita asked, sinking low in the driver's seat. Her tummy bubbled with anxiety at the sight of a cruiser at her home.

"Betty was jogging past and saw the cats in your yard." She pointed to a woman in hot pink running gear and a matching sun visor. "She recognized them because they spend so much time in your window."

"My cats were outside?" Rita gasped. "Are they okay?"

"Well, yes," she said, glancing back at Rita's home. "Betty collected the little lovebugs, then knocked on your door and it opened. The whole place was a mess, so she dropped them inside, pulled the door shut, then came to me, and I called the cops."

A rock formed in Rita's throat. "My house is a mess?" she croaked.

The older woman bobbed her head. "Trashed. The deputy was here in minutes. Must've been in the area."

Her heart hammered and her pulse beat in her ears. Someone had been in her home.

And a deputy was in there now.

Chapter Three

Cole had gritted his teeth and dragged his heels when the call came in from Dispatch about a possible B and E on Maple. Leaving West alone with an active murder investigation seemed irresponsible, but one of the problems in a department with only six deputies was coverage. The next man's shift wouldn't start for two hours unless West called him in sooner. Meanwhile, the homeowner on Maple had left work early and wasn't answering her phone. Cole had reluctantly made the trip to check on things.

The front door was unlocked with no signs of tampering, but the place had been destroyed. The neighbors hadn't seen or heard anything out of the ordinary, but every item in sight was upended, overturned or partially disassembled. Bookshelves were emptied. Drawers were dumped. Yet the television and computer were completely untouched.

Not a very effective robbery. So why break in? And where was the homeowner? He double-checked the name on his notepad. Rita Horn. Maybe this was revenge. Something personal. Maybe the work of a jaded ex or wronged family member.

Whatever it was, it was weird.

He scrubbed a palm over his face. First a body had turned up in the river, and now there was a break-in east of the railroad tracks. In a neighborhood known for its distinct lack of crimes. His exhale was long and slow. What was going on with this day?

The tip of his boot nicked a fallen photograph, and he pulled the thick white frame off the floor. "Well, what do you know?" He grinned. He'd recognize those smart hazel eyes anywhere.

The jaw-dropping redhead worked at the municipal building. He'd taken notice of her last fall while delivering a criminal to court through the rear alley entrance. She'd been handing out homemade sandwiches and bottled water to a throng of homeless people at lunchtime. Her floral wrap dress and high heels had been a stunning contrast to the dirty and disheveled men and women in her care. If memory served him, she'd called several of the people by their names.

He set the frame on the fireplace mantel, feeling much better about leaving West at the docks.

"Here she is!" A voice called from the lawn. "She's okay!"

Cole turned on his heel and went to save the day.

"Miss Horn?" He strode in the direction of a rusty yellow car. "I'm Deputy Cole Garrett. Can you please park your vehicle?"

She nodded behind the driver's-side window.

Her white-knuckle grip and wide eyes worried him. Current circumstances aside, Rita was the poster child for calm and centered. He'd started noticing her every time he made a trip to the courts after that day in the alley. Unfortunately, they'd never made eye contact, and unlike most women in town, she didn't seem to know he existed.

The car rolled slowly to the curb and idled several moments before the engine settled.

She got out, closed the door and moved cautiously in Cole's direction. "What's going on?" Her gaze darted nervously over the scene, catching on his cruiser, then the patch on his jacket.

A gray-haired woman popped up at her side. "I was scared when you didn't answer the phone. Your office said you'd left, but you didn't answer."

"I'm sorry, Doris." Rita soothed the elderly woman. "I wasn't feeling well. I'm not myself today."

"I just thank my stars you weren't home when this happened," Doris said.

"What happened, exactly?" Rita asked again, moving her attention to Cole.

"Your neighbors reported a possible break-in about thirty minutes ago. When did you say you left the municipal building?"

Her eyes narrowed. "How do you know I was at the municipal building?"

Cole put on his most charming smile, hoping to soothe the sudden alarm in her tone. "I've seen you there."

Her cheeks darkened, but she didn't comment.

It was none of his business, but Rita Horn didn't look sick. In fact, she looked fantastic. Her skirt and blouse fit in all the right places, accentuating her curves without giving away the details.

Man, he would love to know her details.

She crossed her arms over her chest, drawing the silky material of her blouse tighter.

Dear Lord.

"I went in early."

Cole swept a hand toward her front door and forced his gaze there, as well. "Would you like to see if anything is missing?" He moved onto the stoop, hoping she'd follow. Honestly, she looked like she might get back in her car and flee. "Any chance you forgot to lock the door this morning?"

"No." Her sweet voice sounded behind him. "I even double-checked the knob."

He angled himself for a look at her. "Do you always double-check or was something different today?"

She pursed her lips.

Cole imagined kissing them apart.

He leaned against the handrail to her porch, allowing her to pass. "I can't help thinking about the fact there hasn't been trouble like this in your neighborhood for quite some time, and it happened on a day when you got sick and left work early. Also on a day you felt compelled to double-check your lock."

"Maybe you're reading too much into this."

He shrugged. "That's possible. It's certainly a side effect of the job."

Rita slid past him into her home, and a zip of electricity snapped over his skin. "Can you think of anyone who might've done something like this, Miss Horn?"

She swept long auburn locks over her shoulder and bundled the strands in one fist. "No." She lowered her arms to lock around her middle. "You can call me Rita."

COLE UNZIPPED THE black duffel he'd left by the door.

"What are you doing?" The fear in her voice startled him.

He raised his palms in a show of innocence. "I'm going to dust the knob and jamb for fingerprints. Maybe replace this old dead bolt."

She lifted a finger. "Can I see what's in the bag?"

Cole felt his forehead pucker as he stretched the duffel wide for her inspection.

"Okay." Her face flushed with the words. "I don't use the dead bolt. It sticks."

"Care if I put the new one on before I go? It won't stop

a professional from getting inside, but it'll slow one down, and in this neighborhood, time is your friend. I have a feeling those people on your lawn don't miss much."

Her lips turned down slightly. "You just happen to have a spare dead bolt with you?"

"No. I've been planning to change mine for months but haven't gotten around to it."

She seemed to mull that over. "Can you leave the door open while you work?"

"Sure." He applied the dusting powder to her knob and jamb. "You sure you can't think of anyone who'd want to get in here?"

"Like who?" Rita lifted a fancy pillow from the floor and clutched it to her chest.

Cole split his attention between her and his work. "I don't know. Maybe a rival or an ex. Maybe a lover's significant other?"

Her shocked expression turned to disgust. "That's awful." She dropped the pillow onto her couch and lined it up with the others. Delicate stitching over a tiny yellow flower formed the words *Suck it up Buttercup.*

Cole smiled.

She frowned. "I don't have any rivals or lunatic exes, and I certainly don't get involved with men who have significant others." She threw his final words back at him. "What kind of women do you normally deal with, Deputy Garrett?"

He smiled at the pleasant sound of his name on her tongue. "You can call me Cole." He stretched to his feet and extended a hand her way.

She eyeballed his hand. "I recognize you from the courthouse."

A smile spread over his lips. "Is that right?"

Rita blushed and slid her thin hand into his. "Can I make you some coffee?"

"That'd be nice." He turned back to the door with a rush of satisfaction.

Rita righted furniture and photos while Cole finished his work on her door and the coffee brewed. The small, inviting space was magazine perfect when he packed up his things. The overall result was very sexy librarian. Claw-footed furniture, books by the boatload and more fancy pillows with goofy sayings like *Hot Mess, Sassy*, and *Hell to the No*.

Cole shook his head. "You might want to think about getting a new knob, too. Maybe something with a code."

"Sure." She rolled the vacuum into view, then wiped a bead of sweat from her brow. "Coffee should be ready."

"Care if I shut the door and test the lock?"

"No. It's fine." She returned a moment later with two fragile-looking cups and set them on the coffee table. "Do you take cream or sugar?"

Cole laughed. "No, but thanks." He made a show of testing the door's integrity and admiring his personal handyman skills. "I think this is all set. I'll let you know about the prints." He dropped the keys to her new dead bolt on the table, then helped himself to a seat in the narrow armchair. "You live here alone?"

"Yeah. For a couple years since Ryan moved out."

Cole felt his jaw lock. "Ryan?" Maybe there was an angry ex out there somewhere who needed a swift kick in the ass. Cole adjusted his position in the little seat and hiked one foot onto the opposite leg. The idea of a man attempting to harm or frighten Rita set his teeth on edge.

"He's my little brother." She flipped the lid on a scrapbook beside his coffee. "There."

A younger, masculine version of Rita centered every

photo. Ryan was tall and gangly, like Cole used to be. At least eight inches taller than his big sister, who was tucked beneath his arm in many of the pictures. "You're close. That's nice. My family's like that. Painfully so."

She smiled.

"Did you say Ryan lived here?"

"Yeah. Until he moved into a dorm for freshman year. I was his legal guardian through high school." Deep sadness swam in her hazel eyes.

Cole found himself leaning forward, suddenly eager to understand her burdens and lighten them.

"Our mother was hit by a drunk driver in Oklahoma. Ryan came to live with me after the funeral."

"I'm sorry. I had no idea." He couldn't imagine losing a parent. Especially not in high school. And he surely couldn't have raised a teenager when he was in his twenties. "Your dad's not in the picture?"

She rolled her eyes and traced the gilded rim of her dainty cup with a fingertip. "No. He's in Kuwait or Afghanistan or somewhere else where people need him." There was no mistaking the disappointment in her tone. She set her cup aside and slid her palms up and down her thighs, then folded her fingers on her lap.

"Do I make you nervous?"

She looked at her feet. "No. Your presence is extremely comforting, actually, but I've had a long morning."

"And you don't feel well," he reminded her.

"Right."

"Anything you want to talk about?" he prompted.

Rita pressed her lips into a white line and shook her head.

He levered himself off the chair and went to fish a card from his bag, leaving his finished coffee where it stood.

There was little left for him to do if she wasn't talking, and West could use his help back at the docks.

She followed Cole to the door and opened it for him. Soft scents of vanilla and honey lifted from her skin and hair.

Cole scribbled his cell number across the back of his card. "If you need anything else or think of something you want to tell me, give me a call. I always answer, and I can be here quick. Meanwhile, I'll add your street to the other deputies' patrol routes."

"No. Don't." Rita's hand flashed up from her side, and curled around his wrist.

He waited for additional information that didn't come. "That's it? Just don't?"

Her home had been ransacked, but she didn't want to know the sheriff's department was keeping watch?

Her face went slack as she released him. "I'm fine. There's no need to send anyone else out. Thank you for coming." She practically shoved him across the threshold, then cranked the new lock behind him.

Cole dropped behind the wheel of his cruiser and grabbed the radio to call in his whereabouts before shifting into gear.

In the distance, a high-end sedan pulled away from the curb and took an immediate turn out of sight. Cole set the radio aside and reversed down the drive. He hadn't noticed the car when he went outside to walk Rita in, and it hadn't been there while he'd worked on her open door. Maybe it was nothing, or his attraction to Rita making him crazy, but something told him he'd better follow that car.

RITA WATCHED FROM her window as the handsome deputy pulled away. Cole Garrett wasn't the man from the docks and her office. She'd have recognized Cole anywhere. He was the one who settled fistfights outside the courtrooms and calmed criminals being loaded into vehicles destined for prison, and the one on his knees beside benches where folks cried over an unfair verdict. Cole Garrett was a peace-keeper and a hero.

When the coast was clear, Rita kicked off her heels and traded her pencil skirt for a pair of blue jeans. She stuffed bare feet into white, laceless sneakers and grabbed her laptop bag and purse.

Five minutes later, she parked Ryan's car against the curb outside a crowded café and wandered inside. On tele-vision, people being hunted always went somewhere with witnesses. The café seemed a smart choice. Even if she wasn't being hunted, it surely felt that way, and her home was too quiet. Too vulnerable. If someone got inside while she was there alone, the invader would have complete pri-vacy to do anything he wanted.

Her stomach protested the thought. "A bottle of water, please," she said to the barista.

"Three dollars." He set her order on the counter.

Rita gave him a five and walked away. She chose a tall table near the back of the brightly lit room and climbed onto a seat with a view of the front door and window, and also of the muted television anchored near the ceiling. She should've told Cole her story. She had to trust someone, and every cell in her body said she could unequivocally trust him. It was stupid that she hadn't. She dug his card from her bag and set it on the table. She needed to stop feeling overwhelmed and start figuring this mess out.

What would she say? Where should she begin?

The white noise of two dozen voices soothed her frayed nerves. She rubbed cold fingertips in small circles against her temples, plotting ways to open the disturbing conver-sation. *Hello, this is Rita Horn. I know we've only just met, but I wanted you to know that I think one of the other deputies is a murderer.*

She rolled her eyes as a silent peanut-butter commercial gave way to live coverage at the river.

She dropped her hands onto the table. Her heart leaped into her throat. She scanned the room full of oblivious people, all pecking at their phone screens or chatting with friends. Rita leaned across the table, wholly focused on the scrolling text beneath the coverage.

"Witnesses reported seeing members of the Cade County Sheriff's Department and Coroner's Office at this location early this morning. Crime scene tape and a number of road blocks have been put in place as the hours progress. Behind me you can see the continued presence of the CCSD. Our question is, why?"

The young reporter on-screen pressed her fingers against one ear and dropped her gaze. When she raised her face to the camera once more, her skin had gone ghost white.

"Sources have confirmed a body was pulled from the river just after sunrise."

Chapter Four

Rita rose on shaky legs as images of the coroner's van crossed the communal screen, a turbulent Ohio River in the background. An old factory and a dozen feline silhouettes anchored the scene.

Her ears began to ring as she strode conspicuously to the door, bumping into people and chair legs while watching the television for any last-minute announcements.

The wind was brisk and nippy as she shoved free of the coffee shop's warmth and safety onto the sidewalk where anyone could see her. Namely a nefarious deputy and the other man from the docks. The one who'd had blood on his dress shirt. She hurried to the little borrowed car and shoved her purse and laptop bag across the console. Rita locked the doors and checked her mirrors before dropping her forehead onto the steering wheel.

Think.

The men she'd seen at the docks had murdered someone. She'd heard the splash. Seen the blood.

And the men had seen her.

She raised her eyes to scan the street and sidewalks around her once more, begging her mind to focus. She couldn't stay at the coffee shop without someone noticing her imminent breakdown. She couldn't go home or back to work. The bad guys had already been there. She paused at the thought. *Bad guys.* Was this even her life?

"What do I do?" she whispered to her windshield. *They know who I am. Where I work and live.* What did they want? To kill her? Why? She hadn't seen anything. Couldn't even identify them. Though she had gotten a good look at the deputy who came to her office this morning and could give a rough description of the other guy—size, height, weight, but not much else. Her gaze traveled slowly to the bag on her passenger seat. *The pen.* What if it was evidence in a murder investigation, and she'd wadded it in tissues and stuffed it in a plastic baggie? There could be fingerprints or DNA evidence or an imperceptible thread. Forensics could find anything, and if the killers knew she had something linking them to the crime, they'd definitely want it back. So what should she do with it?

She considered tossing it out the window.

Her head spun as she pulled carefully into traffic. She should've told Deputy Garrett what had happened. Something in her gut said he had nothing to do with the man at her office or the crime scene. Deputy Garrett was trustworthy, and he would help her. There was no more doubt as to whether or not she'd been present for what she thought she'd been present for. She was a witness, albeit probably after the fact, to murder. And she was in danger.

It was time to do what she should've done all along.

She slowed at the traffic light and dug through her bag for the handsome deputy's business card. She'd call him as soon as she got to wherever she was going. Where was that?

The light turned green, and Rita lowered her foot against the gas pedal. The sun-bleached hula girl on her brother's dashboard bobbled. "Oh, no." A new and terrifying realization slid like ice into her stomach. If the bad guys knew who she was, where she worked and lived, then they also knew what she drove. And her little brother was currently driving it!

Rita applied brute force to the narrow pedal, racing through downtown, then over the bridge and across the river. She dialed Ryan repeatedly from every traffic light and stop sign.

No answer.

Her mind conjured ghastly images of her new silver truck rolled onto its top or sinking in the river, Ryan trapped inside.

"Hi, Ryan," she told his voice mail as calmly as possible. "It's me. Listen. I'm sorry, but I completely forgot I had a thing today, and you can't use my truck. I'll make it up to you as soon as I finish my thing." She cringed. Ryan would never accept her flimsy excuse without explanation, but she couldn't offer him anything more. Bringing him in on her mess would put him in danger. "Anyway, I'm on my way to your place now. I'll just trade you back real quick. Sit tight and I'll be there in ten."

She bit her lip, hating the lie. She'd promised Ryan long ago that he could always trust anything she said, and until now, she'd held tight to that promise. Hopefully he'd forgive her when she was able to explain the gruesome truth.

Rita switched to back roads as the campus came into view. Main routes and intersections were bogged with student traffic and puttering locals. The little hatchback took corners with ease as she cut through the rear entrance to Ryan's neighborhood. Her much larger truck would've barely passed through the narrow alleyways with cars parked on both sides. If his car didn't smell like a gym bag filled with burger grease, she'd agree to trade with him more often.

Finally, the home Ryan shared with two other students came into view.

The only vehicle in the driveway was another old compact.

"No." Rita pulled up to the curb and stared. Where was he? Why wasn't he answering her calls? Again, the scary images beat a path through her mind. *Please*, she sent up a silent prayer, *don't let anything happen to my baby brother*.

Her phone buzzed against her lap and she jumped.

Ryan's name appeared on the screen beside a tiny envelope. He'd sent her a text message.

She released a happy sob and swiped the screen to life.

Taking exam. Can't talk.

He was at school. She wiped her eyes and pulled in long, thankful breaths. Everything was fine. Ryan was safe. She was safe. All she had to do now was switch the vehicles and report everything she'd seen last night to Cole Garrett.

No problem.

The drive though the campus was steeped in nostalgia. Fall was in the air. Mums were in bloom. Even the leafy green trees had begun to change into their pretty fall uniforms. Rita had made memories to last a lifetime on those same streets not too long ago.

Students filled the corners near streetlamps, watching the lights, waiting to cross. Probably headed to class or on another adventure they'd miss dearly someday too soon. College had been Rita's only taste of freedom before becoming the surrogate parent to a grieving teenage brother just two months after graduation.

The main lot for student commuters was nearly full. She circled twice before spotting her truck among a pack of even larger pickups. She pulled Ryan's car into an empty spot several spaces away and tucked his keys under the floor mat. Much as she hated to interrupt him again, especially knowing he was trying to take an exam, she sent a text to let him know his car was there and her truck was off-limits for the day.

Your car is in the lot with my truck. DO NOT take my truck. I'll be back for it. Meeting a friend.

She frowned at the little screen and sent a happier follow-up.

Good luck on your tests!

Rita pocketed the phone and kneaded her shaky hands, then fumbled Deputy Garrett's card into her grip. The sooner she unloaded the truth about what she thought she'd seen last night, and the possible murder evidence from her bag, the sooner she'd feel like herself again.

She double-checked for anyone who looked as if they might be following her, then began the trek across the giant lot toward a busier portion of campus. "Here goes nothing," she whispered, bringing the phone into view and tapping the numbers against her screen.

COLE LEFT HIS cruiser in the middle of the road beside West's and jogged around a line of news vans and local reporters. Crime scene officials tramped the soggy ground near the body recovery site, and a woman in a county coroner's office jacket picked through the area blocked off by yellow tape.

Cole had lost track of the fancy black car after leaving Rita Horn's place, but something in his gut told him the vehicle was significant. The timing of its appearance and haste of its departure were undeniably suspect, and given the break-in, Cole sensed a connection. Maybe Rita had been holding back about who could've wrecked her place, and maybe that certain someone owned a late-model black sedan. His hands curled into fists at his sides. The idea of someone intending her harm knotted his muscles and tightened his jaw.

West caught Cole's arrival and left the quarantined area with an expectant look. "Everything okay with the house? Was it a B and E or false alarm?"

"B and E," Cole grouched. He rubbed the back of his neck and rolled his shoulders, attempting and failing to dislodge the mound of frustration piling there. "It was Rita Horn's place."

West rocked back on his heels with a grin. "That so?"

"Yeah. You know her?"

West smiled. "I believe I do. That's the redhead from the courthouse?"

Cole worked his jaw, unimpressed that his older brother knew Rita existed. Not that he was in the market for a date. West already had a stunning wife, a toddler and a new baby on the way. And he wasn't the sort to have a wandering eye. Still, the conspiratorial look on his face was starting to tick Cole off.

"How well do you know her?" He had three brothers, and they were all known for their ability to get women into bed with a wink and a smile.

"Are you kidding?" West cocked a hip and crossed his arms. "Isn't she the one you used to talk about all the time?"

Cole shot his brother a droll look. "I mentioned her *once*, months ago, and I didn't know her name. I'd hardly call that 'all the time.'"

"Compared to the vast number of other women you never mention, once is a lot. Did you get her number?"

"Yeah. From Dispatch, but she didn't answer."

West barked a laugh and shook his head. "All right. If you're here, then everything must be fine there. So let's figure this one out." West led the way back to the river where the fog hovered like an apparition over the swollen waters, muting the view of a busy college town across the way.

"We know the victim's name was Roger Minsk." West pulled a notebook from his coat pocket and flipped the pages.

"Never heard of him."

"He hasn't been in town long. According to county records, he bought a big house upriver this summer. The maid called the station to report him missing three days ago. I haven't had time to follow up." He furrowed his brow. "She said he was a businessman who traveled."

Cole shook his head. "No one's blaming this on you. He's a grown man. With a maid." His nose wrinkled as the information settled in. Not a lot of folks in Shadow Point kept maids, even if they could afford it. "Who does that?"

West dropped his attention back to the notepad. "Well, this guy, for starters. She didn't have access to his calendar or contacts, so I wasn't in a hurry to worry. I knocked on his door that night and again yesterday. No answer. He was on our list of things to look into if he didn't show up by today. I was hoping he was on vacation."

"Did the maid say anything else?"

"She said she cleans for Minsk twice a week and nothing had changed since the last time she'd been there. It didn't look as if he'd slept in his bed the night before."

"So we don't know when he went missing, but we have a window."

West nodded. "The medical examiner will get us a time of death. I'd say we know the cause."

Right. The gunshot wound to the head was hard to miss.

Cole turned back toward his cruiser. "I'll visit the maid, see what I can find out about the victim, then report back. Maybe I can even get her to let me into his place. Two birds."

"Yep." West agreed. "Do it. I'll be here if you need me. Don't forget to check in. We don't know who we're looking for or what this is about, and I don't like it."

Cole waved a hand overhead, making good time across the empty field, a list of questions for the maid solidifying in his mind.

"Deputy?" West called from the growing distance between them.

"Yeah?" Cole pivoted on his next step, for a look back at his brother, still standing sentinel at the river. He lifted his chin in question.

"Do me a favor and check in on Miss Horn while you're out. See if she needs anything."

"Yep."

West raised one arm in his direction. "Maybe dinner and a movie."

Cole turned away with a smile. "I'm keeping it professional," he called over one shoulder.

Not like West and his wife. They'd reunited last year after a decade apart. One minute, she was involved in a crime spree, and the next thing Cole knew, he was standing witness in a rented tuxedo as the two said their vows.

Pass. Cole wanted all those things one day, but he had a lot of other things he wanted to do first. Find out who tossed that man in the river, for example.

He waved off a renegade reporter headed his way. "No comment." And ducked behind the wheel of his cruiser. This was what held Cole's interest. A puzzle. A mystery. Protecting the peace. These were the things that kept him up at night and got him out of bed in the morning.

He pulled slowly away from the crime scene, taking note

of the smattering of faces in the gathering crowd. Had one of them seen something they weren't willing to divulge? Had they been around last night, feeding cats and playing unwitting witness to murder? If his theory was right about another person being present, he could only hope they wouldn't wash up on the riverbank like Roger Minsk.

Cole's phone buzzed against his ribs, pulling his attention away from the crowd. He freed it from his inside jacket pocket. Rita Horn's number lit the little screen. "Deputy Garrett," he answered, already pointing his car in the direction of her home. A rush of anxiety tightened his grip. If she was in trouble...

"Hi, um, this is Rita Horn. From this morning. I had the ransacked house."

An easy smile curved his lips. She was okay. His foot eased back on the gas. "I remember. How's the lock working out?"

"Okay, I think. I'm not home, actually. I hoped we could talk somewhere in person."

The background noise registered with him, then dozens of voices and...

"Is that a marching band?"

"Uh. I think. I can't see it from here, but it's football season, so I guess. I'm at the college in Rivertown. Can you meet me at the library near the square? Do you know it?"

Cole took the next left toward the bridge over the river. "Sure. Can you tell me what's going on?"

Wind crackled through the phone. Rita didn't speak.

"Go on," he urged. "You called for a reason. Let me have it."

"Okay," she began, then paused once more.

"Rita?"

"I was at the docks last night, and I think I'm being stalked by a murderer."

Chapter Five

Cole's gut fisted. His fingers whitened on the steering wheel, and he rammed his foot against the gas pedal. *Rita was the witness*. She'd fed the cats. *Of course she had*. He shook his head as the cruiser raced across Memorial Bridge. Away from West and the crime scene. Directly toward the insanely captivating redhead who fed homeless cats and people, and raised a teenage brother when she was barely done being a teen herself. Toward a woman whose kind heart and good deeds had just gotten her into serious trouble.

If she was right about being followed, Cole had to reach her before the killer did.

Cole had no idea why Mr. Minsk was killed, but whatever had tainted his life should never have crossed paths with Rita Horn. Not now. Not ever.

Definitely not on Cole's watch.

He eased his foot off the pedal as the small college town popped up around him with its spirit shops and mascot-logoed flags on every lamppost. The pounding of a marching band's bass line thundered in the distance.

Hordes of distracted students took their sweet time jaywalking across the street in front of him, holding him up, keeping him from Rita. He tapped his thumbs against the wheel and considered using the siren, though it had no jurisdiction here. The water behind them had officially yielded his badge void. "Come on," he growled, the fear in Rita's voice still ringing in his ears.

The street cleared, and the light overhead turned red. "Dammit!"

Cole snatched his phone off the passenger seat where he'd tossed it and dialed West. He should've called him sooner. Told him about Rita's confession. Asked where the library was. Now he was wasting precious time and growing unhappier by the second.

"Sheriff Garrett." West answered on the first ring.

Cole rolled his eyes. "Hey. I'm over in Rivertown, meeting Rita. She called to tell me she was at the docks last night."

The line was silent for a long beat before West cursed quietly under his breath. "She bought the cat food."

"Looks like it. At least now we know why someone tossed her place this morning." And why she'd been so on edge. It also explained why she'd left work feeling sick, but hadn't looked it. "She thinks the killer's stalking her."

West swore again. Louder this time. "Why are you in Rivertown? Bring her to the station so we can talk."

The light changed, and Cole inched into the intersection before another swarm of students could hold him up again. "I'm not clear on the *why* yet. She asked me to meet her at the library. I think her little brother is a student here. She could be checking up on him."

"Was he with her last night?" West asked. "Did she tell you anything else?"

"No." Cole scanned the crowded sidewalks. "Where is the library?" He could find it himself with a little more time. The campus wasn't big, but time was something Cole didn't have to spare. "I haven't been here since high school. Were there always this many people?" He checked each passing face for the woman he longed to save, but she wasn't among the crowds.

West gave him blow-by-blow directions to the center of campus.

A white marble fountain stood proudly outside the building marked Library, spraying crystal clear water into the cloudless blue sky. Cole took the last available parking spot and fed the meter a handful of quarters before jogging through the library's front door.

RITA ORDERED A cup of hot tea and took a seat at the window inside a nearby café. The library had been uncomfortably silent and borderline terrifying. Not enough witnesses. She hadn't been able to stay. Her imagination had wreaked havoc within seconds, and she'd darted back onto the crowded, familiar streets for a deep breath of air. A café with large window and view of the library seemed a smart compromise. From here, she'd see Cole's arrival.

Rita pointed her chair at the window. Paranoia crawled over her skin like a thousand baby spiders. She couldn't shake the feeling that she wasn't safe, not even in another town. As if the bridge and river weren't enough distance to protect her from whatever was happening. She inhaled the aroma of her drink and willed the sweet steam to ease her jangled nerves. She also tried closing her lids and counting to ten.

Nothing helped.

Rita let her gaze make quick and continuous loops around the square between sips, checking the street and sidewalks in both directions. So far, no sign of Cole Garrett or any other Cade County deputies.

Good, evil or otherwise.

A clutch of women in blue-and-white hoodies crossed the street, leaving a black sedan in clear view. The vehicle crept along the street outside, dark tinted windows staring back at her, and disappeared around the corner.

Rita worked to swallow the mouthful of suddenly tasteless tea before she choked on it. *Sedans are common*, she told herself.

Breathe. Relax. Deputy Garrett is on his way.

Wasn't he? Her gaze jumped to the library entrance across the street. Where was he?

She pushed the teacup aside and leaned over the table on her elbows, stretching for a look in the direction the sedan had gone.

The little bell over the café's front door jingled, setting her back on her seat. A man strode inside. Too old to be a student. Too casual for a professor. He locked gazes with her, and Rita tilted her head to take him in. There was something in his stride that sent her heart into a fresh sprint. He lifted his brows, and Rita spun in her chair, fixing her eyes on the library outside once more.

It's not him. It's not him, she chanted mentally.

Rita kept the silent refrain going, but couldn't bring herself to believe the words. How could she be sure? She hadn't seen either man's face clearly last night, but the sedan had just rolled by... Rita peeked over her shoulder at the man, now poised at the counter.

The long angles of his arms and lean cut of his waist drew itchy memories over her skin. Was this the same man from her office earlier today? If so, what had happened to the deputy jacket?

The memory of hushed footfalls echoed in her mind, making her breaths shudder.

Her tummy rocked, and an uncomfortable sheen of sweat broke over her goose-pimpled skin. She wasn't built for this kind of life. She'd made herself sick many times with worry, always about her brother's well-being or the health and safety of others. She worried about homeless and injured animals, her fledgling garden and whether or not she'd left the iron on. Those were problems she could deal with. This...

She imagined the man at the counter in a bulky deputy's jacket, marching her way, chasing her through the night. What if he approached her discreetly and pressed a gun to her back? Then tossed her in the trunk and drove her to the river?

Nope.

She gathered the straps of her bags with hasty fingers and slid, nearly fell, off her chair, but the packed-up laptop case caught on the table's edge. "Sorry," she apologized to no one in particular, before stumbling over the table leg and ramming her shoulder into the café door on her way out. Cole or no Cole, Rita couldn't stay. She ducked her head against the number of stunned faces still inside the café, now watching her as she passed the window outside.

The newcomer's eyes were narrow, and his lips were turned down. He made a move for the door, but Rita didn't wait to see where he was headed.

Her flying heart carried her through knots and clusters of students on street corners and outside shops. She darted around a lamppost and into a bookstore she knew had a back exit that opened into a brick courtyard with a gate to an alley. She'd used them both many times during her four-year tenure in Rivertown, perpetually running late to class, often the result of a novel she couldn't put down.

Street noise filled her ears as she landed in the store's rear courtyard. A sprinkle of quiet students in wooden lounge chairs glanced her way, then back to their phones or books, unconcerned by her sudden and probably wild appearance.

Rita followed the picket fence at a crouch. She peeked

over the top once, after a strong internal pep talk to convince herself it was important to see the bad guy before he saw her.

She stopped at the rear gate and pressed her forehead to the cool wooden slats. Anxiety twisted her gut and paralyzed her limbs. Maybe she didn't have to go out there again. Maybe Cole could meet here where she was.

She rubbed her sweat-slicked palms over her jeans, one by one, juggling the phone with each move. Then she hunched her shoulders over her cell phone and sent a text to Deputy Garrett.

Where are you?

Cole's response was immediate. I'm at the library. Where are you?

Of course. He'd gone straight to their meeting place, like she should have. The silence and lack of bodies hadn't frightened him the way it had her.

Rita pulled in a restorative breath and let it out with resolve. Everything was okay now. The library was just down the alley and across the street. She only needed to leave the safety of the fence and get on with it.

She nodded at her screen, then typed On my way.

The phone rang in her shaky hand as she shoved the creaky gate open, creating an escape hatch from the enclosed bookshop patio. Cole's number appeared on her screen.

Her heart settled at the sight of it. "Hi."

"Hey." Cole's voice was strong and steady. "I'm standing outside the library. Tell me where you are, and I'll come to you. You don't have to walk alone."

"I appreciate that. I might be wrong, but I think one of the men I saw last night is here, too."

"Where?"

"Possibly in the café across from the library. I got nervous and left. Now I'm leaving the bookshop on River Drive. I cut through when I thought I was being followed." And if she made it to Cole fast enough, she might make it home without a nervous breakdown.

Rita rolled her shoulders back, borrowing from his confidence.

She stepped into the midday sun and examined the passing faces. "I don't see him now. It was probably nothing. I might be losing my mind, actually."

"You're not." Cole assured her. "You've been through a trauma. Give yourself some credit for brilliance."

"Brilliance?"

"You called me for help."

Rita snickered. "An ego to go with the face. Isn't that always the way?"

"You like my face?"

She smiled against the receiver, enjoying the sudden and blatant curiosity in Cole's voice. He had to know he was handsome. According to the rumors, not that she listened, there were four Garrett brothers, all gorgeous, all lawmen, and all terminally single until recently. But that was fine. She didn't need a date. She needed a protector, and the rumors about the Garretts being unstoppable forces of nature were repeated with as much fervor as those about their sexual prowess.

Those were the rumors she'd put her hope in.

She hurried away from the courtyard. Through a wall of ambling jocks and across the little street. The weight of her situation rolled away as the school's library sign came into view. The door was only ten yards away, just around the next corner. Safety was so close she could throw a stone and hit it. "I see the fountain," she said. "I'm almost…"

The sound of a revving engine cut through her words. A black sedan moved down the street in her direction.

Her mouth opened as the car bore down on her, but only a strangled sound emerged.

"Rita?" Cole barked through the receiver.

Her limbs were leaden as the car tore through the alley in her direction, increasing in speed and chasing students out of its way with a growl.

Her heart ached through to her backbone.

"Rita!" Cole hollered. "Move!" His voice echoed through the phone's speaker and in the air. Cole appeared in the distance, running full speed from the café where she'd seen the creepy man. "Run!"

Adrenaline shot through her limbs like lightning bolts, propelling her suddenly away from the car, around café tables on the sidewalk outside a pizza shop and down the narrow street once filled with students. She pumped her arms and legs as the engine roared closer and lunged for the historic marble fountain moments later, tossing her phone and bags before colliding smartly with the fountain's edge and soaring headlong into the recycled water. Her shins and palms were on fire from the collision before her head cracked against the carved angel's feet.

Her face submerged and, for a moment, there was nothing but icy water everywhere.

She arose with a gasp, pulling in lungfuls of oxygen and scrambling around the fountain's center.

The sound of squealing brakes and screaming people snapped her thoughts back into focus. The car!

"Stop!" Cole's demand rang through the chaos, much closer now.

She wiped her eyes and spun in search of the voice she'd only known a short while, but could somehow pick out of a wailing crowd.

The engine revved once more as the car changed direction and roared softly into the distance.

She collapsed backward into the water, fighting an onslaught of tears. Her limbs trembled and her teeth chattered. She sat upright, knees pulled to her chest, overcome with panic and confusion.

Dozens of people stared openly, pointing their cell phones in her direction. Her brother was going to die of humiliation when he saw the footage and be infinitely angry she hadn't opened up to him about what happened at the docks.

She dropped her head forward and begged her mind to think.

How could she possibly explain this away?

A set of strong hands wrapped around her elbows and hoisted her from the water with a whoosh.

Rita screamed. Her feet found purchase on the ground outside the fountain, and she locked her palms together on instinct to thrust against her assailant's chest, sending him back several steps.

Cole relented, palms up as he widened his stance and waited. "Hey. It's just me." He watched silently as her scrambled brain put the pieces together.

"Cole!" Recognition hit, and Rita flung herself at him. She buried her face against his shoulder and exhaled the suffocating terror from her lungs. "I thought I was dead. I thought he'd kill me right here in front of everyone."

Cole's broad, warm hands found the small of her back and pressed her to him. "You're okay, Rita." His heart thrummed beneath her ear, chest rising and falling in quick bursts.

The sound of her name on his lips sent a shiver down her spine. The soft scents of spearmint, earth and aftershave that wafted off his heated skin didn't help.

She peeled herself away with burning cheeks. "You're soaked." She brushed the sodden fabric of his uniform shirt with shaky hands. "I'm soaked and now... I'm so sorry."

Rita locked her knees in frustration, and the tears began to flow.

"Hey." Cole pulled her back against him and stroked her sopping hair. "I won't let anyone hurt you. Okay? But you've got to trust me." He took her hands in his, and led her away from the wretched fountain and massive crowd. "First, let's get you out of here. I need to call this in, and you need something dry to wear. I've got towels and a first aid kit in the gym bag in my cruiser. How hurt are you?"

"I'm not."

He turned her palm up in his, both their hands now painted with her blood. "No?"

"Scrapes. From the marble."

He nodded stiffly. "What else?"

Her legs were sore and her head was fuzzy. "Bruises. Ow." Her vision blurred. "I think I hit my..." Rita's knees buckled and the world went black.

Chapter Six

Cole stroked wet hair from Rita's face as he buckled her into the passenger seat of his car. This day had gone from strange to downright bizarre in a matter of hours. Luckily, Rita would be okay. "Hey."

Her eyes flitted open then pulled shut.

"Rita?" Cole pressed a palm to her cheek. "You with me?"

She squirmed, apparently confused by the seat belt. Her eyes widened and her arms swung for him.

Cole dodged the blow. That wouldn't happen again. He collected her wrists in one of his hands and put on his warmest smile. "You shouldn't hit lawmen. There's a law against that. Plus, it hurts." He made a show of rubbing his chest where she'd landed the earlier hit.

Color rushed to her cheeks. "Sorry." She squirmed to take in her new surroundings. "What happened?"

"You passed out. I carried you to my car." Cole tugged her safety belt, making sure it was securely latched. "How's your head?"

She groaned.

Cole flashed a penlight in her direction. "Can you follow the light?"

She squinted, but got the job done.

"Okay." He lifted a finger before shutting her inside the

cruiser and rounding the hood to the driver's side. Behind
the wheel, he twisted for a look in her direction. "You were
chased by a lunatic in a black sedan. Tinted windows. No
plates. Any chance you got a look at the driver?"

She shook her head.

"You would've been killed if you hadn't dived into the
fountain. You hit your head doing that. Then you hit me.
Then you passed out. And here we are."

She rubbed her eyes and groaned.

Cole pointed his cruiser toward the bridge, waving to a
set of campus security officers. "Those guys showed up as
I was hauling you off the street. I barely caught you before
you hit your head again." He chuckled. "You were right in
the middle of telling me how well you felt."

"I think I have a concussion."

"You don't." He smiled, happy to know that was true.
She was fine. Slightly banged up, but all things considered,
Rita was stellar. "It wasn't the head injury that knocked
you out, but that goose egg is going to look a lot worse before it starts looking better."

Rita dissolved against his passenger seat. Her fingers
sought the wound. She winced when she found it.

"Shock will do that to people. The fainting, not the
goose egg. Anyway, you're fine now."

"Except someone still wants to kill me."

"Yeah." There was that. He ground his teeth. He needed
to fix that. "You're having a bad day."

She laughed humorlessly, eyes fixed on the world outside her window. "Very bad."

"And you're all wet."

"I need to go home," she said.

"Already on it." Cole took the bridge back to Shadow
Point at half the speed he'd used to arrive in Rivertown.

Rita closed her eyes. "Why are you so calm, and how do you know I'm okay?" Her teeth chattered.

Cole ached to stroke the curve of her clenched jaw. "You're with me now. You're definitely going to make it, Horn."

She rolled her head in his direction, blinking through tear-filled eyes. "And how can you be sure I'm not concussed?"

"Medical school."

Rita's rosebud mouth pulled into a droll expression. "Of course."

"I dropped out," he said, "so I'm not a doctor, but I was a medic in the army, and I've been bandaging up my brothers all my life. My uncle's an EMT, too, so that helped."

Rita straightened in her seat. "Wait a minute. You quit medical school to be a deputy?"

"Law's in the blood, I guess."

"I guess," she agreed. "Clearly also a hero complex."

"Not the first time I've been accused of that. I guess we have something in common."

Rita wrinkled her nose. "What?"

"The hero complex." He watched for understanding that never came, then tried again. "What do you call what you do?"

"Paperwork?"

"No," he corrected. "Feeding stray cats and making lunches for the homeless. You know all their names, and I don't even know all the bailiffs. What do you call yourself, if not a hero?"

A wave of pink spread over her cheeks. "Nothing. I'm just…trying."

Cole worked to redirect his thoughts from that blush and all the other ways he'd like to summon it.

A few creative images came immediately to mind.

Rita's lips parted. She dropped her sweet hazel gaze to her lap before raising her eyes to him once more. "I try to make a difference."

Her words hit Cole in the chest. So much kindness in one small package. How did a woman like Rita Horn go unattached? If Cole were looking for something serious, which he wasn't, and she wasn't an endangered civilian in his care, which she was, maybe there could have been something between them.

Like what? He chastised himself. *Pull it together, Garrett.*

Ten silent minutes later, Cole pulled into Rita's driveway.

Rita unlocked the door and welcomed him inside.

The house was exactly as he remembered. No one had been back while Rita was out. Then again, he'd already known the person responsible for overturning her place was likely the same one driving the sedan across the river.

He helped himself to a seat on her couch while she went to change clothes.

Cole checked his texts and listened to the handful of messages that had collected during his drive back to town. Campus security had conveyed the details of the attack to their local authorities. Rivertown police were interviewing the mass of witnesses and would report to West on the matter.

The phone vibrated in his hand, and West's face appeared on his screen.

"You got something?" Cole moved the phone to his ear.

"Yeah, a pair of empty seats across from my desk. Where are you?"

"Rita's place. She's cleaning up from her fall in the fountain."

"Get her here as soon as you can. Meanwhile, tell me what you learned." The sound of West's creaky desk chair echoed in the quiet background. Cole could practically see his older brother rubbing the stress lines off his forehead.

"Nothing," he admitted, "but we'll head over to the sheriff's department next."

"No!" Rita appeared on the stairs, white as a ghost and looking fit to run. She'd showered and changed at an impressive speed, and from the looks of her, she didn't plan to stay put.

"Why not?" Cole's voice sounded in time with West's through the line.

"Did she say no?" West barked. "Why the hell not?"

Cole studied the fresh fear in Rita's eyes. "I'll call you back." He tossed the phone onto the coffee table and scooted to the edge of the couch, hands clasped between his knees.

Rita took the final few stairs slowly, an apology written on her face. "I'm sorry. I know that's not what you wanted to hear, and you've already done so much."

"Why don't you have a seat," Cole suggested. "Tell me why you look half terrified to go to the sheriff's department. What will happen there?"

"I don't know." She wet her lips and lowered onto the cushion beside him, leaving only a few inches from his knee to hers. "I need to tell you something, but you aren't going to like it."

"Try me." He relaxed his position, trading the forward lean for a casual slouch and pivot in her direction.

She drew her feet beneath her and pulled in a long breath. Her scent drifted to him in a cloud of temptation.

"Rita?" he pushed. "It's okay. You can tell me anything."

Her emotion-filled eyes enticed him to reach for her. She scanned the room before setting her gaze remorsefully on Cole. "The man I saw at the docks last night was a Cade County deputy."

RITA WATCHED AS Cole's expression stretched from shock to disbelief.

"No." He shook his head. "No way."

She released a deep sigh. "Yes. I saw him."

"Who?"

"I didn't get his name, if that's what you're asking, but one of you has been following me all day. To my work. To my brother's school. You'll have to excuse me if I'm in no hurry to deliver myself to him at the station."

"Whoa." Cole raised his palms. "Let's start again. How do you know he's a Cade County deputy?"

"I saw him. The man at the docks, the same one who visited my office, wore a jacket just like yours. Actually, it's possible they were two different men," she corrected. "Either way, I saw the Cade County Sheriff's Department logo on the jacket both times. I'm sure of it."

"What about the man you saw in Rivertown?"

"No jacket." Intuition had told her the man from the café was dangerous, but she couldn't be sure he was the same man from the docks. "And I didn't see him driving the car."

Cole nodded. "That's okay. You remember what he looks like?"

"Yes."

"That's a good start." Cole handed his phone to her. "I believe you saw a man in a deputy's jacket, but it had to be a fake. Folks see a lawman, they tend to look the other way."

Rita bit her lip. Personally, she found the uniform captivating, but she wasn't about to say so.

"There are only six of us," Cole continued. "West, me and four other men I love like family." He pointed to the phone screen. Pictures from a picnic centered the frame. "Move through those. See if your man's in there. The whole team made an appearance that day, and I've got pictures of everyone."

Rita studied each photo, taking in the details, peeking into a day in Cole's life. She had to admit it looked like fun. Volleyball. Horseshoes. Enough food to feed an army and enough people to form one. "This is all your family?"

"Most of it. Not everyone could make it, but quite a few friends showed up, too. Like the other deputies. Everyone stopped in before and after their shifts."

"Reunion?" she guessed.

"Nah. Housewarming for one of my brothers and his new wife." Cole crossed his arms and smiled. "It was a good day."

Rita shook her head in awe. "We've never had that. The military moved our family too often to really grow roots. People were usually nice, but it was always just Mom, Ryan and me. Now it's just the two of us, and Ryan's got his own life across the river."

"Sounds lonely."

"It can be," she admitted. "So I reach out to others."

Cole drifted closer. Conflict burned in his deep blue eyes.

Rita turned her attention back to his phone. She looked at each face carefully. "I didn't get a good look at the man's face last night, but my gut says he's not here. He's shorter and more heavily muscled than these men, built more like the man from the café." She returned the phone to him, then stood and moved onto the stairs. "I have something I want to give you."

His cheek ticked up. He hooked one boot over the opposite knee and opened his arms along the back of the couch. Whatever he was thinking, he kept it to himself.

Her tiger cat sashayed in his direction, blinking curious green eyes.

"Be right back." Rita grabbed her purse off her bed and returned to his side. "I found this on the docks beside a big puddle of blood." Her tongue stuck to the roof of her mouth, preventing her from saying anything more. Instead, she liberated the pen from her bag and handed it to Cole.

Cole traded her the mewing tiger cat on his lap for the evidence in her hand. "This was with the blood?"

"Yeah. I put it in the baggie so it wouldn't get ruined. I think that was what they were after when they broke in here today." She stroked the kitty's head and nuzzled him close to her cheek. "At first I thought one of the cats was hurt. That's why I ignored the no-trespassing sign."

Cole chuckled. He rolled smart blue eyes up at her and smiled. "This pen could be all we need to find the killer. You did good, Horn."

"Thanks." She hid her face in the feline's fur.

Cole watched.

Her puffy white Persian, Snowball, appeared at Cole's feet. She eyeballed the tiger cat in Rita's arms, then turned to the deputy on her couch. Snowball climbed onto Cole's lap and flopped onto her side.

Cole's hands dived into her soft, downy fur and drew out a long enthusiastic purr. "How many cats do you have?"

"Three." She cleared her throat. "I've had more, but these guys get territorial. When I have more than three, it's because I'm fostering until someone else can find a forever home."

Cole's smile waned.

"What?"

"No. Nothing." He set the cat aside and took a spin around the room. He rubbed the top of his head. "Someone knows you have that pen."

"I think so. Yeah."

He turned to face her. "Then we should probably get going."

"Where?"

"Look." He moved cautiously in her direction. "I know you don't want to visit the sheriff's department, but West has questions of his own for you."

Rita stepped back.

Cole flashed an easy, heart-melting smile, and he extended an upturned palm. "I can keep you safe. Do you trust me?"

Rita considered her answer. She trusted Cole. Maybe West. She hadn't recognized any of the other men in the photos. Maybe Cole was right. Maybe the jacket had been a fake. "Fine." Rita collected her purse and laptop bag, dragging both high onto her shoulder. "I can't believe my laptop didn't wind up in the fountain."

Cole dropped his hand, but held the smile. "It was on the cement, right about where you dived in. You're lucky it isn't a pile of plastic bits and keys."

Rita ripped into the bag for a look at her device. Everything seemed intact. "Thank goodness." She smiled in relief. "Wait." A new worry presented itself in Rita's mind. "How do you suppose that black car was able to find me in another town?"

Cole pushed his hands into his pockets. "I saw one like it outside your house when I left today. I tried following, but I lost it in traffic. It could've been following you all morning. Or…" He turned in a sudden circle, lips parted and eyes narrowed. "Someone trashed your house but didn't take anything."

"I had the pen with me. In my bag."

Cole raised his hand once more. "Can I see your bag?"

"Sure." She unhooked both sets of straps from her shoulder and handed them over.

"Did you have both these bags with you all day? Even at work?"

"Not the laptop. I use my work computer while I'm there."

Cole turned the bag inside out, sweeping his hand over the material in a methodical pattern. His eyebrows rose, and his hand withdrew from the bag with a tiny black dot on the end of one finger. "Is this yours?"

"What is it?"

Cole tipped his hand between them, examining the little plastic thing on his finger. "Someone put a tracker in your laptop bag."

Rita covered her mouth. Who would do something like that? Who could do something like that? Not an average thug. The other man's suit and bloody dress shirt came back to mind. "There was a second man," she said, realizing only then that she'd never told Cole about him. "He was dressed up. A suit and tie, but his face was in shadows."

Cole stretched impossibly taller. "I don't know what you stumbled into, but I think it's time I get you out of here." He grabbed his phone and swiped the screen to life. "Pack a bag and let's go."

Chapter Seven

Rita admired the view as Cole parked the cruiser in front of a sensible Craftsman-style bungalow near the national forest. Forgotten barns peppered the rolling landscape, leaned precariously against the horizon. Overgrown fields swayed and stretched in the afternoon breeze, contained loosely by a sturdy-looking pasture fence. They'd negotiated a trade on the way over. She'd agreed to stay with Cole temporarily, just until the killer was caught or a more secure option arose, and he'd agreed to get West to question her at his place instead of the station.

Rita gave her handsome driver an appraising look. "This is where you live?"

"Yeah." He cracked the door and stepped onto the gravel.

Rita watched in the rearview mirror as he popped the trunk and shouldered her bags, arriving a moment later at her door. "You realize you have to get out of the car to get inside the house, right?" he asked through her still-closed door.

Rita joined him on the long narrow drive, taking in the distance to the road and nearest homes, mere dots on the horizon. "This is really secluded."

"Private," he corrected. "It takes my family longer to get here than anywhere else, so they're more likely to knock on West's or Blake's door than mine." He cocked an eyebrow. "I had a place in town for a few years, but I could barely think between doorbell rings."

Rita considered the new information. "I didn't peg you for a loner." More like Mr. Congeniality.

"I'm not," he said, opening the front door. "I love my family. My friends."

"But you like to be alone," she finished.

Cole turned a curious look in her direction. "Yeah."

Rita nodded. "Me, too."

Cole lifted a finger as they crossed the threshold. "Wait here."

Rita watched from her position in the open living area as Cole made a sweep of the home before returning to her side. From where she stood, it was easy to see the kitchen, back door and loft, and a hallway to another set of rooms.

He raised his easy smile. "Ready for the tour?"

Rita hesitated. It had been a long time since a man had invited her to his home. "Sure." Reluctantly she followed him through the modest rooms, mostly decorated in outdoor equipment and pictures of him and his friends doing everything from fishing to hiking. She imagined clinging to his middle as she joined him on one of the mud-soaked four-wheelers or drenched with lake water after a dive off his boat.

Clearly, the stress was taking a toll on her mind.

Cole dropped her bags on the end of a tidy bed in an otherwise messy room. His style was clearly bachelor minimalist, but this room looked like one where he was always in a hurry. Clothes were draped over the hamper and a corner chair. Stacks of jeans lined the wall behind an open closet door.

"Sorry." Cole tossed stray items into the closet and

kicked the door shut. "This room doesn't get a lot of attention. I'm always on my way in or out, so…"

She turned her eyes away from the bed. Either local rumors about his nightlife were exaggerated, or Cole just didn't bring the parade of women here. Either way, she stupidly liked the idea that he'd invited her. "It's fine. Where will you sleep?"

"Won't." The word was out in an instant, and Cole headed back into the hall.

"Why not?"

"Well, for one thing, I don't sleep well. Not since the military. For another—" he turned to look at her over his shoulder "—as long as you're with me, I'm on duty."

"Oh." She caught up with him in the narrow hall. "I can stay at a hotel. You shouldn't lose sleep over me."

He gave a disbelieving laugh, as if she'd hit on some inside joke. "I'll survive."

Cole stripped his uniform shirt off, exposing a plain white T-shirt beneath. He hung the button-down on the back of a chair pulled up to the kitchen island, then went to open the refrigerator. "Let's eat, and then we can figure out what's next."

"You don't know?" Rita climbed onto a seat at the counter and fought a new round of panic bubbling in her core.

"Not yet," he said, no trace of concern in his tone. Cole collected glasses from the cabinet and dropped stacks of ice into them. "It's early and you still have a lot to tell me. Plus, I need to talk with West. He's been on the case since before dawn." A body in the river, a break-in at Rita's, an attempted hit-and-run in Rivertown all before two o'clock. If the pace kept up, it was going to be one hell of a night.

"How long do you think I'll be here?" she asked. "Until morning? Longer? What will people think? How long will

Mrs. Wilcox have to watch my cats? Can I go to work tomorrow or should I call off?"

Cole set a glass in front of her. "Drink this."

"What is it?"

"Ice water." He looked her over carefully. "How are you feeling? Besides afraid?"

She forced her attention away from his lips, ignored the way his T-shirt fit his lean body as if it had been cut just for him, and searched for an answer that had nothing to do with the butterflies in her knotted tummy. "I'm not thinking clearly." That was true enough. She gulped the water. "Probably stress and the head injury."

Cole rounded the counter with concern in his eyes. "What do you mean?" He turned the seat of her stool until she faced him, then crouched to meet her at eye level. "Your thoughts are unclear? How's your vision?"

"Fine. I thought you said I was okay."

"That was before you said you aren't thinking clearly. What if I missed something?" He raised steady palms to outline her face, then brushed away the swath of bangs she'd arranged over the bump on her forehead.

Rita shivered.

"My hands are probably cold," he warned, flicking his gaze to the glass of ice water he'd delivered to her.

"They're nice," she said.

He pulled a penlight from his pocket with a smile and pointed it at her. "Follow this."

She trailed the pen with her eyes. "I didn't mean I couldn't think. Just that I'm thinking crazy thoughts."

Cole lifted a questioning brow, but put the light away. "One more thing, if you don't mind." He leaned closer, running his palms over her neck and shoulders, enveloping her in the deliciously masculine scent of him. "Any unusual pains? Anything that doesn't seem right to you?"

"No." Everything seemed right to her.

"Neck pain beyond the bruises?"

"No."

"Double vision? Seeing spots? Nausea?" His caring eyes drifted back to her face.

Rita's heart pounded maniacally in her chest. Surely he could hear that. *Could he hear that?* She shot her panicked gaze up to meet his.

Cole narrowed his eyes. "Do I make you nervous?"

"Absolutely." Though not in the way he'd meant. Rita had no doubt Cole could protect her from outside threats. It was her reckless heart that worried her. She knew already, maybe had known even before they officially met, that she could easily lose herself to a man like this. They were too rare, the catch every woman dreamed of finding but no one got to keep.

He cocked his head, zeroing in. "Why, exactly?"

She pressed her eyes shut, forcing herself to remember that Cole was only doing his job, and that what she wanted in a companion was so much more than he would ever give. A court clerk had caught her watching him once, and the woman had been quick to let her know she'd graduated with Cole Garrett, and he hadn't even taken a date to prom because he wanted to keep his options open.

If he couldn't commit to one woman for a single prom, Rita's heart was surely doomed.

Then again, maybe a night in his arms would be worth the penance.

"Rita?"

"Hmm?"

"Sandwiches? Soup?" Cole made a pained face. "I have no idea what you eat."

"What?" Her mind scrambled to catch up. "Food?" Shame burned in her cheeks. He was trying to feed her.

To be a gentleman. And she'd been contemplating the value of her virtue.

Cole watched intently. "Are you sure you're okay? You're flushed again. Do you want to lay down?"

"No," she nearly screamed. No beds. "I like sandwiches."

He relented his too-close position with a shake of his head. "All right." Cole returned to the business side of the island and opened his refrigerator.

Rita pulled her wits back together. "I'm sorry I didn't want to go to the sheriff's department. I know I'm putting your brother out by dragging him here instead." She focused on the extraordinary view through Cole's bay window. An array of autumn-touched trees swayed in the distance. "I'm being ridiculous. I should've just gone."

"It's fine," he said with a grin. "Very little puts West out. He's accommodating to a fault."

A cruiser rolled into view on Cole's long gravel drive, and Rita's heart stopped. "Cole."

"What?" He manifested at her side, then marched to the window for a look outside. "Oh. Here he is now."

"How can you know for sure that it's him? What if it's not him?"

"The cars are numbered and his says Sheriff."

Rita worked the information through her mind. "What if someone hurt him and took his cruiser?"

Cole barked a laugh. "Never gonna happen, but that's a funny thought."

She shot him a crazy face. "You guys aren't invincible, you know."

The doorbell stopped Cole from responding. "Hold that thought." He opened the door for the sheriff, a man she also recognized from the courthouse. Equally handsome. Slightly older. Significantly more uptight.

Rita's phone buzzed in her pocket with a text from Ryan. His exams were over, and he still wanted to use her truck.

She responded swiftly, insisting she was on her way to get the pickup now, and Ryan should leave it in the lot. She hit Send, then grimaced internally over yet another lie.

After a brief round of whispering in acronyms, the Garretts approached her shoulder to shoulder, a six-foot wall of testosterone and unwavering confidence.

Rita leaned back in her chair, adding an inch of distance.

West pressed his hat to his torso with one broad hand. "Miss Horn. I'm Cade County Sheriff West Garrett."

Cole rolled his eyes and crossed his arms. "Call him West."

"Please," West concurred. "If you don't mind, I have a few questions about what happened to you today and what went on at the docks last night."

Rita looked at Cole.

"Have a seat," Cole instructed his brother. "I'm making us a little something to eat."

COLE SET OUT an assembly line for sandwiches. He'd wanted to impress Rita with something better than a middle-school lunch, but he couldn't think straight after the way she'd looked at him when he asked if he made her nervous. He'd wanted her to know that she could trust him. That none of the Cade County deputies would hurt her, and whoever she'd seen in that jacket had been a fake.

But that look.

Her cheeks had flushed and her gaze had drifted to his mouth and lingered. The dark, heated expression on her sweet face had done things to him he didn't like. Not with her. The images clogging his mind weren't meant for someone like Rita Horn. She was a good girl, and women like her weren't supposed to look at him like that. They were supposed to want stockbrokers in suits with big-money careers and 401Ks.

Thankfully, West had arrived to put his mind back into work mode.

West took the seat beside Rita. "Did you see a cruiser last night?"

"No. Just the sedan and two men."

"Today?"

"No." She looked to Cole again. A habit she was beginning to develop. One he liked more than he should.

Cole plated the sandwiches and delivered them to the counter. "Cruisers have GPS. West can pull up the history. See if one was near the river last night or your house today."

West nodded. "Already done. None of ours were. I'm trying to figure what else the man with the deputy jacket has in his costume trunk. Good to know he doesn't have a cruiser. I can't have a lunatic pulling folks over." He cast Cole a deflated look. "The width of the track marks near the docks line up with a standard sedan, but that's as much as we can tell about the car that made them."

"I figured." Cole rubbed his hands on a towel.

West took a bite of his sandwich and focused on Rita. "What else can you tell me?"

"I knew the victim," Rita said. She shielded her mouth with one small hand while she chewed. "I saw his picture on the news."

"What do you mean, you knew him?" Cole asked.

West shot him an amused look.

Rita finished chewing before she answered. "He'd visited the municipal building a lot lately. I saw him there several times in the last week or two. I assumed he was a lawyer."

"Real estate developer," West corrected. "Do you know who he was seeing in the building?"

"No." Rita shrugged. "I never spoke to him. He was just hard to miss, so I noticed."

Cole cocked a hip.

West smiled against the edge of his sandwich. "Hard to miss?"

"Sure." Rita looked from brother to brother. "Most folks around here are low-key. Laid-back. They move slower. Talk softer. Smile more." She pursed her lips. "This guy was different. Always in a rush. Back poker straight. Flat expression. Thousand-dollar suit. He was just...off."

West made a note in his pocket-size notebook. "Cole mentioned a person of concern in the café today. Someone who made you nervous. What did that guy look like?"

Cole pressed his palms against the counter. "If we can find him in the criminal database we'll get a name."

West pointed at his brother. "We can use that to see how he's connected to the victim." He turned back to Rita. "Would you know him if you saw him again?"

"Yes."

"I'll log on to the database with her," Cole said. "No problem."

"Good." West finished his sandwich and dusted his hands together. "I'll head down to the municipal building when they open tomorrow morning and pull the surveillance tapes. See if I can find Minsk and figure out where he was going."

Cole nodded. "I'm still going to give the victim's maid a call." He tipped his head toward Rita. "I got off track earlier."

West smiled. "Let me know how it goes."

Cole stared. He could feel Rita's eyes on him. "Yep."

"Well, all right." West headed for the door. "Thanks for the sandwich. Text me if you think of anything else. Otherwise, let's hit this again tomorrow. Thank you for your time, Miss Horn."

"Of course," she said.

West hesitated. He fixed his gaze on Rita and leaned in conspiratorially. "You've had a rough day, but if anyone can keep you safe, it's this guy." He winked at Cole.

Cole made a face. "Goodbye."

West stuffed the brown sheriff's hat back on his head. "I'm going to see if I can make a dent in the paperwork before the next disaster strikes. This has been some kind of day."

Cole agreed. He locked the front door behind him.

"West seemed nice," Rita said, heading back to the kitchen. She delivered empty plates and cups to the sink.

"You don't have to do that." Cole squeezed into the space at her side and turned off the water. "Don't wash my dishes."

She flicked her wet fingertips at him. "You cooked. I clean up."

"No."

Rita turned on him, petal-pink nails latched over the sexy curves of her hips. "Are you always so bossy?"

"Yes." He rubbed his forehead, hating the irrational feeling of attachment coursing through him. Rita Horn was practically a stranger. Beautiful, kindhearted and sexy as hell, but a stranger.

Cole relaxed against the counter. "I can pull up the database after I call the victim's maid. Come on." He motioned for her to follow him to the living room. "Leave the dishes. Make yourself comfortable."

"Fine." Rita curled onto the couch and pulled a pillow over her lap.

Cole punched the television on and went for his phone.

His favorite movie was playing when he returned. "Sorry. That must've still been in the queue."

"Wait." She waved a hand at him. "I love this one."

Cole fell onto the cushion beside her. "You're kidding."

"No. This is great."

He stretched an arm over the back of the couch and worked the screen of his cell phone with his opposite thumb. "I think we're going to be friends."

"Agreed."

Cole dared a look in her direction, ignoring the tightening of his gut. "Am I still making you nervous?"

"Yeah." Rita leaned against his side with a soft sigh.

A low groan wound its way through his chest. "Back at ya."

Chapter Eight

Cole spent the night on his laptop in the living room after Rita had reluctantly agreed to get some rest in his bed. The second half of their day had been significantly quieter than the first, but twice as demanding of his professional composure. Thoughts of Rita in his room had been tough to keep at bay, but luckily the victim, Roger Minsk, had a strong online presence, providing Cole with the distraction he needed.

Minsk had kept an active blog and Facebook account, and he'd contributed to a few dozen online articles about property development. Eventually, the deluge of information was enough to refocus Cole on the case.

Unfortunately, two pots of coffee and eight hours later, Cole had learned nothing about Minsk that was useful in understanding why he had been killed.

"Any luck?" Rita's soft voice and vanilla scent immediately brightened the room.

She shuffled into the living room wearing white cotton shorts and a Rivertown T-shirt. Her mussed hair hung over both shoulders in loose, unkempt waves he instantly ached to run his fingers through.

"A little," Cole said. He moved into the kitchen and poured her a cup of coffee. "Minsk's maid finally returned my call. Alicia something."

"That's good. Oh, thank you." Rita accepted the mug with a puckered brow. "Why are you wearing your uniform?" She sipped the coffee and sighed.

"Good?"

"Heaven." Her sharp hazel eyes popped wide. "Oh, my goodness. I have to call the office." She scanned the room frantically. "I didn't call off. I just never showed up. What time is it? Where's your clock?"

He lifted his watch. "It's only seven ten. Municipal building doesn't even open until eight, so unless you're leaving someone a voice mail, I think you can relax and enjoy the coffee."

"Right." Rita took another appreciative drink. "I guess I'm still waking up."

"You didn't sleep well?" Cole asked, hoping she hadn't been afraid or uneasy about being there alone with him all night.

"Eventually," she said on a yawn, "but my baby brother wants to use my truck to help a friend move, and he's not buying my stories or excuses about why he can't use it. I fielded his interrogative texts until after midnight when I finally insisted he knock it off so I could get some rest before work this morning." She rubbed her forehead. "I just keep lying to him, and that's not who we are. Ryan and I made a pact when he came to live with me. We promised to always be straight with one another."

"You don't want him to use your truck because whoever tried to run you down could mistake him for you in your vehicle," Cole guessed.

"Exactly." Rita dropped her hand and took a long curious look at Cole. "Why are you dressed for work so early?"

"I'm meeting the maid at Mr. Minsk's house in an hour."

Rita blanched. "An hour?" She wrinkled her nose. "All right. I can be ready in ten minutes."

Cole smiled.

"Good. I told West I'd bring you to the station while I interviewed the maid."

"No!" Rita started, nearly spilling her coffee. "I only agreed to go to the station today because I'd be with you. You can't just leave me alone there. What if the killer is a friend or relative of one of the deputies? That would give him access to the jacket and the station. What if he turns up to kill me again and you're not there?" She spun in place and headed back down the hall to his room.

"Where are you going?" Cole called. "Rita?" He followed her as far as the closed door. "Are you mad? Is this a protest?" *What was happening?* Cole latched his fingers behind his head and stared at the ceiling. "I know you're scared, but you've got to trust me or I can't protect you. At least trust my judgment. You will always be safe with my brother." He moved his eyes back to the door. "And don't walk away when we're talking. This is ridiculous."

The door whipped open a moment later.

Rita had swapped her pajamas for dark jeans and a red V-neck sweater. "I'm going with you." She raked a brush through her hair as she headed for the bathroom and began to brush her teeth. "Just because we didn't see the guy from the coffee shop in the criminal database last night doesn't mean he isn't a criminal."

She spoke around the busy brush and load of toothpaste bubbles. "It only means he doesn't have a record. And just because he wasn't in your personal photos doesn't mean he isn't somehow in your circle. So I'm coming to Minsk's place. I'll wait in the car while you talk to the maid. Then you can take me to the station to make a formal statement afterward." She finished up and checked her face in the mirror. "I want to be where you are." A swipe of lip gloss and some eyelash stuff later, she turned puppy eyes on Cole.

Cole processed her demands.

He didn't like taking her out on a call with him, but knowing she was afraid to be without him, even at the sheriff's department, gave Cole a deep ache in his chest.

"Please?"

He rocked back on his heels. "Fine."

"Thank you!" She perked up.

"Don't forget to call off work."

"Right." Rita grabbed her little purple phone off the counter and pecked the screen before pressing it to her ear. Sixty seconds later, she'd delivered the world's worst performance over voice mail, complete with dry coughing and a gratuitous moan. According to Rita, she'd be out the rest of the week.

Cole hoped to have eliminated the threat against her well before that, but he wasn't opposed to having a little extra time with her afterward.

He'd protect her.

She'd learn to trust him. Maybe even see past whatever she might have heard about his usual dating style. Not that he was looking to date Rita.

Was he looking to date Rita?

"Are you ready?" she asked, sliding her feet into little white sneakers.

Not even close, he thought wryly. "Yep. I'll give West a call on our way. Let him know there's been a change of plans."

"Really?" Rita's sharp hazel eyes went soft with relief.

"Come on." Cole opened the front door and held it for her to pass.

The right thing for protocol and the right thing for Rita were in opposition at the moment, and it put him in a tough place. With any luck, no other conflicts like this one would come up, because, given the choice, Cole had a feeling he'd always choose Rita. "Let's go before I change my mind."

The snaking hillside road to Minsk's house wound its way past a smattering of high-end homes overlooking the town. Minsk's property was unapologetically larger than the rest and situated at the top of the mountain, stark white against the towering evergreens and surrounded by an elaborate garden with a wrought-iron fence.

"Good grief," Rita said, leaning forward in her seat as Cole maneuvered the cruiser onto the broad circular drive. "I had no idea this was up here."

A middle-aged woman in traditional gray-and-white servant's attire bustled through the arching ten-foot door before Cole could shift into Park.

He twisted his hat onto his head and gave Rita a warning look. "Wait here."

She rested back against the seat and crossed her arms.

A moment later, he offered the dark-haired woman a handshake and what he hoped was a comforting smile. "You must be Mrs. Sanchez." Her wide brown eyes and olive skin reminded him of his mother's best friend, Anita. Their accents were slightly different, but there was warmth and kindness in both women's eyes.

"I'm so glad you're here," she said. "Please, come." She hustled him inside and shut the door.

The home was enormous. The Garrett boys could've played a nice game of catch in the foyer alone. What would one man do in a house so big? Not that Cole didn't value nice things. He did, but he was also beginning to realize how deeply blessed he was to be surrounded by family and friends. "Thank you for agreeing to meet with me, and for your willingness to meet here."

"He's been gone three days." She lifted the corresponding number of fingers on one hand and shook them.

"Yes, ma'am. I'm sorry we weren't able to find him sooner. The sheriff stopped by twice to check on him, but there was no answer. He'd hoped Mr. Minsk was on a business trip."

"Oh, no," she said. "He was working here. All the time. No rest. No sleep. Then, poof. He was gone."

"Did he keep a home office?" Cole asked. He knew all about the demands of a high-pressure career and lack of everything else that came along with it. "I'd like to take a look at his private calendar and personal computer, as well."

"Of course." She started up a sweeping staircase. "This way."

Cole followed her into a surprisingly plain room with understated furniture and a desk covered in messy files. He lifted the lid on a compact computer. "Is this his only laptop?"

"Yes. He used it all the time. That and his cell phone." Her voice cracked, and she cupped her hands over her mouth.

Cole swiped a finger over the touchpad, and the computer's screen flickered to life. No file icons on the desktop. A quick pass through the drives came up empty, as well. The device was like brand-new. Nothing personal. No history. Strange for a man who'd allegedly used it all the time. Unless... "Have you touched this since he went missing?"

"No, sir."

"Has anyone else been here?"

"Not that I'm aware of," she said, shrugging, "but I only come twice a week."

"Did you notice any signs that Mr. Minsk might've had company in between your visits?"

She raised her shoulders again.

Cole turned his attention back to the clean laptop. Could Minsk have known he was in danger and cleared his files to protect himself? If so, what was he hiding? And from who?

Cole set the laptop aside. He rummaged through the piles of papers, wondering where to begin. There was no way to do the job justice with Rita waiting in the car. "I'm afraid I'm going to need to get some help in here." He looked up to catch the maid's eye. "We'll have to go through everything in detail." Beneath the mountains of documentation was a solid wood desk. No giant paper calendar like Cole had hoped. Of course not. Minsk was a wealthy businessman. He probably kept all his appointments on a cell phone.

Cole took a photo of the cluttered desk and sent it to West. Sorting the mess could take all day. He definitely needed help. Before that, he needed to get Rita to the sheriff's department. She'd be safe there while he investigated. Uneasy, he knew, but safe.

He teetered a moment, torn between needing to leave and needing to stay. A set of blueprints caught his attention near the bottom of one haphazard pile. Cole worked the papers free and carefully uncurled the edges. It was hard to say what he was looking at without context. "Do you have any idea what Mr. Minsk was working on?" he asked Mrs. Sanchez, still positioned at the office door.

She shifted foot to foot. "No. He didn't talk to me like that, but he was a nice man."

He analyzed her troubled stance and unwillingness to enter the room with him. "Are you uncomfortable for some reason?"

"It doesn't feel right watching you snoop through his things. I know he's gone and you're helping but…"

Cole relaxed by a fraction. "I know it's hard, but I appreciate your help."

He turned his eyes back to the scrolled paperwork before him. What was this blueprint for?

Rita said she'd seen Mr. Minsk at the courthouse several times recently. He could have been buying or negotiating a land deal, or researching a property for a buyer. Maybe the blueprint was related to the property, but which parcel and who was the owner?

Mrs. Sanchez kneaded her hands. "Why would something like this happen to such a nice person?"

"I don't know," Cole admitted, "but I intend to find out."

He gave the wiped laptop another long look.

Was Mr. Minsk as nice a guy as his housekeeper thought? Or was he something else? A few days ago, Cole would've said nice guys weren't shot in the head and dumped in the river, but what did that theory say about Rita? Maybe good people were simply in the wrong place at the wrong time on occasion, and Minsk had been one of them. Like Rita.

He spread the plans on the desk and turned them around twice, trying to make heads or tails of the thin lines and chicken-scratch writing. "This looks like the docks." He lowered his face to the awful handwriting along one edge. "Willa. Eleven o'clock."

The maid moved reluctantly into the room. "Mr. Minsk spent a lot of time on the water."

"Does the name Willa mean anything to you? Was she a business partner? Family member? Girlfriend?"

"No. *Willa* is his boat."

He spent a lot of time on the water. And at the courthouse.

There had been talk of revitalizing the docks for years, but nothing had ever come of it. Maybe Minsk had been trying to make that happen.

Maybe, if Minsk spent a lot of time on his boat, there

would be some clues there to help Cole decipher who had killed him and why.

He stared at the blueprint, hoping for the details to snap together, reveal something more than he could yet see.

The ringing of the doorbell turned Mrs. Sanchez into the hallway. "Excuse me," she called over her shoulder, already on her way to the door.

Cole went to the window and pulled back the curtain from the window overlooking Minsk's driveway. His cruiser was empty. The rest of the view was strikingly peaceful.

Was he taking too long, so she'd lost patience, or had she gotten spooked? Either way, he'd known better than to agree to bring her along, and he and Rita would need to have a discussion about what *wait in the car* meant.

Cole rubbed a rough hand over his face, waiting for her voice in the hallway. He needed to get going, anyway. West wanted Rita at the station. Someone else would have to handle Minsk's messy office. He dialed West, then rested a hip against the disorganized desk.

"Where are you?" West answered without greeting. "I've got stuff to do, and I'm down here sitting on my thumbs waiting for you and Rita Horn to show up."

"We're on the way. I stopped at Minsk's house to talk with the maid first. I've got a paperwork catastrophe over here, but I found a blueprint in the mix that might be useful."

"If you're at Minsk's, where's Rita?" West's flat tone was as disapproving as they came. "Tell me you didn't take our only witness to the murder victim's home."

"She agreed to wait in the car." Cole listened to the gonging silence of the cavernous home. His gut fisted with warning. It was time to collect Rita and get moving. "We're headed your way now, but it sounds like Minsk had a boat at the marina. Could be something there that sheds some light. Someone ought to check that out, as well."

"Agreed, now get your witness down here."

The echo of a single gunshot rang through the massive home.

Cole freed his sidearm, a bullet of fear lancing his heart. He crept toward the open office door and peered down the long hallway. Years of military and department training snapped into focus.

"Was that a gunshot?" West asked. His tight voice burst through the forgotten cell phone on Cole's shoulder.

"Shh." Cole hastened toward the staircase. The view from the second-floor balcony coiled his gut. "Maid's down. Single GSW to the head." A pool of blood seeped around her raven hair on the white marble floor. A lump formed in Cole's throat as the image of his empty cruiser thudded back to mind. "Rita's missing." He disconnected without waiting for West's response.

He shoved the phone into his pocket and took the stairs on silent feet. A near-feral need to protect her burned through his limbs. If Rita was hurt in any way, someone was going to be extremely sorry.

A second shot erupted before he reached the foyer, ringing Cole's ears and shattering the window behind his head.

He dropped into a crouch and pressed his back to the wall. "Cade County Sheriff's Department," Cole announced. "Put your weapon down and come out where I can see you."

Three more rounds exploded in immediate succession, following Cole down the steps and trashing the column where he ducked for cover.

Across the open room, a lean man in a bulky coat dashed out of sight.

Cole gave chase, gun drawn, desperate for a chance to take the shot and terrified he'd find Rita in the same condition he'd found the maid.

RITA PRESSED HERSELF behind a stout hedge at the property's edge, leaving only a few inches between her shaking toes and a ragged cliff. She hadn't seen the man in the deputy coat since he'd manifested from the bushes and rung the bell to the house, but she'd counted four gunshots so far.

How he'd missed seeing her in the car was both a miracle and a mystery.

She'd ducked on instinct, huddling into the shadowed space between her seat and the dashboard, praying the killer wouldn't take undo interest in Cole's cruiser.

The first gunshot had set her upright.

The second had propelled her out of hiding.

The third and fourth shots had rooted her feet in place behind the shrubbery as if she was part of the garden.

Cole was still inside, and she wouldn't leave without him.

Tears streamed over her cheeks as she imagined the killer sneaking up on Cole and pulling the trigger while she hid like a coward. She begged her limbs to cooperate and carry her back to the car where she'd stupidly left her phone in the cupholder when she fled. She needed to call for help.

Should she return to the car for her phone? Make a run for the closest neighbor?

Rita leaned around the shrubbery, seeking the nearest home in each direction and estimating which was closer.

"Stop!" Cole's strong voice cracked through the hills.

Her heart leaped in response.

"Come out." Cole moved swiftly in her direction, gun drawn but lowered slightly. He extended a hand to her. "I lost him. I need to get you out of here before he comes back."

Rita shimmied free and grabbed his offered hand in both of hers. "How could you see me?"

"I'm beginning to think I could find you anywhere."

Cole cursed under his breath. He pulled her to him and sighed against the top of her head. "Did you see which way the shooter went?"

"No. I haven't seen him since he went inside."

Cole pulled back for a look into Rita's eyes. Confliction danced over his features. "West's on his way. We're going to get in the cruiser and go. Understand? I'm not involving you in a shoot-out."

Cole led her back through the gardens at a crouched jog. "Stay low," he reminded her. "And don't stop."

"Cole!" Rita froze. She yanked him back, gripping his stubborn arm in both her hands.

The shooter had appeared again in the distance.

"It's the man from the Rivertown coffee house." This time, he wore the deputy jacket.

Cole lifted his weapon, scanning the area.

"There," she whispered, wagging one frantic finger. "That's him!"

The man's head turned immediately in their direction. His arm swung forward, gun in hand. The shot cracked in the autumn air.

"Run," Cole barked, shoving Rita aside and positioning his body between her and the gunman. He returned fire as they ran, but stayed tight to Rita's side as far as the cruiser. He yanked the driver's side door open and stuffed Rita inside.

She climbed over the console and into the passenger seat as Cole revved the engine to life. He spun the vehicle in a reverse circle, tossing Rita against her door, and pointed the cruiser back down the winding road at twice the posted speed.

Sirens cried in the distance as Cole relayed details of the shooting to Dispatch. Apparently he'd been on the phone with West when the first shot rang out.

Her heart hammered against her ribs, threatening to break them. Her stomach knotted, and her hands ached for something to hold. Nothing seemed real. The day had to be a dream. A movie she'd seen years before and nearly forgotten. Anything but reality. This could not be her actual life.

"Rita?" Cole's steady voice seeped into her clouded thoughts. "She's nonresponsive." He traced the line of her arm with careful fingers, then tenderly grazed her shoulder and neck. "I don't see any injuries. She's in shock, I think."

"I'm not," Rita said, jerking her face in his direction.

"Ask West to call me." Cole returned the radio handset to his console, then shifted into Park. He parked the cruiser behind a small white church off the winding road. "Dispatch is taking over. And it's okay to be in shock. It's okay to feel whatever you're feeling. You were shot at. Stalked by an active shooter."

"You saved me."

The corners of Cole's mouth pulled down. "No. I'm the reason you were in danger. You shouldn't have been there. Then you wouldn't have needed saving."

The plea in his tone and determination in his eyes lit a flame in Rita's core. Heat rose and spread from her middle. Cole Garrett was her hero.

Rita unlatched her seatbelt and turned to face him. She raised a palm to the stubble on his cheeks and curled her fingertips against the strong line of his jaw.

Shock flashed in his eyes before quickly becoming something else. "Rita?" His voice was low and gravelly with want.

"Yes."

Cole reached for her then, winding a strong arm over her back and pulling her toward him until she was on her knees, stretching back across the infuriating console.

Her lips met his in a perfect collision of passion and relief. It was the moment she'd been dreaming of since she'd first set eyes on him all those months ago, and it was everything she'd expected and more. Expert hands lifted her in the confined space of his front seat. Greedy and protective, they brought her gently to rest on his lap.

Rita arranged her thighs over his before deepening the kiss. She towered over him, caressing his face in her hands and eagerly opening her mouth when his tongue swept across her bottom lip, asking for more.

The radio crackled beside them as Dispatch announced the need for another car at Minsk's home.

Cole broke the kiss with a groan, leaving Rita breathless and perched awkwardly over him.

She buried her face in the curve of his neck and tried not to think of how to get back into her seat like a lady. "I am so sorry."

His chest went still. "You attacked me."

Rita reared back. "No."

Cole's mischievous smile washed the wave of humiliation away. "Adrenaline makes people do crazy things."

Rita climbed off his lap much less smoothly than she'd arrived. "I think it was your apology."

"Well, then, I am very, very sorry," he said.

She buckled her seatbelt with a grin, hating the rush of heat across her cheeks. "Shut up."

Chapter Nine

Cole pulled back onto the curving country road, his grip tight on the steering wheel. What was he thinking? Kissing her like that. Letting the heat of the moment burn through his professionalism.

Rita gazed out the window, likely regretting the way she'd kissed him or the fact she'd let him drag her onto his lap like they were people who made out in cars instead of what they were. Practically strangers, on the run from a killer.

Correction. Rita was on the run. Cole was on the hunt, and at his first opportunity, Cole would bring this guy down.

Cole's cell phone rang, and he hit speaker. "Garrett."

"Hey," West answered. "I'm at Minsk's. Where are you?"

"Headed to the marina. I think we need to get eyes on that boat before someone else gets to it. If they haven't already."

West sighed heavily. Cole could practically hear him aging. "And Rita?"

"She's here. You're on speaker."

A beat of awkward silence filled the car.

"Hi," Rita said shyly, wrinkling her brow and locking her gaze on Cole.

Cole smiled at the silly look. "Any sign of the shooter?"

"No," West answered, "but we've got a vehicle with no plates around the curve past the house. We're checking it out."

"Black sedan?" Cole asked.

"No. Silver hatchback."

Rita deflated against the passenger seat, allowing her head to roll aside.

"Keep me posted," Cole said. "We'll meet you at the station afterward."

"Sounds good."

Cole tossed the phone into a cupholder and hooked the next right toward the river. He examined Rita's expressionless profile. "If the shooter's anywhere near Minsk's house, West will find him. West's one of the best trackers I know, and the other deputies are diligent. If the shooter isn't long gone by now, he'll never make it."

Rita's face went slack, as if a horrible thought had just occurred to her. "The maid," she whispered.

"I know." Cole lifted a hand to comfort her, but returned it to the wheel. The maid's death was his fault. He should've been with her. He was the one who'd invited her there. And damn if he didn't feel like he'd been one step behind Minsk's killer from the moment he'd laid eyes on his body being dragged from the river. Cole couldn't keep doing this. He had to get ahead of the sonofabitch before Rita was next to pay the price.

A pair of fat tears slid over her cheeks. "He killed her," she said. "For what? Answering the door? What about her family? She could have a husband. Children." The final word was barely a sound on her tongue.

Cole's heart ached for hers. "I'm sorry." Rita had lost her mom senselessly, too. He couldn't imagine what this day felt like to her.

"She shouldn't have been a part of this."

"You're right." And he hated himself for asking the poor woman to meet him at Minsk's home. Cole had wanted her there to provide insight into the man he'd never met. He'd never imagined...

"What happens now?" Rita asked in a small, heartbroken voice. "Who will tell her family?"

"West." Cole answered mindlessly. These were the things his big brother insisted on handling. *My county. My people. My responsibility*, he'd say. "He'll deliver the news and answer whatever questions he can for them. Then, he'll set his sights on the killer and won't stop going for him until justice is done."

Though Cole planned to beat him to it this time.

Eventually, they left the shaded mountain pass in favor of a sprawling two-lane highway that stretched for miles between sun-drenched cornfields. Several raggedy scarecrows and the occasional combine peppered the landscape before they reached the river. Cole flipped his signal and gave the new road a long look. A mile to the east, hidden beyond the curve of a rolling hillside, stood a number of abandoned factories, homeless cats and a recent murder site. Cole drove west, toward Memorial Park, wide waterfront homes and a beautifully landscaped marina.

He pulled the receiver off his dashboard and held it to his lips. "I'm at the Cade County Marina. Checking in." He released the handset and waited.

"Roger that," a grainy voice returned.

Cole made a slow circle around the nearly empty lot before choosing a space and settling the engine. He released his seatbelt and turned his face to Rita, unsure what to say. If he asked her to join him, he might unintentionally lead her onto a boat with a gunman. Though the alternative seemed equally dangerous, he'd already resolved not to let her out of his sight again.

"Ready?" He tipped his head toward the windshield, indicating the row of boats bobbing outside.

She didn't need a second invitation. Rita hustled around the car's hood to meet him. "What are we looking for?"

"Minsk's boat. *Willa*." Cole pointed to a line of red block letters on the closest fishing vessel.

"Got it." Rita kept pace at his side, reading the name of each boat softly as they passed.

A long whistle blew over Cole's lips when he spotted her. *Willa* wasn't a boat, she was a yacht. Coming from Minsk's mansion on the mountain, Cole shouldn't have been surprised, but he was. The largest boat he'd been on outside the military was a historic schooner near Williamsburg. This vessel was something else entirely. Definitely not a fishing boat. *Willa* was seventy-five feet of luxury, from her shining metal rails to her spotless wide-planked deck. "Looks like we've arrived."

Cole kicked a set of freestanding wooden steps across the dock toward *Willa* before stretching one long leg out and pulling himself completely on board. "Your turn." He reached for Rita, who easily accepted his hand. Color flooded her face, and his chest puffed at the response.

He couldn't ignore the way her smaller, softer palm fit perfectly into his larger one, or the way she willingly gripped him back. Maybe she didn't regret their kiss as much as he'd feared. Maybe she liked how their hands, and earlier their mouths, had melded together as much as he did.

What he refused to think about, for now, was how nicely she'd fit across his lap, and how much nicer that could've been without the car and several layers of clothes. A rush of electricity flowed over his skin as her body pressed briefly against his for balance.

"Oops." She released his hand in favor of bracing both palms on his chest to find her footing.

Cole caught her at the curves of her waist. "Okay?"

She dropped her arms to her sides and stepped away. "Yeah."

Cole closed his fingers into fists, hating the loss of her nearness. "Let's see what *Willa* knows."

RITA FOLLOWED COLE through the small cabin door, the feel of his hands still warming her waist. She wet her lips, relishing the tingle left behind from the gentle scrape of his stubble. It was only her imagination that insisted her lips were still flavored with the taste of his tongue.

"You okay?" he asked, clearing her hazy thoughts.

"Yes." She moved into the boat's broad gathering space and paused at Cole's side, arms crossed over her middle in a useless attempt to settle her churning nerves and butterflies.

Cole worked methodically through the piles of clutter on a desk in the corner, then moved to a pile of folders on a nearby credenza.

Rita took in the impressive surroundings. The boat was bigger than some of the apartments her family had lived in while following her dad across the country. Military communities were tight, and there were no secrets, as much by necessity as choice. She'd begun to miss those simpler days since coming home to find her house ransacked. That wouldn't have happened if all her neighbors were soldiers.

She took a few cautious steps around a protruding bar, eager for a better look at the fancy dining area behind it. An oval-shaped table was positioned in the corner and wrapped by bench seating. White china and stemmed glasses were arranged on the table, waiting for a meal that would never come. Piles of lavish pillows covered in rich shades of blue and gold silk buried the narrow bank of seats.

Rita trailed her fingertips over the delicate fabric before moving away. She peeked through small round windows at the distant horizon where dark waters met green mountains and a clear blue sky.

"Bingo," Cole announced.

Rita headed back immediately. "What did you find?" Her pulse raced in anticipation. After the horror she'd seen today, anything seemed possible. Even the things that shouldn't touch her small town. The man in the black sedan. The one who'd murdered two people in two days. He'd changed everything.

Cole spread a blueprint over the messy desk and anchored it at either end with folders. "Look." He took a photo with his phone, then layered another blueprint on top of the first and repeated the process.

Rita leaned closer, one fist pressed to her chest in prayer. *Please don't let these be schematics for a bomb.* A small measure of relief washed over her as she examined the image. "Is that the marina?"

"No, but you're close. This is a stretch of docks on the Mississippi River in New Orleans. I saw a similar blueprint in Minsk's home office. That one looked like our docks. Interesting that he'd have both, don't you think? The Ohio River runs right into the Mississippi River. Two blueprints for properties on the same body of water all these miles apart?"

He peeled back the top paper and waved a hand at the one underneath. "This is a dock in Illinois." He tapped a finger on a line of text along the paper's border. "Confluence with the Ohio River." Cole set his phone down and turned for a final blueprint he'd leaned against the desk's side. He spread it out and took a picture. "And St. Louis." He shook his head, pointing to a similar line of text on this blueprint's edge. "Confluence with the Missouri River."

"I see." Rita struggled to understand the implication. Cole seemed excited over a stack of basic blueprints. That was Minsk's job, wasn't it? "We knew Minsk was a land developer. Maybe he developed docks."

Cole rolled each blueprint carefully and fed them into one another until he had only one thick roll to carry. "Yes, but this information could be very useful in figuring what Minsk was up to before he died. For example, if there's been any bids made on our docks, we can follow that up as a lead, or if the same company has purchased all the other properties, that's worth hunting, too."

Well, put that way, the blueprints sounded like progress. "It's a shame Minsk didn't live long enough to see our docks sold," Rita said. "I remember the explosion that killed four workers there. It was a hot topic the year I moved to town."

Cole turned slowly to face her. "I'd almost forgotten about that. My family attended the memorial service for the fallen workers."

"Me, too," she said. It had been a case she'd followed closely. A major catastrophe only months after she'd moved to Rivertown for school, away from her family, alone in a tiny apartment with a view of the fires that had burned through the night, searing oil patches released into the river by the explosion. She'd carried bottled water and sandwiches to workers for days as they dragged the river in search of the four bodies. Seen the missing men's loved ones sobbing on the riverbanks.

"All four families filed lawsuits, and the company was eventually foreclosed on. The lawyers had proved it was a preventable explosion, and the company couldn't afford the settlement. A ton of families lost their jobs when that place went out of business. It was a mess. The grieving families didn't mean to hurt anyone else. They just wanted to be sure the company didn't let anyone else die."

Cole fixed her with his sharp blue eyes. "I wonder who owns it now. If not the company who went bankrupt, then who?"

Rita shrugged. "The state was supposed to buy it and make it into a memorial honoring those families, but it never happened." She puffed air into thick side-swept bangs, wincing at the reminder of her swollen forehead. "That's how it goes sometimes. Politicians make promises to pacify the people until the heat blows over, then the vows are forgotten." The lost were forgotten. The families… She rubbed her eyes, erasing images of the makeshift memorial created by neighbors for her mother following the crash.

Rita pulled in long breaths and plucked the material of her shirt away from her chest. The air inside the cabin was too stuffy. Claustrophobic. Grief was powerful enough without adding it to the day she was having. She swallowed long and hard to clear her thickening throat and refocused on the docks. "There was going to be a boardwalk with benches that had the lost men's names on little plaques, and locally owned businesses, like ice cream shops and fishing pole rentals. Instead, it's just a big ugly reminder of an avoidable tragedy." And haven to seventeen cats.

Cole's phone buzzed on the desk where it had been acting as a paperweight. "Garrett," he answered, tucking the rolled blueprints under one arm. He flicked his gaze to Rita then back to the desk. "Yeah." He pulled a stack of files toward him, shifting the pages and stacking them up. "Are you sure?" His body stiffened. "We're on our way." He stuffed the phone into his pocket and fixed Rita with sincere blue eyes. "West says they still haven't found the shooter, but someone cleared out Minsk's office while West and the team were tracking the killer through the woods. The coroner was in the foyer downstairs and never heard a thing."

Fear lifted Rita's skin into gooseflesh. "Then this guy's really good. That's very bad."

"Yeah, and he's bold as hell." Cole stacked files ten tall into his hands and rested his chin on the top to steady them. "Grab what you can. We'll come back with help. For now, we need to go."

Rita obeyed, pulling photos from the corkboard over the desk and stacking them on piles of folders as large as her short arms could manage.

A small thud registered in the cabin. Something had fallen on the silent deck beyond the little door. It reminded Rita of the sound made when a package was delivered to her porch.

Except they were on a boat.

"What was that?" she finally asked, half afraid to know the answer.

Cole set the files back on the desk, then unlatched the button securing his sidearm to its holster. "Stay here." He crept silently up the stairs.

Rita followed on his heels, unable to sit still again and wait to be abducted or killed.

Cole swiveled at the waist. He gripped a fist in the air and grimaced. It was the military signal for *stand down. Don't move. Wait.*

Rita had seen the move many times before, and somehow, the visual command was impossible for her to ignore. Her feet froze on the small set of steps to the little door.

Cole shoved the door wide, gun drawn and ready. A string of fervent curses bit the air.

Before he could bark another order, Rita's eyes landed

on a small black device near Cole's feet. Bright red numbers counted backward toward zero. The soft ticking of a clock registering with each change on the display. *17, 16, 15...*

Rita gasped. "Is that a bomb?"

Papers fluttered through the air as Cole tossed the stack of folders from her hands toward the dock. He swung back to face her, this time gripping her wrists and tugging her up the steps toward him.

Rita's feet bumbled forward, catching each rung on autopilot while she stared, transfixed by the device that would end her too-short life.

9, 8, 7...

He yanked her arms, dragging her away from the device when she landed on deck beside it, but her body didn't respond.

"Rita!" Cole yelled, his voice thick with demand and authority. "Move your ass before I throw you overboard."

6, 5, 4...

Her brother would be all alone. An orphan without a sister to watch over him. Abandoned by everyone because his stupid bleeding-heart sister, the only thing he had left, had to feed cats at a murder location.

Something gripped her mercilessly, and she winced with the shock of pain that followed. A powerful jerk hoisted her off her feet and hefted her into the air. Rita's arms flew wide as she sailed away from the boat and crashed painfully into the now-choppy river like an anvil. Her eyes stung and her lungs burned as she broached the surface a moment later, swallowing mouthfuls of disgusting, frigid river water in the process.

Cole followed immediately, launching himself over the polished chrome rail. His arms were around her in the next second, forcing her farther from the boat with each powerful thrust of his legs. He made a show of filling his cheeks with air, then dunked them both underwater.

The explosion that followed shoved them through the water in a powerful undertow. They resurfaced to chaos. Her teeth rattled and her vision blurred. Heat scorched over the river in an invisible wave, and Cole curved himself around her like a shield, pressing her face against his chest and wrapping her in his iron arms.

Smoke plumed and billowed overhead. Debris dropped from the sky and floated around them in a rancid stew of scorched plastic and burning fuel. Rita coughed and hacked, kicking instinctively to stay above water as fragments of torn metal and burning planks shot into the water like missiles.

"Are you okay?" Cole asked, petting Rita's hair and dragging it away from her skin for a closer look at her nonexistent injuries.

"I'm fine. I'm sorry," she cried. "I didn't move. I should've moved." He'd saved her life. Again. Her heart welled with emotion, and she gripped his handsome face in both palms.

The shadow of something large barely registered with her before crashing over them.

"Cole!" But her cry was too late.

The still-burning debris landed across his broad shoulders with a sickening crack.

His handsome face went slack, and his protective grip on her released.

Chapter Ten

Rita caught hold of the dock with one hand as she struggled to keep Cole above water. One hand wrapped under his arm, she pressed her cheek to his.

Cole's eyes flashed open. Shock and confusion raked his brow.

"Be still," she warned through trembling lips. "I don't know how hurt you are."

He began to tread water slowly, attempting to shift away from her. "Are you okay?" His voice was rough and low, his face pinched in pain.

The precious sound was nearly enough to push her under. She pressed her forehead to his and let her tears fall on his cheeks. "I'm perfect," she cried, and it was true.

Cole Garrett's presence in her life had changed everything, and she never again wanted to go a day without him in it. Ten thousand words lodged in her throat and on her tongue, but she could only pull back for a better look at his face and state the obvious. "Be still. You're hurt."

The pounding footfalls of marina workers and nearby boat owners soon rattled the dock. Life preservers and rescue ropes were lowered into Cole's and Rita's reach. A mass of voices churned the acrid air. Moments blurred and time elapsed in a surreal and unsettling way as Rita was pulled from the water by the careful hands of a dozen men.

Cole insisted on climbing out unassisted.

Rita watched the remains of the flaming boat in disbelief. Had she really stood in the below-deck cabin only minutes before? Had someone nearly blown her up?

The distant, lamenting cry of an ambulance wound into a frenzy at the marina's main entrance, then stopped just short of mowing her over in the name of rescue.

Newly arriving deputies and marina security corralled the hodgepodge rescue team and detained them for questioning behind a flimsy line of yellow tape. The ambulance workers had divided themselves between Rita and Cole. Rita got the younger, friendlier one. Cole got a familiar-looking man, at least fifteen years his senior. Rita's guy gave her a quick once-over and an oxygen mask. She was fine. Thanks to Cole.

The other guy's job wasn't nearly as easy. Cole's complaints had started at the sight of him and persisted with fervor. "Knock it off!"

"Hold still," the medic snapped. "I'd be done by now if you'd stop fighting me, or didn't you learn that in medical school."

"I'm fine." Cole wiggled on the ambulance's shiny silver bumper. He was far too large for the seat he'd chosen, but had refused the gurney and all attempts to get him to go into the vehicle willingly.

"Good thing you quit school," the man snarked, dabbing Cole's back with sopping cotton pads. "They'd have kicked you out eventually if you're dumb enough to think people are fine after a bombing and near drowning."

Rita smiled through another round of Cole's fervent cursing, glad he was alive and thankful the medic was ignoring his protests. Her ringing ears made it hard to understand everything he said, but she got the gist.

She tried not to think about the moment Cole's eyes had

fallen shut and his limbs had gone limp. The sickening curl of her gut was something she never wanted to feel again.

Firemen blasted the charred remains of Minsk's boat and walked the dock, taking pictures and scribbling on clipboards.

Rita refocused on breathing in the sweet oxygen from her mask and blowing out the terror that had constricted her lungs and throat more often than not over the last thirty-six hours.

Beside her, the paramedic continued to mumble as he worked over Cole's battered skin.

Cole swatted the man's hands away. "Leave it!"

The older man sucked his teeth and pressed on, cleaning the burns and wounds across Cole's scarred back. "Hold still and suck it up. Let me do my job. You know, you could try being thankful you've still got breath to complain with."

Cole's gaze lifted to Rita's.

She offered a small smile, tugging the blessed oxygen mask away from her face to speak. Her throat ached with emotion, still raw from her cries for help. "He's right. You should let him finish." Cole had only been unconscious for a few seconds, but those moments had felt like consecutive eternities to Rita. The giant hunk of the boat's hull would have killed her if Cole hadn't been there to take the blow. Protecting her at any cost. Guilt clawed her heart, but darned if his bravery wasn't sexy as hell. It had been a long while since anyone other than her baby brother had played the role of her protector.

The fact that Cole probably thought he was just doing his job soured the moment. She did her best to mask the sudden disappointment.

"See?" the medic said. "Listen to her. Maybe she should go to medical school."

Rita smiled. "Besides, if any of that gets infected, you'll have all new reasons to swear."

Cole turned his frowning face toward the water without any more argument.

The paramedic gave Cole a long look before casting Rita a curious grin. "Well, well, well."

"No," Cole said. "None of that." He jerked his shoulder away from the man's touch and shot him a warning look. "Just patch me up so I can get back to work."

The sharp bark of a siren set Cole on his feet, immediately free from the medic's reach. "About damn time."

West appeared at the dock's end, running full speed toward them.

Reporters and spectators moved aside as he hopped the makeshift yellow fence.

He slowed as he drew nearer, both hands anchored to his hips. "What the holy hell happened here?" His growling voice was the perfect mix of fear, relief and outrage. It was the sound of an older sibling whose little brother had been wronged.

Being a big sister, Rita knew that one well. She'd had her *Thank goodness you're okay, now who do I need to flatten?* voice at the ready for nineteen years and counting.

West stopped at her side, flipping his hands into the air. His eyes darted from Cole's scowl to the paramedic's kind eyes. "Well? Uncle Henry?"

Uncle Henry?

"I don't know about the boat," the paramedic started, "but Stanford over here is lucky to be alive. He's got extensive first and second degree burns over most of his back and shoulders, lacerations on the head and neck, multiple contusions—" he made an unintelligible sound "—everywhere. No signs of a concussion, despite the temporary loss of consciousness after being clocked on the head with a hunk of the flaming hull." He shrugged. "I want to take him to the hospital for a thorough exam."

"Cole?" West asked, arms crossed, brows furrowed.

"No."

Uncle Henry lifted his palms, looking exactly like his nephew had a minute prior. "Tell your mama I tried."

"Always do," West said. He embraced the older man briefly. "Thanks, Uncle Henry."

"Don't thank me." Henry tipped his head in Rita's direction. "He blacked out in the water. This one pulled him to the dock and kept him afloat until help arrived."

Rita's face heated. "He threw me off the boat when I was too scared to move. Then he jumped in and shielded me from the explosion. I'm the reason he's hurt."

West rubbed his forehead. "He's hurt because he should've been a doctor."

Cole groaned. "I didn't want to be a damn doctor. Now, if you're all done mothering me, we need to get back to work."

"You're hurt," Henry started. He snapped his mouth shut a moment later and raised his hands in surrender.

"I know," Cole agreed, softening his tone slightly. "I'm cut, burned and bruised, none of which is critical, and we need to focus on what's happening around here. We had a literal boatload of information on Minsk's business and it just went up in flames."

Henry shifted his gaze to Rita and the young paramedic at her side. "Your patient doing better than mine?"

"Yes, sir. Some minor abrasions, smoke inhalation, probably a lifelong aversion to watercraft, but she'll be fine."

Henry bobbed his head and swung his attention back to Cole, a growing look of pride on his face. "Good work, deputy." He slapped Cole's shoulder, then winced. "Sorry."

Cole gritted his teeth until his face was as red as his back.

"Take this." Henry handed Cole a clean, dry T-shirt. "I want it back, so don't get any ideas about keeping it."

West closed in on Cole.

Henry delivered a pile of first aid supplies to Rita. "For my nephew's burns. See if you can get him to change the bandages twice a day and take something for pain." He dumped the packages into her palms, then unhooked her oxygen mask. "Good luck." He marched back to his ambulance and swung himself inside. His sidekick followed.

Rita stared at the creams and bandages. *Back to being somebody's keeper.* Trusting someone else to call the shots had been nice while it lasted, but at least caretaking was a role she understood, unlike how to be the target of a psychopath, for example. She took a seat on the dock and piled the supplies at her side. Yesterday had been rock-bottom bad, but today was unfathomably worse.

She slumped forward, resting tired forearms against her thighs. Her skin and clothes smelled like dirty river water and burned hair. No amount of soap would ever remove it.

"Everything's completely destroyed," Cole complained behind her. "The files. Blueprints. Everything. I took some pictures to send to you, but now my phone is at the bottom of the river."

West sauntered closer to the smoldering husk of Minsk's boat. "Two shootings in two days. A bomb on a boat." Disappointment colored his cheeks and frustration sharpened his words. "What's happening to my county?"

Rita pressed her eyes shut. A lunatic had also chased her down the crowded street of a college town and forced her headfirst into an historic fountain, but she didn't think West needed to be reminded of that right now. She peeled stinging eyes open and concentrated on being alive. Whatever else happened, she'd try not to think too hard about the angry look on Cole's face when he'd awoken in her arms.

COLE WATCHED RITA drift away from them, choosing to sit alone on the dock several feet away rather than stand in their little huddle and listen to him gripe any longer. Not that he blamed her. He wasn't his biggest fan at the moment, either. Throwing her from the boat and shielding her from the explosion was supposed to be heroic. Maybe even epic. It should have been the kind of story he'd relish telling his future grandkids, but instead, he'd become the one in need of rescue.

Rita had saved Cole's life.

Dammit.

"Don't forget the car in Rivertown," Cole grouched. "He tried to run her down on a crowded street in broad daylight."

West's long-winded ramble about the last few days' events was true, but incomplete. He'd forgotten one of the scariest things Cole had ever seen. "The nut nearly killed her in front of a hundred college kids."

Rita shot him a look over one shoulder. The disappointment in her expression was a perfect match for Cole's current feelings. "I can't believe everything's gone," she said. "I'm trying to be thankful we survived, but it really stinks that all those files are a total loss."

Cole agreed. He scanned the gathering crowd of nosy locals and news crews. More than one set of male eyes watched Rita as she plucked river-drenched fabric away from her skin, where it had become somewhat transparent.

He moved into the onlookers' line of sight and returned their stares until they found something other than Rita to gawk at. He turned back to her a moment later, satisfied by his success.

Rita squinted up at him and smiled.

Heat spread through his core, warming him until his chest burned with the same intensity as his back. A sneaky realization poked its way into his thoughts. His irritation with those rubberneckers had nothing to do with protecting a traumatized woman from their stares and everything to do with protecting *this* woman, *his woman*, from their stares. *Dammit*.

Cole rolled his shoulders uselessly, hating the unfamiliar knotting of his muscles and the setting of his jaw. He was jealous. Of strangers. He hadn't been bothered by this particular emotion since high school. He didn't like it then, and he downright hated it now.

Not to mention, he had no business feeling anything personal for Rita Horn. She was a citizen in need of temporary protection and nothing more. Once the threat to her was eliminated, she'd go back to her life in progress, probably glad to be rid of a man who'd toss her in the river, then force her to keep him afloat or watch him drown.

Humiliation knotted in his chest.

He flicked his attention to West, who'd gone the length of Minsk's boat and back, apparently still in disbelief. "Hey."

Concern dragged West's brows into a deep V. "Yeah."

"Before it blew up, that boat had a bunch of blueprints for other waterfront locations like our docks. All the way from Louisiana to Missouri. Any chance you've had time to find out who Minsk was seeing at the municipal building?"

West's wrinkled forehead went flat. "No. I was pulled off that hunt when someone took a shot at you over at our first victim's house. I couldn't find that shooter, but I did find another body about thirty minutes before you were nearly blown up, and now I'm here wondering who's trying to kill you."

Rita bent her knees and hugged them to her chest. "Maybe the bomber wasn't trying to kill anyone," she said.

West hiked an eyebrow and gave what was left of the boat a pointed look.

"I thought so, too, at first," Rita said, lifting a hand to her forehead as she squinted against the sun. "But look at this mess." She waved her free hand at the bits of charred wreckage floating in the water and scraps of torched paper blowing over the dock. "Maybe this was just about getting rid of evidence."

"With a bomb?" West asked.

She shrugged. "I'm just saying. If the shooter came here to kill us, he could've opened the door and gotten the job done with a lot less noise. We know a handgun is his weapon of choice. Why change attack methods so drastically? He could have taken his shot while we walked to or from the boat if he didn't want to climb aboard and look for us. Honestly, I don't think anyone knew we were in there."

West pinned Cole with a meaningful stare.

Rita could be right.

"Cole?" Rita shifted onto her hands and knees, staring intently between the wooden boards beneath her. "Look."

Cole crouched to follow her gaze. "What?"

"It's the pen!" She crawled over the ash-littered deck, keeping close tabs on something bobbing in the water below them. "Why did you have it with you? That was our only evidence! It might have had the killer's fingerprints!"

West dropped into view at Cole's side. "Evidence?"

"The pen," she gasped, stretching an arm off the opposite side of the dock. Dark locks of wet hair clung to her cheeks and neck. "Help!" She scooted on her belly, attempting to reach a bobbing portion of the silver metal in the water.

"Careful." Cole grabbed Rita's hips before she spilled

back into the water. Pain licked his neck and shoulders, fresh cuts and burns protesting the sudden move. "That's not the one you gave me."

"What pen?" West asked. His long shadow wobbled on the waves.

"Got it." Rita backed herself onto the boards beside him. "It's ruined." She held the broken pen daintily between her thumb and forefinger. Heavy tears hung in her sweet hazel eyes. "Why can't one single thing go right for us?"

Cole took a seat at her side. He liked the way she said "us" a little more than he should. At least he had good news. "The pen you gave me is still locked in the cruiser's glove box. I planned to deliver it into evidence when we went to the station." He hadn't expected the day would take any of the turns it had. Though the kiss they'd shared nearly made up for being shot at.

Rita blew out a long breath. "Oh, thank goodness. So, at least we still have that." She dropped her hands into her lap and leaned her shoulder against his.

West's face popped into view. He squatted before them in sheriff mode "I need to know about the pen. Now, please." He took the impostor pen from Rita's hands and twisted it in half. Where a tube of ink should have been, there was a small metal rectangle attached to the pen's top. "A thumb drive?"

Cole's mind jerked into action. Rita had been right to mistake the item in West's hands for the one she'd given him in a plastic baggie. The two were identical. And if the pen in West's hand was a thumb drive... A smile etched Cole's face. What about the one in his glove box?

Rita was on her feet, pacing before him and waving her hands as she delivered the blow-by-blow to West. "It was just lying there by the blood on the docks the night Minsk was killed, so I put it in my purse. Then I gave it to Cole."

Cole stretched to his full height with a grunt. "Let's go see if all those pens were made equally."

West rolled his shoulders back and took long sheriff-like strides as he led the way to the parking lot.

Cole grabbed Rita's hand and fell in line behind his brother. He laced his fingers with hers and struggled not to limp as he kept pace. "This guy kept a clean laptop. Saved files to secret devices. Hid paperwork on a boat. Makes me think he knew he was in trouble."

West grunted. "Minsk probably thought the files were enough insurance to preserve his life. He was the only one who knew where they were, so in theory, his killer should've had to keep him alive if they wanted the information."

Rita squeezed Cole's hand. "If there are files on that pen and the information is worth stalking me, tossing my house and trying repeatedly to murder me, then I bet the killer's name is one of the things you'll find."

Cole broke into a painful jog, easily bypassing West. He couldn't rewind time and save Minsk, but he could bring the killer to justice and make sure that guy never got anywhere near Rita again.

Chapter Eleven

West held the plastic baggie from Cole's glove box with reverence. "This is the best thing I've seen in days." He handed the precious cargo to Cole while he snapped plastic gloves over his hands. "Here's hoping," he said, peeling the bag open and fishing the pen from its tissue cocoon.

West gripped the device on both ends and twisted. The pieces came easily apart. "Hot damn." Just like the busted pen in the river, this, too, was only a clever disguise for a thumb drive. He raised wide eyes to Cole. "I'm going to deliver this to the lab myself."

"Good idea," Cole agreed. No sense letting the only known piece of evidence out of his sight. Who knew what sort of information Tech Support would find on that tiny drive? "We're going back to my place. We'll meet you at the station after a hot shower and change of clothes."

West slid his eyes in Rita's direction, then back to Cole. "All right. If I'm not there, give me a call. I've still got a crime scene at Minsk's house and that mess over there to deal with." He hooked a thumb toward the capsizing boat.

Cole checked his watch. The face was cracked, but the second hand was ticking. "If I can get there before it closes, I'll swing by the municipal building. Maybe someone knows who Minsk had been visiting. I'd like to know exactly what he was up to during his last few days."

West tucked the baggie into the pocket of his sheriff's coat. "Lots to do. We'd better roll."

Cole nodded goodbye to his brother before opening the passenger door.

Rita inched closer but didn't climb in.

Sparks of electricity charged the air between them, and for a minute, he allowed himself to imagine Rita kissing him again. This time in front of half the gawking town instead of hidden in his car behind an empty church. Maybe she could somehow still see him as a hero, even after she'd had to save him when he blacked out.

Rita kicked the toe of her sodden shoe against the ground, her pretty hazel eyes focused completely on the earth. "I'm sorry you were hurt."

The punch to his chest couldn't have hit any deeper. He'd failed her today, and she was as sorry about it as he was. Before he could find the words to apologize, she dropped into the car and pulled her feet inside.

RITA MENTALLY KICKED herself all the way back to Cole's house. *I'm sorry you were hurt?* Of all the things racing through her mind, *that* was what she'd chosen to say? Worse, he'd looked at her like she'd slapped him when she said it, so she'd avoided speaking for the duration of the drive. Unfortunately, she wouldn't be able to hide much longer.

Cole settled the cruiser's engine in his driveway and climbed out.

This wasn't like a random blind date where she could go home and put her awkward words behind her. She was practically living with Cole, at least until further notice, and he rarely let her out of his sight. After the shoot-out at Minsk's house, she imagined her alone time would be relegated to bathroom breaks.

She hustled onto the porch behind him and waited while he unlocked the door.

Cole ushered her inside and locked up. After a quick sweep of the house, he returned with a stack of dry clothes and a towel. "How about that shower?"

Rita's cheeks heated. She looked away in case he could somehow read the explicit thoughts racing through her mind. "You should go first. You're hurt."

Cole's brows knit together. His mouth curled down. "Please stop saying that."

"Why? You *are* hurt." She crossed her arms to stop the tremor building in her gut. Blood had risen in the water as she kept him afloat. She'd seen the gashes on his shoulders, could only imagine the burns on his back or what it looked like now that Cole's uncle had stitched and cleaned him up. The replacement shirt he'd taken, to keep dirty, river-soaked clothes off newly tended wounds, was already patchy with spots of blood and ointment.

Bottom line: Cole *was* hurt. And it was because of her. "A boat exploded thirty feet away from us. My ears are still ringing, and I feel as if I was hit by a truck even though there's barely a mark on me. You, on the other hand…" She left the sentence undone. Where could she even begin? He'd played human shield and nearly paid for it with his life. "Stop saying everything's fine." Endless stacks of emotions piled heavily on her heart, demanding to be heard. Tears stung her eyes and her nose burned. "This is not fine!"

She couldn't stop the sharp sob that broke from her lips. The sound came without warning. Rita clamped a hand over her mouth and turned on her heels for the bathroom where she could drown her worries in a hot shower and wash the stink of river water away. "Excuse me," she cried on her way down the hall. "I have to call Mrs. Wilcox and check on my cats."

She reemerged thirty minutes later, fresh out of tears and ways to fix her puffy eyes. Clean, dry and dressed in her favorite white cotton top and pale gray leggings, she felt almost normal. With any luck, she didn't look like the same frantic nut who'd gone into the bathroom half an hour before.

Her mouth watered as she padded down the short hallway toward the kitchen. The house outside the bathroom smelled like heaven.

Cole stood at the stove, shirtless, pushing sliced peppers, onions and mushrooms around a pan. Rice boiled in the pot beside him. He flicked a troubled gaze her way. "How was the shower?"

"Good." She leaned against the counter behind him in the narrow space, examining the angry red burns and other assorted injuries on his back and shoulders. Beneath today's cuts and burns, a palette of heavy scars rose in permanent welts. Shrapnel. Rita knew those scars well. She'd lived on a dozen army bases growing up, and too many men had similar war wounds. Some had much worse. And they were still the lucky ones because they'd made it home.

Rita had known that Cole was a veteran, but she'd never considered that this wasn't his first run-in with a bomb. "Your uncle gave me everything I need to change your bandages after your shower."

Cole froze for a beat, then went busily back to work at the stove. "Hungry?"

Her tummy rumbled audibly. "Yes."

Cole removed the sauté pan from the stove top and drained the rice before turning to face her for the first time since she'd walked in on him shirtless and cooking. He'd traded his wet socks and uniform pants for bare feet and basketball shorts. The shorts hung dangerously low on his torso, daring her eyes to follow the path of dark hair from his belly button to where it disappeared beneath his waistband.

When she finally found the strength to pry her curious eyes off his body, Cole was staring.

"Everything okay?" he asked through a playful grin.

"Mmm-hmm." She pressed her lips together in embarrassment.

"Good." He inhaled deeply. "How are your cats?"

"Fine. Mrs. Wilcox is meeting all their demands."

Cole grinned. "I made dinner, but I should confess first. There's an ulterior motive behind it."

Rita felt her eyebrows rise to the ceiling.

"I think we should talk about some of the things that happened today," he said.

"Okay."

Cole rubbed the back of his neck, making his chest appear doubly broad. He winced. His arm lowered at a much slower pace than he'd used to raise it. Frustration changed his gentle expression into something resembling the face he'd worn on the docks.

"Why were you angry when you woke in the water?" Rita bit her tongue once the words were out. She hadn't meant to ask so abruptly, but she had to know. She'd upset him somehow and deserved to know what happened.

Cole shifted his weight and let his arms drop to his sides. "I wasn't angry."

"Yes," she argued. "You were. You barely spoke to me the whole time we were on the dock. You snapped at your uncle when he tried to help you. I don't know what I did that made you so mad, but I'm sorry."

Cole crossed his arms and waited. A mask of patience replaced the frustration she'd seen on him earlier.

The more she spoke, the bolder she felt. "Was it because you had to throw me off the boat? Because I panicked and

I couldn't move." Cole wasn't arguing his side, interrupting or diminishing her position. He was listening. And she loved it. "I knew I needed to run, but I couldn't."

He reached for her cheek, brushing away another determined tear. "I wasn't angry with you. I was disappointed in myself. You needed me to protect you, and I failed."

"You were hit with the fiery hull of an exploding boat. It's not like you were home watching the game."

He laughed, and the room seemed brighter. "A blackout is no excuse."

"You saved my life again," she said. "So what if I got to help you out, too?"

"It's my job to protect you. Not the other way around." He turned back to the stove and plated the rice and veggies. "You don't have to take care of everyone all the time. I don't want you looking at me like I'm your little brother. I don't want to be parented."

Anger pinched her chest. "I wasn't parenting you. I kissed you! You think I want to kiss my brother?"

He pushed heaping plates of rice and veggies onto the island beside two glasses of ice water, napkins and silverware. "Eat. You haven't had anything all day, and you're shaking."

Rita moved to a stool at the counter. "Who's the parent now?"

"Not me." He exhaled the words. "I'm the little brother who should've been a doctor."

Rita let the words settle in. "Do you really think that, or are you just repeating the things your brother and uncle said today?"

Cole wiped his hands on a towel and tossed the cloth onto his counter. "I don't regret being a deputy. I was meant to do this, and they know it. I only tried medical school because it made my parents happy. When I left the military, they wanted to see me do something safe, but I'm not a doctor, I'm a lawman." He locked her in his stare. "This is who I am."

"I like who you are," Rita whispered.

Cole made a move in her direction, his smart blue eyes never leaving hers. "I can protect you."

Rita wet her lips. "I know."

A small smile tugged his lips. "Since you're going to be staying here, I think we need some rules."

She forced herself to breathe. His slow, predatory walk was churning her thoughts into mush. "We do?"

"My house. My rules. Ready?"

"Um."

"First, you're my guest. That means I make the meals, shower second and sleep on the couch. You get the bed, hot water and as many of my meals as you can tolerate."

Rita bit her lip against the argument on her tongue. Cole had let her talk when she needed to. It was her turn to listen.

"Second, you're under my protection now, so if something else blows up, it's not going to be you. And if I get knocked out again, don't baby me. Just slap my face and tell me to wake the hell up and get back to work."

Rita laughed. "Fine. Did you really go to Stanford?"

Cole took the seat at her side, stuffing the next closest bar stool beneath him. "For a minute."

"Impressive."

He forked a pile of peppers before lifting a broad and youthful smile to her. "You think so?"

"Yeah."

He stuffed the bite into his mouth and chewed thoughtfully. "You like smart guys. I figured. Suit-and-tie guys with loafers and 401Ks."

"What?" Rita laughed, nearly losing the mouthful of

delicious dinner. "No. I mean, not no, but not only suits. I'm a very nondiscriminatory dater. Or I would be if anyone ever asked me out. No one asks."

"What?" Cole dropped his fork onto his plate. His mouth hung open briefly before curving into a disbelieving smile. "No one asks, or you never say yes?"

"Both, I guess, but mostly the first one."

"Why?" he pressed, inexplicably mystified.

"I can be a little distrusting," she admitted, "and I didn't want the distraction while Ryan was living with me. Now that he's on his own, I'm a little older and a lot of folks are married."

"I'm not married."

Rita's smile widened. "Well, Dad warned me about dating soldiers."

Cole grinned. "Yeah?"

"That's what he said, which is silly because he's a general. Though, in hindsight, it probably saved him a lot of trouble considering my high school years were spent on a series of army bases."

"Your dad sounds like a wise man."

"Really? I expected you to disagree."

"Why? Because I was a soldier?" Cole faced her. "I'm actually a huge fan of whatever has kept you single this long."

Rita poked her dinner, unable to eat with so much nervous energy raging inside her. "I think I was waiting for someone special. A man with brains and brawn. A hero's heart. A strong sense of justice and ties to the community."

Cole slid onto his feet, crowding her personal space. "That's a hefty list."

He grabbed her hips and turned her to face him.

Rita's knees parted on instinct, making room for him to get closer.

"Anything else?" Cole widened his stance, bringing him marginally closer to her height.

She craned her neck for a better look at his handsome face. "Yeah."

Heat from his bare chest radiated out to her, and the look in his eyes turned her bones into putty.

She braced her hands on his shoulders, then slid her open palms against his neck, tracing the strong line of his jaw with her thumbs. "My dream guy would know when to kiss me."

Cole's smiling lips were instantly on hers. Soft and testing at first, then heavy and urging.

She wound her fingers into his hair and hooked an ankle behind his leg, nudging him closer. The little gasp that burst from her lips was met with a low, sexy growl.

The day had just gotten a whole lot better.

Until the ringing landline stilled his mouth on hers.

Cole froze, tightening his fingers on her hips as if she might disappear.

"Do you have to get that?" she asked, hoping desperately he'd decide to carry her to his room instead of taking the call. She'd been replaying their earlier kiss since she'd taken one look at him making her dinner. Shirtless. Could it get any better? Her body responded to his so easily, melding into his touch and matching him, heat for heat, as if this was just one more in a lifetime of shared kisses instead of only their second.

He kissed her again, and she parted her lips for him, inviting him deeper. Cole's tongue swept into her mouth, and suddenly, she could think of several ways this could get better.

Cole pulled back by a fraction and stared pointedly into her eyes. "Yes, but don't go anywhere."

Rita fanned her cheeks as Cole went to grab the landline, still ringing rudely on the wall.

"Garrett." He shifted his gaze back to Rita. "Who's calling?" Color bled from his ruddy cheeks. "One minute." Cole returned to her side, phone extended. "It's for you."

Rita pressed the phone to her ear, more terrified by the look on Cole's face than by anything she'd seen or experienced all week. "This is Rita Horn."

Cole grabbed a T-shirt off the back of a nearby chair and tugged it over his head, then scooped keys and a wallet off the table by his front door.

"Miss Horn," the stranger's voice began, "this is Mercy Medical Center. Your brother, Ryan Horn, has been in a serious car accident."

Chapter Twelve

Rita jammed bare feet into untied running shoes. *Ryan was hurt.* A car accident. He was at the hospital, and she needed to go.

Emergency Room doors...west wing...second floor.

Cole had her purse and jacket over one arm. "Ready?"

"Thank you." She slid shaking arms into the sleeves of her hoodie and zipped it to her chin. A round of powerful tremors rattled her teeth and twisted her stomach. She'd forgotten about the truck. She'd forgotten about her own brother. She was a horrible sister. A terrible substitute parent. *Mom would have never forgotten him.*

Cole opened the front door and held it for Rita to pass.

A moment later, they were on their way to the hospital at unlawful speeds. The cruiser's lights and sirens cleared a path as they moved through the compact downtown streets.

Rita wound noodle arms around her middle, certain that losing Ryan would tear her in two. "The last communication I had with him was through text messages, and I argued with him about my truck. I never argue with him. Why would I do that?"

Cole moved an open palm onto her thigh. "You were trying to keep him safe."

"Yeah," she scoffed, "by lying to him. I promised to always be honest. Always be truthful, but I've been lying to Ryan since the minute I got involved in this mess with Minsk. I broke my promise."

Cole's thumb swept across her skin in soothing waves. "This isn't your fault. It was an accident. And he's going to be okay."

Rita curled her fingers over his and pulled their joined hands to her cheek. This wasn't the first time she'd rushed to the hospital after someone she loved had been in a car accident. "How do you know?"

"He's your brother, right? I bet he's tough."

"He is."

Cole offered her an encouraging smile. "He'll pull through this, and while he's doing that, I'll be with you every step of the way."

The last time she'd been in this situation, things hadn't been okay. Not ever again. "My mom didn't pull through."

Cole gave her a long look. "Do you want to talk about it?"

No, she didn't want to, but the words were already filling her mouth. The fear constricting her chest. "The man who hit my mother was in for his eleventh DUI when he was released due to overcrowding in the jails. A lot of low-level offenders were set free. I guess that was what he was until he killed my mother. Not that he was charged with her death. Wasn't the first time he'd been incarcerated for driving under the influence or the first time he'd been released without a license, only to get behind the wheel again. Drunk."

Cole's strong expression crumbled. Heartbreak swam in his eyes. "I'm so sorry."

"He didn't actually hit her," Rita blabbed on. "Nothing like that. He was just going the wrong way on the highway at night. My mom swerved, attempting not to die in a head-on collision. Ironic, right? The only life she saved was the drunk's. He got off with a slap on the wrist and a stern talking-to. His lawyer argued that he didn't hit her. She'd acted on her own. He said maybe she saw a deer or something. That was the defense's argument. How could we prove that she'd swerved to miss the drunk driver? He got another DUI, a frowny face for driving without a license and some nonsense about not obeying traffic signs. He's probably out there now, doing it again."

"Rita." Cole's voice was husky and thick with regret.

The hospital came into view, tall and regal on the horizon. A giant red cross stretched from the roof with the word Mercy emblazoned in white across its middle.

"I'm fine." Rita released Cole's hand in favor of unbuckling her seat belt and wiping her face. The tears had dried as suddenly as they'd come. "The hospital said Ryan swerved."

Cole left his cruiser in valet parking, but took the key and darted around to meet Rita.

She was already making strides toward the sliding glass doors.

"Where are we going?" Cole asked, taking her hand once more.

"He's in surgery." She racked her brain to remember the voice from the phone. "Second floor, I think."

"I know that one. That's the trauma unit. Come on." He pulled her into a jog, bypassing the giant silver elevator in favor of a doorway marked Stairs.

The second floor waiting room was vast but silent. Bitter scents of burned coffee and popcorn hung in the air, creeping in from the main hall. A sleeping woman tipped awkwardly in one chair, having apparently fallen asleep while knitting, needles still in her hands, yarn on her lap.

Cole kept moving until they reached the nurses' station. "This is Rita Horn. I'm Deputy Cole Garrett. We received a call that her brother, Ryan Horn, was in a car accident. He's in surgery now."

The woman slid a clipboard onto the counter. Her chair knocked against the table, spilling an open bag of microwave popcorn over her workstation. Rita's stomach knotted at the sight of it. "Miss Horn, you were listed as Ryan's next of kin. Is there anyone else you'd like us to notify for you?"

"No. I'll take care of that."

"I don't mind," the woman pressed. "I know this is hard."

Rita shot her a disbelieving look. Did she know? How could she? When was the last time she'd gotten a call like this about her baby brother? Rita bit her tongue against the building tirade. "Our dad's overseas. I don't even know where, exactly." Government secrets and all. She fought an internal eyeroll. Once again she was on her own to deal with a family crisis while the supposed head of the household was off to who-knew-where. "He has a number and an email address that he checks when he can. I'll handle it." She took the clipboard. "What's this?"

"We'll need your brother's complete medical history, insurance and contact information. Also, your brother is an organ donor. If you have any questions about that, I'm prepared to answer them."

Rita hugged the clipboard to her chest. "I'm well informed on that matter. Thank you. What I need to know is how my brother is doing." Tears began to fall once more, ruining her attempt to look strong when Ryan needed her.

"I won't know any more than you do until he's out of surgery."

Rita whipped the clipboard in the air, desperate to smack something with it, and knowing she just looked crazy. A rough sob ripped through her.

The nurse's expression turned solemn. "I'm sorry."

Cole dragged Rita against him, wrapping strong arms around her back and cradling her head to his chest. "Can you tell us anything about what happened?" he asked the woman behind the desk.

"No. Only that he was involved in a car accident. Maybe someone at the sheriff's department will have more details."

"Thank you. You'll let us know as soon as he's out of surgery?"

"A doctor will find you."

Cole led Rita to an exterior terrace on the opposite end of the floor. "I need to make some calls. It's private here."

Rita took a seat, unsure if her legs would hold her up much longer. Beyond the glass, a cafeteria with neon lights promised *Good Food! Cold Drinks!*

Cole worked a phone from the pocket of his shorts and flipped it open. "Burner," he explained. "I lose more phones than you'd think. I have a few of these for emergencies." He pressed the buttons on a tiny keypad, then caught the phone between his ear and shoulder.

Three calls and ten minutes later, Cole lowered into a squat before her. "Lomar was the deputy on scene at Ryan's accident. He said Uncle Henry was the first responder. That's very good news. Henry's the best. I've put a call in to him, too."

Rita lifted her eyes to Cole's, buoyed by the small measure of hope. "Did you talk to Lomar?"

"Yes."

"Was Ryan driving my truck?" She braced herself for the answer she feared was coming.

"Yes."

A rush of breath swept from her lungs. This was the very thing she'd feared most. Ryan had taken her truck, then someone had mistaken him for her and tried to kill him. She didn't need to hear the details to know that was the truth of it. Ryan was a careful driver, and her truck was in sound condition. An accident today, after the day she'd had seemed highly unlikely.

Ryan was in critical condition and it was her fault. "Was he alone?" she asked, realizing the roommate he was helping move might've somehow gotten wrapped up in her mess, too. What if the other kid hadn't been as lucky as Ryan? Ryan had at least made it into surgery.

That was more than her Mom had.

"He was alone," Cole said. "I have some limited details now. They're yours if you want them, but if you want to wait until you know Ryan's out of surgery, there's no rush."

Images of Ryan's crash, or her mind's version of it anyway, raced through her head. He had to be okay. She couldn't live in a world where her determination to help an injured kitten had caused her brother's eventual death.

"I want to know." She pressed her palms against her knees. "I want to know everything you know. Please."

Cole nodded. "Okay. First, why don't you call your dad?" He tipped his phone in her direction. "Then we can move to the waiting area and watch for the doctor to come out of surgery."

COLE FOLLOWED RITA to a pair of chairs near the window. The call to her father had been short and sweet. A message on a voice mail. There was nothing else she could do.

"Okay," she said. "Tell me what you know."

"Deputy Lomar was the responding officer," he began. "Dispatch pulled him from the marina after a witness called to report the accident."

"There was a witness?" Hope lit her beautiful face.

"Yes. A jogger says she saw your truck moving at questionable speeds on the county route between the college and Crestmont Hills in Rivertown."

"That's Ryan's neighborhood."

"The jogger said the truck was speeding and heading into a dangerous curve. She assumed he wasn't paying attention, or maybe he'd been drinking, but when Ryan passed her, she got a look at his face. She described him as terrified. Stiff armed. The truck was loaded with furniture, the hill he was headed down was steep, and she was right, he didn't make the curve at the bottom. He lost control and hit a tree. Based on the damage to your truck, Lomar estimates Ryan attempted a twenty-mile-per-hour curve at more than fifty. Also, there weren't any tire marks on the pavement."

"He didn't use the brakes?" Rita pressed the heels of her hands against red eyes. "I don't suppose the jogger happened to notice an evil psychopath in a black sedan nearby."

"No. There were no other cars at the time of the accident. I think we should count that as a blessing," Cole said. "No one could have maneuvered the truck around traffic at those speeds."

"Right." Rita raked her hands through her hair and gripped the back of her head. "So we can assume someone cut the brakes. Obviously, this was the same person who's been trying to kill me all day, and now they've nearly killed Ryan, instead."

"We don't know anything for certain," Cole cautioned. "Lomar's looking into it now. He'll be here when he finishes."

Rita clenched her jaw. "I just had the truck serviced, and it was fine when I drove it home before Ryan borrowed it. The only way there wouldn't be any tire marks from this accident is if the brakes didn't engage."

Cole leaned closer, lowering his voice as he spoke. "*If* someone cut the brake lines, and trust me, I'm not trying to create a conspiracy theory here, but if that's what happened, given the day we've had, I would agree. It's fair to assume this wasn't a coincidence."

Rita nodded. Good. He was still on her side.

"And if someone wanted to cause an accident," he continued, "they would make sure the damage to the brake line was small and the leak was slow. Someone who knew what they were doing would want brake fluid in the lines when the driver got in, maybe even enough to last while Ryan confidently collected furniture for a new roommate before running out. If he got into the truck and there were no brakes, he wouldn't have gone anywhere, except maybe to a garage, and that would've ruined the criminal's efforts. Wasted his time."

Rita slumped forward. "By the time Ryan was on the county route, loaded down and driving faster, using the brakes for hills and turns, the fluid would've run out, and it would've been too late to stop."

"That's what I'm thinking," Cole admitted. "You know about cars?"

"Just brakes. My first car had soft brakes, and Dad was home at the time. He found the problem and told me what could happen if I'd kept driving it that way. Said I wasted my money on a junker car when I could've walked anywhere I needed to go."

Criticizing his only daughter? Telling her to walk after learning she'd saved for a car? What a jerk. Cole forced a tight smile. "Your dad sounds like a real peach."

"Yep."

Clearly, Rita had gotten her kind and nurturing heart from her mother.

Two long hours later, a man in blue scrubs stopped at

the nurses' station outside the waiting room, then turned to face Cole and Rita when the nurse pointed their way.

Rita leaped from her chair and met the man in the hallway. Cole followed.

According to the man's name tag he was chief of surgery.

"I'm Dr. Keller." He hugged his clipboard in one arm and extended his free hand to Rita, then Cole. "Ryan's surgery was textbook. No complications. No surprises. He's being moved from Recovery to an observation room on this floor now."

Rita lifted onto her toes, craning her neck to see around the doctor. "Which room is his? Can I talk to him now?"

"You're welcome to see him, but talking to him will take some time."

Her jaw dropped. "Why?"

Cole pulled her against his side and curved a protective arm around her waist. He'd seen what she hadn't yet. The tight set of the doctor's jaw. His rigid stance. The slight pinch of his mouth, indicating that he'd delivered the only good news he had.

Dr. Keller shuffled his bootie-covered feet. "Your brother has been unconscious since his arrival. You're more than welcome to talk to him, but he's unlikely to respond. Though I like to think all communication helps, one-sided or not."

Rita crunched her brow. "I don't understand. When will he wake up?"

The doctor shifted his gaze to Cole.

"It's okay," Cole answered the unspoken question. "She can handle it."

Dr. Keller lowered his chin before turning back to Rita. "As you may have been told, Ryan's injuries are extensive. He has multiple fractures to his hands, arms and ribs, plus his right foot and left thigh. There's significant damage to the bones in his cheek, forehead and upper jaw. He'll need additional surgeries to correct those issues later. I was able to locate and stop his internal bleeding, and set several broken bones. It was a good start. Right now, we're concerned about secondary injuries that often occur in situations like these. Sometimes it takes a day or two after a trauma for things to rear their heads. We're watching specifically for signs of swelling or bruising of the brain. The anesthesia should've worn off in Recovery. Now, it's just a matter of when he opens his eyes. We'll know more once he wakes. Any other questions?"

Rita gaped.

Cole hugged her tight. "We want to see him."

"Of course." Dr. Keller led the way to a private room near the nurses' station. "Visiting hours are shorter here than the other wards. The patients need extended time to rest. Also, we ask that they have no more than one visitor at a time. I'm sure you understand."

"No." Rita stopped short. "Two." She faced off with the doctor. "Two at a time, and I'm not leaving until he wakes up. I don't care about your hours. I won't make a sound, and I'll stay out of the way, but I won't leave him."

Dr. Keller made an apologetic face. "Hospital policy says…"

"Sir," Cole interrupted before the man could tell her no. He dragged his badge from one pocket and flipped it open, well aware that he looked absolutely nothing like a lawman in his running shorts and faded army T-shirt. "I'm a deputy with the Cade County Sheriff's Department, and we have reason to believe this young man's vehicle was tampered with. For his safety, we'll need a deputy stationed outside the door at all times, and I'll be staying with Miss Horn.

She and her brother are going through a terrible ordeal right now, and all they have is each other."

The words were sour on his tongue. Rita had Cole, too, and he needed to tell her. She deserved to know the things that had been happening to his heart since their lives crossed paths this week. He'd never felt so attached to or identified so strongly with anyone who wasn't blood related. Hell, he'd never even met Ryan, but the guy lying in that bed may as well have been his brother. At least, that was the way it seemed to his heart as it pounded and his breaths grew shallow. He needed that young man to be okay because Rita needed him to be okay.

"Fine." Dr. Keller didn't look pleased, but he also didn't argue. "Get a chair for the other deputy from the waiting area. You can place it in the hallway outside his door. The security detail is required to stay outside the room, and he can't bother the nurses. They have work to do. I'll allow you to accompany Miss Horn inside the room on a probational basis, but only you."

"Yes, sir."

RITA UNTANGLED HERSELF from Cole's grasp and darted to Ryan's side on autopilot. She dragged her fingers over the cold metal railing, drinking in the sting of antiseptic in the air.

The man in the bed looked nothing like her baby brother, and yet he was exactly that. His face was purple and deeply bruised, swollen to the extreme and distorted by the injuries. His head was wrapped in gauze. Tubes ran from freestanding machines into the crook of his arm and up his nose. Rita recalled the sweet scent of oxygen through her mask at the river and hoped Ryan was as relieved by the clean air as she had been.

She lifted his bandaged fingers in hers. A cast ran the

length of his arm to his palm. "Ry?" She stroked the backs of his fingertips with her thumb. "I am so sorry," she whispered, drying tears as they fell. "This is all my fault, and if you can hear me, you've got to wake up so I can make it right. I owe you a huge explanation, then you can yell at me and tell me how stupid I am." She jiggled his motionless hand in hers. "Wake up and tell me I'm stupid."

Wake up so I know I didn't get you killed.

COLE MOVED TO stand behind Rita. He rubbed her shoulders. He checked the time on a large clock outside the door. The county municipal building would close in half an hour, and no one had been down there to ask what Minsk was doing during his recent visits. Cole wanted to be the one to get those answers.

Rita pressed one palm to her brother's misshapen face. He looked like Frankenstein's monster now, but the swelling would go away soon, and a plastic surgeon would return him to the image Rita remembered. Cole had seen a lot worse injuries heal to near invisibility.

"Hey." He leaned his mouth to her ear. "Any chance I can convince you to make a trip to the courthouse?"

"No."

"Okay." He'd figured.

The minute hand on the clock took another step toward closing time at the courthouse, but there was no way Cole would leave Rita alone again, not even at a hospital. Not even with another deputy as her personal guardian. Protecting her was Cole's job now, and he didn't trust anyone else to get it done.

"I can't leave him." She turned to Cole, burying her face in the contours of his chest. "What if he wakes up and I'm not here? What if he doesn't wake up?" Her chest thumped and rattled with shuttered breaths. "I can't."

Cole stroked the length of her soft red hair. "Okay. We'll stay." Maybe he could sneak into the hall later and make some calls from the nurse's desk.

Rita stroked his chest with one hand. She rolled her head to press a cheek against his tear-soaked shirt. "Do you think there's a chance that this is all just horrible timing? Maybe I assumed the worse, and this was just an accident and it isn't my fault."

Cole pressed a kiss to the top of her head. He gripped her tight around the middle and wished he could give her hope. But he didn't believe in coincidence, and this catastrophe was too spot-on to be anything other than intentional.

"Deputy Garrett?" Deputy Lomar's voice turned Cole's head toward the open door.

Rita tightened her arms around Cole's waist and angled her face away from the deputy.

Cole adjusted his hold on instinct, careful to keep her secure and comforted, even in the presence of another deputy. Especially one who'd been his wingman at more than one bar this month. The only other single man on the job should know Rita Horn wasn't up for grabs. She was Cole's, and he'd be hers in a minute if she wanted him. "Any news?"

Lomar's gaze lingered on Cole's hands, placed low and protectively on Rita's trim body. Lomar knew Cole didn't do PDA. He didn't get involved beyond a bar and a beer. Until now, a *long-term relationship* had meant sharing a bed until dawn. Cole had never made a secret of his intentional bachelorhood. The whole department knew it. Hell, half the town knew it, and by the way Lomar was staring, the whole of Cade County would know about the drastic change in him by dinner.

"You have an update?" Cole prompted, lifting his chin in defiance.

Lomar cleared his throat. "Yeah." His curious eyes jumped back to meet Cole's. "Cade County Automotive was able to confirm the cause of the accident."

"And?"

"Someone cut the truck's brake lines."

Chapter Thirteen

Rita fell asleep at Ryan's bedside to the soft, repetitive beeping and whooshing of hospital equipment. When her eyes opened again, the room was dark. Tiny red and green lights illuminated the corner, occasionally backlit by small screens, assuring her the machines attached to her brother were still doing all they could to monitor him. Her head rested on the edge of his bed, her bottom on the rough cushion of a wooden hospital chair.

She brushed her fingers gently against his bruised cheek. "Come on, Ry. Time to wake up."

Cole shifted in his sleep. His long body was spread over the awful green recliner in the room's corner, limbs dangling, head cocked awkwardly. He'd chosen a seat with full view of the hallway outside, then set up a makeshift office utilizing a Wi-Fi password schmoozed off the nurse and the laptop he'd pulled from his cruiser. He should have gone home for some proper rest, but she was selfishly thankful he hadn't. She'd wanted him there. More than that, she'd wanted him to *want* to stay.

And he had.

Rita's tummy growled and she pressed a palm against her middle to stifle the noise. The green Jell-O and cup of ice chips Cole had delivered around midnight had worn off long ago. She'd been too upset to consider eating anything more substantial at the time, but currently, she'd like a tall stack of hotcakes with a double side of bacon.

Her head ached with every move she made. Her neck was stiff from the awkward position she'd temporarily slept in. She scooped the plastic cup of melted ice chips off the nightstand and sucked down the few measly teaspoons of liquid. She'd cheerfully have gone in search of more, if it hadn't meant leaving Ryan.

The room's door swung open, and a young woman swept back the privacy curtain separating them from the nurses' station on the other side of the observation glass.

Cole had pulled the curtain before Rita fell asleep.

The nurse started. "Oh, hello." She brushed wild brown curls away from her face. Her cheeks darkened, and she darted her attention from Rita to Ryan and back. "I didn't know you were awake. I'm Stacy." She hung a pink stethoscope around her neck. "I'm the night nurse. How are you holding up?"

Rita bobbed her head and forced a tight smile. "Awful."

"Yeah. I figured." Stacy moved to Ryan's side. "It's hard to see our loved ones like this. Most folks stay in the waiting room, if they stay at all." She checked the tubes running to and from him, then tapped the IV bag. "Good." She pulled a small pad of paper from her pocket and made a note, then checked the machines. "Everything looks really great." She turned back to Rita with a warm smile and raised brows. "Your brother's tough. He'll get through this. He talks about you a lot, you know?"

"You know Ryan?" Rita jerked upright, greedy for information. Her pounding head nearly knocked her out. "Ow." She rubbed her temple and cringed.

Stacy moved to Rita's side. "May I?" She caught Rita's wrist in her small fingers without waiting for an answer. "Your pulse is racing. The other nurses said you've barely eaten since you got here yesterday afternoon, and those ice chips don't make much water."

Rita already knew that. She wanted the information she didn't have. "How do you know Ryan?"

"School." Stacy leaned her backside against the bed and gripped the railing on each side of her. "I'm an RN, but I'm going to be a nurse practitioner next year. I take classes during the day, and I see him around sometimes." She lifted her gaze to Rita's forehead where the goose bump looked like the beginnings of a second head.

"Is he happy?" Rita asked.

"Yeah. Always smiling. Funny. Kind."

Fresh tears welled in Rita's eyes. "Thank you for saying that."

"It's no problem. He's a great guy." Stacy stuffed her hands into her pockets. "I hate that this happened to him."

"Me, too."

Stacy stroked the length of Ryan's arm cast. "He's going to be okay. It looks scary now, but this will all heal." She glanced through the window wall, then turned her back to it. "His leg had the most damage. The femur was shattered, but it's not a life-or-death injury, and his brain and spinal column look good."

Rita covered her mouth, outrageously thankful for the details. "Dr. Keller made me think Ryan might not wake up."

"He'll wake up," Stacy assured her. "I know it." She gave him a lingering look. "A career in professional basketball or the military might be out, but he'll be okay."

Stacy smiled at her joke, but Rita ached internally. Ryan had wanted a career in the military and she'd inadvertently taken that from him by allowing this accident.

Stacy finished up and left without a goodbye.

She returned a few minutes later with food. "It's Marcia's birthday today, so we have one of those giant sub sandwiches in the break room. I thought you might like a piece."

Salty scents of ham and cheese wafted out to meet her. Rich, buttery Italian bread. The tangy bite of onions and pickles. "Thank you." Rita accepted the plate with a greedy smile.

"But wait. There's more." Stacy dropped a bottle of water onto the table beside Rita's empty cup. "And…" She dug in her pocket and came out with a two-pack of aspirin. "For your headache."

"How do you know I have a headache?"

Stacy shook her head. "You're squinting and rubbing your temple. You haven't eaten and you're under a ton of stress. If you didn't need some kind of pill at this point, I'd wonder if you were human."

"Bless you." Rita tossed the two aspirin onto her tongue and washed them down with half the bottle of water.

"Don't mention it. I'll be back to check on you after you've had time to eat." She squeezed Ryan's blanket-covered foot on her way out.

Rita really needed to ask him about this woman when he woke up.

She finished the water and sandwich in minutes.

The door opened again, and Stacy reappeared with a folded manila envelope. "How was dinner?" Her attention lingered on Ryan's quiet form.

Rita dusted her palms. "Excellent. Thank you." Behind her, Cole shifted in the too-small chair. He deserved a thank-you for staying with her when he wanted to be out working the case. She didn't like that she'd kept him from it, but she was glad he'd fallen asleep. He needed rest to heal.

Cole yawned. "What time is it?"

Stacy checked her watch. "Four fifteen."

"This is Stacy," Rita explained by way of introduction. "She's Ryan's night nurse and knows him from school."

"Small world," Cole said, sliding to the edge of his seat and extending a hand to Stacy.

"Small town," Stacy added.

"I'm Cole Garrett," he said, "nice to meet you."

She smiled. "Yes, I've seen you around, Deputy Garrett. I'm glad you're here." She turned her attention back to Rita. "I thought you might want this." She extended the envelope in Rita's direction. "This was at the nurses' station. I assume it's everything Ryan had on him when they took him in for surgery. You should keep it until he wakes up." She gave a soft smile. "I'd better get to work. I'll bring another water when I come back. Can I get you anything, Deputy Garrett?"

"Coffee?"

"Sure thing." Stacy slipped back through the door, leaving it ajar.

Cole tracked her movement through the window before turning narrowed eyes on Rita. "Nurses are usually nice to me, but I've never had one taking drink orders."

"I think she's got something going with my brother." Rita turned the envelope over in her hands, examining it top to bottom. Was it nosy of her to want to look?

"Did she say that?" Cole stretched to his feet, brows puckered. He rolled his shoulders and swore softly.

"You're hurt. It's way past time to change your bandages." Rita sighed. She was normally good in a crisis, but lately there had been just too many emergencies to keep tabs on. "She didn't say it, but I can tell."

"How?"

Rita made a face. "Well, don't look so mystified. You can tell when women are into you. Same thing here."

Cole snorted. "I can tell because they say so."

Rita rubbed her eyes to stop them from rolling. She considered judging the women who'd been bold enough to tell Cole Garrett they wanted him, but hadn't she climbed onto his lap yesterday and basically assaulted him?

She let her eyes fall shut. She was jealous of faceless, unnamed women who may or may not have behaved exactly like she had.

"Rita?" Cole nudged her elbow. "You okay?"

"I'm super." She opened her eyes, then flipped the envelope over on her legs and slid a tentative finger beneath the partially glued flap. Either someone had done a terrible job of sealing it, or someone had taken a peek inside. She lifted her eyes to the window wall, locating Stacy in the hallway with ease. Would she have pried into Ryan's personal things?

"Was that already open?" Cole asked.

"I'm not sure." Rita upturned the envelope and shook the contents onto her lap. A wallet. Phone. Loose change. Keys. Nothing unusual.

Cole leaned in. "Anything missing that you think ought to be there?"

"I don't know what he normally carries with him." She opened his wallet and checked for cash. Thirty-two dollars. "He had money." Emotion tightened her chest. "I'm always afraid he won't have enough cash to eat or buy gas or do the things he wants to do." She flipped through the pictures. One of their parents. One of Rita. None of Stacy the potential girlfriend or very nosy nurse. "I'm glad he had some money." There was something else inside she couldn't see. The raised area was among his credit card slots, but sheltered by a small leather flap. She wiggled her fingernail inside and extracted the contents. "Oh, my gosh, he has a condom."

Cole laughed.

She pushed everything back inside the leather bifold and shook her hands out at the wrists. "I didn't even know he was dating. Oh. Ugh. What if he isn't dating?" What if he was a player? A no-commitment type? She bit her lip. *That would make him just like Cole.*

All sex. No strings.

She ignored the ice block sliding through her gut. "Why doesn't he talk to me about this stuff?"

Cole scoffed. "Why would he?"

"Because we're friends, and aren't siblings supposed to talk about things?" She looked to Cole for input. This was clearly more his territory than hers.

Cole rubbed his chin. "I don't know. I've got three older brothers, and we don't talk about sex. Surely you knew he was having sex."

"Stop saying that."

"What? Sex?"

Rita pointed a warning finger at him. "Stop."

His expression rode the line between confusion and amusement. "He's in college. What do you think happens in a town with twenty-thousand single people of age?"

"He's supposed to be in college to learn," she said. "I didn't need condoms when I was in college." She regretted the choice of words immediately.

It was too much information, and it was out there now.

Cole cocked his head. "Never? What exactly are you saying?" A twist of shock and intrigue edged his words. He'd somehow picked up on the thing she hadn't said. An implication that was barely made.

Rita wet her lips, then pressed them tight.

"I mean, it's none of my business, but..." He moved into her space and dropped into a squat before her. "Rita?" His probing blue eyes examined her with intensity, hav-

ing easily and accurately jumped to the borderline embar-
rassing conclusion. "When was the last time you needed
a condom?"

She lowered her gaze. Truth be told, Rita hadn't even
seen a condom in years. Her one and only serious boy-
friend, a fellow senior from her high school *du jour*, had
purchased the only package of protection she'd thought
she had use for, but thanks to his cheating ways, the grand
finale of a goodbye she'd had planned was ruined. Rita's
virginity had stayed intact. Much as she'd wanted that guy
to be her first, there was no room for sharing in her heart.
She wouldn't give herself over to someone who didn't re-
gard her highly enough to be exclusive with their intimacy.
Not then, and not now. After that, she left for college. Then
her mom died, and Ryan became her priority. Work took
second place, and everything else was irrelevant.

"Rita?"

She shook her head. She'd idealized sex for years because it had meant so much to her as a high schooler, but
suddenly the notion of saving herself for true love seemed
juvenile and dumb.

Rita grabbed the envelope hastily and crammed the keys
and change inside. "Never," she admitted. There. She'd said
it. No sense in lying. Why should it matter?

Before she could get Ryan's wallet back into the envelope, it fell onto the floor, knocked aside by her bumbling
hands. The contents scattered, including a folded scrap of
white paper she hadn't noticed before.

Cole collected the things in one big mitt and dropped
them into the envelope. "Sorry. I didn't mean to pry. I
shouldn't have pushed."

Rita took the envelope and reached inside. "It's fine.
What does the paper say?"

She refused to discuss her sex life in front of Ryan, even if he was unconscious.

Maybe Cole had a point about siblings not sharing everything.

She retrieved the neatly folded paper and read the line of uniform text. Her hands began to tremble as she passed the note to Cole.

LEAVE THE PEN UNDER THE MAILBOX AT MEMORIAL PARK. DO IT TONIGHT. COME ALONE. OR YOU'RE NEXT.

Chapter Fourteen

Rage tightened Cole's limbs.

"Stay here." He snatched the scrap of paper from Rita's fingers and went in search of answers. Like how the hell had someone gotten a threatening note into a crash victim's wallet?

Outside Ryan's room, a trio of women in pastel scrubs started. They stared as he held the door wide. He felt his grimace deepen as Lomar's empty chair registered. With Cole inside and Lomar outside, no one should have been able to get anywhere near Rita or her brother. But Cole had fallen asleep and Lomar had apparently taken a walk!

Stacy, the night nurse and note's deliverer, jogged to Cole's side. "What's wrong? Is Ryan okay?" She craned her neck to see into the room behind him, but Cole held his ground.

"Where's Deputy Lomar?"

Stacy looked pointedly at the empty chair. "I don't know. He was there a minute ago. I think."

"You think?"

Stacy swept her anxious gaze back to Cole. "Tell me what happened."

Cole freed the cell phone from his pocket and dialed Lomar. He returned his attention to Stacy as the call connected. "Who delivered the envelope you just brought to Rita?"

The other nurses took a few timid steps in their direction, stopping on Cole's side of their workstation beside an abandoned janitor's bucket. "I believe those were his personal effects," the nurse in blue answered.

"Yes. Who brought them?" he repeated the question through gritted teeth.

The nurses looked at one another.

Cole felt his blood pressure rise. "Where was the envelope?"

Stacy lifted a finger to indicate the opposite side of their curved workstation.

Cole charged in that general direction with Stacy at his heels. "Who could have put it there?"

"I don't know."

"Who has access to this area?" he growled, trying hard not to wake the entire floor with the rush of frustration tearing at his mind.

"Garrett?" Lomar's voice echoed through the phone line and along the quiet corridor to his right.

"Where are you?"

"Here." A set of steady footfalls registered behind Cole and he turned. Lomar putted in his direction, arms bent forward at the elbows, a steaming cup in one hand, giant cookie in the other. He stopped short. "What happened?"

Cole headed for his friend. "Where were you?"

Lomar raised his brows. "Coffee."

"You're not supposed to leave," Cole growled. "You're the protective detail."

Lomar scanned the area, presumably checking each nurse's face for an explanation. "You were inside the room."

"I was asleep!"

"I wasn't gone for two minutes," Lomar barked back.

"I walked to the waiting room to pour a cup of coffee, a lady knitting socks gave me a cookie and you called. That's what happened to me. What the hell happened to you?"

What happened to him? Well, someone had taken the time to type up a threat and place it in Ryan's things, either at the accident scene, somehow, or in the ambulance, the operating room… Cole's mind was cluttered with the number of people who could have done this, not to mention the outsiders he hadn't thought of yet, before the note was delivered to Rita. That was what had happened to Cole.

Stacy returned to his side and pointed to an empty shelf near the printer. "I found the envelope here when my shift started, but you and Rita were asleep. I brought it to her as soon as I knew she was up. It probably came from someone in your office. Someone from the crime scene or maybe the operating room. Why?"

Cole turned on her, pinning her with a warning look. "There was a threat in the envelope with Ryan Horn's things. I need to know who had access to this area."

Stacy fell back a step, finally at a loss for words.

"Us," one of the nurses answered. "We're the only ones on duty from ten until six. Sometimes we see a doctor, but you wouldn't catch a doctor making deliveries."

Then who?

Cole's mind raced. Trauma was a closed ward with a small window of visiting hours and a small number of people who had access. Someone wanted the thumb drive badly enough to take a huge risk delivering that note. Could it be one of the women looking at him now? His eyes roamed back to Lomar's empty chair. Could it be his fellow deputy? Someone present at the accident scene? His fingers curled over the paper, and he forced his mind to work faster.

"Hey," Rita's soft voice sliced through Cole's anger. She

leaned in the open doorway of her brother's room, eyes heavy with tears. "How's it going?"

Cole turned away, unwilling to make her night worse with his lack of information and fully ready to lose his mind.

The abandoned mop and bucket stared back at him. He scanned the area for other signs of a cleaning crew. The floors were dry. The ward was silent. Cole marched to the yellow bucket and peered inside. "Where's the janitor?" He turned wild eyes on the nurses. There was no water in the tub. "Whose bucket is this?"

The ladies looked at one another.

Stacy pinched her lip between a thumb and forefinger, apparently in thought.

"What is it?" Cole asked. "Did you see someone cleaning?"

"I saw a man in a janitor's uniform when I made my rounds, but I didn't pay much attention."

"When was that?"

"Not long ago. Only a few minutes before you came out here."

Adrenaline spike in Cole's system, erasing the dull throb of yesterday's burns and igniting his clarity. "What did he look like?" Cole asked.

Stacy shook her head. "I don't know."

Lomar deposited his snacks on the nurses' station and turned to Cole. "He could still be in the building. You want me to make a sweep of the ward. Maybe the floor?"

"No." Cole turned in a small circle, head tipped back. From where he stood, there were at least three cameras in sight. Cole had a better idea. "Where can I review the footage from these cameras?" There was no way anyone got behind that desk without the cameras knowing.

"Tech Support," Stacy said. "Fourth floor. There's a wing of offices and conference rooms. It's in with Security."

"Got it." Cole pressed the note against Lomar's chest. "Bag that and don't let anything happen to her. I'm going to find this guy."

Rita bobbed on her toes, white-knuckle fingers wrapped around the doorjamb. "Don't leave," she pleaded.

Cole's heart ached at the request. Her fearful expression twisted him inside. Fear for herself, for Ryan, for every patient in the building and probably for Cole. Just one more reason he was falling hard and fast for the selfless red-haired beauty. Rita cared for everyone.

He crossed the space to Rita in long, purposeful strides and planted a kiss on her forehead, hoping the simple touch could convey the things he wasn't yet able to say. "Go back inside and shut the door. Stay with Ryan. Lomar will be right here if you need anything. I'll be back as soon as I can. I won't leave the building without you."

She nodded uneasily, then vanished back into the room and tugged the curtain until only a sliver of her remained visible.

Cole nodded his approval. He hated to leave her, but whoever had followed her this far had chosen to threaten instead of act this time. It seemed to him that that meant recovering the pen she'd found at the docks had taken priority over silencing the witness. She could only tell a jury what she'd seen that night, which wasn't much, but the pen must've had information that someone couldn't afford to have come to light. Whoever wanted it must've thought they'd never get it if they killed her. They didn't know West had already taken that pen for processing.

Cole waved Lomar aside. "Make sure West knows what's going on. We could use some extra boots on the ground if we have them, especially an external patrol of the parking lots and building. If I can't get my hands on this guy before he leaves, we might still be able to catch him making his getaway."

"On it." Lomar dialed Dispatch without missing a beat.

Cole took the stairs to the fourth floor at a run, wincing when the impacts tore at his day-old wounds. He knocked on the security office door with purpose. "Cade County Sheriff's Department. Open up." He held his badge to the glass when a face appeared at the little window.

"Can I help you?" A cheery young woman opened the door and waved him inside.

"I'm Deputy Cole Garrett. I need to see the footage from the second floor trauma ward. Elevator and stairway entries, as well as the nurses' station, over the last thirty minutes."

The girl blinked. "Something wrong?"

Cole could think of at least twenty ways everything was absolutely wrong. "Yes, and we're in a hurry so…"

"Oh." She scrambled onto a rolling chair and swiped her computer to life. "I'm Katie, by the way." Her corkscrew ponytail bobbed and swung as she worked, looking screen to screen on the multi-monitor setup. "Here."

Grainy images of the trauma ward appeared on four screens. On the left, Lomar stood guard outside Ryan's door, keeping careful watch, his eyes on a steady circuit through the space around him. Besides that, the nurses gathered behind their desk. The final two shots showed a still hallway with closed doors for the elevator and stairwell.

"Can you split the screen?" Cole asked. "Cover those four shots at once? Maybe fast forward until we see a janitor." He couldn't afford to miss anything. Rita's life could depend on it.

"Sure." A few more keystrokes and Cole's requests were granted.

He locked and popped his jaw while he waited, looming over the young woman as he searched.

Lomar's head dropped forward, and he jumped to his feet. He rubbed his eyes, yawned and lifted the disposable cup from its place on the floor by his feet.

Cole fought a twinge of guilt at his anger toward Lomar. He'd been on duty as much as Cole since Minsk had turned up in the river. With a small department like theirs, everyone was overworked when tragedies occurred. This many in a row had to be a record.

Lomar arched his back in the top corner of the screen. He said something, and a nurse pointed down the hall. Lomar checked his watch before hustling away, carrying his cup at comic speed as the time-elapsed feed rolled frantically ahead.

"Him?" Katie lifted a finger to the bottom right corner of her screen. Dressed in head-to-toe white and slightly hunched, an older white male motored through the halls. His big black boots shuffled along cartoonishly.

"Yes. Follow him."

The man pushed his bucket as far as the nurses' station, then left it to slide behind the desk briefly. A moment later, he moved briskly away from the camera's reach, disappearing, then reappearing on another camera's feed. He stooped to swipe a dropped cloth as Stacy exited a nearby room. Keeping his back to her, he used the rag to wipe the glass of a framed photo on the wall. Stacy barely looked up before entering the next patient's room.

"Do you recognize him?" Cole asked. "Can you zoom in on his face or ID badge? Get a better shot?"

Katie snorted. "This isn't the movies. What you see is what we've got." She straightened her ponytail, murmuring about hospital funding and tech costs.

The janitor vanished.

"Where'd he go?" Cole barked. He pressed his palms to the workstation beside Katie, leaning closer, willing the image to reappear.

"Hang on." She went back to her keyboard, the picture of calm while Cole's heart threatened to break all his ribs. Her fingers moved at inhuman speed across the keys, sure and confident, the way Cole had felt until Rita Horn's life had collided with his. Now he saw danger everywhere. Not for him, but for her. "There."

The janitor ducked into a windowless door marked Staff. "What is that?"

Katie leaned back in her chair, apparently satisfied with her work. "Supply closet."

When the door reopened, the man who emerged looked nothing like the old bearded janitor who'd entered. This man was tall and clean shaven, wearing a knockoff Cade County deputy's jacket and the same black boots the first image had worn.

Katie swung her face in Cole's direction. "Whoa."

The impostor strode to the nearest stairwell entry and vanished inside.

Cole snapped upright and dragged frustrated fingers through his hair. The killer himself had posed as a janitor to deliver that threat to Rita. Now he was back in faux deputy mode. Cole couldn't imagine the amount of damage a man like that could do in the guise of a Cade County deputy.

"I'm confused," Katie said. "Was that man a deputy

pretending to be a janitor or a janitor pretending to be a deputy?"

"Neither." That man was a murderer. "What you've seen is part of an ongoing murder investigation." Multiple murders, attempted and successful, plus another slated to happen soon, if Cole didn't put a stop to it. "Our discussion and what you've seen here is confidential. I'm going to need a copy of this footage."

"Got it." Katie went back to work on her keyboard.

Cole ground his teeth. The jacket had shocked him with its accuracy. It was a solid facsimile, but still a knockoff. Yet someone had made a clear effort to get it right. If Cole hadn't been so intimately familiar with it, he might not have seen the small differences, either. Rita had been right to be confused by it, but knowing she'd been wrong about a fellow deputy's involvement was still an enormous relief.

Guilt rocked through him for thinking, even for a moment, that Lomar might have played a part in whatever was happening. It wasn't like Cole to doubt his team, regardless of what anyone said. This case was turning him inside out. Mentally. Physically. And emotionally.

"Done." Katie lifted a tiny plastic ninja in his direction. "I copied the footage onto my thumb drive. I included some stills of the man as the janitor and as the deputy. I'm sure your tech team could've done that themselves, but I never get to do cool stuff like this." She waved a hand in a big circle over her head. "Hospital," she added by way of explanation.

"Where did he go after the stairs?"

"I don't know. I could scan the cameras from every floor, but that would take some time. I don't know how much of a hurry you're in. Best guess, though? If he knows his way around, he probably ducked through the laundry area and into the delivery dock. Cameras are limited in those areas. People go out there to smoke because it's forbidden on hospital grounds."

"Do your cameras cover the parking lot and other exits?"

"Yes." Katie went back to her keyboard.

Cole grabbed the phone on the wall and dialed the trauma unit. The killer was on the move, but if Cole and Lomar went right now, they could cover a large portion of the perimeter in a matter of minutes, and the help he'd asked Lomar to request would be on-site before they'd finished.

The sonofagun wasn't getting away this time.

RITA STOOD AT Ryan's bedside, eyes fixed on the hallway beyond the glass. No one would get near them without her seeing them come. She'd wedged a chair beneath the doorknob and moved to her brother's side, prepared to defend him if anyone came through that door uninvited. She couldn't run if things went south, but she could fight. A number of things in the room were light enough for her to lift but heavy enough to knock an intruder out, if needed.

The coward in her said she should pull the curtain completely and hide until Cole returned. The big sister in her said that Ryan couldn't hide, so neither could she.

"You're going to be okay, Ry," she whispered to her brother's tranquil face. "I got you into this, and I'm going to get you out."

She pulled in long, steadying breaths to put the fear at bay, but the thick antiseptic scent of his room seemed heavier and more stifling with each inhalation. She couldn't afford to let emotion take over right now. She had to stay clear of thought, ready to act.

"Please wake up," she pleaded with her brother.

She stroked a line of soft hair off his forehead. If he was awake and well, they wouldn't be sitting ducks. Ryan was fast, strong and smart. He always had the best plans for getting out of trouble. She wiped a fresh tear from her cheek, remembering the antics they'd gotten into together on nights when she babysat him long ago. The way she recalled it, Ryan had also caused most of the trouble they had to get out of.

But not this. This was all on her.

She patted his arm, wrapped soundly in a long cast, then allowed herself to worry about his cast-covered leg. The one Stacy had described as *shattered*. Even if Ryan was awake, how could they hide or run from a gun-wielding, threat-rendering nut with him in such terrible shape?

Still, she just wanted her brother to wake up.

What if he never did?

Lomar strode past the window, leaving his post and making his way toward the nurses' station.

The woman in blue scrubs held a phone receiver in his direction.

Something was happening. Rita inched silently toward the glass.

Lomar stood at the nurses' station, phone to his ear. His back was to her. What was he saying? Who was on the line? Cole? Had he found something on the surveillance video?

Lomar whipped his gaze up to meet Rita's. He lifted a finger, as if to say that something would only take a minute. "Stay there," he said. His stern voice warbled through the glass.

She nodded.

Lomar ran off.

Rita's heart hammered and ached.

"Not good," she whispered. "If that call had been to announce the bad guy's capture, Lomar would've come in to tell me. Something's wrong again," she told Ryan. "I wish you'd open your eyes and tell me what to do."

Rita scanned Ryan's room for the nearest weapon.

She scooped up the paddles on a crash cart stored in the room's corner and rolled the cart into position behind the door. If anyone forced their way in, they wouldn't know she was there until she sprang on them.

She flipped the switch on the cart and watched the lights and gauges hop to life. A low hum vibrated through the room.

Business outside went on as usual.

Nurses carried clipboards and knocked on patients' doors.

Was she wrong? Could everything be fine? Rita lowered her hands to her sides. Maybe the killer had been captured. Or Cole found the janitor and he'd given him all the information Cole needed to put an end to this madness. Maybe Cole caught the janitor but he wasn't talking and he'd called Lomar to help question him. Good cop and bad cop.

There were endless possibilities, and until this week, it hadn't been like her to assume the worst.

She flicked the power switch on the crash cart to the off position and returned the paddles to their bases. The nurses weren't worried. She probably shouldn't be, either.

She gave the hallway another look. *Where were the nurses?*

Rita tugged the curtain wider in search of anyone on the floor. Maybe the woman who'd handed the phone to Lomar knew what had drawn him away.

The elevator across the hall opened for the first time in hours, and a new deputy appeared in its center.

She squinted for a better look at his face. Was he Lomar's replacement? A new shift?

Her heartbeat skittered as his thin lips curled into a sinister smile.

The killer raised his right hand, two fingers extended like a gun, and he pulled an invisible trigger.

Chapter Fifteen

Lomar's earlier call to Dispatch had sent backup to the parking lot before Cole could make it to the ground floor. That covered, he turned on his heel and headed back to Rita. Much as he wanted to be the one to capture the shooter, he hated leaving Rita alone. It seemed as if every time he took his eyes off her, things got exponentially worse.

Cole climbed the stairs as quickly as possible, struggling to move as fast as usual. The cuts and burns on his back and shoulders had begun to scream the moment he'd woken in the uncomfortable hospital chair and they hadn't stopped.

"Anything you want to tell me about the redhead?" Lomar asked, keeping pace at his side.

"No." Cole angled for position in the narrow space, eager to reach the second-floor entry.

"Really? Because you looked pretty uncomfortable in there last night."

"So?" Cole picked up the pace, injuries searing and aching with each swing of his arms.

"You don't do uncomfortable," Lomar said, "and you sure as hell don't spend the night anywhere you don't have to. Don't say it's your job," he warned. "I was right outside the door, and another deputy could have relieved you at any time. Plus, I see the way you look at her. What's that about?"

Cole yanked the door to the second floor open and waited for Lomar to pass. "Can you blame me? She's beautiful."

"Sure, she's beautiful, but she's not your type. This one doesn't seem like the kind of woman who will put up with your shenanigans."

Cole snorted. "Leave my shenanigans alone."

He smiled at the thought of Rita's prolonged presence in his life. What would that picture look like? Would there be a ring and a big white dress in their future? She was definitely the type to wear the big dress.

Cole missed a step in the long hallway as their earlier conversation rushed back to him. Had she really implied she was a virgin?

A virgin. The words rattled nonsensically in his mind. Was that even possible?

And if it was, what did it mean for them? For starters, he'd have to take things slower than he was used to. Help her explore her sexuality. Discover what made her pant and what made her scream. A number of fun possibilities rushed to mind and *damn!* He'd never been in such a hurry to take it slow.

He shook the thought away and forced his feet to move faster, eating up the space between himself and Rita.

The first rays of sunlight had drifted in through the wide glass windows while he was away. The nurses standing behind the desk had also changed in that time. Apparently, dawn had sent the night crew to ground.

All but Stacy.

Stacy had zipped a Rivertown hoodie over her scrubs and taken a seat in the chair Lomar recently vacated. "She's locked in," Stacy told Cole, pointing at Ryan's closed door.

"She knows I'm here, but she's not opening up until she sees you."

The door cracked open. Rita peeked out. "Thank goodness."

She shoved a chair away from the door and pulled Cole inside.

The crash cart had been moved near her chair at Ryan's bedside.

"What happened?" Cole raised a hand toward the cart, but Rita intercepted it, wrapping his arm around her back instead.

She clung to him then, curling her fingers deep into the material of his shirt. "The shooter was in the elevator when the doors opened. He didn't get out, but he pointed his fingers at me like a gun."

Cole's body went rigid. "When?"

"A minute ago?" she squeaked. "Two?"

Cole swore under his breath. "We were sure he was in the parking lot, maybe even off the premises by now."

Lomar was already on his way out the door. "I'll let backup know."

Cole was torn once more. He wanted to help look for the guy threatening Rita, but he couldn't bring himself to leave her. "Listen." He lowered his mouth to her ear. "I think it's time we get you out of here. I say we go to the station and see what Tech has recovered from that thumb drive. Put some distance between you and the killer's most recently known whereabouts."

"But Ryan…"

"Hey." Cole cut her off. "I know you're worried about him, but the way that note reads, whoever's doing this isn't going to go after you or him again until they have that pen. As long as there's a chance you're complying with their request, they're going to watch and wait."

"I can't leave him alone," she said, pushing out of Cole's grip.

"And I can't leave you." Cole worked to sound more supportive and less frustrated. Just because he didn't think someone would kill her immediately didn't mean he wasn't afraid she'd be abducted and forced to tell what she knew about the pen's whereabouts and content. "You have information they want," he continued. "Ryan doesn't. He's safe. You aren't."

Rita turned her attention back to the bed.

Cole's jaw locked and his shoulders squared. "You're coming with me because it's the right thing to do. Staying here will only keep me from helping West and the others find this guy. The longer you keep me here, the longer West is down a man, and there's only six of us to start with."

Rita gripped Ryan's fingers. "I hate this." Anger burned in her voice and eyes. "It's not fair."

"It's not," Cole admitted, "and I'm sorry." He forced himself into her line of sight. "But we can't afford to forget that you're the target. Not Ryan. Being here puts him at an added risk. He's made it through the worst. There's nothing you can do for him right now, and if he wakes while you're gone, I promise to tell him I dragged you away kicking and screaming."

Stacy climbed onto the uncomfortable chair in the corner where Cole had slept. "I could call you," she told Rita. "If you give me your number, I can send text updates. Even if there's nothing to update, I can check in periodically to say he's still okay."

Rita slumped. "My phone's in the river."

"I could text Ryan's phone." Stacy's small smile seemed to loosen Rita's shoulders. "If he had it on him before, it's probably in the envelope."

Rita's hand went to her pocket, covering the telltale outline of a cell phone. "It was. You have his number?"

"Yeah."

Rita stared at the locked screen, entered her mother's birthday, and the lock disappeared.

Lomar arrived a moment later, palms raised. He leaned against the doorjamb, defeated. "No sign of the killer."

"What do you think?" Stacy asked Rita.

Cole owed Stacy something big for calming Rita's heart. "Your shift's over," he said. "How long can you stay?"

"I'm not leaving." Stacy's smile turned sad. "I'm off for the next two days, and I plan to be here until someone kicks me out."

Rita sucked in a long breath and exhaled it slowly. "Okay. I'll keep his phone on. Promise to text me."

"Promise."

Rita kissed Ryan's cheek goodbye, then hugged Stacy before stopping at the open door and staring up at Lomar with worried and fearful eyes.

"I'll keep him safe," Lomar promised. The words rumbled low in his chest like a solemn vow. "Whatever it takes."

She flung her arms around his middle and pressed her cheek to his chest.

Lomar's eyebrows flew up. His hands hovered in the air at her back.

A long moment later, he managed to lower his arms around her narrow frame and return the embrace. He caught Cole's attention and smiled.

Seeing Rita wrapped around another man, even a man he literally trusted with his life, made Cole twitchy. Life-long friend or not, Lomar's big mitts belonged at his sides, not on Cole's woman. He tugged the back of Rita's shirt. "Come on. Before you get him all worked up."

She released Lomar with a soft, "Thank you."

Cole twined his fingers with Rita's and led her into the parking lot, free hand on the butt of his sidearm.

RITA MADE CALLS with Ryan's phone as they motored across town in Cole's cruiser. Her neighbor had too many questions, but ultimately said Rita's cats were fine and she didn't mind watching them another day or two. Cyndi, from her office, was curious but eventually said no one else had come looking for Rita and that she should stop worrying about work and get some rest. Their dad didn't answer his phone. She left another voice mail, this one with Ryan's current status and room number. She didn't bother filling him in on the rest. It wouldn't matter, anyway.

She dropped the phone onto her lap and gave Cole a long look. He was what a man should be. Strong and steadfast, yet patient and willing to bend. "Thank you for giving me the choice to come with you."

He slid his eyes briefly in her direction. "Did I have another option?"

"You could have demanded I come and not left me any freedom of decision."

He furrowed his brow, a look of disgust on his handsome face. "Well, that's a load of manure."

A sudden smile slid over her lips. "Why?"

He glanced her way again. "Why? What? Why's it nonsense for anyone to give you orders?"

Rita shook her head. "No. You're right." Her smile widened. Cole was one of the few men who'd ever been in a position to make demands of her and he refused. He valued her opinions, choices and decisions, unlike her father, bosses, teachers and so many other men who had not. Given her current situation, Cole had every right to insist things be done his way. The fact that he didn't only made her respect him more. She turned back to the astounding autumn day blurring past her window. A cloudless blue sky played backdrop to endless multicolored mountains, thick with changing leaves. Hard to believe awful things could happen in such a beautiful place.

The sheriff's department came into view, and her heart skipped a beat. This was it. Once she delivered the pen to Memorial Park, her brother would be safe again. Hopefully the pen had already been processed for prints, the thumb drive for content, and it was ready for her.

She'd unbuckled before Cole shifted into Park.

He ran around the front of his cruiser and opened her door for her. "Ready?"

He offered her a steadying hand, then gave her fingers a squeeze.

"Yep." Rita was more than ready to finish the mess she'd started by taking that pen from the docks. What she wasn't ready for, on the other hand, was losing Cole from her life once his job was done. She'd actually like to keep him around a while if she could, but no woman held on to Cole Garrett for very long.

Though, horrific circumstances aside, she'd probably already spent more time alone with Cole than most women. Of course, the other women had probably spent a portion of their time with him naked. Ridiculously, she envied that.

Cole Garrett could undoubtedly teach her a few things.

Her cheeks flushed at the thought. Why had she told him she was a virgin? She'd never told anyone. The fact was deeply personal, and not a thing that should have been unloaded on an unreasonably attractive man she wasn't even dating. She blamed Ryan's wallet condom.

Cole opened the front door for her.

Rita tried, unsuccessfully, to untangle their fingers. They couldn't go walking into the sheriff's department holding hands like a couple. What would people think? Surely that wasn't normal. Inexperienced or not, she knew that public displays of that caliber were unofficial announcements of relationships and intimacy. Neither of those things described what she had going with Cole. *A one-sided infatuation fueled by too many emotions and time spent in close quarters.* She tried and failed to imagine him holding hands with other women. Maybe he was just an affectionate guy. Maybe he went through all the pretenses with them, too. At least until morning. "We probably shouldn't." She lifted their joined hands and wiggled them.

"Why?" Cole released the door and stepped aside. He leaned against the building's stone exterior and pulled her against him, spreading his feet to make room for hers. "You don't want to hold my hand?" He released her then, allowing her to back away.

She didn't. "It's not that."

A measure of concern lifted from his forehead. "Am I making you uncomfortable?"

"No."

He frowned. "Are you worried about what people will think?"

Silly as it was, given the much larger things she was worried about… "A little, yeah." She didn't want to be seen as some naive woman who thought she was something special to Cole Garrett. She wished it was true, but people didn't need to know that.

"Right." Cole peeled himself off the wall and straightened to his full height. He swept a hand out, indicating she should go ahead of him as they marched through the sheriff's department door.

A sharp whistle burst through the busy room almost immediately. West waved a hand in the air, motioning for Cole to join him outside the office door. Had he been standing there waiting for their arrival?

The open door beside West had his name and title painted on it.

"Have a seat." West motioned to a pair of chairs stationed across from his desk. An open bottle of antacids sat beside a massive cup of steamless coffee near his keyboard.

Behind them, a printer rocked and grunted in the corner, spewing sheets of paper into a nearly full plastic tray.

Cole passed a small black figure to West, then hung in the doorway as Rita entered. "That's a thumb drive with hospital footage of the man we believe left the note in Ryan's things. I'm hoping our tech team can clear up the picture and identify this guy."

West curled his fist around the little ninja. "I'll get it over there."

"Thanks." Cole folded his arms and scowled at West's busy printer. "What's all that?"

"This—" West made a face at the still belching printer "—is everything from that pen you gave me. I asked Tech to fax over what they've retrieved."

Rita slid to the edge of her seat. "All of that was on the pen?"

West flopped into his chair. "Yep. And do you know how long it's going to take me to sort through it?" He answered his own question after three long beats. "Forever."

Cole approached the printer and slid a handful of pages onto his palm.

Rita rewound West's words. "So, you don't have the pen with you?"

"No," West answered. "Tech needs a couple days to make sure they have everything. I'm also hoping to find a fingerprint on it that doesn't belong to you or Minsk."

"But I need the pen," Rita said, desperation clawing at

her throat. "I'm supposed to take it to the park. Show him the note, Cole."

"He's seen the note," Cole grouched. "You're not making that drop."

"Yes, I am."

His cranky face morphed into a mask of disbelief. "There is no way I'm letting that happen. How can you even think that right now?"

"What happened to letting me make my own decisions?" she asked. Hadn't he just told her not to put up with treatment like this?

"Someone has to step in when you're being irrational. I'm not going to stand by and watch you get yourself abducted or killed. Then I'd be the crazy one."

"I am not crazy," she snapped.

"Then what's your problem?"

Rita sucked air. "What is *your* problem?" She gripped the armrests of her chair, betrayal constricting her chest. This wasn't about her. "My brother is lying helpless and unconscious in a hospital room, and you want me to sit around and cross my fingers and hope the guy who put him there won't decide to walk in and kill him in his sleep? Why would I risk that when I could just do what he asked?"

Cole's chest expanded and fell in deep blasts.

"Ooo-kay." West rubbed his face with both palms. "Let's stay focused on the files for now. We can always get a replica pen, if it comes to that."

Cole swore. Loudly.

West plugged ahead, looking somewhat grayer than when Rita had met him only days before. "I need some help reviewing all these papers." He handed a thick stack to Rita from the mess on his desk. "You've been at the treasurer's office for a while now. I'm guessing you're familiar with most of these forms. I need to know who this data would be relevant to. Better yet, who does it incriminate? Who would go to such lengths to get their hands on it? So far it just looks like a bunch of bank statements and purchase offers."

Rita scooted back in her seat and crossed her legs. "If I help with this, will you let me make the drop with a fake pen?"

"Yes."

Cole grunted.

"With conditions," West added. "You're not going alone. My men will be there, in plainclothes. We'll cover the perimeter and set up takedown points throughout the park. And I'm positioning a sharpshooter on the museum roof as an added precaution." He handed Cole a sketch of what he'd described, apparently having decided on the details before Rita and Cole's arrival.

Cole looked at the drawing with profound sadness. He didn't speak.

Rita turned her eyes to the papers on her lap and went to work making sense of the documents. "These bank transfers go back a number of years."

Three days of fear and frustration fizzled and fled as her mind took hold of the familiar forms. "Wow. This is a three-million-dollar offer to buy the docks from the state." She fed the paper back onto West's desk. "Minsk must've been negotiating the purchase with the governor. I'll bet that was what had him at the municipal building so often. Is the governor in town for some reason? Or is there a liaison of some kind in Shadow Point? I'm not sure how our state government works."

"I'll make some calls," West said, "see what I can find out."

Cole paced the area beside his brother's desk. "That's going to be a problem. Politicians are practically off-limits to us. They have the power to squash an investigation before it has a chance to grow legs. They're slippery, too. Hard to get face time with them. Hard to get a straight answer, even if you do get an interview with the governor. This close to election day, we'd be wise to step extra-carefully."

West steepled his fingers. "If this is even remotely related to the governor, it would explain why the shooter has been so hard to nail down."

"Could be a professional." Cole finished his brother's thought with a solemn nod.

Rita struggled not to swallow her tongue. "A professional what? Hit man? There's a *hit man* after my brother and me?"

"We're going to have to tread lightly," Cole said, ignoring Rita's rhetorical outburst. He gathered another stack of papers and pulled a chair up beside her. "We'll have to work smart. Stay under the radar. Build our case before anyone catches wind of what we're up to. The governor won't want the media seeing our efforts to get to the bottom of this as an accusation against him."

Rita relaxed a bit, thankful to see Cole had rejoined her team.

"Who are all these bank transfers going to?" Cole asked. "Who are they from? Can Tech trace the routing numbers back to an identity on either party?"

Rita reviewed the pages, front and back. "I still don't understand why Minsk was killed. The buyer hired him to make the offers. He was the chosen liaison, so why would they want him dead?"

Cole stretched his legs out and winced. "Same thing can be said about the governor or whoever Minsk was meeting with. All the state had to do was decline or accept the offer. No grounds for murder."

Rita read several more pages, her eyes catching on a repetitive set of initials. "The letters GL appear on a bunch of these papers. Do they mean anything to you?"

"GL," Cole repeated. "Can I see it?"

He took the stack from her hands and leafed through them. "The blueprints on the boat were property of Gray Line Enterprises. Maybe that's the company that hired Minsk."

West typed something on his keyboard. "Gray Line Enterprises is a commercial development cooperative. They own docks in several large cities throughout the country."

"Louisiana, Ohio, Illinois and Missouri," Cole said. "I saw the blueprints in Minsk's office and on his boat."

Rita raised her brows. "Nothing sinister about that. What do they do with the docks they buy?"

West was silent for several minutes as he typed.

Cole leaned in Rita's direction until their shoulders bumped. "Is it the PDA you don't like? Or is it me?"

West's gaze drifted to Cole, then Rita.

"Uhm." She wet her lips and tried to slow her suddenly sprinting heart. Nothing like putting her on the spot, with an audience.

West cocked his head uncomfortably, then went back to work.

Cole shifted closer. "You don't have to be polite about it. If it's me, say it's me."

"It's not you." She whispered as softly as possible; still, the words rang through the silent little room. West's stupid printer had given up its work in time for her answer.

"If it's my reputation, we can talk about that."

Rita's cheeks flamed. "Stop. I don't care about your reputation." Caring for him scared the hell out of her, and knowing he was likely to move on the minute the case was over, thus breaking her silly heart, didn't help. She didn't care who he'd slept with before. His past wasn't any of her business. The notion his future might be, however, twisted her stomach into eager knots.

"Is it your reputation, then?" he asked.

She yanked her chin back, caught completely off guard. "What's that supposed to mean?"

West cleared his throat. "Do you two want me to leave? I mean, it's my office, but this is making me really uncomfortable."

Cole set his hand on the arm of her chair, firmly ignoring his older brother. He turned his palm up, fingers opening and closing in a greedy motion. His blue eyes danced with mischief.

West murmured something about Cole's stupidity, then continued typing.

She pushed his hand away. "I don't have a reputation."

A dare played on Cole's lips. His hand popped back into place. "But you might if you're seen with me. Is that it?"

"That's not it." Not the way Cole had meant, anyway. She just didn't want to be known as the silly girl who played at being his girlfriend when she'd already be dealing with the heartbreaking loss. "Is that why you were mad when we came in here?"

West raised both palms, eyes focused on the computer screen. "Gray Line Enterprises is listed as an import/export company. Looks like they buy unused dock space, then resell it quickly every time. In three of the locations I've searched so far, a storage facility opened within a year. Many of the secondary purchasers are the same on multiple properties."

"Shell corps?" Cole asked, returning his empty hand to his lap. "Do we know who owns the other companies? Could they all be operated by Gray Line?"

"Maybe." West lifted the receiver from his desk phone.

"I'm going to pass this on to Tech Support. They'll have complete histories on all these companies before lunch. What I'd really like to know is why all the properties ended up with a storage facility."

"What do you think they're storing?" Cole asked.

Rita's tummy churned with flashes from her time on the docks. She forced her dry mouth to cooperate as she recalled the stained dress shirt and contents of the blood-splattered car trunk.

"Guns."

Chapter Sixteen

Cole pulled West's truck into the lot outside the municipal building. After Rita explained about the guns and the black sedan's bloody trunk, West had handed over his keys. The possibility of gunrunning in Shadow Point was nearly unthinkable. The fact someone in local government could be involved was worse.

He shifted the oversize pickup into Park and gave his new partner an appraising look. Bringing Rita to the place where Minsk had rendezvoused with his possible murderer was a calculated risk, but it sounded one hundred times better than letting her make that drop at the park. Cole couldn't protect her there, and he couldn't stop her from going if she put her mind to it. Worse, West had looked a little too agreeable on the matter, leaving Cole to agree to plan B.

An undercover assignment.

Rita's brows pinched in concentration. The municipal building was her turf. Cole was only there as backup, and he'd been given strict orders to lay low. Hence the vehicle swap. His cruiser would have drawn too much attention. Thanks to an unexpected night spent at the hospital, he was already deep undercover in his Army T-shirt and basketball shorts.

Rita adjusted the stack of files on her lap and took a deep breath.

"You sure you want to do this?" he asked, torn again. Wishing she'd stayed out of this, but glad to be there with her just in case there was trouble.

"I've got this." Rita pressed the passenger door open and slid into the parking lot.

Cole lowered a ball cap onto his mussed hair and went to meet her. "I've never been to the courthouse in basketball shorts."

"I don't think anyone will recognize you," Rita said. "Being out of uniform puts you out of context here, and the cap adds another layer of cover. Most people won't stare long enough to get a good look at your face. It's bad manners."

He tugged the cap lower on his forehead, curving the bill to better shade his eyes. "What about you? You're supposed to be sick. What will everyone say when they see you?"

She rolled her eyes. "People don't see me."

Cole disagreed. He followed her through Security admiring the curve of her backside in those cotton pants and trying not to make eye contact with anyone he knew.

Everything about Rita was heart-stopping sexy. How could she think no one noticed?

She paused at the bottom of the marble staircase to arrange the folders in her arms. She'd borrowed them from West's office as props. "I'm going to hit up the receptionist at the mayor's office for information. You're going to pretend to be visiting town and picking up literature on the area. Isla's new enough to Shadow Point that she might not recognize you right away."

Rita hugged the folders to her chest. "Isla's an avid gossip. I've gone out for drinks with her and Cyndi before. They talk about everyone. If there's anything juicy available on Minsk or the mayor, or if the governor's in town, like we guessed, Isla will know."

Hopefully Rita was right and Isla would have a significant lead. Then Rita could forget about making the drop at the park. Everything in Cole's gut said that was a horrible idea. "I'll be right behind you," he promised. "Are you sure she won't know me?" Besides, the other option was to wait outside for Rita, and that wasn't happening.

She bit into the thick of her bottom lip. "I don't know if Isla knows you personally, but she certainly knows plenty about you." She started up the stairs without him.

"What do you mean?" Cole kept pace easily, attempting to look as if he wasn't speaking to Rita.

She lifted and dropped one narrow shoulder. "She's got stories. Trust me. I've overheard more than my share." She made a gag face, then turned for the mayor's office.

"Hey." He grabbed her elbow without thinking. Her eyes flashed up to meet his. There was so much he wanted to tell her. Of course, now wasn't the time, but for him and Rita, it was *never* the time. "I think you and I need to talk when we finish here."

"Okay." She wiggled free of his grip. "I guess it won't matter if she recognizes you. As long as no one realizes you're here as part of an official investigation, we're fine."

She strode through the office door, the picture of confidence.

Cole slid into the room behind her and picked up a pamphlet on the history of Cade County.

"Hi, Isla," Rita began, resting her pile of files on the reception desk.

"Rita?" Isla gasped. "I thought you were sick. You should be at home." Her eyes stretched wide. "Or at the hospital with Ryan!"

Rita's limbs twitched at the mention of her brother. Guilt contorted her features, and Cole could practically hear her wishing she'd stayed with her brother.

Come on. Don't get derailed.

"I'm trying to get by," Rita drawled, extra slow and steady, as if she were barely keeping herself upright. "I'm sick, but I'm too worried to rest or concentrate." Her voice cracked on the last word.

"You poor thing," Isla cooed.

Rita patted the folders. "I figured I'd take some work home. Maybe I can distract myself from worrying about Ryan, or at least bore myself to sleep." She slumped slightly and offered a pitiful smile, looking quite effectively put out. "I saw you here, and figured while I was in the building I might as well come and ask you about someone I've been noticing lately."

Isla popped out of her chair and leaned on her elbows over the counter. She shot Cole a curious look before turning hungry eyes back on Rita. "Who?"

"I don't even know his name." Rita sighed. "But he's tall, dark and handsome. Black hair, brown eyes, olive skin. I swear he's a Greek god or something. Always dressed to the nines. Walks like he owns everything, and sometimes I wish…" She trailed off before Isla's line of drool hit the counter.

Cole forced his fingers to ease their grip on the hunting and fishing pamphlet. Rita was improvising, and she was good.

He didn't like it.

"Well, sweetie, I'm afraid I've got bad news." Mischief crawled through Isla's eerie campfire tone. "Your man is gone. Thrown in the river." She raised her eyebrows high and waited for a reaction.

"What?" Rita pressed a hand to her collarbone, utterly overacting. "When?"

"Couple days ago. I guess you've been too sick to catch

the news. His name was Roger Minsk. He used to come in and stand right where you are a few times a week."

"He did?" Rita dropped her jaw. "Why? I thought he was a lawyer or a wealthy businessman."

Isla smiled, apparently savoring the moment. "He was wealthy, all right. A land developer. Came here a bunch of times trying to make a deal about the docks."

"Oh. I hope they're finally revitalizing that area. It's been too long."

"No, now I didn't say that," Isla corrected with a glimmer of fanfare. "Roger was on a mission for some company. They made offers for the docks. He met with the mayor a few times, which is real strange because it's the governor who's in charge of that sort of thing."

"Do you think the governor was here?"

"Hell if I know. That guy's slicker than…" Isla checked over both shoulders and glanced in Cole's direction once more. "Can I help you, sir?" she asked in a sugary-sweet tone.

Cole put the pamphlet away and chose another without looking. Fly Fishing Tours. "Just seeing what your little town has to offer," he said.

"Well, honey, I don't do much fishing, but I'm guessing a man like you would have no trouble hooking a few nice ones out at Miller's pub tonight." She snapped her gum and looked pleased with herself.

"Thanks." He swapped the fishing brochure out for one on local churches.

Isla frowned. "Anyway…" She readdressed Rita in a quieter voice. "I don't know all the details on those meetings, but I can tell you that the mayor stayed late on the nights Roger was here, and he left in a big black SUV that wasn't his. I saw him from the coffee shop across the street when I was having dinner with Cyndi. We thought maybe it was a car service because he was going somewhere he shouldn't be going. Like, maybe he didn't want his car seen sitting outside the gentleman's club, you know?" She raised her eyebrows again. "I never thought that could've been the governor's driver. I'm not sure why the governor would come to Shadow Point for a secret meeting, but it makes more sense than Minsk wanting to talk to our small-town mayor about buying the docks."

"Sounds like a scandal," Rita said.

Isla perked. "I'm thinking the same thing."

Cole suspected *scandal* might be one of her favorite words.

He set his magazine aside and tipped his hat as he left the office. He'd already spent too long pretending to read tourism brochures. It was time to find a place with a good view of the office where he could wait for Rita.

RITA LEFT THE mayor's office a few moments behind Cole. She'd only been able to make her escape by telling Isla she would chase the handsome tourist into the parking lot and get his phone number.

A zip of panic raced through her when she didn't find him leaning against the wall outside the office. She headed for the staircase on quick feet, pulse beating in her ears and mind in full breakdown mode. *Cole saw the shooter and chased him. Cole was caught off guard and whisked away through the side entrance at gunpoint.*

She took a few hasty steps, and he came into view on the first floor, leaning casually against the wall and skimming her with his deep blue eyes. He trailed her with his gaze as she returned to the front of the building and exited into the sunlight. She could feel the heat of him behind her. Watching her. Following her. Dare she think it? *Wanting her.*

He followed her into the parking lot at a lumber, close enough to protect her if needed, far enough away to continue the pretense they weren't together, at least until they arrived at their destination.

He beeped the doors open when she reached West's truck and offered a hand to help her climb inside.

"That was terrifying," she told him, dropping the files onto the floorboards by her feet. "Isla's definitely already on the phone telling Cyndi I was in her office today, and Cyndi will probably have my boss on the line before I finish this sentence. I'm absolutely losing my job for playing hooky."

Cole shut her door and went to claim his position behind the wheel. He gunned the truck to life and smiled. "If Cyndi's anything like Isla, she can't tattle on you until she finds out if you got my number."

"What?" Rita smiled. "How'd you know I said I was going to?"

He laughed, shifted into Drive and pulled away from the building. "I was watching you so closely, I figured Isla would pick up on it. I didn't know you told her you were going to follow me."

Rita smiled back, enjoying the youthful expression on his too frequently distressed face.

Color bled from his cheeks at the next intersection. "Don't look now, but it seems there's a dark sedan following us."

"Where?" Rita checked the rear-and side-view mirrors.

"Three cars back." Cole pulled into the next available spot against the curb and waited. "No front plates. Dark tinted windows." He liberated his cell phone and tapped the screen to life. "We'll let him pass, then get behind him. See where he goes. Meanwhile, I'll get a cruiser out here to play sheepdog and herd him up."

The sedan slowed to a stop in the middle of the road thirty feet back. The two cars in between buzzed past their truck. The sedan idled.

Rita's heartbeat thrummed in her ears and throat. "What's he doing?" She closed her eyes and tried not to imagine the driver climbing into the street with a gun and shooting up the truck. She was with Cole now. He knew what to do. He'd handle this.

She was safe. She was safe. She was safe.

The roaring of an engine sprang her eyes wide. Squealing tires turned her on the seat.

The car pulled a U-turn on the narrow road before tearing away in a fury and peeling out of sight.

Cole returned the phone to his cup-holder. "I guess he really didn't want to pass us."

Rita rolled her window down and leaned against her door, desperate for more air.

Cole's phone rang, and he opened it on his palm. "Garrett."

"Hey." West's voice echoed through the truck cab. "Where are you?"

"I'm on Maple, and I've got you on speaker. Rita's here with me. We're finished at the mayor's office, but I just called Dispatch with the location of that sedan. It was tailing us, but it's headed in the other direction now. I'll fill you in when we get there."

West groaned.

"What do you have?" Cole asked.

"Good news and bad news," West said.

Rita lurched toward the phone. "Bad news first. Then tell us the other thing to cushion the blow."

"Well," West began, "I actually only have one thing. Good news for you, but bad news for Cole."

Cole rubbed the back of his head and swore, apparently reading his brother's mind.

"What?" she asked, leaning closer to the phone.

"I've got a decoy pen and enough men to cover the drop if you're still up for it."

She raised her determined eyes to Cole's wary ones. A wave of uncertainty threatened to steal her resolve.

Walk into a park where I know the man who keeps trying to kill me is waiting? She drew in another breath and let it out to the count of ten. She had to remember what was at stake here. If showing up at the park meant helping the killer be captured, and it would keep Ryan safe, there was nothing she wouldn't try. "Tell me when."

Chapter Seventeen

Rita dropped onto Cole's couch. She'd barely stayed on her feet while they went to pick up the decoy pen from West's office. The terrifying reality of what she'd volunteered to do was like an anvil in her gut, especially since the standard ballpoint West had given her wasn't much of a match for the actual device. With any luck, the killer hadn't gotten a good look at the original, otherwise he'd easily see her delivery for what it was. An attempt to buy time. And if they were lucky, an opportunity to draw the killer into the open for capture and arrest.

"You don't have to do this," Cole said for the fiftieth time. He'd taken a shower and changed into the luckiest pair of jeans on the planet.

"You know I do." She forced her focus to remain on his eyes, ignoring the way his soft gray T-shirt clung distractingly to his chest.

He lowered himself onto the cushion beside her and dropped fisted hands into his lap. "You've already done enough."

"I'll be fine. The plan will work," she assured him. "Either we'll catch the killer picking up the pen after the drop, or we'll be able to follow whoever comes for it all the way back to the killer." *Assuming she had a sudden and profound change of luck.*

He cracked his knuckles, bending and stretching his fingers. A stress-release move she'd performed many times after racing deadlines. "I don't like that the property in question is owned by the state."

"Me, either."

"Or that Isla agreed the governor might be in town. Something about the way these threads are coming together is making me uncomfortable. Dirty politicians are the worst kind of criminal. They have power, money, influence and endless minions to carry out their schemes or provide alibis. This whole thing is shaping up to be a total nightmare."

"Isla could be wrong about the governor. He might have no idea Minsk exists or that our mayor was meeting with him."

Cole flicked his gaze to her. "There was three million dollars on the table, and the middleman is dead. When people have that kind of money to spend and don't get what they want, I worry."

Rita relaxed into the hard length of Cole's side and set an uncertain hand on his forearm. Ropes of hard muscle flexed at her touch, launching a thousand butterflies into her chest.

"Messing with the mayor is guaranteed to get ugly, but given what we have to go on, I don't see any way around it," Cole said. "He'll have to be interviewed, and one wrong move could ruin West's career."

Rita smiled. In the midst of everything, Cole was thinking of his brother first. She stroked the length of his arm and twined her fingers with his. "I wish we could know for sure if the governor has been in town, and if so, why." She tipped her head against Cole's shoulder, loving and hating how easy moments like these had become. How she could pick him from a crowded room in seconds, knew his voice, his touch, his presence instinctively. As if this man, a stranger only days before, had become a part of her, somehow. She snuggled closer and dragged her opposite hand over the firm muscle of his forearm. *I bet the rest of his body feels this good, too.* She imagined testing the theory inch by inch, exploring and searching, marking her arrival at each new spot with a kiss.

Cole leaned forward and caught her calves in his hands, swinging them onto his lap and forcing her back against the couch's armrest, giving her a perfect view of his face. "I've got friends in Frankfort. Maybe they can at least confirm the governor's whereabouts on the days Minsk met with the mayor." He worked his hands over Rita's calves, massaging and stroking the fatigue from her muscles.

A parade of tiny flames ignited along her skin and slowly climbed north.

"It's frustrating to have all those files from the thumb drive and still nothing to go on," he said. "What do you think is so important? What did we miss?"

"Something." Rita mentally revisited the stacks of papers from West's office. "The drop wouldn't be necessary if those papers didn't incriminate someone." But mostly the documents seemed to tell the story of a dock-buying company that wanted to buy another dock. Not exactly a sinister plot.

Cole's hands stilled on Rita's leg, one at her knee, the other slightly higher. "I don't like sending you out there without knowing who we're up against. Truth be told, I wouldn't want you out there even if we did know."

"I'll be fine," she assured him, praying that was true.

"Problem is—" he lifted pleading eyes "—I don't want you anywhere I can't be."

Breath caught in Rita's throat. "So, stay with me."

One stiff dip of his chin said he would.

His soulful blue eyes were saying something else, but Rita wasn't sure what.

Ryan's phone buzzed in her pocket with an incoming text, and she unearthed it hoping for another update from Stacy. If so, it would be the third update since they'd left the hospital.

Rita scanned the message and was relieved, once again, by the content.

"Stacy?" Cole asked.

"Yeah. No changes, but that's okay." She set the phone on the coffee table with a sigh. "I wish he'd wake up, but I'm happy to know his condition is still stable and no lunatics have paid him a visit in our absence."

"She's been on the ball about sending those texts," Cole said. "It's nice. He must be important to her."

Rita chewed her lip. Cole's statement only reminded her of the question she'd been struggling with all day. "What happens when you catch the killer?" she asked. A growing rock of fear lodged in her throat. "I won't need a personal bodyguard anymore."

Cole's intense expression turned to surprise.

Good. He'd understood the question. When this was over, what would happen to them?

A sly smile played over Cole's lips as he raked a suddenly heated gaze over her body. "No bodyguard necessary? You sure about that?"

"Well, I've never needed protecting before," she whispered, squirming slightly under the force of his stare.

"Then who's going to protect you from me?"

Rita pulled in a sharp breath. "I don't want to be protected from you."

Cole's gaze dropped darkly to her breasts. "You sure about that?"

"Yes."

He leaned closer, sliding one broad palm beneath the back of her shirt and splaying strong fingers against her bare skin. Her back arched slightly in response. "You took a strong No PDA stance at the sheriff's department. I believe you said you were concerned about how your reputation would be impacted if you're seen with me. You want to talk about that?" He turned his eyes to her body as his free hand skimmed across her ribs, thumb grazing the thin fabric of her shirt and raising her nipple to attention.

The heat of embarrassment rushed over her cheeks and throat, but Cole's lids drooped hungrily over the change he'd created in her.

"I know your reputation," she said, doing her best to keep her eyes from closing under the extreme pleasure of his touch.

"And you're worried I'm going to walk away because that's what I always do," he guessed. "You think my interest in you will end soon."

"I'm worried about how silly I must look for wishing that wasn't true."

Cole's gaze met hers. His jaw set. His hands stilled. "You don't look silly to me. You look like everything I never realized I wanted, and I want it bad."

"Kiss me," she whispered, desperate to have him closer. "Please?"

Rita arched farther, rising up to meet him. He was too far away, unfairly watching as her body reacted to the slightest of his touches. She wanted more, and if this was the end for them, the last of her time with the most amazing man she'd ever known, then maybe it was time to make the most of it. "Don't stop touching me."

Cole hovered over Rita in one quick move, legs fixed between hers on the narrow couch. He teased her cheeks and jaw with the tip of his nose and the scruff of his chin, leaving a haze of himself on every inch of her face, neck and ears. His expert hands continued their work on her begging breasts.

"Cole." She panted and was rewarded with the sweet taste of his mouth on hers.

He deepened the kiss slowly, intoxicatingly, lowering his body against her until she felt the hard press of him between her thighs.

She ruined the kiss with a ragged gasp for air. Unable to resist, she lowered her hand to his jeans in disbelief, shocked and a little concerned by the size of him.

"Everything okay?" he asked, pulling back for a look at her face.

"You're huge," she stated flatly, contemplating the possibility of losing her virginity to Cole Garrett, a man she admired as much as she desired.

A small light of clarity flashed in Cole's lust-filled eyes. He bumped against her palm with a groan. "I can't believe I'm saying this, but maybe now isn't the right time." His voice was low and hot with need, but tempered by restraint. "We can take it as slow as you want." He traced the ridge of her ear with his tongue.

Her hips rocked against his. "Maybe just a little more?" This might not be the right time for sex, but she certainly had a few questions she'd like answered. "Can you show me how to touch you?"

Cole swept her wrists over her head and pinned them to the couch. "Not tonight." He left a path of wet kisses along her jawline and down her throat to her collarbone where he suckled the tender skin into gooseflesh.

He released her wrists in favor of dragging her shirt over her head and tossing the garment onto the floor. Cole's warm mouth lowered to the spot where her nipple tested her bra, and he rolled his eyes up to her again in question.

One skilled finger slid beneath the thin material, tightening her skin impossibly further.

Rita curled her fingers into the thick of Cole's hair and moaned with indescribable need. "Please."

With a pinch of his fingers, the clasp at her back was released. He swept the flimsy material of her bra away and cradled her bare breasts in his hands. His tongue passed over his lips as he pulled one budded tip into his mouth and lavished it with tender care.

Helpless against the raging fireworks inside of her, Rita bent her knees to grip his hips and arched deep into his mouth. "Cole." She moaned the word, her body squirming, begging for more.

He pulled his shirt over his head and flung it onto the growing pile of their discarded clothing. The heat of him, the clean, freshly showered scent of him, the feel of his hot skin on hers was nearly too much, and he threatened to undo her with each flick of his tongue. Cole was everywhere and yet not close enough.

"More," she whispered, clinging to him with a desperation she'd never known.

Cole's hand toured the contours of her stomach, gliding lower until his fingers vanished beneath the silk of her panties.

"Oh!" Her knees fell wide as he explored the depth of her. Slowly at first, then suddenly more than she could stand. The sensation rode through her like a crashing wave, twisting her hips and drawing out a long, breathy moan of ecstasy.

Rita opened heavy, satisfied eyes, enjoying the prickles of pleasure still coursing over her sweat-slicked skin. He'd barely touched her and yet...

Still stroking and petting her heated skin, Cole watched

as she fell from the climax. He closed his lips over hers in a kiss that nearly made her see stars.

"More." She breathed the word against his lips.

Cole pulled back with a deeply satisfied smile. "Baby, I haven't even gotten started."

COLE HAD WATCHED the tension melt off Rita's face in an explosion of shock and delight. *That's amazing,* she'd whispered, utterly out of breath from a tidal wave of orgasm. It was wrong, and more than a little caveman-esque, but his chest had puffed with pride at the accomplishment. She'd offered him full access to her body and he'd signed those papers in full, delivering her first *and second* orgasms in slow, erotic procession. Whatever else she ever did with any man, those milestones belonged to him. And so did the stubble marks left over every inch of her naked body.

He ground his teeth at the thought of another man near her like that.

Not on his watch.

On his watch, Cole had coaxed her into pieces with the slip of his tongue and skill of his hand, assuring her virginity remained intact, despite her best efforts at handing it over. Which, he hoped, would prove just how much she could trust him.

Cole double-, then triple-checked West's plan for the pen drop while Rita dozed peacefully on his couch. She'd barely slept while they were at the hospital, and he'd done his best to wear her out before slipping away to get them both a glass of ice water. She'd been out like a light when he'd returned.

He hated to disturb her, but they needed to leave for the park soon, so reluctantly, he woke Rita with a soft kiss. "Hey."

A blush crept over her skin. "Hi."

He scooted himself onto the couch in the curve of her narrow figure, careful not to sit on the quilt he'd covered her with. "West says our team will be in place within the hour. Any chance I can talk you out of this?"

She wiggled upright, pulling the quilt with her. "About earlier," she started.

He caressed her flushed cheek with the backs of his fingers. "We should probably talk about that, huh?" They had talked about it, technically, if he counted her begging for more, and his saying yes. Well, eventually, she'd been the one saying *yes*, but he'd given her all he could without crossing the line. Not today. Cole was taking it slow for her. He fought a proud smile.

She averted her gaze, cheeks bright red. "I don't normally do that sort of thing. I mean, we haven't known each other long. We aren't dating." She bit her lip and shut her eyes. "With you, my mind just…" She waved her hands around her head in a little typhoon.

He knew exactly what she meant. "We can talk now," he suggested, struggling to push the sound of her calling his name from his mind.

"No." Rita practically jumped off the couch, clutching the blanket to her remarkably sexy figure. "I should shower now." She baby-stepped backward, away from him.

Cole climbed off the couch and followed her. One step forward for each of her steps back. "Are you upset?"

"No."

"Am I making you uncomfortable?"

"No."

"You sure? 'Cause it looks like you're running away."

She shook her head hard in the negative. "Nope."

He felt his face wrinkle in confusion, mentally seeking a reason for the sudden and drastic change. "Are you embarrassed for some reason?" Hadn't the naked time proved she was implicitly comfortable with him?

"I'll only be a minute." She turned and disappeared into his bathroom.

And that made twice in the last two hours he'd missed a perfect opportunity to tell her he was falling in love.

THE PARK WAS crowded with families when they arrived. Strolling couples, swinging children, people flying kites and throwing balls. Joggers. Bicyclists. Everyone seemed to be out enjoying the final moments of the day.

Above it all, the pale blue sky was dashed with streaky white clouds and fading slowly into the amber shades of a setting sun.

Rita tugged the belt on her white wool coat a little tighter. Her thick red hair was tied back in a messy bun.

Cole kept the hood of his navy sweatshirt pulled carefully over his head, enough to hide his face without fully obstructing his view of their surroundings.

With any luck, the two of them looked like a normal couple out enjoying a walk.

He slid a protective arm behind Rita's back and spoke softly as they moved toward the mailbox. "Do you see the man with the big black dog? That's Lomar," he said. "The suit on the bench reading the paper? Deputy Franks. Hospital security is watching your brother, and I can identify all the men on my team from here. You're in very good hands." He tugged her closer and planted a kiss on her cheek. "See the tall Ken-doll-looking guy over there? The one pretending to talk on the phone? That's my brother, Blake. He's not even part of the sheriff's department. He's FBI, and he can't resist the chance to take down a bad guy."

"FBI? So you're all in law enforcement?"

"Like I said, it's in the blood. Blake married a local nature photographer and moved home last year. He'd been away for a long time before that, dealing with his demons, I suppose. Now he can't seem to stop offering his services." Cole smiled. Both Blake and West had recently fallen in love and it had changed their lives irrevocably.

Cole had even made his share of jokes at Blake's and West's expense on the matter, and now he had plans to follow their lead if Rita would have him.

He gathered her into his arms when they reached the mailbox. Before she could crouch to make the drop, he had something to say.

She looked up at him, clearly startled. "What are you doing?"

"I don't want to find another reason to put this off," he said. "I like what we have here, and regardless of what happens with this case, I don't want us to end."

Her mouth twitched. "Me, either."

"Yeah?"

Rita nodded.

"Don't leave when the case is closed," he told her, a little more sternly than he'd intended.

"Never." She rocked onto her toes and kissed him like she meant it.

Warmth bloomed in his chest. He caught her wrists in his hand and hooked them around his neck, dragging her body more tightly against his. Cole had been with lots of women who didn't matter. He'd never been with one who truly did, and the feeling, he realized, was like a drug. "While you're feeling so agreeable," he said. "I'd like it if you'd have me. And only me." He'd seen her fall apart in his hands today, and the moment had wrecked him for other women forever. He didn't want any man to ever see her like that. That was just for him.

A smile budded on Rita's lips. "Back at ya." She released

him after a small kiss and extended her hand to seal the deal with a handshake.

Cole chuckled, accepting the terms. He rubbed the goofy smile off his lips as Rita crouched beside the mailbox to leave the decoy pen. He'd surely hear about the scene that had played out publicly between them from every single member of his team when this was over.

Rita brushed her palms together. "Done."

"Good. Now let's get the hell out of here." He gripped her tiny hand in his and turned back the way they'd come.

A sharp glint of light stopped him midstride. "Did you see that?"

"What?"

He turned in a slow circle, scanning building tops and shadowed spaces. "A flash. Like light bouncing off a…"

The gunshot cracked through the air, drowning out his voice and scattering people in every direction.

Children cried. Mothers screamed.

Cole swore.

"Get down! Get down!" The familiar voices of his brothers and fellow deputies echoed through the air. "Get down!"

Cole yanked Rita's arm. "Run!"

They broke into a sprint, hands knotted together.

"Straight to the truck," he yelled over the deafening din of panic in the air.

Another shot exploded. Closer this time, blasting a divot of grass before them.

Rita screamed again, digging her feet into the ground and looking like she had on the boat when she'd seen the bomb ticking so close to zero.

"You can do this," he whispered, and her feet began to move again.

Cole cursed himself internally. He'd been blind, thinking only of Rita's safety and his feelings for her. He hadn't taken the time to scrutinize the situation. If he had, he would've realized it was a setup. "This wasn't about the pen," he snapped, overcome with frustration and terror as men and women rushed around them in every direction, making it impossible to get eyes on any of his team members without slowing their run. Hopefully at least one of the good guys had them covered.

This drop had never been about regaining the thumb drive. Nothing on those documents had pointed fingers directly at anyone. No, someone had wanted Rita out in the open, and this was a plot to get rid of the last witness.

Chapter Eighteen

Cole's ears roared with excess adrenaline as he barreled away from the park. How had he not seen the drop for what it really was? An ambush.

Screaming sirens and flashing lights seemed to fill the already thin air as ambulances rushed by them in the opposite direction, pushing traffic onto the berm. A bleating firetruck made Rita turn in her seat, trailing it with her eyes as it disappeared behind them. "Someone called 911," Cole said, by way of explanation. "Probably a witness or bystander." A citizen wouldn't have known that everyone in local law enforcement was already on-site with the shooter. If West or a deputy had made the call for emergency responders, however, it could only mean someone needed an ambulance.

He dragged his phone from his pocket and dialed West on speaker.

He'd put a few miles between Rita and the gunman with no signs of a tail. It was time to check in.

"You okay?" West answered without a greeting.

"Yeah. You?"

"Yeah. Rita?"

Cole slid his eyes toward the trembling woman at his side. "She will be. We saw the ambulances. Anyone hurt? Tell me you caught this guy."

"Nah," West huffed into the receiver. "The guy is vapor. We've fanned out to see if he's still here, maybe trying to blend in, but we've got nothing. Thankfully, no one was injured, but there's no way around a press conference now."

Cole eased the gas pedal off the floor.

"Shooter at a local park." West exhaled the words. "This was bad. And, man, I hate reporters. Luckily, the team's all here."

Was it lucky? Or just shameful that they were all on-site and no one had been able to prevent a public shooting? Cole grimaced. West would be doing public relations cleanup for the rest of his time behind the badge after this.

He rocked his head side to side, stretching the bunched muscles along his neck and shoulders. "And no sign of the gunman?"

"Not yet."

Rita leaned closer to the phone on Cole's open palm, her hands fisted over the material of her coat sleeves. "What about the pen?"

"Gone."

Her pale face went impossibly whiter. "Did he open fire because he realized what I'd done? That I'd delivered a fake?" She flicked her terrified gaze to Cole. "I broke the deal."

"Don't do that," West said. "This isn't on you. The pen was in place at the time of the first gunshot. We lost track of it after that, while we herded folks to safety. When we went back, it was gone. It's possible the shots were meant for that purpose. To distract us."

Cole set the phone on his thigh and reached for Rita with one hand. "What if this was never about the pen? What if the drop was designed to get Rita out in the open? It created an opportunity to eliminate the only person who can identify both men from the docks that night."

"I didn't see both men," Rita said, shaking her head. "Only the one who chased me."

"They don't know that," Cole argued. "From what you've told us, those men have no idea how long you were standing in the shadows. You could've been there when they arrived, could've seen and heard everything that went on, and now you're spending a lot of time with cops."

Rita fell back against the seat, her breath whooshing free in a deep exhale.

Cole could practically see the guilt-ridden thoughts running through her head. "This is not your fault." He gripped her hand. "Hey."

Her sweet hazel eyes glistened with unshed tears.

"It's not," he promised.

"But if I hadn't insisted on coming…"

"No." West's voice cracked through the air, startling Cole.

It was so easy to forget everything else when she was there.

"This is not your fault," West said. "None of it. Not his stalking you, not your brother's accident and not the shooting at the park. Whatever this psychopath does, he's doing it by choice. *His* choice. *His* agenda. You are not to blame for his crimes, regardless of how your anxious heart twists the facts. You got it? Because I want you to hear that. Really understand it."

Cole smiled. He'd seen his fun-loving brother in boss mode more times than he could count, and there was no denying him anything when he got like that. Another reason he made a great sheriff. West could put people at ease without feeling obligated to be their best friend. He got the job done. All of it. And folks respected him for it.

Rita released a long slow breath. "You're right. I need to stay focused."

"Atta girl," West said, his voice going easy and kind. "Cole. Why don't you take Rita somewhere safe while we finish the witness interviews and scan the park? I want to visit some of the nearby buildings for signs the shooter was there. If we know where he waited for her, it could give us another clue about who he is. If he has ties in the area, professional training, anything like that, I can follow it back to him. Lomar's collecting the spent rounds. That'll help, too."

Cole nodded at the phone. "I saw a glint of light before the first shot. Could've been sunlight off a rifle scope."

"Where?"

"East of the mailbox, between the drop location and the parking lot. We were headed back to the truck. A rooftop maybe."

"Good," West said, a rumble of pride in his voice. "That's what we need. Something to go on. You get your lady to safety, and I'll call when we have something."

Rita turned, fear overtaking her pretty features. "Can I see my brother?"

Cole stopped at the next intersection, waiting for West to chime in. Cole was definitely against a trip to the hospital, but West could deliver the bad news this time. He wasn't the one trying to keep her both safe and happy. A more and more difficult task, given their circumstances.

Rita made a pleading face at Cole. "I don't want anyone to go after Ryan again because of what I just did. The note said to bring the pen to the park. I didn't. I brought a fake. The note said to come alone. I didn't. I brought the whole sheriff's department. Ryan's unconscious in the trauma ward. He's helpless and alone. His only protection is a crew of nurses and hospital security. I have to see him."

"Can it wait?" West asked. "Hospital security has the

entire floor locked down, and I trust them. I'd prefer you postpone your next visit until a deputy can go with you."

"Hey." Cole glared at the windshield, easing through the intersection, half expecting the dreaded black sedan to appear in his rearview. "I'm with her. *I'm* a deputy."

"Yeah, and when was the last time you slept?" West asked.

Cole ground his teeth. "Last night."

"For how long?"

Cole pursed his lips.

"I'm guessing it wasn't long," West said, answering his own question with undeniable self-importance. "And correct me if I'm wrong, but whatever insufficient amount of sleep you got was on the same day you were knocked unconscious after leaping off a boat that exploded." He broke the final word into syllables. "Am I right? And I heard Uncle Henry tell you to rest and take something for the pain. Did you do either of those things? Really? Have you even changed the bandages?"

"Are you serious with this right now?" It was one thing to be perpetually teased for being the baby of the family, and completely another to be told he wasn't fit to protect Rita and Ryan until another deputy arrived. "I can do this."

"Of course you can," West said, managing to sound exasperated despite the fact he'd started this. "I know you can. You, out of all of us brothers, always could do damn near anything. But it doesn't mean you should. And it's a proven fact that fatigue wrecks your ability to think on your feet and it slows your reflexes. Would you want anyone else in your condition protecting Rita and her brother? Or do you want to stow your stubborn pride, stop trying to prove something to everyone all the time and just wait until a deputy who's slept longer than four hours in the last two nights gets there to help?"

Cole traded his hold on Rita for a double fisted grip around the steering wheel. He hated to admit it, but West's reasoning was strong, and throwing Rita's safety into the argument made it impossible to disagree. "I'm not trying to prove anything," he said, already defeated. He would wait for the next deputy to arrive before taking Rita to the hospital.

"You are." The zeal had washed from West's voice. "You always have been, but you never needed to. Do me a favor, as your brother, not your boss. Take Rita to Grandpa's cabin or Mom and Dad's place, find a bed with a blanket in a room with a locking door, then get some sleep. I need you healed up and ready to go. We can't do this without you."

Pride stung Cole's throat. "Yes, sir." He closed the phone and set it in the cupholder, unable to look in Rita's direction. He was nearly thirty years old, and his brother's approval never stopped feeling like he'd just won the middle-school fishing derby.

Rita reached for his hand on the wheel and pulled it onto her lap. "That was nice."

Cole laughed. "Yeah. That wasn't bad."

"He's proud of you," she said. "Didn't sound to me like he thinks you're not enough. It sounded to me like he's an older brother."

Cole cleared his throat, not trusting his voice to sound as strong as he needed it to be for her. "Ryan's going to be just fine, but we can head over there whenever you're ready. I'll leave that up to you."

She shook her head. "No. West's right. It can wait. I've still got his phone. Stacy's updates are still coming steady and strong. I know he's safe. His condition hasn't declined, and he's in good hands. I don't want to lead any more danger Ryan's way. How far away is your grandfather's cabin?"

"About twenty miles. A forty-minute trip from here.

Lots of back roads and rough terrain. I haven't been there in years, but it's secluded. Not many people even know it's there." He veered right at the next fork in the road, angling away from shops and local residences onto a narrow finger that would soon be made of mud and gravel.

"Sounds perfect," she said. "I'll call Stacy when we get there and let her know we'll be back tonight unless she needs us sooner. I wouldn't mind a verbal update, either. Texts are nice, but I'd like to hear her tell me he's okay."

Cole watched as she swiveled forward, turning her body back to face the windshield. Was it wrong of him to feel so much pride in knowing her? Her strength of will. Her love for family. Was it wrong of him to want her to be a part of his life permanently, and as soon as possible?

She lifted her sweet-spirited smile to him, light and pure in a moment of sheer perfection. Things were going to be okay.

"Cole." Her eyes went suddenly wide, and Cole followed her gaze though his driver's-side window as a giant truck slammed into his door. Metal twisted and crunched. Glass shattered over them. Cole's arms flew away from the wheel, and his torso jerked toward Rita like a rag doll, thrust away from the caved-in door.

Rita's piercing scream was cut short as their truck rocked briefly onto two wheels before slamming back onto the ground.

The massive tow truck reversed away from them and stopped.

Cole fumbled for the steering wheel and gas pedal. His truck didn't respond.

The silver beast stopped retreating at twenty feet away and shifted loudly with powerful bursts of torque. Broad black tires crept toward them like a predator.

Cole cranked the ignition with all his might. The thing was going to run them over. "Rita?"

She was slumped against the passenger door, unmoving and covered in pebbles of busted glass.

"Rita!"

The angry squealing of tires drowned his best efforts to wake her as the attacking truck raced forward once more.

The resulting collision sent Cole rolling into darkness.

RITA WOKE TO the steady pounding of her head and throbbing of her shoulder. Her hands dangled over her head thanks to the topsy-turvy position of Cole's truck. She struggled to make sense of her new view.

They'd been in an accident!

Beside her, Cole hung limply in his safety belt, fingers resting on the ceiling, trickles of blood racing in crimson rivulets from the gash on his chin, climbing over his nose and closed eyes to his forehead. "Cole!"

She reached for him, uselessly, unable to make contact. Her arms were too short and her seatbelt unforgiving. Pain flashed through her head in bursts of blinding light.

Suddenly, the door at her side swung open with a sickening groan.

"Help him first," she called. "Help the driver. He's not moving. There's blood!"

A man in a deputy's jacket lowered onto his knees outside the open door. "Hello, Trouble," he said.

"Cole!" Rita screamed as the shooter reached for her with black leather gloves. He held her easily in place as he sawed through her seat belt with a giant pocketknife.

Cole's eyelids flickered open as her restraint broke free, dropping her onto her head in the upside-down cab. Her legs and feet crashed over her, connecting sharply with the dashboard and the side of Cole's face.

"Rita." He choked out her name.

Tears blurred her vision. "Help." She forced the word out, knowing there was no help for her. This was it. The killer had won.

Cole swung an arm in her direction, then called out in pain. "No!"

Her assailant shoved his head through the open door and clamped leather-clad fingers around her arms, jerking her roughly toward him. "Time to say goodbye."

Rita scrambled to tether herself to anything, but the jagged shards of broken glass tore through her tender flesh with each desperate move.

"Rita!" Cole struggled behind her, swearing and yelping as he worked to unlatch his seat belt.

"Gotcha." The attacker locked his hands beneath her armpits and hauled her into the rays of the setting sun.

She screamed and fought as he dragged her along the road toward the black sedan parked nearby.

A driverless tow truck sat empty beside Cole's pickup, its bumper lying on the ground below a cracked and broken grille.

In the distance, a man in unmarked coveralls climbed into the passenger side of another sedan.

"How many of you are there?" Rita asked, suddenly realizing that today's shooter may have been someone else entirely. "Are you the one who almost killed my brother? Did you leave the note at the hospital?"

He wound an arm around her ribs and pulled her tight against his chest, pressing the air from her lungs. With his free hand, he produced a black key fob.

The sedan's trunk popped open and memories of the blood and guns rushed back to her. This time, the space was empty but lined in heavy plastic.

"I'm not getting in there," she insisted, applying every

self-defense technique her father had taught her for getting away. Unfortunately, her fuzzy head and wobbly limbs rendered her efforts useless.

He shoved her forward with a jolt, pressing her thighs against the car's open trunk and himself against her backside.

"No!" The pressure of his body forced upon her sent Rita into desperation.

He leaned harder into her, forcing her body to jackknife. One gloved hand covered her mouth, the other was anchored against the plastic-lined trunk floor, leaving her no room to fight and no hope of escape. "Get in." Hot, stale breath washed over her face, sickening her further as she tried not to think about the way his body assaulted hers.

"No."

In one shocking heave, Rita was off her feet and on her back inside the cramped space of the sedan trunk. Scents of carpet cleaners and stain removers bit at her nose and eyes. She clawed at his gloves and jacket as he held her down, wishing she could somehow fill her fingernails with his DNA or at least a useful thread to hang him by when her body washed up at the river tomorrow morning. "Don't do this," she cried. "You don't have to do this."

The man gave a final shove, expelling the oxygen from her lungs once more, then reaching for the trunk lid. "Yes. I do."

Chapter Nineteen

The space inside the trunk was hot and confined. Mixed with the strong chemical scents and darkness, Rita's head screamed for mercy. She traced the trunk with trembling hands, searching for the escape button, but the emergency release handle inside the trunk had been disabled. She couldn't help wondering if Minsk had taken this same ride to his death. Had he gone through the same motions? And, if so, how could she survive if he hadn't?

To make matters impossibly worse, there was nothing available that she could use as a weapon when the car finally stopped. The trunk held not a single item other than her and the plastic, slick with sweat beneath her palms.

Think. She pressed her fingertips hard against both temples and squeezed her eyes shut for clarity. If the car stopped, she could scream for help, pound on the trunk and hope someone heard her, maybe another car or a jogger. So far, the car had barely slowed.

Rita rolled into the fetal position, fighting against the rising panic. A pinch at her hip sent her heart aflutter with new hope. Ryan's phone! Her aching, terrified, addled mind had forgotten the most obvious of tools. A literal help line.

She wiggled the device from her pocket and swiped the screen to life. The backlight burned her eyes, and she squinted against the sudden pain. Rita dialed the only number she could think of, the one she'd memorized just days before. Cole's cell phone.

Her call went to voice mail.

His phone, like hers, was at the bottom of the river.

She didn't know the number to Cole's flip phone.

Nine-one-one. She dialed the new number with growing hope.

"Nine-one-one," a raspy female voice answered. "What's your emergency?"

"This is Rita Horn." She nearly sobbed the words. "I'm in the trunk of a car. I was taken from an accident. Cole Garrett is hurt." Her rambling thoughts spilled through trembling lips.

"Ma'am," the voice interrupted. "You're breaking up. What's your emergency?"

Rita swallowed a whimper. Her bubble of hope nearly gone. "I've been abducted," she screamed the words. "Help me!"

"Miss Horn?" The strange voice perked. "Rita Horn?"

"Yes! Yes. It's me. We were in an accident. I don't know where I am."

"I'm patching you through to the sheriff."

Rita wiped her eyes. Scents of motor oil and exhaust seeped into her senses, mixing with the heat and chemicals, churning her stomach into a vortex.

"Rita?" West's voice crackled through the line.

"Yes!" The Garretts would save her. They were a pack of small town superheroes. She was going to be okay. *Everything would be okay.*

"I can't hear you," he said, an edge of frustration in his voice. "Can you hear me?"

"Yes!"

"If you can still hear me, stay on the line. I won't hang up. We're starting a trace now. Cole's on his way to the hospital." West's voice cut out. The air went still. Background noise and rustling wind through the receiver. Gone. Snatched away when she needed them most.

"West?" She jerked the phone away from her ear and stared in disbelief.

The phone's timer ticked upward, tracking silent seconds as the call continued, her ability to communicate gone.

Tears poured over Rita's cheeks.

Cole was going to the hospital. What if he was badly hurt? What if his injuries were worse than she'd imagined? What if he was seriously, permanently injured, or worse?

The steady hum of the sedan's tires on pavement eventually changed into the loud crunching of gravel, and the mostly smooth ride grew intensely rough and bone rattling.

She gritted her teeth against the pain as her aching body jostled and bounced inside the hot trunk. Rita listened closely as the car's engine soon settled and a door opened and shut. Footfalls ground through the rocks outside before a quick beep released the trunk lid.

Rita slid the phone up her coat sleeve and curled her fingers around the hidden device. She shut her eyes and went limp.

Sunlight rushed over her face. The sharp golden glow was a hammer to her throbbing head. "Wake up," the man growled.

Rita feigned a coma. Dead weight was harder to carry, and he couldn't force her onto her feet again if she was unconscious.

"Come on." Angry hands circled her biceps and yanked her upright.

She let her head loll over one shoulder, determined to pull off the con. If she was lucky, he'd skip shooting her and simply toss her into the river where she'd have a fighting chance.

The man leaned closer and patted her cheek sharply, stinking up the already rank air with his nasty breath. Wherever they were, it didn't smell like the docks. It smelled like manure.

"Up you go." He jammed his shoulder into her ribs and tipped her over him like a sack of potatoes.

"Stop!" Rita screamed and kicked, realizing her plan to slow him down by being still was foiled by her small size.

New plan. She thumped his back with both fists and wailed into the endless countryside.

"Hey!" he shouted. "Knock it off or I'll knock you out."

Rita went still. Her chest heaved with desperation. Could West hear her pleas through the phone tucked up her sleeve? How long could she hold on to her lifeline before the caveman beneath her took it away?

She let her lids close on a silent prayer, then gave one more wild round of squeals and kicks. When her assailant began to threaten and complain, she released the cell phone, aiming it toward the sedan.

Ryan's phone collided with the gravel and bounced before rolling to a stop beneath the car.

"What are you doing?" He flipped her off his shoulder, wrenching her arm behind her back and surely dislocating her shoulder. "Walk!" He gripped her neck with hot, meaty fingers and shoved her forward along a dirt path.

Rita strained for a better view of her surroundings. Where was the river? Everywhere she looked were overgrown fields and rolling hills of long-abandoned farmland. An armless scarecrow hung cockeyed on a wooden stake, impaled long ago and left to guard against nothing but the wind.

There would be no chance of swimming to shore now.

No chance at surviving or being found. They weren't at the river. They were in no-man's-land.

A dilapidated old barn rose on the fiery horizon, its weathered boards dark with age and neglect. Its concave roof gaped with a hole the size of a tractor.

"You don't have to do this," she said, trying those words again as she dug her feet into the hardened earth.

The man shoved her forward in giant bursts of force, eventually knocking her through the yawning doorway and into the ominous structure.

Rita batted her eyes, adjusting to the dimmer light. The sinking sun bathed the space in eerie shades of crimson and scarlet, casting long shadows over the floor and illuminating dust motes like falling embers ready to set her world ablaze.

Bits of ancient hay swirled along the ground, caught in the breeze blowing in from the field. Dirt and animal hair floated in the air, peppering her senses with the overwhelming scents of death and decay. A rickety wooden chair stood in the room's center.

The man stepped away then. He removed a handgun from beneath his jacket and pointed it at her middle. "Sit."

Rita stopped. "Cole will find me," she warned. And he would.

Though whether he'd find her alive or dead was yet to be known.

"I don't think so." Her abductor smashed one large palm hard against her shoulder, eliciting a yelp and successfully bending her knees. The chair rocked with the shock of her collapse upon it. "He was a little tied up last I saw him."

"Then the sheriff will find me," she said, "or another deputy, another Garrett, but someone will come, and you'll pay for the things you've done." Newfound bravery worked through her core and pushed free of her lips. She had nothing to lose, and delaying her death might mean saving her life.

He kneeled beside her and produced a length of rope. "Quiet."

Rita slid her hands deep into her sleeves and gauged the distance to the barn door. Her mind raged with impossible questions. Could she outrun him? Would he shoot her if she tried? Was she willing to find out? "You should let me go and spend your time getting out of town before you're arrested. This could be your last day as a free man. Is killing an office clerk really how you want to spend your time?"

"Not really. Hands behind your back. Unless you want a hole in your forehead like the others."

The others. Like Minsk and his poor maid.

Rita dropped her arms at her side. "My shoulder," she winced, biting into the thick of her lip. "I think it's out of the socket. I can't move it any farther."

He yanked it back for her.

She screamed in agony. Black dots danced before her eyes and her stomach rolled. "I'm going to be sick."

"You'll feel better soon." He tightened thick scratchy rope around her wrists with speed and precision.

"Why are you doing this?"

He rose to his feet and stared blank-faced at her for a long beat. "Family."

Family? What did that mean? "Well, you don't have to. Whoever's making you do these things is just using you, and you can stop. The Garretts can help you."

He blinked through a sudden look of remorse. "No one can help me."

"Give us a minute." A long shadow stretched toward them. The slow Southern drawl crawled over Rita's skin. "Finally, we meet."

Her abductor tucked the gun into a holster on his side

and walked out the way he'd come in, giving the new arrival a wide berth.

Curiosity and defiance stiffened Rita's spine and narrowed her eyes.

The newcomer was tall and broad, a faceless silhouette. The waning light rode slowly over him with each new step, illuminating shiny black shoes, then gray suit pants and a dress shirt that stilled Rita's heart. His shape and stride confirmed her worst nightmare. This was the man with the bloodstains on the docks.

"Hello, Miss Horn." He tipped his head in greeting.

"You," she seethed. This was the man pulling the strings. The one who'd called the shots that nearly killed her brother. And Cole. And her.

"Who are you?" she asked. He wasn't the mayor or the governor; she'd easily recognize both, and he was neither. "What do you want from me?"

"I tried to scare you off," he said. "Tried everything, but nothing worked. You had to show up that night. Become a witness. Steal evidence, then run. You stopped going to work. Stopped going home. If only you would have cooperated."

Rita squinted at the middle-aged stranger. There was something familiar in the line of his jaw. The set of his eyes. Had they met before?

"You really don't know who I am?" he asked.

"A sociopath?" she guessed.

He pulled his chin back, looking significantly put off by her answer. "Think harder, Miss Horn. You work at the municipal building, don't you?"

Her jaw dropped. Recognition hit like a bat to the forehead. "Senator Sayers?" She'd walked by his portrait, hanging beside the ones of the president and governor, many times a day for several years.

He smiled. "See. I knew you were smart."

So, they had been right to suspect an elected official's involvement. They just hadn't thought far enough up the food chain.

Rita shored up her nerve and prayed to look more composed than she felt. Something about the senator told her that he'd have little patience for a panicking woman who shed tears and begged forgiveness. "Why are you doing this?"

"You wouldn't understand."

"Try me." Rita forced back the bile pooling in her throat. Pain, fear and nausea circled in her gut and lightened her head by the minute. Scents of rotting wood and hay stirred with sunbaked animal hair and excrement. It was only a matter of time before she was sick or passed out.

If it came to that, would he kill her while she was unconscious?

The senator chuckled. He locked his hands behind his back and looked briefly at the ceiling, as if debating where to begin.

"I'm sure you weren't always like this," she prompted, her voice warbling with fear.

"I made a bad decision ten years ago." He stared past her, apparently lost in thought. "Sometimes it's impossible to put bad things behind us."

"What kind of bad decision?" she asked, hoping to stall the inevitable. Rita worked her wrists against the restraints, resolving to break free and make a run for it. Better to die trying than sitting helpless in a chair. "What's haunting you, Senator?"

A sad smile formed on his lips. He dragged his gaze back to Rita. "It wasn't long ago that I was young like you. Had a bright, limitless future ahead of me. I was an aspiring politician with big dreams and impossible goals. No money," he sighed. "I accepted a huge endorsement for my campaign with a single string attached. I couldn't allow the docks to be renovated. No one could buy them. No one could rebuild. I had to use my position to keep them as they were. Unused and abandoned. It seemed simple to me. They'd literally asked me to do nothing."

"You had to know that wasn't good," Rita said. "Why would someone give you money for something like that, if not for something nefarious?"

He made a strange face. "It's hard to say now what I was thinking then, before I'd been through so much. Maybe I wanted to believe in easy money. Maybe I wasn't yet jaded. Whatever the reason, I accepted the money and agreed to their terms, moved to Frankfort after the election and forgot about this insignificant little town. The company who'd supported my campaign sent money regularly. It was nice."

"Gray Line," Rita muttered.

The senator's mouth opened. His bushy salt-and-pepper brows crowded together. "Yes. Eventually, curiosity got the best of me, and I pushed for details. When I saw the guns and realized what I'd done, I demanded more money." He shook his head sadly. "They threatened me. Threatened my family. My career. My world. They said I ought to keep quiet and be thankful they were only moving the guns along the river and not through my state."

Rita continued to struggle with her bindings, fighting through the blinding pain in one shoulder as she worked the rope with her opposite wrist. She only needed to loosen it enough to slip free. "Then Gray Line made a move to buy it themselves."

"By then I'd learned enough to know that if the state sold to them, they'd put up a storage unit and keep their supplies here. The potential income of the operation would triple, plus the problem would no longer be limited to secret river rendezvous. Now, the crime would be on our shores, I wouldn't see any extra cash for it, and if anyone found out, I would be the villain."

"So you had Minsk killed? Why? He was just a middleman."

"He overheard me encouraging the governor about renovating the docks. It's ultimately his call, and I figured if Gray Line wasn't interested in upping my cut, I'd force them out, talk the governor into making good on his campaign promise to revitalize the area. Then Minsk showed up, claiming he had a potential buyer. I knew who he worked for. I had to stop him. What else could I do?"

"You could've gone to the authorities. You should've come clean."

Color torched the senator's face. "Everything's not that simple!" His voice roared through the rickety barn, sending hidden birds into the air. "I could've come clean, and Minsk could've reported it all back to Gray Line or the local media. He could've gotten me killed or revealed me as a traitor to my constituents. I'd facilitated the use of our docks by gunrunners for years."

He balled his hands into fists, looking suddenly heartbroken. "Killing Minsk should've bought me time to figure this out. Instead, you showed up and made everything worse. That thumb drive you stole had years and years of documentation. I know you've already given it to the authorities because you used a fake in the drop today, and the entire sheriff's department was there when the shooting broke out. It stands to reason that the sheriff would have sent it straight to Tech Support. I can't have anyone figuring out Gray Line has been running guns, so I've asked my contact at the FBI to collect the pen for me. He'll claim jurisdiction, and that will clean up the evidence. Except for one problematic eyewitness."

Rita worked harder at the fraying ropes, raking them along the jagged rungs of her chair. "Maybe you and I can make a deal. Let me live, and I'll never say anything about what you've told me. You'll kill me if I do."

"I'm afraid it's far too late for that." He raised two fingers to his mouth and puffed out an earsplitting whistle.

The shooter reappeared in the doorway, backlit by a hazy twilight sky and slowly rising moon.

The elongated shadow of a handgun stretched firmly from one hand.

Chapter Twenty

"Wait!" Rita called out to the senator's retreating figure. "It doesn't have to be like this. Just tell the truth!" She rocked and jerked in her seat, begging her ties to snap and her body to be free. "Come back!"

The senator didn't stop, and he was soon outside the barn.

The shooter moved in front of the chair. "Close your eyes."

Rita's bottom lip quivered and her stubborn chin inched higher. She could see the differences in the fake deputy jacket now. Not to mention that the real thing was worn by a hero. This one was the costume of a monster. She locked eyes with her soon-to-be executioner. She hated the mockery of the uniform all the more, knowing how important it was to Cole and his family. "Why pretend to be a deputy? What's your point? If you're trying to blend in, why not wear something less eye-catching?"

He smiled. "You're wrong, because no one looks twice at law enforcement. I can go anywhere in this jacket, no questions asked. People step aside and don't interrupt."

The distant click of a closing car door swept through the night, followed closely by the gentle purr of an engine. Apparently the senator wasn't staying around for Rita's disposal.

The gunman widened his stance. "Now, close your eyes."

"No."

He rolled his head over one shoulder, then fixed her with an impatient expression. "Look, lady, this isn't personal, but if you cooperate, I promise never to visit your brother again. He can heal up and live his life like this never happened."

Rita stifled a sob. She let her lids drift shut. Her hands fisted at her back, the frayed rope biting into her skin. Her time was up.

"I'm sorry," she whispered, hoping everyone she'd let down could somehow know this wasn't what she'd wanted. She was supposed to watch Ryan grow old. She'd wanted justice for those who were hurt by the senator's selfish and sinister behavior. Most of all, she'd wanted a chance to tell Cole Garrett that she loved him.

Rita imagined Cole's face, his warm smile and the haven of his protective arms as she waited for the end to come.

The gunshot boomed like thunder, ringing in her ears and stealing her breath. Fear radiated through her in bone-crushing shock, but the pain didn't come.

A muted thud lifted her eyelids.

The gunman lay at her feet, a growing puddle of his blood staining his faux deputy jacket.

"Rita!" Cole Garrett limped forward from the open barn door, one arm in a sling, one foot in a boot cast. "Are you okay?"

She gave the fallen gunman one more look. His unseeing eyes confirmed it. "Yes," she sobbed. She was going to be fine.

A wail of relief rolled through her. "You're hurt!" She rocked on her seat, struggling to free her pinned arms. "How are you here? Are you okay? West said you went to the hospital."

Cole kicked the dead man's gun away, then kneeled at her side.

"I'm fine." The distant drone of sirens grew steadily in the distance. "We traced the call." He cut quickly through her ropes, freeing her wrists, then massaging them gently in his hands.

Rita squeaked from the pressure. Tears ran over her cheeks. One arm hung limply at her side. "It's out of socket," she said, doing her best to be strong for the man who was always strong for her.

"Here." Cole stripped the sling from his shoulder and hooked it over Rita's head. He slid her aching arm into the hammock and adjusted the length of material behind her. "Uncle Henry's already on the way."

Rita cradled her arm in appreciation and relief. "Thank you." She pressed her cheek against his chest and cried.

Cole kissed her head and stroked her hair. "You're safe now, and I won't let anyone or anything hurt you ever again."

Rita held him tight, melding herself to him before she fell apart.

"You were so smart to hide Ryan's phone," he said, nuzzling his cheek against her head. "I don't know what I would've done if I hadn't found you in time."

"I love you," Rita blurted. "I know it's soon and it's silly, but it's true, and whatever you think about that is fine, but I need you to know."

Cole pulled back an inch, a peculiar look in his eye. "Yeah?"

Someone cleared their throat nearby.

Rita looked for the interruption, and discovered West at the barn's entrance, gripping the senator's elbow. The politician's hands were cuffed behind his back.

"I hate to break this up," he said, "but I'm hoping Miss

Horn can provide a formal statement about why Senator Sayers was caught racing away from her abduction site."

Cole moved back into her line of sight, successfully blocking out her view of West and everything else. He waved a hand overhead, dismissing his brother. "You said you love me?"

"Very much."

He bent his knees and let loose a rodeo-worthy hoot! He feathered kisses over her nose and cheeks, smiling with every press and release of his lips. "I love you, too."

"You do?"

"Oh, yeah." He looped his good arm over her shoulders and turned her toward the door. "You want to get out of here? Maybe visit a hospital?"

She laughed.

Together they shuffled toward the carousel of red and white lights flashing in the evening sky. An ambulance pulled up.

"Maybe Uncle Henry can give us a lift," Cole suggested.

"That's fine. As long as I don't have to ride in a trunk."

SNOW AND HOLIDAY music drifted in the air outside Rita's home. Her driveway and half the street were lined with cars in both directions. Cole straightened his jacket before knocking. Thanks to a double shift, he hadn't seen Rita in nearly twenty-four hours, and his chest was already flooded with warmth in anticipation.

She was sure to be smiling tonight. Ryan had finally been released from the recovery center where he'd spent the last three weeks regaining his strength and coordination. According to Rita, he'd already rescheduled his dropped classes for after Christmas break.

Dogged determination was definitely in the Horn genes. Rita swept her door open, pouring the warm scents of holiday cookies, casseroles and hot chocolate over Cole's senses. She greeted him with a kiss and a smile. "Come in," she urged, tugging his sleeve and nearly vibrating with enthusiasm. "I can't believe how many people are here. I don't even know all these people. I think half of them are named Garrett!"

Cole stole another kiss, then scanned the crowded room. Her neighbors had dibs on the kitchen table, chatting and laughing around steaming mugs and full plates. A few office workers from the municipal building were chatting animatedly in the corner. Ryan and Nurse Stacy were tucked up close on the couch, a fuzzy cat on each of their laps. A middle-aged man with Rita's eyes spoke animatedly to the couple. "Is that your dad?" Cole asked, downright shocked when she nodded. Her dad had said he was coming home when he'd finally returned her calls, but the only one who'd believed him was Ryan. "Well, I'm glad he came," Cole said, and he meant it.

"Me, too, I think. He says he's going to retire," Rita said. "I'll believe it when I see it, but so far, he seems to be trying to make up for lost time. He even apologized for not choosing us over duty more often. I liked hearing that."

"I bet you did." Cole slung an arm over her shoulders and kissed her head. "I will always choose you."

Rita smiled, and the room grew brighter.

Cole gave the crowd another long look. Rita was right, the other fifteen or so people were Garretts. Cole had personally invited them to come.

"They all showed up to welcome Ryan home," she said. "Can you believe it?" She pressed a palm to her heart. "Is this what it's like to have a big family? Because I love it. Your dad invited Ryan to go bass fishing. Your mom brought so much food I won't have to cook for a week."

She wiped the pad of one thumb under each eye. "I miss my mom so much it hurts."

"I know." Christmas was a rough season to be alone, but if things went Cole's way today, Rita would never be short on family again. He wrapped her in his arms and smoothed a hand over the length of her hair, marveling at how this one woman had so irrevocably changed his life.

"There you are." West's voice boomed through the room. He left a kiss on his wife's forehead, then wove a path to Cole's side. "Time for those announcements?"

Rita furrowed her narrow brow. "Announcements? Do you have news about the senator?"

"Attention!" West tapped his fork against his little plate. "I have some news that many of you will enjoy hearing. I know I did."

Slowly, the room quieted. A sea of expectant eyes turned in West's direction.

"First of all," he began, "I want to thank Rita for opening up her home to all of us. Given what she's been through, some folks might be inclined to never open their door again."

The crowd chuckled.

"And speaking of men I wouldn't invite inside," West continued, "I received news today that Senator Sayers is in jail awaiting trial without bail. The state believes they've got enough evidence to put him away for a long while." He turned his attention directly to Rita. "It seems the thumb drive you delivered into my hands has provided the ATF with everything they needed to make multiple arrests within Gray Line Enterprises, a known gun-trafficking organization that they've been watching for more than two years. My big brother Blake was able to use your tip that someone from the FBI would try to collect the drive from Tech Support, and that guy was arrested, as well."

Rita beamed. "You're kidding."

Cole began a slow clap that rolled through the room.

Her brother pounded his hands together and chanted her name.

Cole grinned.

Ryan had admitted to taking her truck after being told not to for a bunch of little brother reasons. One, he only needed it to make one trip, so what could go wrong? Two, she hadn't moved it from the lot where he'd left it at his school, so she obviously didn't need it back right away. And, three, he couldn't reach her by phone to beg some more, because unbeknownst to him, her phone was in the river by that time.

West extended a hand in her direction for a formal shake.

Rita accepted. "Thank you."

Isla, from the mayor's office, was next to make a scene. "I've got something, too," she hollered, sliding to the front of the crowd. "The mayor announced today that the governor is taking control of all monies seized from the senator's business with Gray Line and reallocating the funds to reclaim the docks!"

Rita's jaw dropped.

"There's more." Isla beamed, clearly enjoying her moment in the spotlight. "He was so moved by your love for those stray cats that he vowed the first business opened there will be an animal shelter."

Rita's eyes glistened. "That's amazing! Thank you."

Isla gave the crowd another smile, then sashayed away looking quite proud of herself.

Rita turned to Cole with a look of sheer joy.

Cole's heart thundered in his chest. The announcements were made. Rita was happy. Now, there was only one thing left to do.

"Rita Horn," he began, a ridiculous quiver wiggling in his chest. "Knowing you has changed my life, my world and my dreams."

West tapped his fork against his plate. "It's happening."

Cole ignored him and pressed on, retrieving a small gold band from his pocket. He looked into Rita's wide hazel eyes, then slowly he lowered onto one knee.

Rita's head began to nod in agreement.

"Now wait." Cole smiled, his chest tight with elation. "I haven't asked you anything yet."

"Yes."

Everyone laughed, and Rita's gaze jumped toward the crowd.

Ryan lifted a slow thumbs-up to his sister.

She turned back to Cole with tear-filled eyes. "Yes."

Cole gathered her trembling hands in his. "I realize we haven't known each other long, but I'd like to know you forever."

Fat tears spilled over her cheeks. "Yes."

He stood and offered her his handkerchief. "Marry me," he said.

Rita rose onto her toes and planted her lips to his in a shameless display of love and desire.

The crowd erupted in cheers of utter delight, but Cole was certain there would never be a happier man alive than him in that very moment.

* * * * *

COMING SOON!

We really hope you enjoyed reading this book. If you're looking for more romance, be sure to head to the shops when new books are available on

Thursday 10th January

To see which titles are coming soon, please visit

millsandboon.co.uk/nextmonth

LET'S TALK

Romance

For exclusive extracts, competitions
and special offers, find us online: